THE WEIGHT OF COMMAND

THE WEIGHT OF COMMAND

MICHAEL MAMMAY

Copyright © 2023 by Michael Mammay

All rights reserved.

No part of this book may be reproduced in any form or by any electronic or mechanical means, including information storage and retrieval systems, without written permission from the author, except for the use of brief quotations in a book review.

For everyone like Kiera Markov who needed to step up and did.

1

The war started while I sat on the toilet. If my mother heard me say that, she'd tell me it wasn't ladylike. But she's not here, and I'm not a lady. I'm a soldier. A soldier who ate grilled pork from a local roadside stand, which makes me a stupid soldier. I'd been doing peacekeeping duty on the gods-forsaken planet of Tanara long enough to know better. But since that poor culinary decision saved my life, living with a little dysentery was probably a small price.

The sound came first, a deep thump in the chest, a rumbling reminiscent of one of the intense thunderstorms from my family's farm on the outer-rim colony Desicair. A short time later, the prefab latrine shook, and dirt scattered from the ceiling. I scrunched my face, trying to hold off a sneeze. Maybe it was a seismic event. Except Tanara didn't have those, and it rarely had thunderstorms. Whatever it was, I didn't want to be sitting there with my pants around my ankles waiting to find out.

Footsteps slapped on the raised walkway between the latrine buildings, and I rushed to get my pants up. Shouts sounded in the distance. I couldn't make out the words, but they had an urgency that started my heart pounding. A chill ran up my spine despite the heat, and I didn't think it was the food poisoning. Something bad had happened. I was sure of it. But at that moment I couldn't conceive of how bad, and my mind raced through mundane scenarios such as vehicle accidents or weapon misfires.

If only.

Dust hazed the air when I hurried outside, as if a massive wind had swept through and not settled yet. The footsteps and shouting had gone, leaving an oppressive silence. In the quad, a couple of food wrappers littered the usually pristine ground. I walked toward headquarters, the gravel baked into the dirt acting like pavement under my feet. Whatever had happened, they'd know there. Three soldiers ran past in front of me, more dust swirling around them, weapons at the low ready. Was there an intruder? It seemed unlikely. That had never happened here. I couldn't generate a sense of alarm, because I couldn't conceptualize danger in this place that had always seemed tame. Yet something at the back of my mind was whispering ominous thoughts.

"What's going on?" I called.

The third soldier in line slowed and turned, walking backward, almost bouncing with energy. He pointed to the horizon behind me. "There's been an explosion, ma'am. A fucking big one."

A gigantic black cloud blotted the sky, reaching as high as an aircraft would fly. "What the—?"

"Lieutenant, I have to go..."

"Right. Carry on." I hustled toward the task force headquarters, glancing back every few steps at the cloud. Even at that point, I knew what it was, I think, but my mind couldn't completely process it yet.

A guard stood outside the door of the three-story windowless building, the largest on the compound, his weapon unslung and ready. Someone had stepped up the defense protocol since I'd last entered, two days prior.

"Ma'am, please state your rank and name for voice recognition."

"Lieutenant Kiera Markov."

"Thank you, Lieutenant." He gestured toward the hand pad for the door, which hadn't been active in the seven previous months of my tour. A guard and a biometrically locked door. They'd stepped up the defense protocol a *lot*. Shit. Not good.

I entered the Operations pit and let my eyes adjust to the dim light. Most of the illumination came from the massive screens along the front wall that toggled through maps and information. I scanned them, trying to glean what I could. Without a terminal, I couldn't control the flow of data, which made it hard, but my neural implant kicked in—I triggered it subconsciously, I guess—and started parsing information, a little flicker in my mind.

"Ma'am?" A tech sergeant stood at a respectful distance, and I glanced over my shoulder to see if I was blocking someone's view. "We're going to start an operations sync briefing, if you want to sit in."

"Sure." I turned toward the back wall to take my spot as a junior officer. No need to get my own update when they'd cover everything in the sync anyway.

"Ma'am?"

"What?"

"You can sit up here." He gestured to a row of terminals on the first raised level, positioned to look over the top of the first-line operators. The command row. That made sense. The colonel had traveled with all the staff to a luncheon sponsored by the ambassador from Argaz, so most of the officers were gone. I was supposed to go, too, but given the condition of my intestines, there had been no way, so I'd stayed back, allowing the watch officer to attend. It was an annual event and supposed to be a great time, where the Argazzi plied the leadership of the peacekeeping force with the best food their country had to offer.

"Right." I walked up four steps and down the aisle, taking a seat at the operations officer's terminal. It didn't matter if the commander wasn't there; you didn't sit in the colonel's seat. I put on the headset and a moment later, Sergeant First Class McNamara, now on Watch, started broadcasting to the group. I knew her in passing, but not well. I did know her voice, having heard it often enough. She had one of those professional, newscaster-like timbres. On top of that, she ran the basic operations of the Ops center, and she acted as moderator for the briefing, standing down front but broadcasting over the loudspeaker from an invisible wireless microphone. She'd pass the comm to different briefers and analysts as needed.

"At 1744 hours a large explosion occurred here." A red circle appeared on the giant front map screen around what looked to be a small grouping of buildings set apart from any other structures by a good bit. "Satellite sensors indicate that it was a low radiation nuclear weapon in the three-kiloton range. We detected no delivery system, which likely means it was there on the ground and triggered on site."

A nuke.

Shit.

I think I'd known it outside when I'd seen it, but I hadn't let myself believe it. Why would I even imagine that could be true? There hadn't been a significant attack on Tanara in forty-eight years of peacekeeping.

Tanara only even existed because seven hundred years ago someone had discovered enough lithium on it to make it worth the money to terraform it and settle it, and nobody beyond the two million or so people who lived there ever gave it a thought. At least until the two major nations on the planet—Argaz and Zarga—started fighting each other and cutting off production of the vital element. But that was half a century ago. In the present, our unit performed more of a ceremonial role than a tactical one, invited in by both sides to keep the other honest as part of the treaty that ended their war. Neither side really wanted to fight, and us being here gave them a good excuse to avoid it. The Federation gladly supplied the troops to Tanara in order to keep the lithium flowing to the rest of the galaxy.

"We've triangulated the location to the compound hosting the ambassador's dinner. We've tried to establish communications with forward elements there but had no success. We're not sure if that's EMP from the blast or…"

I didn't hear anything else she said. Another voice took over, briefing something about the potential source of the explosion, then another about the lingering effects. My vision blurred. All the officers in our task force had been at that dinner hosted by the ambassador. It was a tradition that every unit had continued for the last forty years.

Tears welled in my eyes, and I struggled not to let them fall. Officers didn't cry.

My family.

As an unmarried officer, that's what my unit was. All my friends were army friends. More than friends. Sisters and brothers. No communication. A nuke. They couldn't be dead. I stared at the monitor without seeing. I don't know how long I sat there before I tuned back into the sound in my headset. McNamara, the watch NCO, had taken the brief back.

"Priority of work is to continuing security protocols and establishing a temporary chain of command. Pending your closing comments, ma'am, this concludes the briefing."

I looked up after several seconds of silence. McNamara stood there and three or four other NCOs had turned in their seats to look at me. She wanted me to give closing comments. Holy shit. Was I in charge? I couldn't be. I was a scout platoon leader. But there were no other officers present, so I guess I was. My voice cracked when I spoke. "No comments."

2

I remained in my seat for several minutes after the briefing concluded.

All my friends, the entire leadership, dead. "Lieutenant Markov? A word, ma'am?" Master Sergeant Hearns stood about two paces away. I knew him vaguely—everyone did. He worked for the command group, taking on a lot of the routine duties to run the building, sort of like a mayor. He wasn't in charge, but he was somebody you didn't mess with, especially as a junior officer. Not unless you wanted your ass handed to you by the XO.

"Sure." I stood and followed him out of the pit and down a hallway into the command group area. Cheap furniture dotted the large, open room with just a few clerks occupying desks outside the doors of the private offices of the task force leadership.

"Give us the room," announced Hearns. He had a voice that didn't allow for debate, and the junior soldiers scattered quickly, leaving us alone.

I stood there, head down. Jaks, Cooper, Rodriguez, Rostov...so many more. They couldn't be gone. For some reason, I thought about Rodriguez and the time she'd swapped out Cooper's pants for a size smaller, so he'd think he was gaining weight, and I almost laughed, which would have been pretty fucked up.

"Ma'am, I need you to get your shit together." Hearns stood close enough that I had to look up at him. The dark-skinned man dwarfed me even though I'm one point eight meters tall and weigh eighty kilos. He stood a head taller than me and had shoulders like a bot-tank.

I took half a step back with one foot to put some space between us. "Excuse me?"

He watched me, unblinking, the overhead light reflecting from his perfectly bald head.

There was a good chance that I'd lost every friend I had in the world, and this motherfucker was staring me down. I steadied myself and tried to keep an even tone. "It's a lot to process."

"We all lost people, ma'am. But you're in charge now, and if the soldiers see you losing your bearings, this whole place is going to collapse."

I started to snap back at him, but then stopped and considered my words in light of who I was talking to. I outranked him, but he had positional authority. "Master Sergeant, I've got two years in service. You've got twenty. I'm not in charge of anything."

"Twenty-two, ma'am. And yes, you are."

"Right. Twenty-two. You should do it. Until the others get back."

He shook his head. "They're not coming back, ma'am."

I stood there with that for a few seconds. I knew it already, but hearing him say it out loud made it more real. "I can't. You take it."

"No, ma'am. You're the officer. You've got the brain implant, and you've got the academy training."

"You have real-world experience. That's more important than all my training." It sounded whiny as it came out of my mouth. He was right. All the experience in ten lifetimes wouldn't add up to everything I could access via the expensive interface the army had implanted in my skull.

He stood there silently, waiting. I think he knew he had me.

I met his stare. "You'll back me up?"

"Absolutely, ma'am. Here." He held out an insignia.

"What's that?" I asked.

"Major's rank. I got it out of one of the Ops officer's desks. Nobody's going to follow a lieutenant for long."

"I can't wear—" The door from the pit whooshed open, followed by running steps.

A short, bald, male soldier ran up. "Master Sergeant, ma'am, we need you in the pit. Something just took out our satellite links."

Hearns and I made eye contact for a second before hustling after the soldier. I squeezed the metal rank tight into my palm, letting it dig into the skin.

"Ma'am, we've lost everything." McNamara launched into her briefing before I even stopped moving. "Surveillance, long-range communications, space-based weapons. It's all gone."

"Do we know what happened?"

Before she could answer, a klaxon sounded throughout the pit.

"Ma'am, now someone's attacking our local network, trying to breach the base security system," a female voice announced from the back of the room.

Everyone stared at me, and for a few seconds I couldn't respond. My heart raced and my breath got short, and I scrambled for something to say. Anything. I didn't understand it before, but in that moment, I knew that I was in charge. Nobody teaches that. It's not in any leadership book. They sure didn't cover it at the academy. But there we were. Things had gone to shit, and twenty people stood, staring at me like I had some magical answer. And I couldn't move, couldn't think. Everything was coming too fast.

"Ma'am," said Master Sergeant Hearns, softly.

"Give me a second," I said, holding up my hand to keep him from saying anything else. Hearns was right. If I didn't keep my cool, nobody else would either. I took a deep breath to calm myself, to buy a second to think. Every part of me wanted to lash out, to find out who attacked us and destroy them. I took another deep breath. We didn't even know who did it. I had a guess, but it was only that. The Zargod didn't like us, and I didn't like them. They were a bunch of arrogant bastards. Add to that the fact that the luncheon was on the Argaz side of the border, and that was a lot of evidence. But I needed proof.

That would come later. First, I needed to deal with the imminent threats. Two problems. We'd lost satellite connectivity, and someone was attacking our network. I needed to address the more immediate problem first. The local one. Satellites wouldn't matter if someone compromised our security and we got overrun.

"Switch all security systems to manual and lock down the base. Full guard. Throw everybody out who's not part of the task force, no exceptions."

"Ma'am, the vendors are going to protest," offered Hearns, softly, so only I could hear him. Right. We had a bunch of shops on the base run by Zargod entrepreneurs that provided goods and services—a place for soldiers to spend their money in the local economy without venturing out into the city.

"Fuck 'em. We'll apologize later," I said. "We need to secure ourselves until we know what's going on."

"Roger," he said, louder.

"Trace the cyberattack if you can. I need to know where the enemy is."

"Roger, ma'am," came a response from the back of the room.

I closed my eyes for a minute and accessed my implant to help me visualize the surrounding area. Our base was located in the small city of Tanzit, about thirty klicks south of the border with Argaz. It sat on generally flat terrain with a narrow river bisecting it. Outside the city things quickly tapered off to grasslands and low, rolling hills. Nobody spent the money to terraform unoccupied land beyond what was necessary. It made for an easy search pattern for drones. "We need eyes up. Watch," I said, speaking to McNamara and trusting that she'd pass the message to the appropriate station, "launch half the surveillance drones and get me a view in every direction. Get two of them over into Argaz to get eyes on the blast site. I need to know what we're dealing with, and if anyone survived."

"Yes, ma'am," said McNamara.

"Once all that's moving, let's figure out what happened to our satellites, and when we can get them back. We can't sit around blind and out of contact." *And the sooner we get in contact with someone, the sooner someone else can take charge.* I leaned in closer to Hearns and spoke quietly. "Spin up the quick reaction force. I don't know how recently we've exercised them, so I want you to go out and put eyes on them personally. Make sure they're square. If we find survivors at the blast site, they're going to need help."

"Yes, ma'am."

I hoped they'd be ready, and that everyone would respond, but we weren't really prepared. We had the equipment and the soldiers, but nobody had challenged the task force in the almost five decades of the mission. We'd be relying on training, not practical experience.

"Have them ready to go by the time we get sensors over the blast site."

"Yes, ma'am." His tone told me I was saying things I didn't need to. He had it.

"Sorry," I said.

"We've got this," he said, as he turned and headed out to the task I'd assigned him.

The pit jumped to life as McNamara spoke commands into her headset. I became quickly aware that everyone in the room had a job but me. I'd let instinct take over as I gave orders, but now I stood there alone and awkward, unsure what to do with myself. Part of me wanted to go to a workstation, to dive into the intelligence and dig for the nugget that would throw light on the problem. That was something I knew how to do. Instead, I tried to remember what I had seen the commander do in the past.

"Watch," I said.

"Yes, ma'am."

"I'll be in the XO's office if you need me. As soon as anyone gets anything on these attacks, no matter how small, I want to know it. You can ping it directly to my implant." It would be at least twenty minutes until we got surveillance on the blast site, and that would only happen if everything went right.

"Yes, ma'am."

I turned and walked back to the command suite, imitating what I'd seen the Colonel do in the past. He'd give his orders and then get out of the way so people could work. As I passed through the door, I reached up and unpinned the lieutenant's rank from my collar, then weighed the major's insignia in my hand for a moment before pinning it on. My implant unhelpfully provided the information that it weighed three-point-one grams. It was probably my imagination, but it felt heavier.

3

I tried to sit at the XO's desk but quickly gave that up for the visitor's chair. Even that felt like an invasion. I didn't belong there in his space. McNamara needed to work with the analysts, and I knew that she'd call for me when she had something, but I needed to do something. I'd never been good at sitting still. I tried to work through the nuclear attack in my mind, figure out who was likely to have been behind it. One of the two nations made the most sense, at least on the surface, but the more I thought about it, the more skeptical I got.

The Zargod were the most likely culprits since the attack had taken place in Argaz. They were a patriarchal monarchy where rulership had stayed in one family for more than two centuries. Wealth was focused mainly within a few families—those who had begun the lithium mining companies—though a lot of that money had trickled down to other citizens, to the point where immigrants did a lot of the actual work now. The problem was, an attack like this didn't fit their nature. The Zargod weren't really fighters; the war fifty years ago had proved that. But it was more than that. It was *beneath* them. They saw themselves as too cultured to debase themselves with that sort of thing. Or at least they seemed to.

The Argazzi seemed less likely since the attack happened there. But maybe they had used that as an alibi. They were nominally a collective, but realistically it was something else. On the surface, they were the opposite of the Zargod, completely opposing the amassing of wealth by individuals, and outlawing family inheritance. In theory. Yet there were still those in power and those who weren't, and that didn't seem to change. They had elections, but there was only one party, and candidates usually ran unopposed. A lot of the power ran through the mining collective, and while everybody was, by definition, equal, those involved with that particular enterprise were more equal than others. But they were also ridiculously bureaucratic. For them to agree to something as rash as a nuclear attack…well, I just didn't see it.

I lasted seventeen minutes, turning thoughts over in my own mind before I couldn't take it any longer and headed back to the pit.

"Battle stations," McNamara yelled when I came through the door. The two or three soldiers who weren't already in their chairs glued to their screens scrambled to their seats. "Space, report," she said once I approached.

Space's voice came over the speaker before I reached my seat in the command row. "Still no contact with any satellites. That includes the entire quantum communication network. We've lost all off-planet communications and primary GPS systems as well as all space-based observation systems."

I put on my headset, so I could hear without the clutter of the room that came with listening to the speaker. "What happened? Did we just lose the link?"

"Still working on it, ma'am," she answered. "We can't be sure."

"How soon?" I asked.

"Estimate that we'll know more in ninety minutes. Two hours at the outside."

I tapped my fist against the desk. "What's your best guess?"

The net stayed silent for several seconds before she answered. "If I had to guess right now, I'd say the satellites are gone."

"Gone? As in destroyed?"

"Yes, ma'am. But like I said, we can't confirm."

I shook my head. "Who could have…how…"

"We don't know, ma'am," said Space.

"Roger," I answered after a few seconds. There were too many things we didn't know. I squirmed in my chair, unable to get comfortable.

"Cyber, report," said McNamara.

"The attack against our network is contained, ma'am. It was kind of primitive. Not much of a threat."

Primitive. It sounded more like the Zargod. "Can you trace it?" I asked.

"Yes, ma'am."

"Do it," I said.

"Already working, ma'am," Cyber replied. "We'll have a tight location in thirty minutes, tops. We've already got it pegged down to about a half-kilometer radius."

"What's there?"

"There are several blocks of mid-tier housing."

I interfaced with my implant and quickly located the area he was talking about. "Good work." If we could get a location...at least that would be something on which I could focus my attention and get my mind off our losses. I wanted something to attack.

"Ops, report," said McNamara.

"Drones are up, ma'am," said Ops. "We should have eyes on the blast site in two minutes. The quick reaction force is spinning up. Ground force will be ready in fifteen. Airborne force in twenty-five."

I resisted the urge to tap into the drone feeds via my implant. I could wait for them to come up on the screen. "Okay." That seemed slow for the QRF—the ground force was just four hover vehicles that held five soldiers each with a couple of air-cycles tacked on for recon—but it wasn't as slow as I'd feared, given their lack of use in the past. It didn't matter. I didn't think I would launch them until we had a better handle on what had happened, anyway. No sense sending people into a nuke site unless there was someone to save. Even with a low-radiation nuke, the residue would affect them at close range, and with no satellites, we wouldn't have accurate radiation readings yet. I mentally tabbed into my implant and ran a quick check on radiation dispersal rates in a dry, grassy climate for several different types of bombs. I appreciated the efforts and professionalism of the staff and how fast they'd acted to find what I needed to know, but with my implant, I could do some things easier on my own.

"Drone feed is on the main screen," announced Ops.

"We're not going to be able to get an overhead," said another voice. Probably the drone operator. "There's too much smoke and turbulence. Switching to side-looking aperture."

The pit went silent as the first images of the bomb site showed on the large screen up front. I pressed my lips shut and breathed through my nose, trying to suppress my reaction. Black smoke dominated the frame, thick and evil, gusting across the rest of the image and obscuring the site. The camera flipped to an alternate view that showed the ground at a wider angle. Debris littered the area, a few mangled vehicles standing out from the less identifiable rubble. Smoke blocked the picture entirely for two or three seconds but then cleared.

A crater. A black smear at least a kilometer wide marred the green and brown of the surrounding grassland.

I turned my head away and looked down at the floor, my stomach flip-flopping. I reached up slowly and took off my headset. Nobody could have survived that. Pressure built behind my eyes, and I ran my hand through my dark hair. The familiar movement brought to mind a memory of Jaks—one of my best friends, now dead. She'd cut off her long hair in favor of a more utilitarian cut like mine. She just got tired of all the work it took to maintain it on a deployment. But afterward, she couldn't keep her hands off of it, constantly running her fingers through the four or five centimeters of hair at the front.

Someone came to stand close enough for me to sense their presence, and it broke me out of my daze. It was McNamara, a light sheen of sweat at her temples shining beneath her close-cropped black hair. "What do you want me to tell the QRF, ma'am?" she asked, not speaking into her microphone.

I paused for a moment, then replied quietly, not wanting to disturb the silence. "Have them continue to ready status, but don't launch them. Hold them at Ready One for fifteen minutes. After that, back them down to Ready Two. I want them to finish going through the full process." Ready One would have them on immediate alert, sitting in their vehicles. Ready Two meant they could roll out the door and take off in five minutes or less. I didn't think we would use them, but I hesitated to stand them down right away. If I *did* need them soon, I'd look foolish calling them back up again. I told myself it would be good training for them, regardless.

McNamara nodded. "Yes, ma'am."

She stood beside my chair for a minute, both of us looking at the screen, watching the smoke.

"What do we have off base right now?" I asked. "Not including people who went to the ambassador's party. Anything else?"

McNamara spoke quietly into her microphone and then waited a moment for a response. "We've got one logistics convoy out. They're due in early morning the day after tomorrow. About thirty-four hours from now."

I nodded. Logistics convoys traveled mostly at night so that the big vehicles didn't impede local traffic. "Do they have an escort?" I had a good idea about the answer before I asked, but I wanted the time to think.

"They've got small arms, ma'am. That's it."

"Notify them of what's happened, once we can establish comms. We should probably launch some sort of escort, right?" I kept talking, not waiting for an answer. "Let's do that. Launch an escort six hours before they arrive…does that make sense? Where would that put them in relation to us?" I tried to figure the distances in my head and visualize a map, but I couldn't, so I started to call it up with my implant.

"We'll figure it out," McNamara said. "I understand your intent. We'll determine the best rendezvous point and launch at the appropriate time."

"Right," I answered. "Give them two ground platoons including at least two bot-tanks, plus air cover."

McNamara leaned down, so she could speak softly. "You sure about the tanks, ma'am? That's a lot of firepower inside the city."

I hesitated for a second, but then forced a quick answer. I didn't want to look indecisive. "I've got no idea what is going on out there, Watch. But they hit the command gathering and potentially hit the satellites, so we can't afford to risk it. If someone tries to ambush our force, I want to give them a hard fucking target." I paused. "But your point is a good one. Have Master Sergeant Hearns meet the leadership of the escort before they depart to check them out."

"Yes, ma'am. Do you want me to give him instructions on what to check?"

I appreciated her gentle prompt. Of course, I needed to tell him that. I couldn't assume he would know what I was thinking. "Ask him to assess their state of mind. I'm worried that after the attack…we've all lost friends. We're all angry. But we don't know who our enemies are yet, and we can't afford to add more problems by taking a shot at civilians who don't deserve it. Have him reinforce that." After all, I felt that way myself. It was only natural that the soldiers would want revenge as well.

"Yes, ma'am."

Cyber's voice cut through the room's chatter. "Watch, this is Cyber." I snapped my headset back on to listen closer.

"Go, Cyber," said McNamara.

"We've tracked the origin of the attack on our defense system. It's three kilometers from here."

I stared at the red dot that showed up on the map on my screen, right in the middle of the city that surrounded our base. Zargod territory. It matched my guess. The nuke had detonated on the Argazzi side of the border, and since they and the Zargod had hated each other for longer than the peacekeeping mission's fifty-year history...well, we didn't have enough intelligence to accuse them, but the corrupt assholes were definitely the most likely suspects. The Argazzi were corrupt too. They just weren't so smug about it. Theirs was more of a legal, corporate corruption. Zarga was a patriarchy that believed women had no place outside the home. Like I said...assholes. Part of me hoped it was them. If we could prove it, I'd make them pay.

It was a stupid thought—I knew that even as I had it. Commanding a brigade was way beyond my capability, and the smart thing to do was to be as conservative as possible and hold on until our higher headquarters could ship in new leadership in a few weeks. But a few weeks was a long time, and a lot could go wrong before we got relief.

"Watch, have the heads of all the Intel disciplines meet me in the small conference room in five minutes." I stood and walked out of the pit.

4

I stood at the head of the table with five analysts seated at it, all of them looking at me, waiting. Two women, representing Commo and Human Intelligence sat on one side with a man from Cyber between them. Across from them were two men, representing Imagery and General Intel. They spanned the ranks between Sergeant and Sergeant First Class, and I spent an extra second looking at each one. I didn't know them yet, but I needed to remember them going forward. I felt a bit like a fraud, standing in front of them having never really received this sort of briefing before. Then I remembered that since their bosses had died in the attack, all of them had stepped up to these new roles recently just like me. That helped me focus.

Hearns stood against the wall to my left, not interfering, but positioned so I could see him. I wondered why he chose to come. Something in his body language struck me as confrontational, as if he thought somehow that I required a chaperone, but if he had a problem with me, he wouldn't have insisted that I take charge. Maybe it was my imagination. I couldn't spare the time to unpack that with the analysts waiting.

"Tell me who tried to breach our network," I said.

The Cyber analyst stood without hesitation. Sergeant Alexie. He had brown skin and a short, dark haircut that curled a little on the top. "Ma'am, we don't have enough information to answer that." His voice marked him as the same person who had briefed me back in the pit.

"But you have a location."

"We have a building, ma'am." "How sure are we that it's the right building? A hundred percent?" I asked.

Again, Alexie didn't hesitate. "Ninety-nine. More than ninety-nine. It was a clumsy attack. Amateurs."

Amateurs didn't add up. Someone had touched off a nuke. That alone meant we were dealing with a high-level actor at least at some point in the chain. But still, someone had hit our network, which made them a valid target. That suited my purpose. I wanted a target. I wanted out of the headquarters and into the action. "It has to be Zarga behind the attack, right?" I asked.

"I can't say that with any confidence, ma'am," said Alexie. He was a young man, maybe two or three years older than my twenty-three. A light sheen of sweat coated his forehead, and he blinked several times. He probably wasn't used to being grilled by the commander.

"Any chance that it's a trap? Could someone have made it look like a hack from that location to try to draw us out?"

Alexie looked down at his fidgeting hands. "I don't know, ma'am. Maybe? It seems unlikely, but I really don't know."

"Okay. Thanks." I looked at Commo, a pinch-faced soldier with dishwater brown hair pulled back in a tight bun, seated next to Alexie. My implant provided her name as Lewellyn, keeping me from having to glance at her nametag. "What have we picked up from other communication coming out of that area?"

"Nothing I can clearly categorize, ma'am. High transmission traffic. Panicked. I've got the language programs working on everything, but so far it's consistent with seeing a giant nuclear cloud." She spoke with confidence. No hesitation. I believed her. If someone had the audacity to attack our network, they probably had the sense to keep quiet about it on systems that we could monitor.

"Imagery?" I asked.

Sergeant First Class Klauss, a tall, pale-skinned man with recruiting-poster hair spoke. "Nothing out of the ordinary, ma'am. I ran it back four hours before the blast and picked it up again once we got drones up to replace the satellite feeds. We had a gap, though."

"How long?" I asked.

"Twenty-two minutes."

Twenty-two minutes right after the blast. Anybody getting in or out of the area would have done it before that, so it probably didn't matter. "Anything from Human Intelligence?"

"No, ma'am," answered Sergeant First Class Diaz, a copper-skinned woman with broad shoulders and a buzz cut. "We've got word out to our local sources, but nothing back yet. We'd have to get really lucky to pick something of value up on this. We expect to get a lot of calls but for most of them to be just rumor."

"Yeah." I paused and thought through everything we had. It was thin. We had the hacker located, but the attack itself didn't make sense in relation to the nuke and the potential attack in space. The right answer—by the book—would be to turn the intelligence over to Zargod authorities and let them chase it down. But I didn't trust them. The Zargod were corrupt on a *good* day, and today was anything but good. At best, they might go to the scene and take a bribe to look the other way. At worst, if they were responsible for the attack, they might sanitize the scene and ensure we found nothing.

There was another option. We did have the right, according to the treaty, to conduct unilateral action in situations where we'd been directly attacked. I'd checked. But I sure would have appreciated a stronger case. I tried one last gambit, hoping that I could tie the three attacks together, even while knowing I probably couldn't. "Which side has the capability to pull off a nuclear attack?"

The last analyst in the room, a pasty male with a bit of a double chin hesitated before speaking, looking like he'd rather have been somewhere else. "In theory, ma'am, neither. The tripartite treaty prohibits nuclear weapons above point-one kilotons on the planet. The one from earlier was approximately thirty times that size."

I took maybe ten seconds to think about it. We didn't have enough to justify unilateral action. But at the same time, if I was going to command this unit, I needed the respect of the soldiers. They wouldn't give it to me...I'd have to earn it. Soldiers respected action. I'd get some blowback from the Zargod, but I wanted to take action, and what could they do to me?

"Okay, we're going to hit the building. We'll do a cordon and search. We'll isolate the building with a supporting force and take a team inside to search the residences in question. Anything more you can gather in the next twenty minutes, send it directly to my implant."

Hearns pushed himself off of the wall, looking like he had something to say, and I braced myself for his rebuke. He'd know as well as I did how flimsy my case was. But he caught himself before he spoke.

"Master Sergeant Hearns," I said. "You have thoughts?" He hesitated still. He didn't want to contradict me in front of subordinates. "Speak freely. I want everything in the open. Nothing said in here leaves the room." I glanced around at the analysts, making eye contact with each one. "Understood?"

A chorus of *yes ma'am*s returned.

"Ma'am..." Hearns paused, cleared his throat. "It might be a mistake to take soldiers out into a civilian area right now. We've lost a lot of people, and the mood...our soldiers want revenge."

Of course they did. I wanted it too. Not against civilians, but against those responsible for the deaths of my friends. Even if the cyberattack wasn't tied to the nuke, we needed information and searching that building might provide it. But more important, I'd at least show our soldiers that we were doing *something*. Militarily, it was a bad reason to push a mission. But the near-term success of our unit relied on more than just the correct tactical decision. "We'll go in soft. We need intel, and we've got a clear source from Cyber."

"Ma'am, I don't think we can count on the proper restraint from our soldiers at this time." He kept his voice even, respectful, though something more forceful boiled just beneath the surface. He was right. There was tension between the Zargod and the peacekeepers on a regular basis, and recent events had amplified that.

"We've got to act," I said. "Line soldiers aren't going to see the intel. They're just going to see the inaction if we don't do something. What kind of message do we send to our force if we just sit here?"

"Ma'am...the risk—"

"That's why I'm going to lead the mission myself," I said.

"That's out of the question," he said, then pulled back, realizing what he said. "Ma'am," he added, belatedly.

I looked at everyone in the room except Hearns. "Not one. Fucking. Word. Got me? Nothing leaves this room." I couldn't have word of a division between Hearns and me getting around. From the way he stared down all the analysts, Hearns knew it too. Good. At least we agreed on *something*.

"Yes, ma'am," they responded. Good. We'd find out if they meant it based on what rumors started circulating. Like it or not, they were my inner circle now, and I had to be able to trust them with sensitive information.

I turned to Hearns. "You just told me this was risky. I'm going myself to mitigate potential issues."

"Yes, ma'am, but you're our only officer. There's too much risk."

"And that's why I'm going. I want to be there to control the situation." That wasn't the only reason, but I couldn't say that I felt like a fraud as a leader, and this was my way to prove I wasn't. This was a mission I understood—something I was good at.

Hearns hesitated for a few seconds before backing off. I don't think he came to see it my way. More likely he realized he couldn't oppose me in front of the others any longer. "I'll have an assault team ready to go in twenty minutes, ma'am."

5

I walked toward the assembled force, shrugging to try to get my body armor to stop digging into my shoulder blades. I hadn't worn it since training before we deployed, which made it stiff. I had my assault rifle clipped to one shoulder. I didn't expect to use it—the last thing we needed was a firefight downtown—but there was no way I'd leave the compound without it in the current circumstances. Despite the discomfort, I could feel the tension sloughing away. I was out of my element running a brigade, but this—a platoon-sized patrol—this was my jam.

About forty soldiers stood around in front of six vehicles: four troop transports with guns mounted on forward turrets and two bot-tanks, with a command vehicle—mine—and two air cycles sitting off to the side. The tanks weren't completely autonomous, but they might as well have been. The systems ran fully automated, and they only carried a passenger to circumvent the laws against armed drones. Technically, the pilot could override the computer, but that only happened when there were civilians around—like if you took them on a mission into the middle of a city to surround a building. We probably didn't need them, but I wanted them with us to send a message. I wanted the Zargod who saw us to know how serious we were, to understand that we were not to be fucked with. There was some small chance that this was a trap, the cyberattack bait to draw us out into an ambush. If that was the case, we'd make them regret it. At the same time, bringing tanks carried risk, so for safety's sake, I used my implant to send a message to the vehicle commanders, giving orders for them to stay extra tight with their weapons. That wouldn't bother the soldiers. We always stayed tight. We were peacekeepers, after all.

I tried to pick out the noncoms as I walked up. The nondescript gray body armor made it tough to ID the leaders, but watching the way they interacted in the group gave me a clue. Four soldiers listening to one talk probably meant the platoon sergeant and four team leaders. I should have thought to have people that I knew put on the mission. I now had about four thousand soldiers in my command, and while there were maybe a hundred I'd recognize, I didn't actually *know* more than thirty or so. That's just how it went with officers and enlisted. Regardless, I hadn't thought about that when building the team, and I didn't want to go back and make a change now. It would make it look like I didn't trust the team that Hearns had picked for me. Plus, we didn't have time. The intelligence was getting stale on the origin of the cyberattack. A smart enemy would be long gone by now, but I held out a little hope since Cyber had called the incursion amateur.

"Major Markov! Major Markov!" I didn't recognize my new rank until Hearns called it the second time. He jogged up with four soldiers in a neat two-by-two formation trailing behind him.

I took a few steps and met him as he drew up. "What's up?"

"Got your security detail here, ma'am." The soldiers behind him stood at rigid attention.

"I've got a whole combat patrol here, Master Sergeant. I think we're good." The brigade commander always traveled with a security detail, but as a lieutenant, I'd never used one before. I was just one member of a team. Besides, with the enhanced abilities my neural implant gave me—faster reactions and access to nearly every form of hand-to-hand combat known in the galaxy—I'd be a tough match for all four of them together in a fair fight. Never mind that the brigade commander had the same implant.

"Humor me, ma'am," said Hearns.

His tone pissed me off a little, and my first reaction was to push back. I was the commander, and everyone here worked for me. But this was still Master Sergeant Hearns, and regardless of our legal command relationship, he held a lot more power than I did and had a lot more experience. Plus, he'd caved at our last confrontation, so it was my turn. I didn't want his hand-picked crew—it seemed less like a security detail and more like babysitters—but I nodded. "They're good?"

"I got them recommended from people I trust," said Hearns.

"Okay, I'll take them. But if they get in the way of the mission, I'm going to stash them in a vehicle and leave them there." It was petty of me to say. We both knew that wouldn't happen.

"They know what to do, ma'am." Hearns tried to hide a smile at his victory and almost succeeded, but not quite.

I grunted at him and walked over to my new security detail. "At ease." They shifted from rigid attention to only a slightly less rigid stance with their legs shoulder-width apart.

"If you're going to work for me, the first rule is that you work for *me*. Nobody else." They were Hearns's soldiers—I couldn't change that right now—but I needed to start making them mine.

"Yes, ma'am," they said in unison. The male soldier on the front right flicked his eyes quickly to where Hearns stood, a couple meters behind me and to my left.

I glanced at his nametag. "Murphy, do you have a problem with that?"

His eyes snapped back to me and went wide. "No, ma'am."

"If that's going to be an issue, tell me now and I'll get someone else. You go where I tell you to go, and you stay out of the way. This is a combat patrol. I need to lead it, which means I'm not going to hide in my vehicle. I'm going to be exposed. There's no help for that. You just keep your eyes open."

"Yes, ma'am," they chorused.

"If someone shoots at me, you find them and shoot back. Murphy, heaven help you if something goes down and you try to jump on me like a human shield. I'm going to punch you in the nuts."

That drew a smile from all of them, and a snicker from a tall man named Gonzalez, whose helmet seemed to swallow his narrow face. I took in the other two. Xiang was the final male soldier and Zillakovavich the only woman. I had seen Xiang around before, but I couldn't place where. It was a small base, so it could have been anywhere, and nothing about his appearance stood out as memorable. He was average height, neither good-looking nor ugly, and I imagined he could disappear easily in a crowd.

"Zilla is fine, ma'am. Or Z." She must have noticed me staring at her name.

"Got it. Thanks. What's your role?"

"Gunner, ma'am. Weapons specialist." She was the shortest member of the team, but she had broad shoulders and heavy arms.

"You can hit what you mean to?" It wasn't a real challenge. She wouldn't be there if she couldn't. But I wanted to establish a connection, and soldiers liked to be challenged.

She met my eyes. "Every fucking time, ma'am."

I nodded, and then met the eyes of each of the other soldiers in turn. No fear in any of them. I didn't want a security detail, but if I had to have one, this one would do nicely. "Fall in with the patrol," I told them. They snapped to attention and took off at double time.

"Thanks, ma'am," said Hearns. "Better safe than sorry."

I nodded, but at the same time I was thinking that he and I had to get more on the same wavelength, or the entire unit was in trouble.

I studied the troops as I briefed them on the mission. I kept the parameters simple, the tactics basic and by the book. We hadn't worked together, and the last thing we needed was a miscommunication over procedures to get in the way. We were isolating a rectangular building in an area full of similar structures with wide roads and square corners. That section of Tanzit was almost a grid, which made the tactics simple. We'd put a bot-tank at corners one and three of the building and a fire team at corners two and four. That left two teams to clear the inside, which was more than enough. Add in my four shadows and we had serious overmatch on any expected threat.

But something nagged at me as I briefed them on the final details, like who would take over if I went down, and other contingency plans. I couldn't put my finger on it at first, but it slowly dawned on me. They were paying attention. That doesn't sound strange, but it was. They weren't showing the casual interest of a routine mission, but the rapt attention usually reserved for chow or the latest holo-game. Soldiers paying attention to my briefing. Shit just got real. The tension reverberated in the looks they gave each other, the extra checks of weapons. Hearns had warned me that the soldiers weren't mentally in a good place to be out on mission, and now I could see it.

"It's important that we go in with the right demeanor," I said. "We've got intelligence that leads us to this building, but we don't know anything for sure. Success here is defined as a quiet mission, nobody hurt, no shots fired. In and out, as peacefully as possible."

Doubt started to creep into my mind as we broke up and headed to our vehicles…something in the way the troops responded, I think, though I couldn't say exactly what. Nervous troops made dangerous missions, and I couldn't shake the feeling of unease this group gave me. My gut warned me to call it off, but after I ordered it…to go back on it…I had the authority, but I don't think I had the guts. They'd see me as indecisive, and as a lieutenant pretending to be a commander. I couldn't have that. I'd done it to myself. I wanted out of the headquarters and into my own element, and I'd forced the decision. Now I wasn't sure.

I signaled the team to mount up.

Better to drive on than look weak.

6

We encountered minimal traffic traveling the paved streets as we moved through the twisty roads in the old part of the city that abutted our base. They were mostly clean and well repaired, meaning we didn't cross into any of the poorest sections. We rode in a command-and-control vehicle—basically an armored hover car. Murphy drove, I had shotgun, Gonzalez and Xiang rode in back, and Zilla manned the turret. We passed a few pedestrians scurrying between buildings, and one group of five or six children playing on a sidewalk, but with things generally quiet, I turned my attention to my team. If Hearns wanted them with me full time, there was no better opportunity than the present to get to know them.

"Xiang, you look familiar. Where have I seen you? What did you do before Master Sergeant Hearns tapped you for this job?"

"I'm not sure where you would have seen me, ma'am. Maybe the mess hall?"

"Given how much you like to eat, that does seem likely," said Gonzalez.

"You two know each other?" I asked.

"Yes, ma'am," said Gonzalez. "We're from the same infantry company."

"What about the others?"

"No, ma'am," said Murphy. "It was just me from my unit."

"How'd you get the job?" I asked.

"I don't know, ma'am. My platoon sergeant just called me over and told me to put on a clean uniform and double time it over to brigade."

"What about you, Zilla? Are you from the same unit?"

"No, ma'am. I didn't know any of these guys. Not really. I'd seen Murphy around—you can hardly miss him with that red hair and pale skin. He damn near glows in the dark. But that's it."

I glanced to the driver's seat to see Murphy's reaction, and he was smiling, taking the dig in stride. "You're all infantry, then?"

I got a chorus of *yes, ma'am*'s in response. That made it less likely that they were purely spies, and more likely that Hearns really *was* just trying to keep me alive.

"So Gonzalez, Xiang—you know each other. Anything I need to watch out for?" I kept my tone light, wanting to make them comfortable enough to open up a little.

Gonzalez took the bait. "Well, ma'am, you need to watch out for Xiang."

"*Shut up*, Gonzo," said Xiang, but he sounded more embarrassed than angry.

"Yeah? Why's that?" I asked.

"Well, he's slept with like half the women in our unit. And probably a quarter of the men."

I snorted, trying to hold in a laugh.

"Shut *up*, Gonzo!"

"It's okay, Xiang," I said. "I'm not a prude. Tell me something about Gonzalez."

"Uh...well, he mixes music."

"Yeah?"

"Yes, ma'am," said Gonzalez. "I can play some through the vehicle's intercom system if you want. I always keep a fresh mix on me."

"I think I'll pass for now," I said, and while I didn't mean it as a joke, the other three soldiers burst out laughing. That helped me. I'd been really tense leaving the base, but getting around soldiers again—remembering how much fun that part of things was—helped me relax.

We talked a bit more, until we reached our target area when the tension crept back into my neck and shoulders and I focused on the terrain. We were doing this thing, and I was in charge of it.

The curving streets of our part of the city were gone, replaced by square blocks with wide, paved streets. Sidewalks lined either side, and a slew of identical two-story red brick buildings filled almost all of the empty space, four to each rectangular block—two the long way, two the short. One block had a small corner store, which appeared to be abandoned except for the smoke from some sort of grill coming up from behind it, but beyond that, it was just the apartments.

The thing that stood out the most, though, was that it was utterly empty. It looked like a dystopian film, where some sort of plague had wiped out civilization but left all of the infrastructure intact. A few empty vehicles were parked on either side of the street, but there were no people. Not a pedestrian, not even a kid or a person walking their dog. The only sign that the neighborhood wasn't deserted was one woman watching us from the open second-story window of an apartment building, but even she disappeared, closing the window as we moved past. Strange. Were the streets empty in reaction to the nuclear attack earlier in the day, or did they know we were coming? Or both?

Arriving at the target building, teams quickly secured each corner of the block and assumed overwatch positions where each one could see down two sides of the structure. The rest of us would isolate and search the target. My terminal provided a map but no schematic of the inside of the building since we'd lost our satellite data link, so I studied it as soon as we approached, trying to validate my plan. I never gave a thought about how much we relied on that technology until we no longer had it. But I had to make do until we could get our backup system working.

The low, rectangular building had twelve windows per floor on the long side and six on the short side. Given the moderate affluence of the residential neighborhood, I judged four apartments per floor for a total of eight. Cyber had isolated the attack to the back left of the building from our current perspective but couldn't give us the floor. That made two possible residences. We'd hit the bottom floor first while ensuring nobody left the top.

Our vehicle lurched to a stop in front of the building and settled down onto its feet. Murphy might have been a good infantryman, but he wasn't a natural driver. I waited for the team behind the building to secure their side and for the assault team to take their place near the door. Once they signaled they were set, I flung open my door and hopped out, joining Gonzalez and Xiang, who'd dismounted before me. Murphy and Zilla would wait with the vehicle, providing covering fire if we needed it. Not that I wanted Z opening up with a heavy weapon in the middle of the city.

My boots clacked against the street, loud enough to echo in the silence, the only other noise was the whirring engines of our combat vehicles. Somewhere someone was grilling meat from the smell of it, but I couldn't tell from where, as what little breeze there was seemed to swirl and come from every direction at once.

A member of the assault team attached a device to the electronic keypad that controlled the front entrance, and a few seconds later another flung the door open. We probably should have knocked, but there was too much risk of someone destroying evidence. We had to go fast.

As more of the team moved to secure the entry, locals started to poke their way out of surrounding buildings. We'd spent enough time in their city over the last half-century where it didn't take long for curiosity to overcome fear, I guess. But they had nothing to be scared of. They saw us every day, albeit without the bot-tanks, which we didn't normally take into the city. They tore up the roads and blocked traffic, which just pissed everyone off.

On a prearranged signal, Gonzalez, Xiang, and I joined the second team entering the building. We hadn't worked together, but we'd all had the same training and fell into rhythm naturally. The foyer opened into a wide hallway with a scuffed tile floor. The recessed light fixtures on the ceiling almost three meters overhead were spaced just a little too far apart to give even light. As I had predicted, the hallway only had four doors, two to the left and two to the right. That was good. No surprises. At the far end of the hallway, four soldiers stacked on the wall outside the suspected residence, while five more guarded the hallway and two kept watch on the stairs that led to the second floor.

I gestured with my head and my two security guards led me toward the target. I lowered the visor on my helmet with a thought through my neural implant, and my heads-up display flickered to life, outlining friendly soldiers in dim green.

The four soldiers hit the door harder than they needed to, but otherwise executed a textbook entry, each soldier tucked right up against the one in front of them. Once they entered, I couldn't see them because of the wall between us, but their outlines stayed on my HUD, relayed from their own helmets. They moved perfectly, quartering the first room, then clearing each subsequent space. I could gauge a vague outline of the shape of each room from their feeds, but it didn't give me any detail. I moved my team closer. I wanted to get in there as soon as we got the all-clear.

"Entry clear," came across the radio. A woman shouted in Zargod in the background of the transmission, and once the broadcast cut off, her voice still carried through the door.

I toggled the translation program in my implant—I could understand and speak dozens of languages with its help—but her words were too garbled to make out even with the computer assist. She was pissed; that much came through from her tone. Hard to blame her when soldiers came crashing into her house. In theory, men ruled Zargod. In homes—this home, at least—that didn't appear to be the case. We needed to search and get out before we did too much damage to local relations, but some of it couldn't be helped.

The whole team knew what we wanted: any electronics, especially computers. The lady would probably yell even louder when we started taking her stuff. We'd give her a receipt, but I doubted somehow that would mollify her.

Crack.

What the fuck was that? I hesitated between steps.

Gunshot.

Shit.

I ran for the door, trusting my team to follow. A scream joined the yelling woman, then other voices.

"Shit, Darnell, what did you do?" Comm transmission. My implant identified it as the team leader.

"He showed red!"

"What the hell happened? Was that a shot?" The patrol leader checked in from his position leading the covering force outside.

I reached the door and entered, ignoring Gonzalez's best efforts to get in front of me. "Clear the net," I broadcast over my comm. I needed to concentrate on the situation in front of me. We could inform troops not in the apartment later.

A boy of about nine lay in the door to the next room, a woman—perhaps his grandmother—kneeling over him. The child squealed in pain as she tried to touch his shoulder to check the wound. A terrified soldier stood three paces away, waving his weapon wildly at nothing. My heads-up confirmed his name as Darnell. Three Zargod men stood against the far wall, cursing us, but not moving as two soldiers covered them with rifles. Their voices jumbled together so that my program didn't give me a clean translation. Fuck that software. I swung my attention back to the child on the floor. A rivulet of blood ran into a small puddle on the tile. I stared at it, unable to move. The simulators I'd trained on never did that. The blood. They didn't capture the way it pooled. And they didn't use kids.

"Ma'am! What do we do?" The voice over my headset snapped me back into focus. A female voice, the same voice as before. The team leader.

Shit shit shit. I needed to think. "Everybody quiet!" I said it in Zargod, using the broadcast function of my helmet to make myself heard over the yelling.

Everyone stopped for a heartbeat, apparently stunned into silence. Things snapped into focus.

"Darnell, get your fucking rifle under control," I said, switching back to standard language for my own soldiers. He quickly pointed it toward the floor. "What happened here?"

"The kid burst through the door just as we were getting ready to clear through," said the team leader—Lippett—her voice steady. "Darnell fired a shot which struck—"

I waved my hand to cut her off. "Got it. Get a medic in here to treat the child. Darnell, why did you fire your weapon?"

No answer. I glanced at the boy on the floor again. He had a shoulder wound.

"Darnell!" I grabbed the soldier by the shoulder of his body armor. He whirled on me, his weapon swinging with him. Gonzalez came a split second away from leveling him, but I beat him to it with my heightened reflexes, grabbing the barrel of Darnell's rifle and twisting it down and away.

He paused, his eyes darting back and forth. He had raised his visor.

"What happened?" I asked again, locking my eyes on his, speaking calmly.

"He shot my son!" yelled one of the men against the wall in Standard, so all the soldiers would understand.

"Be quiet!" I broadcast in Zargod, without turning my head. Rude, but I needed to get answers fast. I felt the whole operation slipping out of my control. "Darnell! For the final fucking time. What happened?"

"Like I said, he showed red!" Darnell shook, his weapon unsteady in his hands.

Darnell's HUD had identified the child as hostile? Usually that meant the target had a weapon or a bomb, but it could also trigger off of other algorithms that recognized intent. I had no idea if Darnell was telling the truth—if the child had really shown with a red outline—but we could play back his feed later and find out. Regardless, he shouldn't have shot a kid.

He shouldn't have shot at all in this situation. This was supposed to be a simple fucking mission!

And there was a child, bleeding on the floor, the medic just reaching him and starting to assess his injuries. That was bad. Bad for a lot of reasons. The obvious one, of course, is that you don't shoot fucking children. But in this case, it was bad beyond that for the situation it put us in. Because when you *did* shoot a child, people got really, really mad about it. And they weren't wrong.

Part of my brain screamed to just get out of there, but it was too late. We'd done the damage. Like it or not, we had to mitigate it, and unfortunately, that meant I was going to make things worse before I made them better. "Search the child," I said.

"Ma'am?" Lippett turned her head to me.

"Darnell said the boy showed red. Make sure the boy doesn't have a weapon." We were going to pay the price for this mistake. We'd have to answer questions from the Zargod leadership, who were going to be righteously pissed. I was going to have to have answers to those angry questions, and that meant checking the child, despite the fact that it was going to set the family off even more.

Lippett hesitated. I don't know if she was processing the order, or just didn't want to search a wounded child, but after a few seconds, she moved. She tried to guide the grandmother out of the way, but the woman resisted. "Stay away from him," she shouted, my translator getting it clearly that time.

"Ma'am, please back away from the child," I said in Zargod, mustering all the command I could put into it. The soldiers didn't have the translator built into their brains like I did. They all knew a few common phrases, but under this pressure, I couldn't count on that.

Grandmother stood and stared me down. She looked like she wanted to say something, but then she pushed past me and toward the door.

This was going to shit in a hurry. I thought about having the soldier at the door stop her, but I didn't act fast enough and then it was too late. Probably for the best. She didn't plan on stopping, and if we put our hands on an old woman we'd have made things worse. The men against the wall would have had to act, forcing us to act in response. "Hold your fire. Civilian coming out," I announced over the comm unit. The last thing I needed was another nervous soldier pulling a trigger.

"They shot my baby!" Grandmother yelled in the hall, her voice getting farther away as she repeated her cry.

"All clear," reported the team leader. She'd searched the wounded kid while the medic continued to work.

"How is he?" I asked.

"He's lost a lot of blood," said the medic.

"Stabilize him the best you can."

A report came across the comm. from someone out of my view—a female voice. "Ma'am, people are starting to fill up the hall."

Shit. This was *really* getting out of hand. "Roger. Do not engage under any circumstance."

"Copy."

The team leader signaled over another soldier who pulled a med kit and started working on the boy. I willed them to go faster but knew that if I said anything, it would just add stress.

"People are starting to file into the street from this building and ones surrounding it," a male voice said. The patrol leader, from outside the building. I needed to make a decision, fast, before things got beyond my control. I wanted the tech we came for, but I didn't think it was here. Moving to the upstairs apartment to search it with all the civilians gathering…that wouldn't end well.

"As soon as the medic's done with the child, we back out of here," I told the team with me. I got nods in return. I didn't need to tell them. Everybody had the same idea. If we hung around long enough for a mob to form, we were in trouble. Sure, we had the weapons and the body armor, but nobody wanted to open fire in a crowd. "Darnell, you go now. Join the team in the hall and keep your weapon pointed at the ground."

"Roger, ma'am." Darnell moved, dragging his feet as he went.

"He's as good as I can make him," the soldier treating the child said after a couple long minutes. He'd sprayed on a coagulant, bandaged the wound, and put the boy's arm in a sling.

"Roger. Prepare to exfiltrate."

Lippett signaled to her team, and they moved in practiced unity, keeping cover on the men against the wall.

I looked directly at the man I assessed to be in charge of the family and spoke in Zargod. "If the boy needs further medical attention, bring him to the base. You understand?" We had better medical facilities than the locals but taking the kid with us would just incense them more at this point.

He met my eyes, unblinking, for several seconds, then spit on the floor. I didn't need a translation to know what that meant.

"Let's move," I said.

"We're coming out," Lippett broadcast over the comm.

Perhaps fifteen civilians had gathered in the hall, shouting in Zargod, raising their volume if anyone made eye contact. I searched the commotion for Grandmother so I could tell her about the offer of medical aid, but I couldn't find her.

We pushed through the people in the hall, who melted back when we approached, making it easy. By the time we reached the door, about a hundred people had gathered around four soldiers who tried to maintain a line between the entrance and the crowd, their weapons held square across their chests to form a wall.

"That's them. They shot Milo!" Grandmother shouted from the front of the mob. The crowd howled, fists in the air, a cacophony of voices that my translator couldn't parse.

I looked over at Gonzalez who was on my right shoulder. "On my signal, make us a path out of here. Don't shoot, but be as rough as you need to be."

"Yes, ma'am," he answered.

I pulled my pistol out and fired into the ceiling—unlike my rifle, the bullet didn't have enough power to penetrate to the next floor of the well-constructed building. The crowd quieted for a moment, stunned, some of them drawing back. Gonzalez used the distraction to his advantage and waded into the crowd, using his long arms and weapon to clear a path. The soldiers with us took his lead, making a wedge, driving through the angry civilians, shoving them out of the way. Murphy had the vehicle door open when I got there.

"Get us the fuck out of here," I ordered once Gonzalez and Xiang made it in. Murphy took off at an even pace, accelerating only after he cleared the crowd. I silently thanked him for his restraint. So much had gone wrong, so even the smallest thing going right seemed significant. I said a silent thanks to Hearns for forcing the security team on me.

Beyond that, I'd managed to get the worst of both worlds. I'd pissed off the locals, *and* I didn't get any intel on the people who breached our network. Hearns was going to have a field day with that. He wouldn't say 'I told you so.' He wouldn't have to. He *had* told me so, and we both knew it. I doubt I'd ever be able to forget it. The thought of seeing him filled me with anxiety.

My security team stayed silent on the trip back, the atmosphere of the outbound journey completely gone. I wondered what they thought. I couldn't ask, of course. It wouldn't be appropriate, and they wouldn't tell me the truth anyway. They'd say it was okay. At least to my face. But behind my back? I wondered. Did they still see me as the young officer who was willing to take action? Or was I the fuck-up lieutenant who was pretending to be a major?

Honestly, I wasn't sure myself.

7

It was sunset when we reached the gate of our base. We made it without incident except for one of our vehicles hitting a parked civilian vehicle. Thankfully it was unoccupied, so we left it. It sucked, but they could file a claim and we'd compensate them for the damages and their time. On any other day, that would have been a big mistake for my patrol. Today? It wasn't even close.

I'd spent the entire trip on the comm, sending instructions to have our people contact the local authorities and tell them what happened on the mission. I was sure they knew by now, but hopefully making the effort to reach out would score us some points. We'd hurt a kid, which ideally should have been the focus, but practically speaking, that was in the past. We couldn't change it. So we needed to mitigate the consequences.

Soldiers swarmed in the yard just inside the gate. Apparently, news of what happened had traveled throughout the unit. Great. Word of my failure had spread; just what I needed. I'd have to talk to Ops about that. They should have kept it as a need-to-know, even though it would have gotten out eventually from the soldiers on the mission.

Lippett and the platoon sergeant, a shorter, dark-skinned man named Whitcomb, met me as I exited my vehicle. Murphy and Gonzalez herded other soldiers away from the area so that I could talk to the two noncoms.

"Orders, ma'am?" asked Whitcomb. He was senior, and Lippett's boss.

"Secure Darnell and get his helmet to Intel immediately. I need to

THE WEIGHT OF COMMAND

know what his video feed from the incident shows."

"Yes, ma'am," said Whitcomb. "You want us to put him in D cell?"

I paused. Darnell wasn't accused yet, just under investigation. But I didn't want him walking around. I especially didn't want him talking to everybody in camp about what happened until we had some clear answers. Detention cell, though…that would look like I'd already judged him guilty, and I'd risk a revolt. "I think not. But put him somewhere safe and keep an eye on him. He's been through a significant emotional event, and I don't want him hurting himself."

"Yes, ma'am," Whitcomb said. He kept his face neutral, so I couldn't tell if he agreed with my decision or not.

"I especially don't want him talking. Do whatever you've got to do to convince him that it's in his best interest to keep his mouth shut until we know more."

"Roger, ma'am." This time, I thought I saw a hint of agreement cross Whitcomb's face, but that might have just been wishful thinking on my part.

When I entered the pit three minutes later, McNamara met me before I reached my seat. "Ma'am, what happened out—"

I cut her off with a raised hand. "Have we got any satellite contact back?"

"No, ma'am. No off-planet communication."

"How long until someone notices that we're off the net?"

"They've already noticed, I'm sure of it. They had to have."

"Then how long before they get someone here to see what's going on?"

McNamara thought about it for a few seconds, though I'm sure she already had the answer in her head. She was too good at her job to have not considered it. "If they dispatch a ship after being out of communications for thirty-six hours as per standard protocol, and if there is a ship ready at the closest military base…twenty-five days."

"That's if everything is perfect," I said. "So let's call it four weeks as most likely."

"Probably smart, ma'am."

"And then let's add another week because I have shitty luck."

McNamara wisely didn't respond to that, and we stood in silence for a moment.

"We need two-way communication off planet. I can live without satellite surveillance—we have drones for that, and we can put up aerial relays for on-planet comms, but I *have* to report the nuclear incident to headquarters, which means I need a functioning quantum communicator. I assume we've checked on civilian options?"

"Yes, ma'am. Our intel points to *all* satellites being out. Something hit ours, but it hit everything else in orbit too."

I nodded, acknowledging the information. This was getting bigger by the moment. "Get the staff working on ideas for how we achieve that. Tell them they've got four hours and I want to hear their best solutions."

"Yes, ma'am. What do you want us to do about the situation with the patrol you led?"

I let out a breath. What could we do? I could try to get in touch with the senior father—the man who ran the city—but my people had already contacted the authorities, so what would I tell him that he didn't already know? "Let me know the minute that Intel has looked at the video from the helmet. Until we get that information, anything else we do is premature." I'd jumped into enough hot water for one day. I didn't need to rush into any more.

"Yes, ma'am."

I turned to where Hearns stood, hovering a few paces away, brooding. Might as well get that ass-chewing over with. "Master Sergeant Hearns, join me please." He fell in beside me as I strode out of the pit to the command suite.

I led him into the XO's office—I still couldn't think of it as mine—and shut the door behind us.

"What happened out there, ma'am?"

I half sat on the edge of the desk. "I fucked up."

"You didn't shoot the kid."

I hesitated. I expected him to blow up at me, because I *did* fuck up, but instead he was giving me an out—the chance to blame it on Darnell, or the technology. It felt like a trap. I wasn't falling for it. "No, but I saw it in the soldiers before it happened. The nerves. You told me about it, and I absolutely saw it. I should have called the mission off, but I didn't have the guts. The result was inevitable."

"I should have pushed harder for you not to go," said Hearns.

I sat there, confused. While I appreciated the sentiment, we both knew he was full of shit. He was being nice, trying to take some of the blame off of me. But I couldn't for the life of me figure out why. If ever there was a time for *I told you so*, this was it. After several seconds, I decided to just put it out there. "Why aren't you yelling at me? You told me not to do it, I did it anyway, and you were right."

Now it was his turn to pause, his brow furrowed. "You're the commander. It's your call. On top of that, you already recognize your mistake. Would me pointing it out help you in any way?"

I considered it. He was right. After all, we'd shot a kid. I didn't need him to tell me how fucked up that was. But we were past that, and I had to focus on what happened going forward. I'd get plenty of recriminations from the Zargod when I faced them—rightfully so. But right now, it was just us, and I needed to do what helped the unit. "I'm just trying to figure out how you and I work together."

He took a few seconds. "I think we do our best to communicate so that we stay on the same page."

At that moment, the comm box on the desk buzzed. I pressed the button. "Markov."

McNamara spoke through the speaker. "Ma'am, the external cameras are showing civilians gathering outside the main gate."

"Shit. Already? How many?"

"At least two hundred, but more are showing up every minute."

"I'll be right there." I cut off the comm and turned to Hearns. "The unit knows I screwed up. I made the call on that mission against your advice, and it went to shit. I think it would help if you told them that you came in here and read me the riot act."

"Ma'am, that's none of their business. You're the commander."

"But it is. They've all got opinions—today more than ever—after the nuke. They need something that makes sense. If I was a lieutenant and I screwed up, you'd have spoken your mind, right?"

"Probably, depending on the officer and if they were worth developing."

"Right. And even though I pinned on Major, everybody knows I was a lieutenant yesterday."

His face lit up in understanding. "And if I let you know you screwed up, I show everybody else that you're worth developing."

"Exactly. And our story is that I admitted my mistake and promised to take better input from people with experience." It wasn't all a lie. I needed to do that.

Hearns considered it. It would give him credibility, too, as the guy with the guts to tell the commander the truth. And I'd have to pay it off—

have to listen to him in a public way for the next couple of days. I didn't mind. Soldiers would appreciate an officer who could learn from a mistake. At least I hoped they would.

Hearns met my eyes for a long few seconds, thinking it over. "That's how you want to play it?"

"If you're okay with it. Unless you have a better way?"

He thought about it for a moment. "No, ma'am. I don't have a better way."

My shoulders sagged in relief because I needed the idea that I was worth developing to be more than an illusion. I needed Hearns to actually believe it. If I lost him, I'd lose everything.

"Thanks. Start brainstorming some experienced ideas for what I do about this mob that's forming at the gate. Somehow I don't think the city fathers are going to be as forgiving as you are about shooting a child."

Back in the pit, McNamara waited for me with a taller, pale woman with her hair pulled into a disheveled bun. "This is Tech Sergeant Berghof. She's an expert on helmet software, and she reviewed the footage from Darnell's system."

"Excellent. Berghof, what have you got?"

"Ma'am...it showed red."

"So Darnell was telling the truth." I didn't know if that made things better or worse. It certainly made them better for Darnell, but I didn't think it would help with the crowd massing at the gate. "What could make a friend-foe identifier read red when it should have read white?"

"A trained actor can sometimes defeat the recognition software," Berghof replied. "It picks up on intent from facial cues, as well as other biometric factors."

"What about a nine-year-old kid?"

"Almost certainly not, ma'am."

"I thought not. What else have you got?"

"The technical specs allow for a small percentage error."

I nodded slightly. "It can just fail to function properly?"

"Yes, ma'am."

"How often?"

"About one time in a hundred thousand."

I rubbed my eyes with the heels of my hands and ground my teeth. "So that's pretty unlikely." I couldn't write this off as a simple software malfunction. Could I? Sure, I believed my luck was absolute shit, but those odds defied reason.

"Yes, ma'am."

"Berghof, what's your best guess at what caused Darnell's heads-up to read wrong?"

"Ma'am..." She took a few fidgety steps.

"Spit it out. The damage is done," I said.

"My first guess would always be human error, but the video doesn't support that."

"Sure. What's the next most likely possibility?"

"Honestly, ma'am? The next most likely possibility is that the kid had a weapon."

"Except he didn't. I had him searched." For everything that I'd done wrong so far, at least I'd done that. It was callous, and it pissed the family off, but it had been important. We could rule it out unequivocally. But it didn't give us an answer, and I didn't know what to do. No way had we hit a one-in-a-hundred-thousand glitch at exactly the moment when it would hurt us most. "Is there any chance that someone hacked Darnell's heads-up locally? Is that even possible?"

"In Zarga? I mean...anything is possible, but it's extremely unlikely. Our HUDs are built to resist the best cyberattacks in the galaxy. And... respectfully...Zargod technology isn't nearly at that level."

She was right. Zargod culture didn't put a high value on high-tech pursuits. They preferred things less complicated. They would say they were more civilized, more refined. I might suggest more arrogant. But we all had our biases. "Keep digging, Berghof. Pull the entire thing apart if you have to, but find out why it showed red. And more important, make sure that that glitch isn't in any of our other helmets."

"Yes, ma'am."

I turned to McNamara. "What's the status of the gathering at the gate?"

"Continuing to grow. Nothing violent yet, but they're pretty fired up."

"What's our best option?" I asked.

McNamara keyed her microphone and spoke into it, "Sergeant Anthony, attend." A short, slightly overweight male soldier with pale skin hustled down from the back row to join us. "Sergeant Anthony is with PsyOps. He's got potential courses of action." With everything that was going on, McNamara seemed to have an answer for every question, and I appreciated her organizational skills. I should have told her that, but it didn't seem like the time or place. Instead, I waved Hearns forward to join us from his spot hovering just out of the way. I wanted him to hear whatever PsyOps had to say. "Give it to me."

"Ma'am, I want to send a team with a speaker and a translator out to one of the guard towers. Our message to the crowd will be that they should disperse, and that if their leaders present themselves, we'll talk to them directly to try to resolve any grievances they have."

"You think that will work?" I tried to keep my skepticism out of my voice.

"No, ma'am. It almost certainly won't. But it will turn their focus inward because none of them will be able to agree on who is in charge. It's a cultural thing with them—they're very formal when it comes to leadership. We've done facial recognition, and none of the city fathers are there. The others will argue among themselves, which will buy us some time. It's already getting dark."

I nodded, and then glanced to Hearns. "What do you think?"

"I don't have enough expertise to go against Sergeant Anthony's opinion, ma'am. I say we go with the subject matter expert."

"Roger." I turned back to Sergeant Anthony. "Aren't they eventually going to figure it out? And when they do, we're back to the same problem, right?"

"Yes, ma'am. But it buys us more time to prepare a response."

I was inclined to listen to Anthony—and more inclined to listen to Hearns—but I wanted to understand more about the cultural aspect. I'd spent nine months here, but really hadn't interacted more than basic transactions. I needed to fix that. "You don't think I should go talk to the crowd?"

"Absolutely not, ma'am," said Anthony. "If you do that, it sets a precedent, and they'll show up with a mob any time they want to talk to you. They don't expect that kind of access from their own leaders, and we don't want them to see you as anything less than a leader."

"What happens when the crowd's leaders do sort themselves out?" I asked.

"*If* it happens, we wait for them to present at the gate, and then we turn them away because they aren't the city fathers. You're the commander, and you're in charge, so it's only right that you talk to someone as senior on their side."

"That will work?" I appreciated his answers. They were contrary to what I thought initially, which just went to show how much I had to learn.

"Yes, ma'am. They'll be pissed, obviously, but it's how they would do it to us, and more important, it's how they would treat each other. It is how they *expect* you to act. And at the same time, it's better that they're pissed off about not getting to meet you than focusing on what we did wrong in that apartment."

"Okay. So we send out a team with a speaker. Let's say that works. What happens next?"

"They'll go to the city fathers. Or, more likely, they already have. There's a good chance that the city fathers are the ones who ordered the protest. So we wait. If they want to see you, they'll let us know tomorrow. That will give us information about how important they really see this matter."

I turned to Hearns one more time before giving my final guidance. "Are you still good with Sergeant Anthony's plan?"

He considered it for a few seconds before speaking. "Yes, ma'am."

I nodded. "Okay. Make it happen. Watch, anything new on the nuclear attack?"

"No ma'am, no new intel."

"Nothing?"

"We've got AI synthesis of photos of the blast zone, but they don't measurably alter what we already knew. And while we haven't put people on the ground at the detonation site because of the localized danger from the event, we don't think we're going to find any remains of the device. And even if we did, our teams that analyze explosives don't have nuclear training."

Well okay then. My confidence level in McNamara went up a bit, and I made a mental note for the future. When she said there was nothing new, she'd done her homework. "What about our logistics convoy?"

"Still on schedule. We got a comms drone up and were able to make contact with them via relay. Expected arrival is around 0400 plus one day from now, and we're still on track to launch an escort when they're six hours out."

I found myself standing there with no more questions, unsure what to do next. My hair was plastered to my forehead, and I realized how gross I felt from being out on mission in body armor. "Okay. I'm going to go get cleaned up. Buzz my implant when the team is ready with options for establishing communications to the other side of the galaxy."

8

I let myself cry for exactly one minute in the shower—one of six stalls in what used to be a shared space but now belonged to just me. I actually set a timer, because if I didn't, I might not stop. There was just too much. It was the only place nobody would see me, and while I couldn't let it show on the outside, I really needed it. I'd lost all my friends, and on top of that I somehow now had responsibility for four thousand lives and didn't have the experience to deal with it. I'd already made mistakes, and I was afraid I was going to make more. And even thinking that was wrong. If I focused on potential errors, I'd hesitate and be less likely to take any action at all. Part of me wanted to sit on the tiled floor and just let the water wash over me for an hour.

But I didn't. I stepped out and towel-dried my hair. I kept most of it cropped short, so it didn't take much effort, though it was getting a bit longer than I liked in the front. I'd have to use a little extra product to keep it swept up and back until I could find time for a trim. I checked myself in the mirror and liked what I saw—my strong chin, broad shoulders, the definition in my arms. I was a mess on the inside, but nobody would see it. They'd see the hard exterior because that's all I'd show them.

I wrapped my towel around me for the walk back to my room. I needed to consider getting myself lodging in a building closer to the headquarters, now that I was in charge, but that would require cleaning out the room of one of the senior officers, and I didn't want to think too hard about that yet.

The junior officer barracks was a one-story building with a low ceiling that consisted of a single long hall with rooms down each side and latrines at either end. Since I was the only one living there now, it had a graveyard feel.

The minute I stepped out of the latrine into the hall, something felt off. I don't know what triggered the thought. Maybe a sound, maybe something in the way the air moved. But I knew I wasn't alone. My heart pounded in my chest, and I silently cursed myself for leaving my pistol locked in my bunk room, four doors down the hall. I breathed evenly and tried not to overreact, walking down the hall as if nothing was wrong. I wasn't helpless. My implant gave me exceptional reactions and a whole host of unarmed combat programs. Unless the invader had a gun, I liked my odds, though I'd never fought in just a towel and flip-flops before.

Remembering the cameras at each end of the hall, I used my implant to patch into their feeds. It took a lot of practice to be able to walk normally while looking at video from another source, and I found myself thankful for the eight months of specialized neural implant training all officers received. It took me about three seconds to find the intruder hiding in the recessed doorway one past mine, and about one more second to identify him. I moved closer before revealing that I'd seen him.

"Murphy, what in the space-fuck are you doing here?" Murphy screamed, a little too high-pitched for a man his size. His face turned a shade of red that almost matched his hair, though whether it was because of the scream or the fact that I'd caught him stalking around my barracks, I couldn't tell. "Ma'am...you startled me."

"That'll happen when you're creeping around while someone's in the shower."

He stammered. "It's...Ma'am...it's not what you think."

"Really? What *do* I think?"

He stood gawking, unable to form words.

"I'd love to do this all day, Murphy, but I have a job. Why are you here?"

"Master Sergeant Hearns told us not to leave you alone, ma'am."

I frowned. "Told whom?"

"All four of us. Me and Gonzalez and Zilla and Xiang. He said one of us should guard you at all times."

I started to snap at him but held it back. It wasn't Murphy's fault. If

Hearns gave him a legal order, he had to follow it. I couldn't tell Murphy to buzz off without countermanding Hearns, which was something I'd recently promised not to do. Hearns knew that too. He'd got me. Asshole. It wasn't all bad, though. My building *was* deserted. Even when he was doing things behind my back and pissing me off, Hearns had a good point.

"Okay," I said. "You can guard me, but you stay outside my door. I don't know you well enough for you to see me naked." *Nobody* had seen me naked in a couple of months, which was something I wouldn't have minded fixing under normal circumstances. But these weren't normal times, and Murphy wasn't an option, regardless.

His face reddened even deeper if that was possible.

"I'm going to get changed. Once they call me for the briefing, we'll head over to headquarters."

Hearns looked at me like a man waiting for a beating when I entered the pit with Murphy by my side, but I ignored him. We'd talk about it later. McNamara had two other noncoms with her, waiting to brief me.

"Ma'am, a quick update before we start. Sergeant Anthony deployed a team with a loudspeaker, as discussed, and the crowd is beginning to disperse."

"That's good," I said. It was a welcome relief to have *something* go right.

"You remember Staff Sergeant Lewellyn from Commo," McNamara continued, indicating a female noncom to her right. "To my left is Sergeant Tuchs, from Space Ops."

I took the XO's seat. "Give me some more good news."

McNamara's face tightened. She wasn't going to give me good news. "Ma'am...along with losing comms with the satellites, we can't reach the Wakobi spaceport, either."

"You can't contact the station here planetside?" The planet of Tanara was served by a single space elevator located about three hundred kilometers away. We should have had multiple ways to contact them.

Lewellyn spoke up. "We can still contact the base station, ma'am. But they can't contact the orbital anchor station or any of the way stations."

Shit. Why hadn't I thought about that earlier? Why hadn't anybody mentioned it? "That...correct me if I'm wrong, but that shouldn't be possible. They're hard-wired in through the elevator itself."

"Yes, ma'am," she said. "They should have comms, but they don't."

"Does the elevator itself work?" I asked.

"They have full function at the base station, but both the freight and the passenger trams are up in space, and—"

"And we can't contact them."

"Yes, ma'am, that is correct."

I looked at McNamara. "Why am I just hearing this?"

She had her arms drawn in around her, but she still met my eyes. "No excuse, ma'am."

I hesitated. I'd been too harsh. She had a hundred things to manage, and she'd missed this one. It was like Hearns had told me earlier in the day—he didn't need to yell at me, because I already knew. So did McNamara. "It's okay. Just tell me what happened. Why'd we miss it?"

"We... I just got focused on other things. Between the nuke and the cyberattack and coordinating for the convoy—" Her voice trailed off. "Like I said, ma'am. No excuse."

"How long have you been on shift?"

McNamara glanced at her device for the time. "About fifteen hours."

"That's not going to work. Do you have relief?"

"I do, but without the Ops Officer, I'm in charge of the pit. I want to be here."

I nodded. Any good noncom would. But she couldn't do it without a break. Nobody could. I needed to remember that for myself as well. "You are going to have to trust your subordinates," I told her—again, applying it to myself as well. We had at least a month before we would see reinforcements. We had to make do.

McNamara let her arms fall to her side, and some of the tension came out of her face. "Yes, ma'am. I'll get on that as soon as we're done here."

"Please do," I said, in as soft a tone as I could manage. "I'm going to need you, and that means I need you to take care of yourself. Now...what do we think is going on with the orbital stations?"

"Ma'am, if I may," offered Sergeant Tuchs.

"By all means," I said.

"Our best guess from Space Ops is that someone set off an extra-atmospheric EMP. Or, given the satellite pattern, more likely several of them, because they'd have to hit the entire constellation, some of which would have been on the opposite side of the planet. We considered a natural phenomenon—solar related—but given the proximity in time to the nuclear detonation on the surface, that seems unlikely."

"And the same EMP would take out the spaceport?" I asked.

"It would be a lot more difficult," said Tuchs.

"More difficult than delivering a nuke down here on the planet?" I asked. He considered it. "Yes and no. More complicated, yes, but less secure, so if they had the technology to make a big enough EMP…the orbital stations, and especially the anchor station, have some pretty serious radiation shields up there, since people live on them and they're outside the atmosphere. They have to deal with solar radiation on a constant basis."

"Shit." If someone could deliver an EMP big enough to take out a space station, what else could they do? And who the fuck would *do* that? "But there's still power at the ground station."

"Yes, ma'am," said McNamara. "We checked on that. Separate power supplies. The ground station provides most of the power, but the space station has its own supply. Relying on power from outside the station is considered too risky."

"So the people on the station…" It dawned on me what the power outage meant. Life support systems. I felt like I might puke.

"It doesn't look good, ma'am," said McNamara.

"How many aboard?" I asked.

"Daily crew is right around two hundred on the main station, with a much smaller crew on each of the two intermediate way stations. That doesn't include passengers. We checked flight schedules, and while we can't be sure, no ships were supposed to be there. Tanara only gets one ship in every ten days or so. It's not a busy station. We may have gotten lucky."

Something in the back of my mind gnawed at me. It didn't feel like luck. "How often are both trams up top at the same time?"

The three looked at each other, each apparently hoping that the other had an answer. It was McNamara who finally replied. "We don't know."

"Find out. There's something off about all of this. The timing of the attack on the ambassador's party with, potentially, an EMP in space…or multiple EMPs. That would have taken a hell of a lot of coordination, don't you think?"

"Yes, ma'am. Definitely not something you throw together at the spur of the moment," said McNamara.

Tuchs held up his hand.

"You're one of my primary advisors now, Tuchs," I said. "You don't have to raise your hand. Just speak up if you've got something to add."

"Yes, ma'am. They couldn't have timed it to the elevators. I mean, they could have, but they had a really small window. The celebration that drew all our officers—that's a once-a-year event. At most, they had a two or three-hour window."

"Great point, Tuchs." Maybe my first thought had been off. Maybe it *was* luck. I couldn't let myself be paranoid. On the other hand, I didn't want to blindly accept it, either. We weren't even one hundred percent sure it was EMPs. "We need more information. What are the people at the base station telling us?"

McNamara answered. "The lead engineer there said they're trying to get the entire operation shifted to ground power. It might be too late for the people in space, but it would at least let them get the trams back."

"Do they have a backup plan?" I asked.

"Yes, ma'am. They're spinning up an emergency tram. They have a maintenance rig that's designed for doing work in atmosphere. They're trying to modify it so it can go all the way to the space station. They plan to work through the night on both options and give us a report in the morning."

"Okay. Keep me posted. If there are people up there and they're alive, going to get them is our absolute priority." The nuke and the loss of commo were massive issues, but lives had to come first. Not that I had a lot of hope that we could get to them. The anchor station—the one with the most people aboard—was something like forty-thousand kilometers above the surface. Even if we got a tram working, it would take days to make it up there. How much oxygen did they have? What other systems might fail and cause catastrophe? I did a quick search via my implant, but I didn't have that information. It wouldn't normally be something I needed. When I got a minute, I'd do a deeper search and pull it up. I waited for Tuchs and Lewellyn to depart, waved McNamara away, and indicated to Hearns that he should come closer.

"Ma'am, about the security detail—"

I raised a hand for him to stop. I could have made it hard, but I decided to play it a different way and be gracious. I think seeing McNamara hang her head in shame even though she'd been doing great softened my attitude a bit. Like her, Hearns was doing his best. Like me. "Don't worry about it. If you want me to have security, I'll have it. But it *did* catch me by surprise since Murphy was hiding in the hallway like a dumbass when I came out of the shower."

Hearns sighed and shook his head

"So in the future," I continued, "I'd appreciate you letting me know before you do something like that. But we'll figure stuff like that out as we go."

"Yes, ma'am," said Hearns. "Do you have orders?"

I considered it. I didn't, and that was a problem. "What do you think should be our priorities?"

He hesitated. "I'm not the right person to answer that. I'm normally the mayor. I make the base work. I'm so far removed from operations off the base that I'm almost useless for that. You want *my* list of priorities? I want all the primary staff noncoms and other key leaders moved into the senior officer barracks so they are closer to headquarters. That includes you, and it includes me. Like you said to Mac, people have got to sleep. And when they do, if they're close, they can get back here quicker. That's the kind of thing I think about."

I nodded. He had a point, and I appreciated that while he was admitting his limitations, having him handle that was something I didn't have to think about. Everybody had a job. "Can you make that happen for us?"

"I'll get a detail on that first thing in the morning. I don't want to disturb sleep for those who can manage to get it tonight."

"That's smart."

"What are you going to do now, ma'am?"

I waved for McNamara to rejoin us. Hearns said Operations wasn't his area of expertise, but it was hers. "I need to stop and think. There's been a nuke, a cyberattack, and something up in space. They might not be coordinated, but it seems too coincidental for them not to be. But what I don't know—what I have absolutely no clue about—is who might be coordinating it and why. When the nuke happened, I immediately thought terrorist attack. But nobody has claimed it. So now I'm thinking that they did it on purpose to take out our officers. But to what end? We're a nothing mission on a nowhere planet."

"The lithium, ma'am," said McNamara.

"I get that," I said. "But what about it?"

"I don't know. But when something happens on Tanara, that's always the answer. It's the only thing anybody wants from this place."

It was blunt, and a shitty thing to say, but that didn't make it wrong. The Federation wouldn't have footed the bill for a peacekeeping mission if the planet was poor. Life didn't work that way. "But taking out the anchor station *stops* the lithium," I said. "That's not in anybody's interests."

After a moment of silence where we all thought about it, Hearns said, "Ma'am, if we can't put together the big picture yet, maybe we should focus on the individual things we need to do. I've always found that if you handle the small stuff, the big stuff becomes clearer."

"Good idea," I said. "Priority one is the space elevator. There might be people alive. I want a combat patrol on standby, ready to move in fifteen minutes, starting at first light tomorrow. Mission is to secure the ground station of the space elevator. Expect resistance. I want the closest thing we have to a doctor and at least three medics on the mission, and I want as much gear as we can get that would allow someone to survive in space. If they get that maintenance platform in shape to get to the space station, we need soldiers and medical personnel on it. We've got no idea what the situation is up there." We only kept a small military detachment on site—it was mostly a civilian-run facility—and if we were going to put people into space, I wanted it to be soldiers.

"We can do that." Hearns keyed in some notes as he spoke. "Though I don't know how much we have in the way of kit that's rated for space. I'll check, and if we don't have it I'll get the printers working on it. But are you sure we should send another mission off base at this point, given what happened last time?"

I tried not to wince. He wasn't being an asshole—he had a point, and I hadn't explained my rationale. "We don't have a choice. There are lives at stake, and while there's risk, we've got to take it."

He nodded once.

"Second, we've got to deal with the aftermath of the shitshow I caused out in the city. The protest has dispersed, but Sergeant Anthony said the leaders would probably be back tomorrow."

"Roger," said Hearns. "We'll get things set up to receive the city leadership."

"And let's keep an eye on the nuke site. There were no survivors, but I'd still like to get a team in there once it's safe enough."

"Roger," said McNamara.

"We should probably make contact with the Argazzi government, too," I added. "See if there's any sort of aid they need. It was mostly our people affected, but it *did* happen on their soil and they had some people there. I can take care of that." I knew exactly who I'd call. While I had exactly no contacts among the Zargod, I'd run several missions on the other side of the border, and I'd met a few people. One, in particular, stood out. She worked for the government, and I had her contact info. Sure, she hadn't given it to me for business reasons, and I'd never gotten up the nerve to use it, but maybe it could help me now.

"Last thing," I said. "Make sure that you get at least four hours sleep tonight. And before you ask, I will too. Right now, I'm heading over to Intel. I need to look at the terrain between here and the elevator, and I need the human intelligence team to get me prepared for whatever might happen with the local leaders tomorrow."

"Yes, ma'am. You okay taking Murphy with you?"

Hearns offered me an out, and I appreciated it. I still didn't think I needed an escort, but I hoped acquiescing would buy me some future points with him. "Sure. It can't hurt."

"Thanks, ma'am," said Hearns.

"Thank you too." I caught Murphy's eye and nodded for him to follow me out to Intel.

9

News from the space elevator early the next morning set my priorities for me. They had constructed a rig that could move a dozen people up to the space station. It wasn't nearly enough, but at least we could get some supplies moving, establish communication, and get an assessment of the situation. More important, we could deliver oxygen and safely move people down. So I gave the order to launch the team we'd prepared.

But first I had to contend with the protest outside the gate. They had dispersed for the night, but locals started to trickle back at first light, and by sunrise, there were two or three hundred people around the gate. They posed no physical threat to a military convoy, but the last thing I wanted was to accidentally run somebody over, and I could see them throwing themselves in front of vehicles, or at least trying to block the road. We came up with a pretty simple solution—or, I should say, Hearns did. He prepared a patrol and sent them out the front gate, and, as expected, they bogged down among shouting protestors. Meanwhile, I saw the real mission off from a previously unused back gate. I was sure that the protestors would find it eventually, but for this one time, it worked like a charm. No resistance.

I'd sent four hover vehicles with turret-mounted weapons, two transports for the team and equipment that would go to space, and a bot-tank. I'd considered leaving the tank behind because of the potential collateral damage if it engaged. I'd also considered sending two. I settled on one because it provided enough firepower to blow through almost anything someone could throw against the patrol along the route. Given the lengths someone had gone through to disrupt us recently, it only seemed prudent.

My true focus, though, was assessing the soldiers. I was sending heavily-armed trained killers into the civilian space and, given what happened at the apartment and with our recent casualties, I wanted to make sure I didn't have anybody with the wrong attitude. And I was serious about it. I pulled two soldiers off of the mission because I didn't like the way they answered my questions, and I replaced them with others I had ready for expressly that purpose. A couple of the noncoms stared at me after I did that—at least when they thought I wasn't looking—and I got it. They had their own people, and they trusted them. I was probably overreacting. But I really didn't trust *anybody* right then, and none of them were bold enough to challenge me directly about it.

Not going to lie, I almost went myself. If I wasn't so worried about what Hearns was going to think, I probably *would* have. Leading a patrol was my comfort zone. But I'd made that mistake once, and I couldn't make it again. Not if I wanted people to keep following my orders, especially since there were pressing things to do on base that only I could do.

The first was to make contact with the Argazzi government. I took a minute to fix my hair so that it swept just right, and I made the video call from my office. It was 0715 hours, so I didn't expect my contact to be ready for the day. She might even still be asleep. But I didn't want to wait.

Liana Trieste surprised me by picking up after only one buzz. Not only was she not asleep, she was completely put together, all high cheekbones and perfect makeup, her blonde hair up in a tight bun. She wore a gray suit jacket with a white blouse that had enough frills to look feminine but not enough to seem unprofessional. She looked so good that I had to force myself to keep my hands still, resist the urge to fix my hair again.

"Kiera. Holy shit! You're alive!"

I hadn't even thought about the fact that she would have thought I was dead. Hell, I didn't even consider the possibility that she'd ever given me a second thought. After all, we'd only met twice, and both of those were random encounters in a coffee bar. Okay…being honest, the first meeting was random. The second time was me taking my patrol back to the same place, which was near where she worked, hoping to run into her again. But that's a technicality.

"Uh...yeah. Hi. I am." Great job, Markov. Real smooth.

"I'm glad you called," she said, overlooking—or at least pretending to overlook—my oafish response.

"Yeah?"

"Yes. After the attack yesterday, our government tried to get in contact with your unit, but all the lines were dead."

Dead. She didn't mean it, but that hit me like a punch in the gut. "Yeah...everybody is dead."

"I'm so sorry."

"Thanks." What else do you say to that? "Look, the reason I'm calling—"

"Hold on," she said, cutting me off. "Before we get into that, can you give me the contact information of whoever's in charge now? It'll make me look great with my boss if I can come up with that."

"Actually, that's why I was calling. It's me."

"What do you mean?" she asked.

"I'm in charge."

"You..." her voice trailed off for a second. "Oh! Oh." She paused again, and the weight of what that meant hit her face. "I'm so sorry."

"Yeah. So I was calling to try to set up a call with someone important, figure out if there was anything we could do to help with the aftermath of the attack."

"I can help!" She said it with a little too much enthusiasm, but I wrote that off to her trying to compensate for the awkwardness. Or maybe that was me.

"Thanks. I'd really appreciate it. I've kind of got a lot of balls in the air over here."

"I bet. Is there anything else I can do?"

"Well...can you...what's the reaction been like over there? To the attack? You know, what's the leadership saying?"

She hesitated, but from her horrified look, I figured that it wasn't good. "Uh...I think it's better if I leave that to the people in charge to discuss with you. I...you know, I don't want to overstep. I'm sorry."

"Nah, it's cool, I get it. I need to run anyway." I wasn't lying when I said that, but when I replayed the conversation later in my head, which I would do multiple times, I'd wonder why I said it. It wasn't at all cool.

After an awkward pause, she responded, "Okay. Hey."

55

"Yeah?"

"I'm glad you're alive."

"Thanks," I said, smiling like a goofball.

"If you need somebody to talk to, well...you've got my info."

"Thanks. I'll do that." I snapped off the connection with a warm feeling. I wasn't sure I'd call her again—there was a lot going on—but just the fact that I could... It was good to have a friend. Someone I could talk to who didn't work for me.

An hour later, I was meeting with Corporal Collins from Human Intelligence discussing how to handle the meeting we expected to have later with the city fathers, when I got a priority alert from McNamara, calling me to the pit. She wouldn't have interrupted unless it was an emergency, so I grabbed Zilla, who was my current escort, and headed there at a fast jog.

"What've we got?" I asked as I entered, not waiting to get to my station.

"Ma'am, two and a half minutes ago, our patrol headed to the space elevator took contact from an unknown enemy."

"What?" I stood there, stunned. As much as I'd considered it, I hadn't really thought it likely. I probably should have. "Is everyone okay?"

"Nobody's dead, ma'am. Beyond that, we're still getting an assessment. But I thought you'd want to be here."

"You thought right." I headed to the commander's station and sat down. I hadn't been there for more than a few seconds when Intel came over the speaker.

"We've got video from the patrol."

"Put it on the front screen," said McNamara.

The room went silent—not that it was loud before that—as we all watched the attack together for the first time. The video opened with the bot-tank exploding, a quick flash of flame and then a roiling river of black smoke.

"Back that up and slow it down," I ordered. Whoever was controlling the video did it without responding. At five percent speed, a streak of light appeared for a few frames just before the explosion. A missile with a flat trajectory, coming from their left side. "Okay. Run it," I said.

The source of the missile came into view as the camera slewed, probably with the turret of the vehicle filming. For a moment it was hard to make anything out as fire erupted all around and whatever was out there opened up with both pulse and conventional weapons. A second missile flashed once, then brighter a split second later as the patrol's countermeasures detonated it short of its target. A few missiles streaked the other way, slamming into the source of the carnage, which rocked and ceased firing for a second, allowing it to come into focus.

"Is that a Mark Thirteen?" I asked without broadcasting, more to myself than the staff. A Mark Thirteen was a combat drone and highly illegal on planets inhabited by humans under the Drone Accords.

Zilla, who was standing behind me, said, "Yes, ma'am."

Before I could consider it anymore, the bot sprang back to life, firing only pulse weapons this time. It only made it a few seconds before two more missiles slammed into it, driving it down into the grass already burning around it. Black smoke blew across the picture, obscuring our view, and then it cut off.

"That's all there is, ma'am," said the technician over the speaker.

I turned to Zilla. "You sure about that being a Mark Thirteen?"

"Yes, ma'am. I study all my potential targets."

"Intel, we make that as a Mark Thirteen. Do you agree?" Nobody on this planet should have one. But then again, they shouldn't have nukes, either.

"Yes, ma'am. With ninety-nine-point-eight-seven percent certainty."

Well, fuck. That was pretty certain. Suddenly the meeting with the city fathers didn't seem nearly as important. Somebody was trying to keep us from getting to the space elevator, and they wanted it badly enough to employ sophisticated combat drones. And if they wanted to stop us, that made it even more urgent for us to get out there. But first I had to discuss it with Hearns. I stood and looked around, finding him at the back of the pit. He'd seen. "Get the team ready to move," I told Zilla, and then I headed over to him.

"It's obvious to say it, but there's something going on here that we don't understand," he said as I approached.

"I need to go out there. I'll fly," I said before he could protest. "Find me a couple of intel techs who can assess that drone wreckage and I'll take them with me."

"Roger, ma'am." If he disagreed, it didn't show in his body language.

"From there, I'm going to head to the space elevator with the patrol and see this mission through. There are people up there. We've got to get to them."

"Yes, ma'am." He paused. "Be careful. We need you."

"I won't take any unnecessary risks. Can you handle the city fathers when they show?"

"I'll stall them until you get back," he said.

I nodded. "Am I doing the right thing? I'm not being rash, am I?"

He gave it some thought, as if it hadn't occurred to him already. "I think this has to be the priority. Like you said, lives are at stake. What's more important than that?"

"Roger. Thanks."

Nineteen minutes later, when we landed fifty meters away from the patrol on the opposite side from the smoking drone, they had already established security and some soldiers were approaching enemy wreckage, spraying everything with coolant before they approached to protect against ammunition cooking off. We were a long way outside the city and the open grassland and low, rolling hills gave us good visibility in every direction. My team fanned out behind me as we dismounted the aircraft, and a lone soldier walked to meet us. We met him halfway.

He raised his visor, revealing a dirt-streaked face and a perfectly-trimmed mustache. "Ma'am, Staff Sergeant Markiton. This is my patrol."

"What happened, Markiton? Where'd the drone come from?"

"It popped right up out of the grass, ma'am. None of our scanners picked it up until it fired."

"That model is all polymer and it has a lot of stealth tech," I said.

"Yes, ma'am. After that, it was all just reaction. The whole thing was over in ten seconds."

"How are your wounded?"

"Jennings—he was the bot-tank crew—is lucky to be alive. He has a couple of broken bones, a hell of a concussion, and two ruptured eardrums. He's stable. We called for a medevac, but they said we can exfil him on your bird."

"Roger. Anybody else?"

"Lopez is going to need a few stitches in her chin. She ate her turret weapon when her vehicle lurched, and we've got three others with mild concussions. But other than that, we're in pretty good shape."

THE WEIGHT OF COMMAND

I stopped and observed the unit at work. Soldiers were working in pairs, collecting the biggest parts of the enemy drone. One pair swept up the rest, getting plenty of dirt along with the components. "I want the whole thing. We need to analyze it and hopefully find a clue to its origin."

"Roger that, ma'am. What do you want us to do once we've got it? Push on or RTB?"

Should they return to base? I thought about it. The drone had been here, waiting. Someone knew we were going to come this way, and they'd set an ambush. There might be another attack ahead. But it wasn't really a choice. If our enemy didn't want us at the space elevator, that's where we needed to be. "We push on. My crew and I are taking over one of your vehicles. Evacuate all your injured, including the concussions, on the aircraft. We'll take their spots."

Markiton considered it, maybe deciding whether he should push back on that order or not. He wouldn't be happy to have the boss joining his patrol. "That leaves me with one too many, ma'am. If it's okay, I'll send Allouette back with the injured. He's healthy, but he can take charge of the retrograde and make sure all my people get treated when they get back."

"Roger. Make it happen. We can't recover the bot-tank—not that there's much left of it. Hard to believe the bot-tank crewman didn't fare worse."

"It's a good design. Shunts the blast away from the crew compartment."

"It is. Recover anything sensitive, blow anything left that the missile didn't destroy in place. Let's try to be moving in ten minutes."

"Roger that, ma'am."

Going forward was a risk, of course. It was only another seventy-five kilometers, but now we didn't have a bot-tank. I called for air support to fly patrol over our route. I should have done that from the start, but it seemed like a waste—a needless show of force. I wouldn't make that mistake again.

The soldiers probably saw it—the mistake—but nobody said anything. Zilla certainly saw it. I got the feeling she didn't miss much, and not just with her weapons. I made a note to talk to her when we weren't as busy. Her insight might be useful. She was a junior enlisted and she had a job, but she'd also be wherever I went, and I wasn't going to stand on protocol when there was something that might help us win.

We first spotted the space elevator after twenty klicks or so, as it manifested out of the haze into a smudge on the horizon. From there it continued to grow and resolve as we approached, and while I didn't think the soldiers would lose focus on their jobs after the drone incident, it was hard not to fixate on the looming monolith.

"Are you planning on going up, ma'am?" asked Xiang.

"Not initially." I wanted to go—a leader should lead from the front, and plus, it would just be really cool—but I couldn't think of anything that I'd do up there that I couldn't do from the ground. Once I had the away team's assessment of the situation, I could always follow them up later if it made sense.

By the time we reached ten klicks out, the elevator dominated the horizon. I leaned forward to look up to where it disappeared somewhere far overhead. It really was a marvel.

I happened to be looking right at it when it exploded.

A fireball flashed, and then the base station disappeared in a gout of smoke and dirt. I stared, unable to turn away, hardly able to believe what I was seeing. The sound of the blast, hard and deep, shocked me into action about thirty seconds later when it reached us.

"Max speed," I called across the net. "Let's get there and help the survivors." Even as I said it, my implant had already calculated the size of the blast and predicted the damage. Survivors were unlikely.

"What the fuck was that?" asked Murphy.

"Truck bomb," said Zilla. "A big one."

"How would they get through security?" Murphy stepped on the accelerator to match the increasing speed of the vehicles in front of us.

"No fucking clue," said Zilla.

I didn't know either. But the estimate of eight tons of explosives that my implant fed me gave me some ideas. You didn't have to get that close when you had a bomb that big. I watched the elevator, and then queried my implant for information about what would happen if the cable broke. I'd never considered it before, and whatever happened, it wouldn't be good. If it was falling, continuing to drive toward it would be a really bad idea.

"Does it look like the cable is still attached, Zilla?" I asked. From her vantage point in the turret, she had magnifying optics and the best view.

She took several seconds to answer. "I think so. I don't see anything moving, but it's hard to tell with the smoke and dust."

"Roger." We were traveling almost due south, and if the cable had broken at the bottom, I wasn't sure exactly what would happen, so I ran some simulations in my implant. The results varied depending on where the cable broke, but regardless of that, for a near-equatorial elevator, the majority of damage would occur on an east-west axis. I flipped to the convoy network. "If it looks like that cable is coming unanchored in any way, don't wait for orders. Turn around and haul ass due north."

A chorus of rogers answered me as we continued to speed toward the potential danger.

We had to slow about a kilometer out, as debris lay in and along the road. The hover vehicles could move off-road—of course they could—though it burned a lot more power to do that, as the roads were specifically designed to reflect the most energy from the hover system. Our drivers picked their way around bricks and chunks of hot, torn metal, and it took us several minutes to traverse the remaining distance. The east wind blew at about twelve kilometers an hour, carrying the majority of the smoke off to our right, which allowed us to get pretty close. "Pull up short and run full scans, including for drones and any other electronic signatures." Given the totality of the wreckage—the building was just gone—the extra minute we took wasn't going to matter to anybody living.

"Roger," called the lead vehicle.

We didn't find an enemy on site, but we did find three people alive, miraculously, thanks to the physics of explosions that had somehow spared them. All three were in critical condition, so we weren't able to get any information from them. Reports indicated that there should have been nineteen other people on duty. We found what we thought were six bodies. Whether others were off base when it happened or simply disintegrated in the heat of the blast, we couldn't immediately know, but I called it in to Watch so she could track down the status of everyone assigned.

We had some time before civilian authorities started to arrive. I didn't know where they'd come from, but there was nothing within fifty klicks in any direction. I'd leave it to McNamara to coordinate with the Zargod in that regard. Onsite, I set the team to a variety of tasks. The medic supervised the air evacuation of the wounded, while one of the engineers from what was going to be the space team tried to get an assessment of the damage to the cable and elevator. Unfortunately, with the remnants of the fire and debris from the base station, she couldn't get close enough to get an accurate answer due to the heat and smoke.

"Ma'am," called Murphy, on a private channel. "Base wants to talk to you. Master Sergeant Hearns."

"Send it to my personal."

"Ma'am, are you okay out there?" asked Hearns.

"It's ugly. I want a full company out here as soon as you can send them, with all the digging and construction equipment they can bring. Once this thing cools down, we need to get in and check the integrity of the cable."

"Roger that. I think you should probably head back this way as soon as you can. Things are escalating with the protests. PsyOps expects that the city fathers are on their way. I can stall them if I have to, but if there's nothing for you to do out there onsite, we could use you here."

A siren from an arriving civilian fire suppression vehicle forced me to hold my next communication for a few seconds, which gave me time to consider his recommendation. "Okay. Send a bird for me. I'm leaving the rest of the team here until you can get that relief mission onsite, but I'll fly back with Zilla."

"We'll have a bird on the way in five."

I didn't want to leave the site of the explosion, but in the end, that catastrophe had already happened. I needed to move on and hopefully prevent the next one. We were at war with somebody. The problem was, I still didn't know who.

10

On the fifteen-minute flight back to base, I got an update on the situation with the protest. The city fathers had indeed shown up just moments after I'd talked to Hearns, and now five of them were waiting for me. I really could have used a little downtime to process things, but the situation didn't allow for it. Instead, Ops sent me a video of their arrival so I could identify them and start preparing on my own as I traveled. After that, PsyOps would brief me when I got off the aircraft. I played the vid through my implant and zoomed in on the faces to compare them to the database. Five men, dressed in slacks and open-collar shirts. For all that they were formal about food and wine and ceremony, the Zargod didn't dress up for anything other than funerals and weddings. Only three showed up in my files of leaders, including the senior father. Anthony hadn't expected him to show, so we were already behind in our assessment.

I knew him, though. Or at least knew *of* him. Family name of Romero, they'd been one of the early investors in the lithium business, and they'd held on to some measure of power ever since, at least locally. The two unidentified men were probably lower-level leaders, or maybe one was a relative of the wounded child.

I expected that they'd push for a payment, and they'd insist that it would go to the family. On the surface, that made sense. But once they left, the family would be expected to give a cut to both their local father and the senior father. That was just the price of doing business in Zarga. And while I understood that as part of their culture, it sat wrong with me. It just felt corrupt. But there was nothing I could do about it. We'd screwed up and injured a kid, and there were provisions in place for how to compensate for that. That sounds cold-blooded, especially when a child was involved, but that's what both sides had agreed to half a century earlier, and it worked.

Hearns, Anthony, and Corporal Collins met me as I stepped off the bird onto the landing pad, and we walked quickly to get away from the whine of the engines so we could talk. Collins was responsible for meetings with local leaders, so he took a position right at my side. His section had been especially hard hit by the nuke and, because of that, he more than almost anybody else other than me had had to assume much greater responsibility.

"The five men are waiting in the fancy conference room," said Collins. I knew where he meant. The room had an official name, I'm sure, but nobody ever called it anything but the fancy conference room. It was decorated like a local leader's parlor, with sofas as the prominent furniture and oil paintings on the walls and stood apart from the headquarters; the colonel and other senior leaders used it when they had meetings with locals. That kept us from having to give the visitors access to restricted areas where they might see something they shouldn't, and in theory, it made them comfortable because it fit their style. But if it was me? I'd have done it in our style, more sparse and efficient. It wasn't like we were going to fool them into thinking they weren't on a military base. Besides, if we were going to negotiate, having them a bit uncomfortable would be an advantage, and it seemed strange to give that up.

"Why is the senior father here?" I asked.

"Anything I told you would be a guess, ma'am. I really didn't expect it."

That wasn't particularly helpful, but it seemed pointless to chastise him for it. It meant *something*, and not knowing was putting me behind the eight ball before I even started. "So best guess it for me. Any idea you've got is better than what I have now."

"If I had to go out on a limb, ma'am, I would say it means that they want something more than the standard compensation."

"What do you think they want?"

"I don't know, ma'am. I'm sorry, but I'm a little over my head at this level."

I could understand that. We reached the door to the fancy conference room, and I led the way in followed by Xiang and Gonzalez, who would take up positions just inside the door. I didn't need their protection, but the locals expected the protocol, and I didn't mind the demonstration of power. I was at a disadvantage already, in their culture, being both a woman and significantly younger than any of them. So I'd take whatever help I could get to even the playing field.

Inside, the four soldiers waiting with the guests snapped to rigid attention. The seated locals didn't rise, but they did fall silent. I had to give it to Collins—or Hearns—for that one. Smart play, having the soldiers' actions let everyone know who was in charge.

"Senior Father, this is Major Markov, our commanding officer." The interpreter, a civilian who worked for us named Ricky, introduced me in Zargod. I didn't need an interpreter, of course, and the city fathers probably knew that, but in case they didn't it made sense to keep that edge secret. Even if they did know, an interpreter slowed a conversation down naturally, which gave me more time to analyze things before I had to respond.

The senior father made a point of remaining seated for several seconds, before finally standing to greet me. I took it as an intentional slight. The others followed suit. He looked me up and down the way someone might look at something disgusting they'd stepped on in the street, his lips twisted in a sneer, and I wondered if anyone had informed him that he'd be meeting with a woman. I hoped not. I hoped it made him uncomfortable. He had white hair and a weathered face. He could have been anywhere from sixty to eighty, though my data told me he was seventy-two. "You're very young to be in charge," he said.

He had a point. At twenty-three, I probably wasn't half the age of anyone in his delegation, or even anybody he dealt with on a regular basis. That didn't stop his words from bothering me. "We've had a lot of casualties lately."

He sniffed. "Yes. That seems to be going around."

I forced a smile, though probably not a good one. "Please, won't you sit?"

The fathers sat on three of four sofas that made a square, and I took a seat alone on the fourth. After we were all comfortably seated, I gestured for Ricky to come sit beside me.

"I was wondering if you had any information about yesterday's nuclear attack." I figured I'd take the initiative before they could get me on my back foot and reacting to their agenda. It's not like we could ignore that topic. Or, I thought we couldn't.

The senior father had other ideas, and he looked down his nose at me. "You speak business before we have wine? What are we, uncivilized Argazzi?"

I wanted to kick myself. I was focused so much on the problem at hand that I'd forgotten the cultural formalities. I was saved any further embarrassment by two soldiers who arrived with stainless steel platters holding small cups of wine, just a little bigger than a shot glass, but bell-shaped and on a short stem. They moved with precision, like they'd practiced. Part of me felt bad for having them act like servants, but another part of me wanted to hug them for cutting the tension and giving me a moment to recover. They served me and the senior father simultaneously, indicating that, at least in our eyes, we were equals. Then they served the other men, and finally Ricky.

When we all had glasses, we raised them to each other, and without a word we each took small sips—which was counterintuitive when the entire glass held like fifty milliliters, making me want to just toss it back. But we all set our glasses down on end tables, unfinished.

"You have Zargod wine," said the senior father, his tone hinting at approval. I found myself appreciating that, and then hating myself that it mattered to me what he thought.

"It's the best," I said. That might not have been *completely* true, but they *did* have a talent for it. Not nearby—the climate wasn't right for it—but there was one elevated valley in Zarga where all they did was produce wine, and they had it down to an art form.

"Not the best vintage," said the senior father, "but of course, you can't be expected to understand that."

And just like that, we were back to me not liking him. I gave him a fake smile and didn't say anything.

"You asked—before the wine—about the attack yesterday. I would be happy to discuss that with you."

"I appreciate it," I said.

"We should set up a separate meeting for that; I will make it a priority. But today we have to address your egregious actions against Zargod citizens."

I did my best not to react. It wasn't like one could divorce the nuclear attack from our action that injured the child. Without the first, the second would never have happened. But it didn't seem like a good idea to mention how it affected my mental state, and before I could formulate a counter, he continued.

"You raided a home in violation of all our agreements. You spit on fifty years of a relationship."

This I was ready for. "We have the authority under the tripartite treaty to conduct unilateral operations on both sides of the border when it pertains to the protection of our own forces. We were attacked."

"You lie," said the short, fat man sitting on the sofa next to the senior father. He almost spat the words. I scanned him fully with my implant since he was one of the two I didn't know. I could upload him to the intel database later.

"I'm sorry, we've not been formally introduced." I didn't want to respond to his obvious emotion, and I wanted his name for our files.

The senior father raised his hand before the man could reply; he sagged back, the venom taken out of him. "I apologize for those words on behalf of my party. He speaks out of turn. But it's an emotional subject; the family you attacked were his people. It's understandable."

I wasn't sure it was understandable as much as I was sure it had been scripted. I would have bet good money that the senior father had told the man to make an emotional outburst so that he could come in and act rationally.

"I understand that you're upset," I said. "But there's no reason for the crowd outside. You can send them back to their homes and we can take care of this."

"We appreciate you seeing us. But our people will remain outside your gate until we get satisfaction."

"We'd be happy to reach an accommodation," I said.

The senior father smiled a fake smile that accentuated the cracks in his face. He looked like a salesman who knew he had an ignorant customer. Perhaps he did, because I had no idea where he was going next. "We're glad to hear it. There's much to accommodate."

I fake-smiled back but didn't respond. I upped the intensity of my implant so I could detect breathing and heart rate—an unadvertised feature that allowed me to detect lies and bluffs. Implant officers made great card players. So good that nobody would play with us, because we could pick up every tell.

After a moment, the silence became uncomfortable and the senior father spoke. "You people run through our city like it's your own personal playground."

I met his eyes and didn't flinch, but I still didn't respond. He hadn't asked a question, and it didn't do me any good to volunteer information. I wanted them to list their demands before I countered.

His heart rate increased, probably from annoyance. "You've done irreparable damage."

I drew my lips into a thin line. "There have been accidents before. There are claims procedures established. You know this."

The senior father flung his wrinkled hand into the air. "Pah! Claims. You violated our rights. There must be more."

I remembered my civilian engagement training and paused for five seconds before responding. "In our almost fifty years here, there has never been a situation like this. We had intelligence that led us to that location."

"I want to see the intelligence," he replied.

"We're not going to make that available," I answered quickly. He knew that. He almost smiled when I said it but caught himself. He was using the demand to get at something else and I'd fallen into it. I was overmatched. At least I knew it. It didn't solve my problem, though. All I could think about was how to get out of this without committing to something I couldn't deliver. If he'd said we should double the standard payment for injury, I'd have accepted and run out of the room.

The senior father took up his wine and had another sip, and I followed his lead, leaving us in silence for a few seconds until one of the side-sofa men spoke solemnly—the other one for which I didn't have an identity. "My family has suffered tragic damage today."

So he was the patriarch of the family we'd raided, though in their culture that didn't necessarily make him the injured boy's father. Family to the Zargod was more of a social unit than a biological relationship. And I'd made another mistake. I should have asked about the boy. I thought about correcting that now, but I wasn't sure if I'd just make it worse. I decided against it. I'd just say I was sorry. "And for that, I apologize. We'll gladly pay reparations for the injured child."

"The indignity of the invasion," he continued as if I hadn't spoken. "My family's reputation is forever tarnished." Now he was just laying on the bullshit to drive up the price. Or, at least, that was my considered opinion. Thankfully we'd run this scenario in training. At the same time, my implant's read on his biometric information indicated that he very likely believed what he was saying. So that was confusing. I guess there was nothing to do but ask.

"So if not reparation, what would salvage your family's honor?" I asked.

The senior father held up his hand again, slightly this time, and the man, who had been about to speak, remained silent.

"We want the offending party turned over to us," said the senior father.

I meant to wait five seconds before replying, but I didn't make it. "No." There was no way I was turning one of my soldiers over to Zargod justice. The treaty absolutely said we didn't have to, and there was no precedent. We'd investigate, and if he'd made a mistake—which I didn't believe—we'd punish him. If we turned him over to them—well, I didn't know what they'd do. But if I had to guess, they'd hold a very public trial and use it to demonstrate their power over us.

The senior father paused for several seconds. "A very hasty answer."

He was right, of course. I should have taken my time with it. But no amount of time would change my decision on that. *No* Federation commander would turn their soldier over in this situation. And the senior father knew that when he made the demand. Asshole. We weren't going anywhere with this, and again, I smiled, this time for real as I decided to push back a little. "You know the young. We're hasty."

He sniffed. "Yes."

"You also know our policy on discipline. Our soldiers aren't subject to Zargod law." That's what my training said to do. Stick to facts that both sides understand. Yes, I didn't care much for his culture and he definitely didn't care much for mine. But we did have a treaty.

"An outdated agreement that has no basis in the current environment," he said.

"A governing treaty that specifies the actions of three parties," I countered.

He stared at me for several seconds without speaking. "Are we at an impasse?"

My implant indicated that he was running another gambit, perhaps to try to move in another direction. I just wanted to get this done. I had lives at stake up on the orbital stations, and every minute I spent here was one that I wasn't working on that problem. To put it bluntly, I didn't have time for his bullshit. "There's no impasse. You can file a claim, and we'll pay reparations for the injury to the child. We will expedite it. We will also compensate the family for any damage done to their home and add an extra payment of forty percent for their inconvenience."

I watched the men to try to pick up tells, see how they reacted to the idea of extra money. I was offering them a legitimately good deal—one beyond what the treaty and other agreements required. I didn't get a chance to read them, though, as the senior father stood, and the rest of his party joined him quickly. I marked it for a bluff. They had my offer, and he wanted to get more. I remained sitting for a few seconds, just to say my own little "fuck you." Childish, I know, but it made me smile on the inside for a moment. Finally, I stood.

"We still demand that you turn over the man responsible."

"I understand that demand, and you know my position."

Something in him hardened. "You've not heard the end of this. Our people will remain at your gate until you see reason."

I nodded. "I suggest you tell your people to be careful. This is a working military base with heavy machinery. I'd hate for there to be another accident."

All of the men glared at me, and I didn't need my implant to tell me what they were thinking. I probably shouldn't have said that but screw them. We had fucked up, yes, but we didn't mean to shoot the kid, and I was truly sorry it happened. But he'd live, and there was nothing I could do about it now except follow the rules and pay out the established restitution. They had about as much chance of me giving up Darnell as they did of getting into my pants. But they knew that. What they really wanted was something else. The problem was, I didn't know what it was.

Hearns walked up and we watched the men walk away together, slowly, as one of them had a slight limp. "You think that was a good idea, antagonizing them?'

He was absolutely right. I'd let my frustration with the events of the past twenty-four hours get the better of me. It pissed me off. "What was I supposed to do? I'm not handing over Darnell. We've got forty-plus years of precedent on our side." Even as I said it, I knew where I went wrong.

"You could have thrown them a bone, though, ma'am. Give them something so they can go back to their people and save face."

"They didn't ask for anything else."

"Do you think they actually thought you'd hand him over?"

I blew a big breath out through pursed lips. "No. Of course not. He was being insincere. That was just their starting point, I know that."

He nodded. "He was, and it was. Which was opening it up to you to make an offer."

"But they didn't respond when I offered them extra money."

"It wasn't what you offered, ma'am. It was how you offered it."

I started to snap back at him but held it. He was probably right, even if I didn't see it. "So how should I have done it?"

"Ma'am...I'm just going to put it out there, and you can do with it what you want. But your disdain for the Zargod is evident."

"And their disdain for us—for me—isn't?"

"Sure it is. But you're in the position of power, so it's up to you to be the bigger person. You don't punch down."

"You think he picked up on that?" I asked.

"You think he didn't? I know he doesn't have an implant, but the man has seventy-plus years of life experience. And you're not that subtle."

Again, he was right, and this time it sank in. I wasn't ready for this job, and because of that I had made things worse. "So what do I do now?"

"You make it right. These guys can make life difficult if they want."

"How do I do that?"

Hearns shrugged. "I don't know. That's why you're the commander. But you've got people around you who can advise you."

I left unsaid that they had failed to do that, that they had rushed me right out of the aircraft and into the meeting. Because that was my fault. I should have insisted on better preparation. "I need a cultural advisor—someone who understands these old men. Didn't the Colonel have a guy who gave him advice on dealing with the locals?"

"He did, ma'am. He took him to the dinner and we presume he's dead along with everyone else."

"Shit. I'm sorry. But I also need a new one. How do we do that?"

"Normally we'd put in a personnel request up through headquarters and they'd hire someone—probably a Federation citizen who had been born here but moved away.

"But we can't get a message through," I said, completing his thought. "So think outside the box. What's another option?"

"You could always ask the senior father if he has a recommendation," said Hearns. He held out for a couple seconds before he cracked a smile.

I laughed. "I'm sure he'd get right on that. Although...I wonder if that would work. It might make him think he had influence here."

"Right up until you didn't give him what he wanted, at which point he'd have another point of leverage."

I nodded. "Right. Shit, this is complicated. I need some ideas on what I can offer to the senior father that isn't Darnell's head."

"The businesses, ma'am." Anthony said. He and Collins had been walking with us but had remained silent up until then.

"What do you mean?" I asked.

"Ma'am, when we sealed the base, we threw out all the locals who normally work here—everything from cleaning staff to the people who run the small shops that cater to soldiers. Those shops do good business, and the city leaders get a cut."

I was perturbed that he hadn't told me that *before* the meeting, but I tried not to let it show. Instead, I vented about the system of patronage. "Can't I just offer the senior father a bribe directly and cut through all the middlemen?"

"That's not how it works. They'd be offended if you tried," said Collins.

"You really think opening the businesses will do the trick?"

"I don't know. But that might be a good first question for that cultural advisor."

"Right," I said. "Find me somebody. Meanwhile I'll see what I can download to my implant that might help."

"Yes, ma'am," they all responded.

"Find me as soon as you have an answer. I'm heading to the pit to get an update on the space elevator." I didn't mind if they took some time to come up with a solution for my problem with the locals. It was better to delay some before I went crawling back to the senior father anyway.

11

When I got to the pit, McNamara called for an update, which suited me, because I wanted a report on the viability of the elevator cable so we could figure out our next steps with that and assign a semi-permanent guard force to protect it. But when Ops started briefing, they opened with a completely different topic.

"Ma'am, we're getting rumblings from Argaz. Specifically, they've called up reserve troops, and we're hearing comms traffic that indicates increased military activity and a potential rollout from base locations."

It took me a few seconds to process that. With everything else going on, I hadn't even considered a possible reaction from the Argazzi. "Have they offered any explanation?"

"There has been no public mention of it at all. Intercepts of internal communications show that they're calling it an exercise. I'll turn the analysis of that over to Intel."

"Ma'am, this is Tech Sergeant Kennedy, from the Analysis section." I couldn't see her from where she was briefing, so instead, I focused on the map she put on my screen and listened through my headset. She highlighted five locations. "These are the bases affected by the orders we've seen. We haven't seen upgraded activity there because we don't have visual assets in place, but we *are* seeing an increase in communications that are consistent with an increase in optempo."

"Do you buy the idea that it's an exercise?"

"No, ma'am. Someone just set a nuke off on their soil. The timing is too convenient." She responded quickly and sounded confident in her assessment. I happened to agree with her. What I didn't know was what to do about it, so I talked it out as a way to process it.

"It's hard to blame them. I'd be pissed if I were them. At the same time, if they take aggressive action, it could dictate a response by the Zargod, and that's just going to make things worse." First the Zargod, and now the Argazzi. Couldn't anyone just cooperate for a couple of days and let me get my footing? I had too many problems and no solutions. I needed help. Thankfully I had a staff, depleted though it was. "Watch, get the Plans team together and have them quickly work up a couple of courses of action in response to the Argazzi. Intent is to de-escalate. Everything is on the table—we just need them to stop and give us time to figure out what happened.

"Yes, ma'am."

Just passing that action off lifted some of the weight from me. I didn't have to have all the answers. I had people to help me with that, and I needed to let them. "Tell me about the space elevator."

"They're still working on it, ma'am. They've just started removing debris. We don't expect an engineer's assessment for a few hours still."

"Security is good?"

"There are some issues with the local police about responsibilities, but the team leader on the ground says that he's got it under control. With no way to regain the communication link, I've got Commo working on a direct beam option."

"Will that work? Will it let us talk to the survivors on the orbital stations?"

"It should if they're prepared to receive. Commo seems pretty sure that those facilities will be trying exactly the same thing if they can generate enough power."

"But we don't know how much they lost in the attacks."

"Exactly, ma'am."

"Okay. That's good work. Keep me informed, and let me know immediately if we establish comms. What else?"

"The logistics convoy is ten hours out. They're aware of the potential issues within the city. The drones we sent to scout for them haven't picked up anything out of the ordinary so far. We will launch the ground escort in four hours to meet them and escort them through the city, pending your guidance. Additionally, they're arriving under cover of darkness. So far, the demonstrations have stuck to daylight. So that should help."

"That sounds good. If we can do something to get them in away from the crowd, do it, but if not, we don't have much choice."

"Yes, ma'am. Nothing further."

"Roger. I'm going to depart the building for a couple hours and get a workout. Message me on my implant if anything changes." It probably seemed like I was running away from my responsibilities, and I considered explaining myself to McNamara, but I didn't. There was too much happening and I wasn't making good decisions. I needed a short time away to clear my head and think, and for me, that meant the gym.

Gonzalez insisted on accompanying me to the gym, but I told him that if he did, he had to work out too and not just stand there and watch me, so he was spotting me as I bench pressed about forty-five minutes later when McNamara buzzed me.

I racked the bar—80 kilos—and answered my comm. "Markov."

"Ma'am, you got a call from the Argazzi. They want to see you."

"That's good. I gave them the contact info, and I hoped they'd use it. They want to come here?" Visions of my previous meeting with the Zargod made me cringe at the idea.

"No, ma'am. They won't come here because they don't want to cross the border. They want you to come to them."

Of course they wouldn't come here. The question was, did I want to go *there*? My gut said no because every time I'd left base something bad had happened. On the other hand, I was much more at home in Argazzi culture than Zargod. I also didn't want to rush into a decision without advice. "What does the staff think?"

"Split, ma'am, but the majority think you should meet them, with the thought that you can forestall rash action on their part."

I considered it. It was about 350 klicks to where they'd likely want to meet—I couldn't imagine Argazzi leaders leaving the city and meeting me in the forest. I could fly and be there in under an hour, but I wasn't sure I wanted to do that. If I had an enemy out there—and I did—they'd expect me to fly. No, I'd drive.

"Roger. Give me fifteen minutes to get a shower and kit up. Have a ground patrol ready to go by then. I don't want to fly. If something goes down, I want at least a little bit of firepower with me."

"On it, ma'am."

The drive took us about two hours—we made good time because the first part of it was open grassland, and when we transitioned to wetter country and a combination of verdant forest and jungle, we had a wide, well-maintained road. The Argazzi cared a lot more about their infrastructure than the Zargod, who preferred things more rustic. It seemed strange, that dichotomy, given that both nations were very well funded by the lucrative lithium trade. I considered calling Liana Trieste from my vehicle as we drove, to see if she could give me any information about the meeting, but I didn't want to put her in a bad position with her boss. And, if I'm being honest, I was a little bit nervous.

We pulled up in front of a modern-looking twelve-story building, all faux granite and tinted glass. It had been a few weeks since I'd been into Argaz proper, and it always struck me how very dissimilar it looked to the places I'd visited in Zarga. It was like we'd passed out of a previous century into the present. In this case, it also made me question their capabilities in other areas—specifically if they could hack a military helmet. My team had told me they couldn't, but looking at the civilian foot traffic, all glued to their devices or using enhanced lenses, I couldn't help but wonder.

A man and a woman stood atop a set of wide stone steps, both dressed in immaculate charcoal business jackets over dress pants with razor-sharp creases. Neither showed in my database when I scanned them.

Xiang, Gonzalez, and I dismounted and walked up the stairs to meet our greeting party.

"Good afternoon, Major Markov," said the woman. "I'm Katya Kastinsky, legal counsel with the Argazzi federal government. This is my colleague, Darvin Cook." She spoke in Standard, so I didn't need to translate through my implant.

"Nice to meet you." I wasn't sure why they'd sent lawyers out to meet me. I'd been expecting politicians or maybe the military. I'd have liked to bring my own lawyers, but they were officers and had been at the party. All I had left were legal clerks, and while they could handle most of the unit's business, they wouldn't help here.

"We'd ask that you not bring weapons inside the federal building." She smiled, but it was thin and perfunctory.

I considered it quickly, not wanting to hesitate and make things awkward. By leaving our weapons, they were taking responsibility for our security, which culturally they took seriously. At the same time, as a soldier of the peacekeeping mission, I had no obligation to follow their rules under the treaty. And they, as attorneys, knew that. So this was a test. But to what end? Was I supposed to insist on my rights, or acquiesce to show that I was amenable to ceding those rights to help relieve the tensions? I needed them to see the treaty as sacrosanct, but I also wanted their goodwill. I decided to split the difference. I unstrapped my sidearm and handed it, along with my assault rifle, to Gonzalez. "Leave these in the vehicle, and the two of you carry sidearms only inside the building."

I glanced at Kastinsky, but she gave no reaction. She also didn't protest my decision. I wasn't sure if I'd passed the test or not, which was a bit disconcerting. She gestured me through the door that Cook held open via palm-reader.

The inside of the building seemed to dampen sound despite an abundance of polished marble. The Argazzi tended to spend their money on visible trappings like that. Our footfalls didn't echo in the wide hallway down which Kastinsky led us, and I wondered how they did that. We stopped in front of a huge set of double doors made out of some sort of heavy wood. They swung outward without any action on our part, revealing a large conference room dominated by a long, polished-wood table, around which six men and three women stood, waiting. My eyes went to one woman first. Liana Trieste. She was even taller than me and wore a charcoal pantsuit and a white blouse with a little bit of frill. She had her blonde hair in a perfect bun and her makeup was immaculate, just like it had been when we talked early that morning. She looked like an actress playing the part of "Powerful Executive" in a high-budget video. And I had no idea what she was doing here. I knew she worked in the Ministry of Foreign Affairs, but I didn't think she was senior enough to be in this meeting. But maybe that was just a bad assumption on my part based on her age; she was maybe four or five years older than me.

Maybe her making first contact with me got her enough credit with her bosses to get her a seat at the table. Or maybe one of her bosses was trying to use her connection to me to their advantage.

Yeah…that second one seemed more likely. Call me a cynic. Either way, I wished I could talk to her for a minute and figure it out, but there was no good way to do that. Everybody was looking at me, which made me feel awkward. Trieste looked good though. When I considered it, really most of the room looked good. I'm not sure if it was planned or random, but it was a significantly above-average-looking group of people. That made me feel even more awkward, standing there all ungraceful in my uniform. Mostly it meant that I needed to focus and get my head in the game.

Kastinsky gestured me inside toward the opposite end of the table, and then followed me, moving to stand behind the seat to my right while Cook took the one to my left. I motioned for my two escorts to remain outside the conference room. My boots sank into the plush carpet, and I couldn't help but think how much it had cost to furnish the opulent room. The table alone probably ran five figures.

"Greetings, Kiera. Major Markov. Thank you for coming," said Trieste. That she was first to speak and sitting directly next to the person at the head of the table…that meant something.

"Thank you for having me." I hesitated because my implant was telling me she was a deputy minister, which was significantly higher up than I had thought, and it threw me for a second. "Deputy Minister Trieste," I added awkwardly.

For her part, Trieste went on as if I hadn't stumbled at all. "This is Minister of Foreign Affairs Arwin Dantler. My boss." The man next to her wore a suit just a hair darker in shade than hers, also with a white shirt, open at the collar. He had salt and pepper hair and the kind of rugged good looks that suited a man in public office.

"Good to meet you, Minister."

"Shall we sit?"

"Yes." I almost wanted to laugh at the ridiculous five meters of table between us. They clearly meant it to intimidate—what other conclusion could I draw, facing eleven people who looked like they just stepped out of a corporate fashion catalog?

As soon as we all got seated Trieste said, "We're glad you could come on such short notice. But of course, the emergency circumstances warranted it."

"It's no trouble," I said. "There's no precedent for this."

"Exactly so. I'll get right to the point. We here in Argaz would like to know what you intend to do about the attack on our sovereign land by the Zargod." It was a blatant gambit and the fact that they tried to soften it by having Liana deliver it offended me a little. Like I'd be flustered by a pretty face. It offended me a little more that it was kind of working.

I stalled by reaching for the water pitcher on the table in front of me. I turned my crystal tumbler right side up and took my time pouring. This was an entirely different type of confrontation than the one with the Zargod, both more direct and more subtle at the same time. But I was more schooled in this method, as it was culturally closer to my experience in the military. "Do you have evidence regarding the source of the attack?"

The man sitting directly to Trieste's right responded. "I'm Harvey Latterbin, Second Deputy to the Minister of Intelligence."

"Good to meet you, Minister Latterbin." Ministry of Intelligence—I wondered if that made him the party guy. I mean, they were all party members or they wouldn't be here, but I wondered if he was the *real* party guy. The one the others worried about.

"*We* don't have any specific evidence that we can share, but it doesn't take much deduction to figure out the culprits." *That we can share.* He wouldn't have said that without specifically planning it, which meant he was implying that they did have information, but that I couldn't have it. Or he wanted me to infer it, even if it wasn't true.

I turned up the fidelity on my implant sensors to get a better read on the room. They were going to deal in half-truths, and I needed more than that. "While that does seem like the most obvious answer on the surface, we can't be sure. As you probably know, there was an attack this morning on the space elevator. That happened on Zargod land. Should I assume that that means that the Argazzi initiated the attack? Perhaps in retaliation for the nuclear attack?"

"The space elevator should be considered international land!" a youngish man with sandy hair halfway down the table blurted. Several other members of the delegation glared at him, but my reading told me that he felt no shame at that. It had likely been intentional, rehearsed to sound like an emotional outburst.

"But it's not," I said, keeping my voice even. "So I find myself in a situation where I either consider the nuclear weapon an attack by Zarga followed by a retaliation by your nation"—I let that hang in the room for several seconds before continuing—"or I consider the possibility that there are other actors at play in the region." I'd originally come up with that gambit on the drive because I knew I was going to need something to at least slow down the Argazzi delegation and keep them from pressing me. But the more I thought about it, the more I believed that to be the case. It was in neither Zarga's nor Argaz's interest to attack the space elevator. At the same time, I knew that their first ask wasn't their true purpose. They couldn't believe that I'd simply take their side and sanction the Zargod.

"We wouldn't want you to act without evidence," said Trieste, positioning herself as a voice of reason. My friend in the room. "And we understand your situation as well, being recently promoted into your position." Now she was implying that I lacked experience, which was true. I knew the game she was playing, and it shouldn't have bothered me, but if I'm being honest, her condescension got to me a little. I'd have taken it better from the others, but with her, it stung. I kind of wished I could tell her to just get to the real point of the meeting—assuming they had summoned me for a reason and not just to posture. Another part of me wanted to find a closet and crawl into it. Because like it or not, I cared what Liana thought about me.

"What evidence do you have related to the nuclear attack?" asked the man immediately to the left of the minister. That made him the second most important person at the table, so I scanned him and got his identity as Joran Yakina, but his title showed only as Government Official. Interesting. That probably meant *he* was the party guy. Their spy. The real power in the room.

"We haven't found anything definitive yet," I said.

"But you have found *something*."

"We haven't."

He stared me down, and I tried to get a read on him via my implant but couldn't. Seeming to realize what I was doing, he said, "You're not the only one with an implant, Major."

Good to know. I hadn't considered it, as civilians with implants weren't at all common, and strictly speaking, nobody on Tanara should have one because of the technology embargo on non-Federation planets. But people emigrated or found new employment, and while there were regulations, there were also ways around them. Especially if you had money, which Argaz most certainly did. And Yakina was *definitely* the party guy.

In a practical sense, it meant that I wouldn't get any extra information from him, as two implants trying to read each other would constantly adjust in a never-ending battle that could only end in stalemate. "Regardless, I don't have any intel on the bombing. I was hoping you did."

"And I was hoping you would be honest with us," said Dantler. Yakina sat back in his seat, ceding control back to the minister. "But you first said you haven't found anything definitive, but then changed your story to not finding anything at all. Which is it?"

I gave him a flat look and counted to five in my head before responding. He was baiting me, and I couldn't fall for it. I'd at least learned *something* from my earlier meeting with the senior father. I needed to keep calm, but I couldn't tell them the truth. I couldn't tell them that what I really wanted was for everything to calm the fuck down for a month until I could be suitably relieved by somebody qualified for the job with a full staff to help. "If I had anything that I thought relevant, I'd share it."

He sniffed as if trying to demonstrate that he didn't believe me without actually saying so. "We'd like to propose a pact of information sharing, as it regards the attack in our country."

"I'd be open to that," I said. "Send your points of contact to my Operations center and we'll put the appropriate people in touch."

"Do you have the appropriate people?" asked Yakina, and I got the feeling that we'd gotten to the real point of the meeting.

"Of course." I kept my voice neutral, choosing to ignore the intended insult.

"Most of your officers were killed in the attack."

"That's true." I considered taking insult, putting him on the defensive for his callous statement, but instead, I decided to let it play out a little longer, to try to figure out where he was going with this.

Dantler jumped back in. "Forgive my colleague, *Major* Markov, but our records do indicate that you were a lieutenant a few days ago. It's a reasonable question...whether you have the experience to handle this situation...on your staff, I mean." The way he said it made it perfectly clear that he didn't only mean on my staff. He meant my personal experience as well. Sure, he was right, but it still pissed me off. I didn't need to come all this way to be insulted. I glanced at Liana, but she was staring down at her hands, looking like she wanted to be anywhere else but at the table. This wasn't her fault. Her boss was using her, but she wouldn't have any control over what he said.

"We make do with what we have."

Yakina took back over. "Yes, forgive me, Major" —he didn't emphasize the rank the way Dantler had—"but you're very young."

I didn't respond at all this time. If he wanted to try to lead me down a path, he could do it without my help. They'd eventually get to their point and then we could start negotiating.

"It has to be difficult, commanding such a complex unit with your experience."

"I have a lot of good soldiers to help. They're very capable. I have the easiest job in the brigade." I faked a smile. I'd heard a lot of commanders repeat that platitude. Nobody believed it, but nobody ever contradicted it, either.

"We would like to make you an offer—some of our more experienced officers to serve with you on an interim basis. Just until you get the reinforcements that I'm sure the Federation has dispatched."

I wished that I could read him, wished that I could determine if he knew that those reinforcements weren't coming right away. I scanned the minister at the head of the table but got nothing from him. If anyone knew, it was Yakina. Definitely a spy. Which meant that the offered officers—if they were military officers at all—would be spies as well. So this was their agenda. It almost made me appreciate the Zargod city fathers. At least they just wanted payment. "That's a very generous offer," I said.

"You'd remain in command, of course," said Yakina, as if that was my only doubt. "The officers would work directly for you."

And they'd report back to you, I thought. It seemed best to stall. After all, I only had to hold out for a month. "I'll consider it and get back to you later this week."

"We have them ready to return with you right now. After all, we wouldn't want your lack of capability to lead to a difficult situation."

I hesitated, considering my options. I could lie and say I didn't have room for them in my convoy, but they'd just offer to fly them. I knew what I wanted—no way was I bringing a squad of Argazzi spies into my headquarters—but I didn't know how to say it. The Argazzi wouldn't make a show of taking offense the way the Zargod did, and they couldn't protest outside my gate, but they'd show their displeasure in other ways. What I really wanted was their help figuring out what happened with the nuclear attack. Second to that, I wanted them to end their military activity until I had a better handle on my other problems. They probably knew that. There was a significant chance that they'd ramped up those operations knowing that I would learn of them, all to get me to the table to negotiate. And if I gave in and made concessions to get them to stop, there would be nothing to keep them from doing it again down the road to get something else they wanted.

THE WEIGHT OF COMMAND

That I knew all that was good on one hand, in that I could recognize the situation for what it was. On the other hand, I didn't have a solution that addressed my problem without giving in to their demands. Having to make a decision, I decided it was best not to try to be subtle with the Argazzi. That was their game, and I wouldn't beat them at it. Instead, I took it head-on. "We've noticed that you're increasing your military activity."

If I'd expected to catch them by surprise with the non sequitur, I'd have been disappointed, as a woman on the right side of the table answered immediately. "I'm Julia Sevenstein, from the office of the minister of defense. The actions you've seen are part of a routine training exercise."

"Even the call-up of reserve soldiers?"

She didn't show anything visibly, but the increase in her heart rate showed her lie. "We initiated that when we thought there might be a follow-on invasion after the nuclear attack. Now that we've seen that the Zargod aren't marshaling forces, we're canceling the reserve call-up."

"But you're continuing the *training exercise*," I said.

"That's correct."

"Major Markov," interrupted Yakina the spy, "you didn't answer my question about the immediate acceptance of Argazzi officers to round out your staff."

I had to give him credit for timing because it was unclear if he meant to push me for an answer or just wanted to bail out his ministry of defense before I asked more questions and caught them in more lies. "If I accept the officers, can I be assured that you'll put off your training exercise?" It didn't get any more direct than that.

"Major Markov," Dantler interjected. "Surely you're not implying that we're conducting a military exercise in order to get concessions from you."

"No, of course not." Now he was treating me like I was stupid, and I wanted to reject the offer out of principle. But I'd fucked up the meeting with the Zargod because I let them manipulate me, and I wouldn't make that mistake again. I smiled at him.

"Minister, if I may?" Yakina said, and when Dantler nodded, Yakina continued, addressing him, though it was clearly meant for me. "Having our officers involved with Major Markov's operations would greatly help our security situation. Perhaps we could come to an agreement?" He said it as if they hadn't planned the entire charade ahead of time. I wanted to roll my eyes.

Dantler played his role perfectly, though, acting as if this was a completely new thought to him. "Why, I suppose you're right? What do you propose?"

"Major Markov accepts our help, and we postpone our military exercise. What say you, Major?" Yakina looked at me. We were beginning the real negotiation now. Dantler would nominally make the agreement, but Yakina was the power in the room.

I paused, playing up the idea that I was still considering it. "I'm open to anything that will improve relations between us. Let's talk specifics."

"We have eleven officers with a variety of specialties ready to go. You take them on, and we agree to postpone our military exercise—"

"*Any* significant military exercise," I said.

He looked at me, perturbed at the interruption. "*Any* military exercise, for a period of time that we can discuss."

I knew the time period I needed, but it didn't matter, because I couldn't accept his offer. No way could I keep track of eleven observers, at least some of whom would be spies at best, and trying to undermine me at worst. I could maybe handle one. But I also couldn't come right out and refuse, because that would risk cutting off the negotiation. "That's a good offer, but logistically, I'm not sure how I'd make it work. As you would expect, we've got systems and feeds at varying levels of classification. It will take too much time to integrate foreign officers, as I'd have to figure out how to use them effectively while not exposing them to things beyond their level of approval. If you give me a couple of weeks to make an assessment, I can get back to you on how many we can accept." *And if a couple weeks turned into a month, well...shit happens.*

"You need the help now," said Yakina, "and we need the assurance—"

"But..." I cut Yakina off intentionally. They were treating me like a child, and while I was not going to blow up at them, I was through with it. "I have a couple of areas specifically where I can use help immediately."

Yakina did a poor job of hiding the skepticism on his face. That was the problem with an implant—it was easy to get complacent knowing that people couldn't figure out your thoughts with their own implant. But it didn't keep someone from reading your face the old-fashioned way. "Go ahead."

"I'll take two officers." I had people working for me, and they were doing fine, but in some cases, they couldn't easily replace the level of education or training that an officer might bring to the job.

"Two," he said, unpleased.

"I'd like one of them to be an engineer who can lead the technical effort in assessing and possibly repairing the space elevator." I didn't mention that that officer would reside at the elevator itself and be nowhere near our base. But they could probably figure that out.

"We can provide that," said Yakina, looking a little mollified. If nothing else, they'd have first-rate intelligence on the progress of the most important economic infrastructure on the planet.

"And I need a plans officer." This one would be trickier, but I saw actual value in having someone to whom I could feed information and who could lead the staff to come up with solutions for me. They'd be inside my headquarters, but there was no way Yakina was going to accept any proposal that didn't give him that. I'd work out how to keep the spy in the dark later.

Yakina considered it for a bit, probably deciding if he could get more out of me. If he had countered, I'd have accepted three, but he decided against it, apparently more worried about timing than number. "And you'll take them back with you?"

"Have them sent out to my convoy. I'll call out to my people and tell them to make space."

The eleven-member delegation continued to pepper me with questions, but nothing registered as important. They had gotten what they wanted—as much as I was willing to give—and they had agreed to delay their military exercise.

When the meeting broke, I tried to get to Liana, get a word with her—if not in private, at least semi-privately—but my two lawyer handlers chivvied me out, and when I tried to make eye contact with her, she wouldn't meet my gaze. Maybe she was sorry for her role in what had just happened or embarrassed that her boss used her. Maybe she thought I was the enemy and wanted nothing to do with me. Either way, I hated it and wished I'd made use of her number *before* some asshole had set off a nuke.

The ride back was uneventful, which left me brooding over the meeting and Liana and the unknown enemy. My crew left me to my thoughts, but, perhaps sensing my mood, they kept things light as they conversed with each other over the intercom where I could listen in. Soon I was distracted by their banter and Murphy's boast that he could eat a dozen pancakes in two minutes. None of the others believed him, but I would have put money on him if a commander could ethically do something like that. It just didn't seem like the kind of claim a guy would make without knowing. Too specific.

Eventually they got around to me—more specifically, trying to get information from me. Xiang led the effort. He was the bold one. "So, ma'am. How did it go with the Argazzi?"

"Not bad. They thought they were pretty slick, but I had a good read on them." I couldn't share all the details, but there was no harm in that much. There was an understanding with a commander's crew that they wouldn't share information. Sure, they still would, but only in a general sense, and I didn't mind this getting out. "There was some give and take on both sides."

"Is that how we ended up with two Argazzi officers riding back in the convoy with us?" asked Zilla.

"Yeah. That was the part I had to take," I said.

"It seemed pretty calm. We couldn't hear anything through the door," said Xiang.

"I'll remember that you're listening the next time I leave you outside." I kept my tone light as I said it, making sure that he knew I was joking.

"If you need to replace him, ma'am, you'd be doing us all a favor," said Zilla.

"I'm hurt, Zilla," said Xiang. "I thought we were cool."

"Eh. I could take you or leave you. Some new blood would make things interesting."

"Careful, Zilla," said Murphy. "Xiang isn't used to rejection. You might make him cry."

"Don't be jealous, Murph," said Xiang. "You should want me to stay. If you hang around me long enough, maybe some of what I've got will rub off on you. I figure that would take…I don't know…five or six years, tops."

"I'm sorry, Xiang," said Zilla with absolutely no sincerity. "I didn't mean to damage your ego."

"It's okay. I've got plenty more of it left. So ma'am—what happens now with the Argazzi and the Zargod?" He really was smooth, turning it back naturally to what they wanted to know. The Argazzi could have learned from him.

"I don't know, Xiang. I really don't know."

12

It was nearly dark by the time we made it back to base, which was fortunate for us because apparently it was still a daylight-only protest, and that left us unobstructed. I headed immediately to the pit to get an update, after which I'd hope to get some much-needed rest. The four hours from the previous night wasn't cutting it. McNamara had anticipated my desires and had a briefing ready to go as soon as I entered. They started by filling me in on the nuclear attack. We'd finally gotten a team out to the blast site in radiation suits; it was a low-yield blast, so the danger was localized, but still present. They hadn't found anything, but would head back in the morning to continue to sift through the area.

The team then informed me that while the elevator base station was a total loss, the cable itself appeared to still be serviceable. I told them to have the Argazzi engineer transported out there the next day for a second set of eyes, but for the moment it seemed to be good news. We'd just have to figure out a way to make it work again, and to figure out who attacked it in the first place. No organization had taken responsibility, which made a terrorist attack seem less likely.

Intel was working all their various sources to try to figure it out, but so far, much like with the nuclear attack, they hadn't come up with anything. We also had nothing new on the cyberattack against our base, though we were still maintaining enhanced systems and physical security, in case somebody came after us directly again. It was hard for me to focus, because so many things had happened in the last day and a half, and while we had quality analysts, we didn't have the trained leadership to prioritize tasks. I knew that it fell on me to establish those priorities, but I was struggling to even prioritize myself. That continued when I got to the last item of the briefing.

"Ma'am, the logistics convoy has left its final rest stop. Lieutenant Perston estimates their arrival at approximately 0430 tomorrow," said McNamara.

A chill ran through me. "Who?"

"Lieutenant Perston. He's leading the logistics mission."

Nobody in the pit appeared to share my reaction. They didn't seem to grasp the importance of another officer still being alive. I hadn't even thought about the personnel on the logistics convoy among all the other fires I'd been trying to put out. The fact that it was Dirk Perston...well nobody else would understand the significance of that in the same way I did. On the one hand, it was another officer, someone who could share the burden. On the other hand, he and I had history, and it wasn't good. And now he was going to arrive back to see me playing at being a major. I could only imagine his reaction.

"Thanks, Watch." I turned to find Hearns. "Can I see you in the XO's office?"

"Roger, ma'am."

I waited until we were inside with the door closed, but Hearns spoke first. "Ma'am, you probably should start referring to this as your office. Or you can take the commander's—"

"Why didn't someone tell me that Lieutenant Perston was still alive?" I said, cutting him off. I was being an ass, but I couldn't help it. This was huge.

Hearns hesitated, perhaps assessing his culpability in the oversight. "Ma'am...I didn't think about it. The manifest is routine data, and readily available. I didn't even check it myself."

I started to speak, but held back, took a deep breath. I hadn't thought to check, so it was hypocritical to expect him to have. We both should have known that there'd be an officer in charge. Regardless, there was nothing for it now except to deal with the situation. "Perston is senior to me."

"You were both lieutenants. You've been promoted, so you're senior."

I shook my head. That wasn't how it worked. When two people had the same rank, the person who reached the rank first was senior. "He was two months senior to me. He is in charge."

Hearns considered it. "No, ma'am."

"Excuse me? We can look it up, but I know I'm right." I knew Perston well enough to be sure. All lieutenants knew where they stood in relation to others in the unit when it came to seniority. It was a thing.

"What you were is irrelevant. You're the commander now, not Perston. The noncoms won't accept him as commander."

"They can't just *not accept* him," I protested. "This is the military, and that's how things work."

"Ma'am...nothing here is how anything has ever worked. There's no precedent. Perston is an asshole who is only out for himself. Nobody is going to follow him. This isn't theory; I know this for a fact. I know people who have worked for him, and it's not good."

My face heated, and I was pretty sure Hearns would notice that it had turned red. But he wouldn't know why. After all, his assertion that Perston wasn't acceptable was another way of saying that I *was*. And that was flattering. I had no idea what criteria or whose opinion went into that assessment, but I did know this: noncoms know things, and I took pride in the fact that they chose me. Even if it was only a two-person race.

I wanted to elaborate on how I knew Perston was an asshole, but I wasn't sure how much I should share. We didn't like each other, but it was personal—a rivalry gone wrong back in our days at the academy—and it didn't seem appropriate to drag that into the light in front of the unit.

It hadn't even been a big deal to me at the time. Perston had an ego, and he'd made it known to everyone who would listen—and some who wouldn't—that he intended to win the tactics practical exercise, which is the most prestigious event of the junior year at the academy. They even gave you a medallion for taking first. And it wasn't even that he expected to win—everyone expected him to win—it was how he acted about it. As if it was his entitlement. When I beat him out, he didn't handle it well. And I, being who I am...well, maybe I rubbed it in a bit. Long story short, he'd violently resented me ever since. Could I not get just one problem that was simple? Something I could just punch and be done with it?

"He's not going to accept it," I said.

"He doesn't have a choice, ma'am."

"How do you figure? Certainly, there are some people loyal to him. When he insists on taking charge, some people are going to take his side. The people on his own team, at a minimum. We can't afford to have divi-

THE WEIGHT OF COMMAND

sions within the unit, and the easiest way to avoid that is for me to step aside."

"Ma'am, and I mean this with all due respect, you don't get a choice in this either." He said it in a way that senior noncoms have where it's clear that all due respect, in this particular case, is none.

Then, perhaps sensing I still wasn't sold, Hearns spoke, less harshly this time. "Ma'am. I've got this. I'll speak to the senior noncoms tonight and make sure there's no doubt about how this is going to go. Trust me."

"Fine. So how are we going to handle it?"

"Get some sleep. You and I will meet the convoy when it comes in. Just follow my lead." Hearns must have seen the lack of confidence on my face because he spoke again. "Ma'am. Trust me."

After a few seconds, I nodded. It was a hard thing for me to do, trust. But he didn't want to hear that. "Okay."

I woke up at 0315 and I couldn't go back to sleep. After lying there for fifteen minutes, wide awake, I got up and took a long shower. One of the perks of moving to the senior officer building was that I had my own shower and toilet. I'd never thought about that before—as a junior officer, that never happened—but it really made life better. I thought about going into the pit to check on the night shift but decided against it. They wouldn't have anything new since the brief that McNamara had given me, and it would just put stress on them for no reason. There were plenty of real things to cause stress without me adding to it.

At 0415, I headed out to meet Hearns. I stood next to him, shifting my weight from one foot to the other as the logistics convoy rolled in, tires crunching on gravel. You didn't get that sound from combat vehicles, which hovered instead of using wheels. The deep thrum of large truck engines echoed off the cement walls of the base. I'd never considered just how long a convoy of supplies to support four thousand soldiers might take to make its way through a gate and into an orderly assemblage. I had questions for Hearns—such as how much Perston already knew about the situation—but Hearns had said to trust him, so I didn't ask. I would wait and see what happened and react from there.

The way that Perston stomped across the gravel yard toward us gave me an indication that he knew most of it. He held his helmet crooked in one arm, and his dark hair was matted to his head. He was tall—almost as tall as Hearns, but not nearly as thick. He looked skinny, the way that his uniform was clinging to his ribs, but even grimy from the road his fine features shone through. His eyes bored into me as he approached. I met them, refusing to turn away.

"What the fuck is going on here, Mark?"

"You mean 'ma'am,' don't you sir?" asked Hearns.

Perston looked ready to snap something at him, so I interceded before he could. "There was a nuclear attack on the celebration dinner. We lost all our officers and a lot of senior noncoms."

"I know *that* part. What I mean is *that*." He pointed to the major's rank on my collar.

I hadn't been sure how I was going to react to this confrontation, but I found that I was a little pissed off. We'd lost a lot of people, and Perston just brushed that aside as if it didn't matter. Before I could respond, Hearns stepped forward. He didn't quite put himself between us, but he did insert his bulk in a way that caused Perston to take a half step back. Despite them being close in height, Hearns dwarfed him.

"Major Markov has been promoted, and she's in command, sir."

"That's not how this works, *Master Sergeant*. Someone doesn't get to grab a new rank, put it on, and declare themselves in charge."

"She didn't." Hearns's voice was calm, which contrasted sharply with the over-excited whine of Perston's. "The soldiers of this brigade promoted her."

"The soldiers of the brigade? They have no authority. *You* have no authority."

"We do now," said Hearns.

"When headquarters hears about this—"

"We have no communications off-planet," said Hearns, cutting him off.

Perston stood there, stammering, as if trying to figure out what to say to that. He was right, of course. When we did reestablish communications, headquarters was going to have an opinion, and that probably wouldn't end favorably for me. But for now, we couldn't talk to them, and there was nothing Perston could do about that. For my part, if I got that judgment from headquarters, it would mean that I'd found a way to reestablish communications. That was more important than who was in charge. Although I might have been the only one in our trio right then that believed that.

"I'm not accepting this," Perston said, finally, trying to sound calm but mostly failing. I hoped I didn't sound as whiny as he did when I protested to Hearns. I probably did.

Hearns smiled, but it was one of those terrifying smiles of someone who doesn't give a fuck what you think. "You've got two options. One, you can pin on this captain's rank that I have right here in my pocket, take your place as the executive officer, and do your best to help Major Markov run this brigade."

"Not happening—"

"Or two, I can beat your ass, and you can spend the rest of your time here in a cell for insubordination, and we'll let headquarters figure that out once we find a way to get through to them."

Perston hesitated, glanced at me, and then back to Hearns. He couldn't read me with his implant, but he could read Hearns. But if he did, all he was going to glean was that Hearns absolutely wasn't bluffing. Finally, Perston spoke. "I haven't gotten any sleep that wasn't in the front seat of a vehicle for the past two days. I need rest." With that, he turned and walked off without looking back.

"He's not going to accept it," I said.

"He's going to be surprised when he finds out that his stuff isn't where he left it because we've moved his room into the senior officer building."

I snorted, and a half-laugh got out. I understood Perston's situation, and I felt for him. But it wasn't like it was great to be me, either, with the weight of an entire brigade on my shoulders.

I was up and I had a full complement of problems and no idea where to start, so I was somewhat relieved when the senior supply sergeant, Master Sergeant Cantrell, tracked me down and answered that question for me. Before that, I had seen the protest outside the gate as an inconvenience, but not something that really demanded attention. I'd been mistaken.

While the protestors didn't do much to slow down our military vehicles leaving the base—they just waved signs and yelled at them—they were keeping all civilian vehicles from entering. They weren't physically stopping them, but their presence deterred any civilians from even trying to deliver their goods. Since we got most of our food from local sources, that was going to be a problem sooner rather than later. Soldiers would start to notice today, with certain items missing, like fresh fruits and vegetables, but it wouldn't really be a major issue for another two to three days. At that point, we'd have to switch to military rations, and I didn't need anyone to tell me what that would do to morale. Given my precarious leadership situation, and the situation of our unit in general, that was a non-starter. I needed to solve the dispute with the Zargod to create the freedom to work on my other pressing issues.

So that became my mission for the day. I put everything else out of my mind for the moment and convened a meeting in my office with McNamara, Hearns, and Corporal Collins from Human Intelligence.

"Where are we at finding a cultural advisor who can help me?" I asked.

The three of them stayed silent for a bit, fidgeting and looking anywhere but at me.

Collins said, "The senior father is going to block anyone we try to get—"

"I know that," I said. "But we can't let him dictate our actions. We need to find someone outside of him."

Collins nodded. "I'm sorry, ma'am. I don't have anyone."

"The lady who used to run the local coffee shop here on base speaks our language. Mrs. Zukov. She always seems to know what's going on in town," said McNamara.

"Yes!" I said. "Great idea."

"As a woman, she might present an issue with the locals," said Hearns, but his tone was deferential. He wasn't trying to crap on the idea, just presenting a potential roadblock.

But the fact that she was a woman made her perfect for me. I needed to know how to work with a patriarchal system—one that I found difficult to understand—and who better to help me figure that out than a woman? "She might. But I also have to believe that a woman who runs her own shop in a culture like this has to have an idea of how to get men to do what she wants."

"We couldn't use her for formal events," said Collins.

"I'm not really planning anything like that in the near future, given that someone nuked the last formal event." I stood and started pacing. "Can we get her in here so I can talk to her?"

"I can call her," said Collins. "We have her contact information from the shop documents."

"How are we going to get her past the mob at the gate? We don't want to paint a target on her," said Hearns.

"Ask her," I said to Collins. "Make the situation clear, ask her how to do it safely, and then get back to me."

It didn't take him long. Fifteen minutes later, Collins knocked on my door.

"Give me the good news," I said.

"She wants us to detain her, ma'am."

"Say what now?" I looked at him, but we didn't have the kind of relationship where he'd be joking. "Okay. Get Master Sergeant Hearns. We need to talk this through."

Collins did what he was told, and we reconvened after just a couple minutes. "It could be a trap, ma'am." Hearns leaned back against the wall, bringing him down a little closer to reasonable height. "She could be working with the local leadership to set us up. We take her, she denies telling us to do it, and the senior father has another thing to hold against us."

"It's possible." I pursed my lips; it's a habit I have when I'm trying to think something through. "But she didn't know we were going to call. She'd have had to have instructions before that."

"They could have anticipated our move," said Hearns. "Or something similar. They could have contacted all the businesses that used to be on base."

It was possible. I had to decide if it was worth the risk. My gut told me that there was no way that the senior father was some sort of political genius with plans on top of plans, but I worried that was just my bias talking. I'd underestimated him before. I didn't like the guy, so thinking of him as smart was distasteful. I'd like to say that I fully weighed all the pros and cons, but in the end, I made my decision because I didn't have any better options.

"Tell Ops to spin up a patrol and go detain Mrs. Zukov."

If it was a trap, it was a complex one because they picked Mrs. Zukov up without a hitch. Sergeant Anthony had ridden along on the mission and been in phone contact with her, and she guided them straight to where she was waiting on a street corner. Now she was sitting across from me on a sofa in the fancy meeting room—the same place where I'd blown the engagement with the city fathers. It seemed ridiculous, using that big room for just the two of us. I'd insisted on nobody else being there, which had drawn a protest about my safety, but I'd held firm. Mrs. Zukov looked like she was about sixty, her hair more gray than its original black. She stood just a little over a meter and a half tall and weighed maybe two-thirds what I did. I figured I could take her in a fight if it came to that.

For her part, she didn't seem worried at all to be alone with me. She just sat there, sipping her wine, which I remembered this time, and waited for me to speak. It was oddly effective. Something about the woman just made me want to tell her everything and have her tell me it was going to be all right. Maybe she could help me figure out what to do about Perston.

"I need your help," I said, in her language.

"I understand," she said in mine. "We should speak in your language. It helps me practice. I didn't have schooling, so I make do with experience." She took another sip of wine. "You've made a bit of a mess of things."

I laughed. She certainly was direct, but that just made me want her advice more. I needed someone who would tell me like it was. "As Corporal Collins told you, I'd like you to work for me. As my advisor."

"Too quick to business. You're all like that, you soldiers. Take some time, talk to people."

I knew that from my cultural studies, but for the life of me I couldn't make myself do it. I couldn't think of a single casual topic that she and I might have in common. "Uh...have you always lived in Tanzit?"

"Since I was girl. My father moved us here when I was nine. Ever since." She spoke slowly, not completely adept with the language, but understandable.

"How long have you run the shop here?"

"Again with business." She smiled, I think sensing how uncomfortable the situation was making me. "You're good-looking young woman. You have husband?"

I didn't answer for a second, a little shocked at the change of direction, and also the outright lie about my looks. Sure, I was in shape, hard and strong, but nobody would seriously call me attractive. "No, no husband."

"Good," she said. "Me neither. He died."

"Oh, I'm sorry to hear that," I said.

"Don't be. He was shithead. You, you don't marry. Live for self."

THE WEIGHT OF COMMAND

"Is it difficult running a business here as a woman?" I asked.

"Not so difficult." She finished the last of her wine. "Have to let men think they are in charge. Easy enough. Men are stupid. You just have to pet them."

"Pet them?"

"Pet them. Like cats. Make them think that they are important."

"Ah. So how do I pet the city fathers…make them think they're important?"

"Give them what they want," she said.

"I have a feeling that what they want is to see me publicly humiliated, and I can't do that."

"Bah. You are like them. Too much pride getting in the way of getting things done. Me? I just want to run my shop again."

I considered it. Was it just my pride getting in the way? No, I had more at stake than that. I had a unit to run, and to do that, my soldiers had to respect me. If the colonel was here, he could have acquiesced, brought himself down, and everyone would have called him brilliant for doing it. With me, they'd see it as the young woman being too weak to handle the job. "I'm in a difficult situation. It's more than just pride. I have to lead soldiers, and I can't afford to look weak."

She thought about it and nodded. I expected her to tell me I was too prideful again, but she surprised me. "This makes sense."

"So what do I do?"

She thought some more. "What do you want?"

"I want the demonstrations to stop so that we can go about our business."

"Yes. Now more important. What does *he* want?" She didn't say who she meant, but she didn't have to.

"I don't know…to feel important?"

"Yes!" She waved one hand in the air, and I found that her approval warmed me. "He wants to *look* important. Not to you. To the people. And what do the people want?"

I didn't know, and immediately I knew that was my problem. I should have figured that out from the start. "They want justice for the boy we injured?"

Mrs. Zukov rolled her eyes. "No."

"I don't know. I *should* know, but I don't. Could you just tell me?"

"They want to re-open their shops on the base, to resume their jobs delivering goods and removing trash and such. The boy…he'll get better.

The money?" She shrugged. "The money matters. It matters to me, as shop owner, and it matters to city fathers, who get their cut."

I stared at her. "That's what *I* want. I want the shops open and the workers back. I want our trash pickup and our food vendors. I want to go back to normal. If we all want that, why are we stuck here?"

"One man doesn't want that."

"Why doesn't he want that? Doesn't he serve the people?"

"Yes and no."

"How do I get him out of the way?"

"I told you. Give him what he wants." She shook her head as she said it, as if she was a teacher and I was a recalcitrant student.

I thought about it. What he wanted was to seem important to the people, and what the people wanted was their economy back. "So you're saying I should contact the senior father and tell him that I want the shops open again and the workers back on base."

"Just so." She smiled, and it warmed me.

"But if I ask him for that, isn't he going to hold it over my head? Isn't he going to use that as leverage to demand more?"

"He will try," she allowed. "But he cannot. There is lot of pressure on him from the people. He may ask for more, but that's just bluff. You stand strong, and he will give you what you want. He will act like big hero to the people. All will cheer for him. Then they go back to work."

I thought about it for several seconds. She wasn't lying—my implant verified that. She believed every word of what she was saying, and she hadn't minced those words. All I had to decide was if what she believed was right. In the end, it was an easy decision. I believed she could get things done. "I'll call him."

"No," she said. "Go to him. Just him, not the others. Nobody to tell a different story from him."

"And if I go to him, it shows the people that he has power, which is what he wants."

"It shows that you respect him," she said. "Which you should. He's a man, and arrogant, but overall? Not bad man. There are many worse."

I sat with that for a few seconds, taking her words for the chastening that they were. I was so busy trying to get what I want that I'd forgotten that basic dignity that I owed him. I was an asshole. "Thank you, Mrs. Zukov. I will. About the job as my advisor—"

She waved her hand at me. "I have a job. I run coffee shop. If you need me, you send for me."

I smiled. It was a comforting feeling. There wasn't anybody I truly felt was on my side unequivocally, and of course Mrs. Zukov had her own motives. But she felt like the closest thing to an ally that I had, and that helped. "Will it be any trouble for you that we brought you here?"

She waved her hand again. "Natalie Zukov knows how to take care of herself. I tell them that you asked me questions, but I told you to talk to fathers."

"They'll believe you?" It seemed too simple to work.

"Possibly not. But they cannot prove. You don't worry."

13

With Mrs. Zukov gone, I made a call to the senior father and used my implant to address him in his own language. He hesitated when I said I wanted only him and not his retinue, but after a minute or two of protest, he agreed to meet me the next morning at his office. Mrs. Zukov had been exactly right about that. When I proposed coming to him, he nearly jumped through the comm-link to say yes. For him, he could use that to bolster his status in the city. At the same time, it didn't hurt my status, because I could sell it as us showing that we're not afraid to go out into the city, even with their protest. My soldiers would see it as strength.

With that settled, I turned to handle some of my other problems. Our efforts to reach anyone in the orbital stations had so far failed, and nobody could explain why. We got direct laser comms set up. Nobody answered. That's all we knew. I didn't have a direct way to deal with that —but it fit a pattern. More and more I was seeing it as the enemy, whoever that was, denying us the ability to communicate and restricting our freedom of movement. If that were true, their intent might be to isolate us. Or maybe that was just a step in a greater plan that hadn't revealed itself.

With no solutions for that problem, the plans officer-slash-Argazzi spy seemed like the easiest thing to get sorted, so I decided to talk to her. Anything to avoid having to talk to Perston again. *That* was a mess that I wasn't going to straighten out any time soon, though I'd have to try.

I found Captain Ana Song in a small conference room that soldiers were converting into a workspace for her. She was reading from a tablet when I entered, and she stood. Two soldiers were assembling a printed desk against the back wall.

"Give us a few minutes, would you? Pull the door behind you." I asked them and then waited until they left.

Song was average height—maybe ten centimeters shorter than me—with a slender build and delicate features. She was pretty, which led me to wonder if the Argazzi had done that on purpose. If they knew I was attracted to pretty faces, would they try to use it to influence me? Or was I just seeing ghosts—figments of my paranoia-fueled imagination—around every corner? She had one of those ageless faces that could have been anywhere from twenty to forty years old, but I figured that as a captain she'd be a bit older than me at a minimum. Not that it mattered.

I almost felt bad for her. Her leadership had dumped her into a difficult spot, probably without much notice, and now she was away from all her support systems. I'd thought about the enemy isolating me, but she'd been isolated as well. Even her communications back to her own base were subject to our control, as even if she had her own equipment, we could easily jam it.

I'd perused her file via my implant on my way over, though I didn't trust it much since it came directly from the Argazzi, and they could have doctored it to say whatever they wanted. I'd figure out what I really wanted to know—how much I could trust her—on my own. My starting position was *very little*.

I took a seat across the conference table from where she'd been sitting and gestured for her to sit as well.

"Are my people treating you well?"

"Your soldiers have been respectful, if not particularly helpful." She paused, seeming almost embarrassed. "I shouldn't say that. They've given me workspace and are working to get me everything—a lot of—what I've asked for. And the soldier assigned to me as a liaison—Private Mahar—has been nothing but polite."

"What have you asked for that we haven't provided?"

She pointed to the tablet. "This isn't attached to anything. Someone loaded it with information, and I can read what they put on it, but nothing else. I understand why, but it's not very useful."

"I'll see what I can do for you."

"It's okay, ma'am. You've got a lot on your plate without having to worry about me. I'll get by." She was sincere, which I hadn't expected, and I decided right then that I liked her. It was a snap decision, and perhaps I'd regret it, but that's how I work. I wanted to trust her because I needed someone to trust, but needing it and having it were very different things. But I could take a step. After all, you have to show some trust to receive it in return, and how would I know if I didn't give her a chance?

"We'll set you up with secure communications back to your base, and you have my word that it will go unmonitored."

She narrowed her eyes, clearly skeptical. "How can you do that?"

I shrugged, trying to come off as casual, though I felt her skepticism and didn't blame her. "We've both got jobs to do. As of now, I think we're mostly on the same side. If that changes, I'll let you know and we'll reevaluate the comms situation."

"Yes, ma'am." Her look told me she still didn't believe me, and my implant confirmed it.

"Look. We both know why you're here."

"Yes, ma'am. I assume we do." That she didn't deny her primary mission as a spy said a lot for her in my book.

"The way I see it, it isn't reasonable for me to expect you to help me do mine if I don't help you do yours." I let that sink in for a few seconds. "At the same time, I can't give you access to everything. Technical specifications of systems, intelligence collection information—that's still off limits."

Captain Song nodded, and then hesitated, waiting to see if I was going to say more, and when I didn't she said, "I need to say this…while you're not wrong about the job I've been assigned, I absolutely want to maintain the peace that your organization is here to support. So in that regard, we have overlapping interests."

It was my turn to nod. She meant what she said; I couldn't detect even a hint of deception in her. "Thanks for that."

"Ma'am…you mentioned helping each other. So far, you've told me what you're willing to do for me. What is it that you want in return?"

I smiled. Smart woman. Of course I wanted something. "I want you to find a way for me to communicate off-planet."

She sat there, stunned. She hadn't known. Our lack of comms was a big piece of information to share, and she had to realize that. It would certainly go in her first report home. It was okay, I think. I couldn't see how it hurt me to let the Argazzi know that if they didn't already. After all, they might already know and simply have not filled in Captain Song. They'd also lost all off-planet comms, so it stood to reason that they'd at least suspect that we didn't have it either. So what seemed like a huge piece of intelligence to Song at the moment was really more just a confirmation. "Yes, ma'am."

I liked it. She didn't ask how she was going to do that. She just said yes. I needed somebody like that, someone who would take the mission and work it without guidance. I had too many things to think about already. But I could at least give her some parameters.

"Our enemy—and I'm not defining that enemy because I don't know who it is—has attacked our ability to communicate at every turn. While our primary objective right now is to restore the space elevator to functionality in order to regain comms, I think that's an easily predictable course of action. If I was the enemy, I'd work to stop it. So I think we have to plan for that. Part of that planning will be defensive. Obviously, we're not going to just sit still and let them stop us. I've got our intelligence assets searching for anyone acting against that mission, and we'll work to thwart them."

"So you want me to work on alternate courses of action."

"Exactly."

"What are my assets?" She gestured around to the sparse furnishing of the room. "There's not much here that's going to help."

I considered it. I couldn't afford to assign people to screen everything she did, but at the same time, she was right. I couldn't expect her to come up with a solution to a technical problem without access to resources. "You're in charge of what you access, but I'm putting you on the honor system. Access what you need, but don't cross the line into things that don't apply to your mission. You also can call in whatever staff you need to work with you, as long as you don't take them off of missions that I prioritized. Work with the heads of each department to determine those priorities and who fits best for what you need. Mahar can facilitate that for you, and if he can't help on his own, send him to see Sergeant First Class McNamara in the pit."

"You want *me* to work with the staff?"

"I do. I don't have the time or resources to dedicate to monitoring everything you do. You know well enough what lines you shouldn't cross." She still didn't believe me, so I continued, "Every so often I'm going to check on what you've accessed. And I'll be able to tell, I promise. And if you've crossed the line, you're done. I'll set you back in a sterile conference room with no outside sources at all."

Her eyes widened as the threat sunk in. "Yes, ma'am."

"I'm serious. One strike and you're out."

"Roger that."

"Great. Update me in a day or two." I didn't really know how it was going to work out—it was a risk, for sure—but given my situation, having someone specifically working on that project took some pressure off me. I had a lot of noncoms who were experts in their field, but I didn't have a lot of people who could synthesize that knowledge into something with a more general purpose. Something told me that Captain Ana Song could do that.

After I left, I headed by Intel and asked them to do a background check on Song and the other officer the Argazzi assigned to us. I said I trusted her, and I did—but what I didn't trust fully was my own judgment. While I was there, I asked them to dig up what they could on Liana Trieste and Mr. Yakina as well. I had a feeling I'd be dealing with them a lot, and the more I knew, the better.

I couldn't put off talking to Perston any longer. I had hoped that after he calmed down he'd have sought me out, but I should have known better. Counting on an asshole like him to be the bigger man was like counting on a dog not to eat a steak left out on the table. I should admit here that I'm an asshole as well. If I'm being totally honest, Perston and I were more alike than we were different. Most young officers are when you get right down to it. We're arrogant and we're competitive and we want to get ahead. As it turns out, those are kind of the traits you need as a junior officer. There might be a little space in the room for someone quiet and competent, but that space usually got taken up by brash and loud.

Add to that that Perston and I knew each other pretty well, even beyond our days back at the academy. We were lieutenants in the same unit and while he'd been commissioned a couple months before me, we were from the same cohort year, and we had the same group of maybe fifty friends and acquaintances. All of whom were dead. There were two sides to the situation, though. Since I was a lot like him, I had a pretty good idea how he was going to react. But also, I knew how I'd take it if our situations were reversed, and it wasn't good.

But there was nothing to do but face it, so I queried the system to find out where he was and then headed to his room with Zilla in tow as my security. It was the last place I wanted to meet, but if I summoned him to my office, I'd just make the situation worse. And I certainly didn't want to meet somewhere public. Anywhere we went, people would be watching. Anything they saw me do would spread through the unit like a particularly virulent STD.

I stood outside his room for longer than necessary and then knocked. I waited for maybe thirty seconds. In my head, I pictured him standing there, deciding whether to open or not. He'd have patched into the camera feed with his implant, so he knew who was standing at his door. Finally, he opened it.

"Come to gloat?"

I reassessed my previous thought and decided that maybe he'd just been trying to think up a good opening line. He should have taken more time. "Don't be a shithead."

He stood in the door, blocking it so I couldn't come in, and we stared each other down for what felt like a long time, having our own little alpha asshole contest. He'd cleaned up since his return and stood there in shorts and a t-shirt, a bit of shaving cream that he'd missed under his ear. I didn't tell him; I can be petty like that. Besides, it made me smirk on the inside and distracted me from his pretty face, which I didn't need confusing me. Finally, he stepped back to let me enter into the small room. It had a tile floor, a bed, a utilitarian wardrobe, and a desk. A small door at the back led to the shower and toilet.

"It's bullshit. You *know* it's bullshit," he said.

He wasn't wrong, and I did understand the sentiment. But the fact that all the officers in our unit were dead, and the thing he opened with was that he wasn't in charge said a lot about him. I shut the door behind me. "Sure."

"It *is*," he said. "You know that if we'd both been here, we'd have looked at each other and we'd both have immediately known that I was in charge."

I wasn't so sure about that. I hadn't made the decision. Hearns had.

Would he have made a different one if both Perston and I had been here? I couldn't say. But I didn't want to have that discussion with Perston. It wouldn't help, and I didn't want to fall into the trap of trying to rationalize the situation. "I didn't even realize that I was in charge until somebody looked at me expecting orders."

"You know what I mean. Every lieutenant alive knows their relative date of rank."

That he chose the word "alive" seemed particularly crass, but I decided not to call him on it. I had to watch my attitude, not focus on the fact that he was an insensitive dick. He *was*, but my focusing on that wouldn't help the situation. He and I needed to come to some common ground for the good of the unit, and he wouldn't make that happen, so I had to. Part of me wanted to throw down and slug it out. Maybe if we did that, afterward we could get to a better place. We'd be an even enough match in a fair fight, with both of us having the same training as well as implants to enhance our reactions, but if I hit him first…I banished the thought. I needed to stick to the job at hand, which was much bigger than our ego problems.

Instead, I played to his vanity and made it about him, just like Mrs. Zukov had said to do with the city fathers. "So what do you think we should do?"

He had been looking away but snapped his head toward me. Good. I had his attention. "What do you mean?"

"You said it's bullshit. So what do we do about it? It doesn't do any good to stand here and complain, right? It's all about what happens next."

"Sure. Yeah."

"So what happens next?" I asked.

He thought about it, scrunching his face up a little like he hadn't even considered it until I asked. "I don't know."

"Do you want me to call a formation and announce my abdication of command in favor of you?"

"No." He spit the word like a sullen teenager, but he didn't hesitate, which surprised me a little bit. Maybe he realized that I didn't actually intend to do it. But I doubted it. It was exactly the kind of ego-stroking thing that he *would* believe, as ridiculous as it was.

But I wasn't letting him off the hook. For this to work, he needed to come up with the answer himself. That's the only way he'd accept it since he saw himself as more competent than me. Which, maybe he was. I

THE WEIGHT OF COMMAND

didn't think so, and Hearns *definitely* didn't think so, but we had different specialties, and it was hard to say. "Why not? I'll do it. I'll do it right now."

He thought about it for a few seconds, and I started to second-guess myself, but finally, he spoke. More of a whine, really. "Because the soldiers won't accept that."

"You don't know that. Just because Hearns said it—"

"I checked, Mark. Okay? Does that make you happy? I asked some of the noncoms that I trust, and they told me the deal. Hearns was telling the truth, and the vast majority of the soldiers who matter support him. Is that what you wanted to hear?"

It *was* what I wanted to hear. I liked to have my ego stroked too. Like I said, he and I are a lot alike. but I couldn't let him make it about me. "So I'll ask you again. What do you want to do?"

He looked at me, and tilted his head to the side. "What do you mean?"

"What role do you want?"

"Hearns said I was the XO. I don't think I get a vote."

"He said that, but you do get a vote. There are a lot of different kinds of XOs in the galaxy, and they all handle the role a little differently."

He considered it but didn't speak, so I continued. "Let's be real with each other. I don't see you being my trusted advisor behind the scenes."

He snorted, and I knew I had him. If he could laugh about it, he could support it. "I suspect not." It was too bad. I could have used a trusted number two, somebody to bounce my ideas off of and to confide in. But that possibility had been shot to shit four months ago as soon as I rolled out of his bunk and refused to ever get back in it.

"So what makes sense to me is that I give you a role that gives you a lot of autonomy in one area, and where I don't have to give you a lot of orders. I think that would be useful for both of us." What I mostly meant was that it would be more tenable for him, letting him salvage some of his pride and not throwing it in his face constantly that I was his boss. Giving him an option was a risk because if he said he wanted to take over operations, I'd have to try to talk him out of it. But I knew his specialty—he was a logistics officer—and I counted on him focusing on his strength. Please, just let him think this through and answer for the good of the unit this one time. "So tell me. Where do you think you'd do the most good?"

He considered it for more than a minute, pacing around in the smallish room, walking to the opposite side of the bed to get some distance from me. I moved back toward the door both to give him more space and to try to give him the hint that I had places to be. I didn't, but I didn't want to be there any longer than necessary. "Logistics."

"Yeah?"

"Yeah. Give me logistics. It's what I'm good at, and it's not your strength. I'll take all the supply, maintenance, and movement stuff off your hands."

I tried to keep my face neutral, but inside I wanted to do a happy dance. Finally, something broke my way. Since he came up with it on his own, he'd be invested. "It's yours."

"I'll take the Four Shop personnel to help me. Master Sergeant Cantrell can be my right hand."

Him taking the supply, food service and maintenance personnel worked for me. I hadn't had much time for them anyway. "Roger that. Cantrell is going to tell you that we're running out of food. I'm working on that."

He looked like he wanted to say something, pulled back, and then said it anyway. "Yeah? Work fast. Morale will go down in a hurry if we have to go to military rations."

I'm pretty proud of myself for not saying *no shit*. "I'll work fast."

"I'll call you 'ma'am.' In front of the soldiers. It has to be that way."

"Thanks, Dirk."

"You got it, Kiera."

I closed the door behind me, and Zilla, who had been waiting for me in the hall, fell in half a step behind me as I walked away. I considered what had just happened. It had been too easy, I think. I didn't trust Perston. Not completely, anyway. I did believe that he'd assessed the situation and taken the only course he could. But I didn't believe he accepted it. It wasn't in his nature to just let it go, to support me. What remained to be seen was how that would manifest. Unfortunately, all I could do was wait and see. He'd been smart that way. By saying the right things, Perston ensured that I couldn't just sideline him. But I could watch him.

"Everything okay, ma'am?" asked Zilla.

"I'm not sure."

"There was no yelling."

"You were listening?"

"Yes, ma'am." I liked the fact that she didn't even pretend she wasn't.

"I supposed that's natural."

"I figured that maybe Captain Perston would push back, so I was listening to make sure there was no trouble. You know, in case I needed to come in and help you kick his ass."

I laughed. "Zilla, this meeting didn't happen. You hear me? Nobody needs to know about it."

"What meeting, ma'am?"

I chuckled again, but I believed her. I don't know why—maybe it was the ridiculous air of competence she had—but I trusted her to keep her mouth shut. I trusted my crew. Sure, it would have been nice if I could have trusted Perston. But at least I had somebody.

14

I set out early the next morning with my team and four escort vehicles to head to a 1000 hours meeting with the senior father at his house-slash-office. I left us a significant amount of time to clear any possible protests, but the city stood quiet. Like the sea a day after a storm, it appeared like none of it had ever happened. I had little doubt that the senior father had been the one to end the protest, but what I didn't know was his motive. Was it a demonstration of his power, or was it something more sinister? After all, if he could end a protest, he could start it again at a time and place of his choosing. For that reason, I switched up our route and we drove most of the way around the city to approach his compound from the other direction.

We passed by the main market, where heavy foot traffic headed into the rows of colored canopies and semi-permanent wooden sheds. A few families who had shopped early headed home, the women carrying their burdens as the men herded small children. A group of older boys played a game with a ball on a patch of bare dirt, pushing and elbowing but not fighting, as if they knew the lines and didn't cross them.

The apartment buildings of the city shifted to single-family dwellings made of red brick as we slowly wormed our way toward the senior father's compound, where we stopped outside a wrought iron gate. A guard came out of an oversized gatehouse that sported similar wrought iron bars on its windows and he manually retracted the gate, pulling it

THE WEIGHT OF COMMAND

toward himself on tiny wheels. He didn't speak to us—he hardly looked at us—which meant he had his marching orders already. That he was alone at his post and carrying only a sidearm said a lot about the expected threat in the area. I knew from study that there were exactly six houses inside the gated compound. Four of them belonged to the senior father and members of his extended family, while the other two housed other influential city leaders. Each house was its own walled compound inside of the greater one, and the wide streets had room for four cars to pass at once—yet we were the only vehicle moving.

"Nice digs," said Gonzalez.

"I wonder if this guy has any daughters he wants to marry off," responded Murph.

"You're disgusting," said Zilla.

"Didn't bother me when my mom said it, doesn't bother me when you say it," said Murphy.

We left our escort vehicles at the gate and continued on to our destination alone, and it wasn't lost on me that it was a perfect spot for an ambush. But that wouldn't happen. We had a contract, the senior father and I, consummated when I agreed to visit him on his turf. That made him responsible for my security and any failure in that would fall directly on him, culturally speaking. It was an unwritten rule of the Zargod that I appreciated. Not that the shame on his family would do my corpse much good.

We pulled up outside his compound at 0947 and waited a few seconds for the gate to open. This one was automatic, presumably controlled from inside the house. We pulled into his compound into a wide gravel lot, and it crunched when Murphy lowered the vehicle's feet to park. I waited for Gonzalez and Xiang to dismount first, pausing for their all-clear before stepping out myself. I left my rifle in the vehicle with Murphy and Zilla but kept my sidearm strapped to my side. I wasn't sure how the senior father would react to that, but that was policy and I stuck to it. My two escorts kept their long guns. I wanted to see if the senior father would make an issue of it or not.

We walked to the left side of the building, away from the main entrance toward a less ornate door that led to the office, where Xiang knocked. A heavy-set young man with dark hair and a thick mustache opened it and stood back as we entered. I made a note of the weapon slung over his back, as well as the other young man in the room who was short and wiry and also carrying a rifle, but not in a way that he'd be able to quickly use it. They both wore them more like badges of office than as weapons. Despite their radically different builds, they had a look about them that suggested they were brothers, or possibly cousins. Before I could ask, the senior father walked out from the inner office and greeted me, his arms wide, as if we were long-lost friends. Seen in his own environment, he seemed somehow bigger and smaller at the same time, standing several centimeters shorter than me with his white shirt sticking to his narrow ribcage, but with his energy filling the room.

"Major! Welcome!" His change in attitude made me wonder if we had an audience beyond his two guards and mine. He gestured to the two identically dressed young men, their khaki pants and white shirts passing as a sort of uniform. "These are my nephews. They will stay out here while you and I talk."

"That's good. Xiang and Gonzalez will wait out here with them if that's okay."

He didn't even glance at my security team. "Of course! Come."

I followed him through the door and the tile floor turned to a carpet that had probably once been expensive, but now appeared worn. He left the door partially open behind me, probably for cultural propriety. It was fine. I didn't mind his guards—or mine—hearing whatever we said. I couldn't rule out a recording, regardless, so anything I said I'd be willing to abide by.

"Please. Sit." He gestured to a fabric-covered sofa that sat a little too low to the floor for me to be comfortable at my height. He walked around behind a desk that was almost too big to be real as if the size of the desk generated power or something. "We'll have wine."

"Of course." I remembered Mrs. Zukov's words about not jumping right to business, and I tried to be patient. I settled back into the couch as well as I could but kept my feet and knees together in front of me uncomfortably. I wondered if the couch had been designed to be a torture device on purpose. A few moments of awkward silence later, the smaller of the two nephews brought a tray with two small glass wine cups on it, offering it first to his uncle, and then to me. Just in case I didn't know who was more important.

He took one sip and then set the cup down on his desk. "Very nice. The '62 vintage. So smooth, but so full at the same time."

I was in a hurry to get through the formalities and get to business, but I had to admit, it was some damned fine wine, like an explosion of flavors in my mouth. "It's exceptional."

THE WEIGHT OF COMMAND

"I trust your meeting with Mrs. Zukov went well."

I hid my mouth with a second sip of wine to give myself time to process his opening gambit. He was trying to fluster me—that much was clear. But of course he knew about the meeting. Someone would have seen her and reported it. Whether he was intending it as a threat or just to wrong-foot me, I couldn't be sure. "It went well, Senior Father."

"Please," he said, interrupting, "call me Father Romero."

"I will. Thank you, Father Romero. Mrs. Zukov suggested that I contact you." I gestured around. "And here we are. I appreciate her advice."

"Of course. You saw that I've had the protests stop."

"I did." I also noted that he said *I've*. Whatever his game, he wasn't subtle. "I also noticed a brisk business at the market this morning."

"Yes, yes," he said, waving his hand to dismiss it. But he'd heard me, even if I *was* subtle. The end of the protest helped his city as well as me because the citizens could get back to their lives. "We can keep it this way."

"I'd like that."

"You will open the shops on the base." He had this weird phrasing that fell somewhere between a question and a statement.

"I will give the order today," I said.

"Good. And you will pay the mother of the injured boy." He paused. "As a gesture of good faith."

"We will. I'll have someone help with the claim so we can expedite it."

"Good. Good. I will bring her here and host a lunch to help smooth things over." He glanced at me as if waiting for me to object.

I knew what he was doing. He was having her there so that when we paid her, he could take a cut—after we left, of course. He'd make it clear to them that they were getting paid because of him, and that they owed him. And they'd accept it because that's how their patronage system worked. Part of me wanted to let him know that I knew, but it wasn't worth it. I needed this problem out of the way, needed peace locally so I could focus on restoring communications and on the fact that someone had nuked our officers and tried to kill one of our patrols in the desert with a drone. And it would also keep me from going back to the scene where we'd injured the kid in the first place, which I definitely wanted to avoid. If we showed our faces back there, we might trigger a *legitimate* protest. "Of course. That would be good of you. It will make things easier for us."

"Good." With that settled, he took another sip of his wine. "We should talk about the road."

"The road?"

"The road in front of your base. The trucks coming and going, they cause a lot of traffic to back up, and your drivers, they don't let our vehicles pass in the middle of their formation."

There it was. I'd known he was going to ask for something beyond what we had already pledged to give, but I hadn't known what. I didn't know anything about the road, but I was sure it involved money for him. But I could deal with that. I had the purse strings, after all, and what was the point of having funds if you didn't use them to further the mission? Besides, roads took a long time, and I only had to work on them for a month. After that, it would be somebody else's problem—somebody who had the right experience to deal with this. "What do you think we should do about it?"

"You could expand the road," he offered.

"I can have my engineers look at that possibility."

"You should use local labor. It will make the people like you more." And there was how he'd make his money. By selling jobs.

"I can have my legal people look into it to see if we're allowed to do that." I hesitated, faking a lack of confidence, even though I knew it was standard practice to hire locally whenever possible. I was following Mrs. Zukov's advice, and I wanted him to feel smarter than me. "I'm new to command, as you know, so I don't know all the rules yet. It may take a little time."

"Of course, of course. It's nothing. You'll do your best. Will you stay for lunch?" Before I could respond and beg off, he continued, "You'll stay. Arthur!" The bigger of the two nephews poked his head in. "Get us lunch. You'll eat with us."

"I really shouldn't," I said. "I have my soldiers waiting out in the vehicle."

"We'll bring them lunch too. We'll get street food."

I almost laughed. My last experience with local street food hadn't gone well, but I really did love it. Lunch it was.

I checked with my escort before we departed to make sure they had everything under control before we headed back to base, and I directed them to take another circuitous route, just in case. The bot attack in the desert was still at the back of my head, and if we had to be a target, we at least could make ourselves a difficult one. The road took us around the far side of the market, where the foot traffic was about half of what we'd seen on the way in, either because of the different location or the timing.

"Slow down as we pass through here," I ordered. "I don't want—"

Something exploded to our direct left and I let the transmission drop. It took a second for me to process it—it had felt close, in the way that unexpected explosions always feel, but my implant told me it hadn't been.

"Talk to me Zilla. What do you see?" I asked on internal. From her spot up top in the vehicle, she'd have the best visual.

"No contact." If the explosion had startled her, it didn't come across in her steady voice. "Smoke is coming from the market, near the middle, on our left at seventy-five degrees. Something blew up there."

"Stop the convoy. Let's assess," I said over the platoon net.

"Roger."

Once we stopped, the screams became audible, and a few seconds later people were running in every direction, but all of them away from the explosion. One man was limping, his face bloody, and he was holding pressure on his arm. The first people ran past us, and I wanted to grab someone to ask what had happened. It could have been as simple as a propane tank going up—some street food vendors used it to cook with— but the fact that it happened when we were right here made me suspect something more sinister.

And then it clicked.

With our presence here, people were going to blame us for the explosion. My first instinct was to get back to base as fast as we could, and I was just about to give that order, but I thought better of it and took a second to assess my options. Either way, we were screwed. If we sped off, it would make us look guilty, but if we stayed and tried to render aid, a mob might form and come after us, putting us into an awkward situation where we had to defend ourselves.

Shit.

People slowed as they saw us, some visibly rerouting to go around, but an uncomfortable few stopped to stare. I had to make a decision and I had to do it fast. I came up with a third option. "Reverse course and head back the way we came. Take us to the senior father's compound."

To his credit, the platoon sergeant for the escort didn't hesitate when he said, "Roger, ma'am." The lead vehicle pulled a U-turn, going up over the curb on the far side of the street, and we all followed suit. To people onsite, it would look like we were running away. And we were. But we weren't heading for base. We were going back to Father Romero's compound. I didn't like it, putting myself further in his debt, but if anyone could control the narrative around the explosion and make people believe we weren't at fault, it was him. But I'd have to ask.

The guard at the compound gate didn't immediately come out when we arrived this time, probably because he wasn't expecting us. Instead, he stared out his big window for several seconds. I jumped out to meet him as he moved to the door and Xiang swore, scrambling to get out and catch up to me.

"We need to see the senior father," I said.

The tall, thin soldier had his weapon holstered, which was a good sign, but he didn't move toward the gate. "You were just here."

"It's an emergency. I need to see him now." Scenarios flashed through my mind as I considered what I was going to do if he didn't let us in. I could force him, of course, but that would probably make things worse. Thankfully he saved me the decision, and moved toward the gate, though he certainly took his time about it. I looked behind me to see if anybody had pursued us. I'm not sure what I expected, but of course there was nobody.

I ordered all five vehicles through the gate this time and remounted in my own. I took a few seconds to order the four escort vehicles to stay there and secure the entry, just in case, and then headed back to the big house.

The gate was open when we got there, and Arthur the nephew came running out of the business side of the house to meet us as we pulled up. He had his weapon off the sling and in his hands but kept it pointed down and away.

"I need your uncle. It's an emergency," I said through my open window, just after we pulled to a stop. Unlike the guard at the gate, Arthur reacted without hesitation, running into the main house. I got out of my vehicle with my two guards and waited. And waited. It was several minutes before the door opened and Father Romero strolled out, still buttoning his shirt. Perhaps he had decided on a nap after we left.

THE WEIGHT OF COMMAND

He listened patiently as I explained what had happened, considered it for a moment, and said, "Come to the office. I'll make some calls."

His calm struck me, as I sat on the uncomfortable sofa and listened to him work. He only raised his voice once, and that was to energize an underling who had apparently not had the appropriate sense of urgency about the task he had been assigned. Despite our differences and my inherent dislike of the Zargod system of government, I started to see why he was in charge. It would have been easy to lose his cool—his people had been attacked, and some of them were hurt—but he took it in stride.

After fifteen minutes and seven calls, he sat back in his chair and laced his hands behind his head. "Now we wait." He smiled, just one corner of his mouth going up, as if to reassure me or something, and I had the strange feeling that we had gone from sort-of-adversaries to co-conspirators in the course of an hour. I had to watch that because we were absolutely *not* friends. But I can't deny that in that moment, where I'd been a little panicked about what would happen, I was happy to have him on my side. Strange how that works.

We sat there in silence until, about five minutes later, the phone beeped. I made a conscious effort not to try to listen in to the opposite end of the conversation as he received the report. They spoke in Zargod, but of course that was no barrier for me.

"Yes. Okay. Okay. Yes. Call me back if you get more. Okay." He turned to me. "One person is dead. A woman. One of the vendors. Several are injured. More than ten, fewer than twenty, though we may not know that for sure if people left on their own."

I nodded. "If there is anything we can do to assist—"

"There is one thing," he said, cutting me off, but then stopping before making his request.

"Anything," I said.

"One witness said that she saw something come from above right before the explosion. Does that make sense to you?"

The way he asked the question, I could tell that he had his own idea already but wanted to lead me to my own conclusion. "Like a missile?" I hadn't seen anything, hadn't heard anything before the explosion. The ambient radars in our vehicles hadn't picked anything up or someone would have mentioned it.

"I don't know. It seems like a thing that a person wouldn't make up, though, don't you think?"

"Xiang!" I called, and a few seconds later he stuck his head through the door. "Get on the comm back to base. See if they have anything on the airspace around the market during the time of the explosion." I almost said attack, which was a good indication that I was already thinking about it the same way that Romero was.

The phone beeped again, and this time he listened without speaking. When he hung up, he shook his head, indicating that he didn't have anything new to share.

"You don't think this was an accident." I copied his speech pattern subconsciously, phrasing it somewhere between a question and a statement.

He shrugged. "It could be." But he clearly didn't believe that.

"Do you think it would be possible for me to get an explosives forensic unit in there to look at the site? We might be able to determine what happened, evaluate the residue of the explosion, look for surviving pieces." I had my doubts since people were surely disturbing the scene even now, but it was worth a shot.

"I think it's best if you don't." He paused as if deliberating on what to share, and then continued, "I can't be seen to be working with you too much."

I started to make a smart-assed remark about him not minding working with me when there was money involved, but I swallowed it. He knew the people, and if he had to do that, he had to do it. After all, who the fuck was I to tell him what was best when it came to leading his people? I had different issues with my own leadership situation, but I most assuredly had issues.

"I will pass along anything we find, though," he said quickly, as if sensing my displeasure.

"I understand."

We waited in silence until Xiang interrupted. "Ma'am, they've got something. Video from a drone."

"Get it to me on a tablet."

Having anticipated my request, Xiang entered and handed me a ruggedized device, the video already queued up and waiting. It was a shot from a long way away, and the market was not the focus of the surveillance, but at the twenty-two-second mark a shadow flashed down the left side of the screen. A second later smoke and dust rose from the market and the video shifted, now centered on the explosion. I scanned it back, played it again, paused it during the dark streak just prior to the explosion. I used my fingers to enhance it. "What is that?"

"May I see?" asked Father Romero.

I handed the tablet back to Xiang and motioned for him to show the man. While Romero was watching, Xiang turned back toward me and silently mouthed the word "drone." I considered that, and when Romero had finished watching, I made a decision.

"Go ahead, Xiang. Tell us what you know."

He took a couple steps back so he could face both of us at the same time. "Ma'am, the video analysts believe that it's a small drone. They told me a lot of stuff about trajectory and velocity and things, but I don't remember it all. Zilla has notes on it out in the vehicle if you want me to get her."

"That's okay. You can leave us now." After waiting for him to leave I addressed Father Romero. "I trust my analysis team. They have the right tools for this, and if they say it was a drone, it probably was." There were other questions, the most notable being whose drone, closely followed by was this drone the cause of the explosion? It sure seemed like it. If it was, that made it an illegal drone, though that legality became murky if it wasn't itself carrying a payload and instead slammed into something else explosive at high velocity.

"This cannot stand!" Father Romero slammed his hands against his desk and shot to his feet.

I stared at him but didn't feel the need to intervene, as I marked the outburst as performative. Even if it wasn't, he had people injured and dead in the attack, so if he wanted to rant, I'd let him.

"This is clearly an attack by the Argazzi!"

I widened my eyes at that. Not what I expected at all. "Why do you think that?"

"Those uncultured bastards blame us for the nuclear attack, so now they are trying to get revenge."

"What makes you think they blame you for the attack?" I asked. They did. I knew that because they'd said it themselves, even if they didn't fully believe it. But Romero shouldn't know about that.

"You don't understand the culture here! It's their way. Anything bad that happens, they blame us."

I didn't mention that he was doing the same thing, blaming them. I wanted to deflect this line of thought but didn't want to antagonize him. "I think it's too early to jump to that conclus—"

"They know we didn't do it, but they're exploiting the nuclear event to attack us. They've been looking for an excuse for a long time."

I resisted my immediate urge to dismiss his accusation as baseless and considered it. He was right that I didn't have a total grasp on the culture, but I didn't see the benefit to the Argazzi of attacking like this. I'd talked to them the day prior, and we'd come to a reasonable understanding. At least I thought we had. Still, I couldn't totally rule out Romero's conjecture.

But I was seeing a bigger picture developing. At least the outline of it. The nuke, the drone attack on our convoy, the attacks on the space elevator, and now this attack on a civilian marketplace. Granted, that one didn't fit the pattern exactly, as it didn't seem to have a purpose beyond terror. But the fact that it was a drone made me doubt that it was just a random thing. I didn't think Romero would add much to that picture, but having seen him in action leading his people, I decided to give him a chance.

"Why would they do that? What do they gain by setting off an explosive in the market?"

"I told you! Revenge."

"But is it? Is one dead and ten to twenty injured fit revenge for an attack that killed hundreds?"

He started to reply immediately but stopped. He sat down, appearing to consider it. "Who did it then?"

"I don't know, but I don't want to jump to conclusions. Is it fitting to attack civilians in retaliation for a nuclear attack against mostly military personnel?"

He sighed. "No. That would lack honor. The Argazzi have very little of that, but this would be too far, even for them."

He had calmed down, and that helped, but at the same time, I didn't have an answer to who *had* done it. What would be the purpose? It wasn't the casualties, which, given the circumstances, were light. I needed to get back to base and see if some organization was taking credit for the attack, which might mean it was a terrorist act. I could do it from here with my implant, but that meant taking my focus off of Father Romero, which would be rude. And I didn't think I'd find anything. Terrorist acts weren't common in Zargod, as Romero said; they didn't fit the cultural standards regarding honor. I hadn't heard of any in my time there, and none jumped out from my study before we started the peacekeeping mission, either.

"I can't say who did it or why," I finally admitted. "But I'd like us to try to keep an open mind about it." What I *really* wanted him to do was to keep his people from jumping to conclusions, because the last thing I needed was tension between the two nations. But I didn't feel that I could come right out and ask him for that. It might insult him, and even if it didn't, at a minimum, he'd take it as an opportunity to make another demand of me.

"And I don't want to immediately exonerate the corrupt cowards from Argaz," he replied.

"I assure you, we won't rule them out. I will talk to them myself as soon as I get back to base."

He looked at me, assessing. "What can I do to help?"

I understood that he meant what could he do without being seen doing anything, and what could he do for a price, but that was okay. I had an answer. "Find me a piece of that drone. As much of it as you can. I know it will be hard, but anything we can get might help us figure out who initiated the attack. You can get it to me without anybody knowing what you did with it."

He nodded. "I can do that if we find a piece. I will do what I can."

15

It was nearing dinnertime when we arrived back at base, and I dismissed my team to go find food while I went in to check on everything I'd missed. Murphy broke off from the group to accompany me, and I let him. Zilla promised to bring us each a plate, which wasn't her job but was something I really appreciated because otherwise I probably wouldn't eat. I couldn't leave the headquarters for the better part of a day like I had without expecting work to be piled up waiting on me when I returned. I didn't know what *kind* of work, having not been a commander before, but I knew the command group worked late every night.

My soldiers didn't disappoint me. News of my return had spread, and there were multiple people waiting in the outer office of the command group as I entered. One of the clerks called people to attention, and I put them at ease without slowing my pace. I surveyed the group because it wasn't a first-come-first-serve situation. I knew that much. They'd see me when and if I decided, which, on the one hand is a bit of a power trip, but on the much more realistic hand was just another thing I had to decide. Perston was one of the people waiting, and while I might have enjoyed making him stand there while I dealt with other things, that would only cause trouble. I called Hearns in first, though. Even Perston couldn't complain about that.

THE WEIGHT OF COMMAND

I filled Hearns in about what had happened in the market and how I handled it as I ditched my gear and slumped into my chair.

"Things are under control here," he said. "Tech Sergeant Berghof is waiting outside. She's got the most pressing business."

"Understood. I'll probably still take Perston first."

"Roger." His voice held no judgment. He was a long-serving noncom. He understood.

"I'd like to find someone to manage all that." He gestured toward the closed door that led to the outer office.

"Sounds good. Make it happen."

"I've already selected someone. I'll bring her by for you to interview."

"You picked her, so she's fine. My only requirement is that she's someone who can keep from gossiping about what she hears around here."

"I think she is, ma'am."

"Then put her to work. I trust you. I'll talk to her on the job."

"Yes, ma'am. I'll have her here after dinner."

With that, he departed and directed Perston to come in. Perston wore a clean, pressed uniform, contrasting starkly with mine, which was sweat soaked and rumpled from wear under body armor all day. "Ma'am," he said, with a little too much emphasis. I couldn't tell if it was mocking or if he was just making sure people outside the office heard it. Unlike with Hearns, I kept the door open.

"What's up?"

"I won't take much of your time." He passed three tablets over to me. "I just need your authorization on these three documents. Routine logistics actions."

I wanted to tell him that he should be approving stuff like this himself, but that felt lazy, so instead I took the first one, inserted my chit from around my neck, and pressed my thumbprint into the authorization block. I repeated the step with the next two, and then pushed them all back across the desk. "Anything else?"

"No, ma'am. Thank you." He turned and left having spent less than a minute with me. He had made it really easy, and as I thought about it, I started to get suspicious. Why had he done that? Was it to try to show that he was making an effort, or was there another purpose? I didn't have time to think about it, as there was plenty of other business waiting.

"Tech Sergeant Berghof!" I called.

Zilla appeared at the door with a covered plate in her hand. "Ma'am, if I could bother you before she comes in, I've got dinner."

"Just set it out there on one of the desks. I'll get it when I'm done."

"You sure? I've got tater tots."

That caught my attention. "You got tots? How'd you manage that?" Tater tots were hard to come by because whenever they served them, they ran out early. That was possibly because it was something that even a cook preparing food for four thousand people couldn't screw up. Or maybe I just liked tots and thought too much about that kind of thing.

"I know a guy. You want it?" Zilla gestured with the plate.

"Yeah, bring it in. Thanks." I didn't know who Zilla's magical tot fairy was, and I didn't care. I took the lid off and popped one of them into my mouth. "Mmm. So good." Sometimes the smallest thing can really help your mood. I was usually pretty good about the fuel I put into my body—I didn't eat sweets at all—but greasy carbs? Yes, please.

Berghof entered carrying a plastic tub filled with a conglomeration of tech-looking stuff, including what I assumed was the helmet of the soldier who had shot the child. She hesitated, looking around, and I gestured to my desk, so she could set down her burden. Her hair was disheveled, almost completely out of the regulation bun, and at that moment I appreciated the contrast to Perston, whose hair had, of course, been perfect. Berghof had been working, and it made me feel okay about my own appearance.

"Pardon, but I'm going to eat while you talk. What have you got for me?"

"Ma'am, I've analyzed the helmet from the attack, as you ordered." She glanced behind her. "Can I close the door?"

I nodded and swallowed my next bite. "So you have something. You can sit if you want."

"I'd prefer to stand, ma'am. I get nervous."

"Of course. Just tell me what you know in your own words. Don't worry about how it comes out. If I have questions, I'll ask."

"Yes, ma'am." She swallowed. "I think the helmet was hacked."

I paused with a tot halfway between my plate and my mouth. It seemed impossible. "Who could have done that? I thought that the Zargod didn't have the capability. Do the Argazzi?"

"That's just it, ma'am. I don't think they do. It took me a long time to find it, but there was a backdoor in the coding in the helmet's IFF." She gestured with her hands as she talked, her nerves gone now that she was into her subject.

"A backdoor..." The IFF was the software routine in the helmet that identified friend or foe. The implications of that stunned me.

"Yes, ma'am. It bypassed all the defenses in what is normally a pretty foolproof system and allowed access for someone to change the programming in almost any way they wanted."

"This backdoor...it exists in all of our helmets?"

"I knew you were going to ask that, and I don't know the answer. But I pulled one hundred helmets and tested them."

"One hundred helmets? When was the last time that you slept?"

"Uh" —her mouth hung slightly agape as she thought about it—"what day is it?"

I laughed. "Okay. That's great work, but you make sure that you rest after this. What did you find?"

"Of the hundred helmets, there was one that had a similar code error."

"This is unbelievable. We need to check—"

"Yes, ma'am," she said, cutting me off in her excitement. "I've already started a recall on all the helmets in the brigade. I can check them all within nineteen days."

"That's not fast enough. Can you teach other people to check them?"

She hesitated at that, stumbled over her words, a little flustered. "Yeh...Yes, ma'am. It's just code, and now that I know what to look for, any tech who works on programming at a high level can do the work."

"How many can you handle? How many other techs can you supervise?"

"Uh...I...I don't know? Ten?"

"Okay. Ten it is. They will be in your work area at 0800 tomorrow. Because you are going to sleep tonight." This was a big issue, a problem, but as a commander, it was a simple one, because there was only one answer, and it was very clear. "Tomorrow you'll train up your people. I want you to start with the helmets of soldiers who leave the base most frequently. I'm going to inform Ops that *nobody* leaves the base without your approval on their equipment."

"Yes, ma'am."

"You've done great work, Berghof."

She smiled. "Thank you, ma'am."

"Who had the second helmet? Anything suspicious there?"

"No, ma'am. It was a mechanic who almost never leaves the base."

"Interesting. So it was probably random. Do you have any idea how the backdoor got there?"

"I've been thinking about that. We don't do any of the programming ourselves on this sort of equipment, so the only way it could be an inside job is if someone with the right equipment and skills got physical access to each helmet individually. I checked the logs of all the helmets signed in over the last month, and neither of the two with the coding flaw has been in for service. I specifically asked the soldiers they belonged to."

"What does that leave?"

"Well, unless someone has been running around and sneaking off with helmets to modify them, it means that it happened before we got them. Either at the manufacturer, or at some point in the distribution process."

I considered it. Soldiers were issued their helmets at initial training and kept them throughout their time in the service, so if it happened before they got to our unit, that would mean that it wasn't just us, but every unit in the military. That seemed like a bit of a stretch, but it sure did make me wish that I had a way to contact someone off-planet to find out. Or to warn them. Maybe after Berghof checked every helmet I'd have enough information on my own to make a better assessment. Then I had a hunch. "Are all the helmets made by the same company?"

"Yes, ma'am. Falon Systems."

Huh. So much for that idea. I'd thought maybe if there were multiple manufacturers, we could trace the flaws to a single source. "Okay. What does the backdoor allow?"

"I'm still working on that. But at a minimum, it makes them much, much more susceptible to hacking from the outside. And I think that's what happened with our shooter. I think someone local to the scene hacked his helmet and screwed with the IFF."

"How close would they have to be?"

"That depends on the power of the rig they were using. Inside the building? I could create something to do the job from parts you could buy at a local tech store. From kilometers away? That would take some serious hardware."

"I don't suppose there's a way to trace where the hack came from?"

"No, ma'am. Unfortunately not."

I sighed and nodded. "Okay. That's not on you. You've done great work here."

"Thank you, ma'am."

"Consider yourself promoted to Sergeant First Class."

"Ma'am?"

I smiled. "You've earned it. You're working above your pay grade, and you deserve to be recognized."

Her pale face reddened. "Yes, ma'am. Thank you, ma'am."

I really didn't know if a commander could just promote someone. Hearns would know. But I wanted to do it, regardless. She really had earned it. "I need to be up front about this—I don't know if I actually have the authority to make that stick once" —I gestured around—"all this is over. But you have my word that I'll do everything in my power to make sure that it does."

"Yes, ma'am. I understand."

"And in the meantime, it will help you with your authority as you work with your new team tomorrow."

"Yes, ma'am."

"Okay. Now. Tell me one more thing. What are you going to do as soon as you leave here?"

"I'm going to go get something to eat, I'm going to get a shower, and I'm going to go to bed."

"Good. Make it happen."

I took another meeting where I got an update on the space elevator, where they were still working on clean-up after the explosion, and an update on the nuke, where I learned that the onsite team still hadn't found anything useful beyond a bunch of readings that gave us a better estimation of the physics of the device itself. After that, I closed my door, taking exactly ten minutes to finish my tots as well as some sort of vat-produced protein. As I ate, I reviewed the reports I requested from Intel yesterday.

The two officers the Argazzi sent us appeared to be exactly that: Army officers. There was nothing in their careers or lives prior to being assigned to us that suggested they were anything else. They surely still reported to someone back home, but the fact that they weren't professional spies was nice. The information on Trieste and Yakina wasn't quite so benign. Trieste had been a mid-level bureaucrat in the Ministry of Foreign Affairs a week ago. The department had undergone a huge shakeup after the nuclear attack, a lot of which was by necessity. There were forty-seven Argazzi casualties that day, and forty-one of them had been from that ministry.

But Trieste's promotion was still somewhat of an anomaly. She'd been promoted at least two levels above her previous station, and there were several people who had been senior to her that were still alive and *hadn't* been promoted. The intel report didn't speculate as to why that happened, but the facts were the facts, and I had my own ideas about the reasoning. But I didn't know what to do with the information, so I filed it. Yakina was a quicker report. Despite their best efforts, Intel didn't find anything on him. He barely existed. That alone confirmed my suspicions about his position in the Argazzi government.

When I opened my door again, the outer office was empty except for one staff sergeant, who was busy organizing things on top of a desk, and Murphy, who was emptying all of the recycling bins into a larger one.

"Where did everybody go?" I asked.

The woman looked up from her task and snapped to attention. "Ma'am. I'm Staff Sergeant Chao. Master Sergeant Hearns assigned me."

I nodded. The help he had promised. "At ease, Chao." I gestured around. "Where is everybody?"

"I screened your appointments, ma'am. They either didn't have anything important to present, or they were underprepared, so I sent them away." I hesitated, not knowing how to respond to that. I didn't doubt her, but I did need to let people meet with me if they had business. Perhaps sensing my confusion, Chao continued, "Don't worry, ma'am. There was nothing that won't wait until morning, and they'll be better prepared when they arrive. If it's okay with you, I scheduled your first meeting for zero-eight-hundred. If possible, I'd like to meet with you half an hour before that so I can brief you on your schedule for the day."

"Sure. That sounds good." Chao seemed so sure of herself that I'd probably have said yes even if I didn't agree. "Murphy, what are you doing?" I asked.

"Murphy was under-utilized, ma'am, so I put him to work. I hope that's okay."

"Uh…sure. I guess I'll just be in my office if you need anything."

"That won't be necessary, ma'am. You can go get cleaned up and take the rest of the night off while I organize things here. I'll have a soldier joining me presently, and one of us will remain here until twenty-two-hundred hours. We'll buzz you via your implant if anything requires your attention."

THE WEIGHT OF COMMAND

I didn't know what to do with that, so I stood there for a few seconds before speaking. "Uh…great. Is it okay if I take Murphy to escort me back to my quarters?"

"Of course, ma'am. He's yours whenever you need him. I just didn't want him sitting around doing nothing while he waited."

I nodded. "Okay then. I will see you at zero-seven-thirty."

"Good evening, ma'am."

I showed up the next morning ten minutes before I was scheduled to meet with Chao because, if I'm being honest, she intimidated me a little bit. She was already there, and another soldier sat at a desk that hadn't been there the night before. They both stood when I entered.

"Ma'am, this is Private Jacobsen. He will be here to cover things when I have to be out of the office. Like me, he is now part of your personal staff, and while I would appreciate you giving him tasks through me, if I'm not available, he answers directly to you and nobody else."

I had a feeling that a lot of people were going to answer directly to Chao. "Good to meet you, Jacobsen."

"You as well, ma'am." He was my height, which meant he was a hand taller than Chao, but she still seemed to take up more space.

"Coffee is ready, ma'am," said Chao. "We can go over your schedule whenever you're ready."

With all the problems facing our unit outside, having things organized on the inside took more weight off than I could have imagined. "Great. I'll get a cup and we can get started. Is it okay if we do it in my office?" I don't know when I started thinking about it as my office, but at some point, I had. That seemed significant.

"As you wish." Chao waited for me to get coffee and then followed me into the office.

I took a seat and then gestured for her to close the door behind her. "You can sit if you want."

Chao approached my desk and slid a tablet across it and then retreated to a chair, accessing a tablet of her own. "Ma'am, this is your—"

"Before we start, Chao—" I cut her off before she got going because if I didn't establish some rules with her, she was going to run right over me in the name of efficiency.

She immediately quit talking and prepared to take notes. "Yes, ma'am."

"I want to make sure we're both clear on our relationship."

A hint of a frown flitted across her face and disappeared, snapping back into professionalism. "Yes, ma'am. I've been told in the past that I'm too aggressive."

I started to launch into the speech I'd prepared in my head lying in bed the night before, but then stopped. "What? No, that's not it. You do things your way and I'll tell you if there's a problem. But what I wanted to talk to you about is loyalty."

"Yes, ma'am." She seemed relieved. "I was worried that you were mad about me throwing everyone out last night."

"I was a little surprised, but I'm willing to give it a shot to see what happens. But what I have to have—one hundred percent—is your discretion. Jacobsen's too. If you're going to be here all day, every day, you're going to see me at my best and at my worst. I can't have it getting out to the unit that I lost my shit if I have a bad moment. Because if I've learned anything in the past couple days it's that I'm going to have some bad moments."

"Ma'am." Chao hesitated. "I speak for Jacobsen in this, as well as myself, because I picked him personally. We are your personal staff. We are on your team, and nobody else's. I don't care if you're right, wrong, or somewhere in between." She paused again to think. "I should say that I do hope that you're mostly right, and if I think you're not right, I'm going to privately tell you that."

I agreed with that and nodded for her to continue.

"But if I tell you privately that you're wrong and you make a decision? I don't care if you say the sun is green. If that's your final decision, then as far as Jacobsen and I are concerned, the sun is fucking green. And I'm going to destroy anybody who walks in here and tells me that it isn't."

I laughed. "Hopefully I won't be that bad." At the same time, it surprised me how vehement she was. After all, Hearns had assigned her. I figured she would owe him some loyalty. But that was a testament to him as well as her. He hadn't picked who *he* needed. He'd chosen who *I* did.

"Ma'am, I'm not naïve. I now have positional power, and other people are going to know that and try to use it to their advantage. That's not going to happen. They'll figure it out soon enough, I promise you that."

I nodded because I didn't trust myself to speak. With everything that was working against me, having someone unequivocally *for* me had me ready to cry. To cover that, I picked up my tablet and looked at my schedule. It seemed pretty standard, with updates from Intel, Ops, and Engineering in the morning, but one thing jumped out at me. "You scheduled me time to go to the gym?"

"Yes, ma'am. Fourteen hundred to fifteen hundred. That still gives you time to come back and get any follow-ups required from earlier meetings before dinner."

"Thanks. This looks great." And it did. All of it. And for a short time, I thought maybe we'd make it through the next few weeks unscathed until we got relieved.

That feeling continued for two days as I took my briefings, gave guidance, made all my meetings and meals, and marched along precisely according to the schedule of Staff Sergeant Chao. If anyone else in the command had a problem with how she managed my time, it never got to me. The only issue was the continuing low quality of meals. I had put off talking to Perston about it because I didn't want the confrontation, but he saved me the trouble when he brought the issue to me himself, though that probably wasn't his intention. I left my office when I heard him yelling at Chao.

"What's going on?" I asked, keeping my voice calm despite the obvious tension between the two. They were standing up, facing each other across Chao's desk. Thankfully the room was empty besides the three of us and Xiang, who was my protection detail for the afternoon.

"I just need your signatures on these documents," said Perston. Belatedly he added, "Ma'am."

"And I told the Captain that you weren't signing anything until I looked at it first, ma'am," said Chao. "To ensure that it is accurate and complete."

"I'm not funneling my work through your power-hungry functionary," said Perston.

I wish he hadn't done that. If he had come to me privately about it, I could have worked it out with him, but by challenging me in front of the others, even if they were sworn to keep secrets, he forced me into a confrontation. Because he was telling me what to do, and if I allowed that, I was setting precedent. He'd know that, too, if he wasn't such a hothead and had just thought about it. But he didn't, so I didn't have a choice. "Yes, you will," I said. "We're establishing staff processes for efficiency, and this is how we're doing business from here on out."

Perston turned and glared at me, and I thought he was going to say something. He stared me down for several seconds, and then he snatched his tablets off of Chao's desk and stormed out.

Chao looked at me to see if I was going to do anything, but I didn't know what to do. I hadn't been prepared for it, and I couldn't come up with anything in the moment that would make it better. Apparently, Chao couldn't abide that, so she popped off with a command voice that would have stopped a bot-tank in its tracks. "Captain Perston!" How so much sound came out of one average-sized person, I don't know, but it had no effect on Perston, who kept walking without even as much as a glance back.

"Let him go," I said to her. "He and I still have some things to work out, and you don't need to be in the middle of it."

"Yes, ma'am," said Chao, without even a hint of attitude. At that moment, I appreciated her even more.

"So? What's next?"

16

The answer to *what's next?* came to me while I was on the treadmill of all places. My mind drifts when I run, but with things coming at me from every direction, I'd been tied up in short-term problems and unable to relax. With Chao taking over my schedule and getting me into a routine, I was free to think again. And when it finally hit me, it hit me so hard that I stopped my machine.

"Holy shit."

Dutifully, Gonzalez turned his treadmill off too, so he'd be ready to move if I was. "What is it, ma'am?"

"I've been thinking about this all wrong."

"About what?"

"Workout is over. We've got to go." I didn't bother changing, instead running from the gym to headquarters.

Chao shot to her feet when I entered the office. "Ma'am, what's going on?"

"Call a meeting of all the intel branch heads, Ops, and Sergeant First Class Berghof. I don't care which conference room. I just need to talk to them ASAP."

"Roger, ma'am."

It took about ten minutes before they were assembled. I was being a bit melodramatic, rushing over without showering or changing. It had taken me forever to see the thing, and it wasn't like another fifteen minutes would alter the situation, but I felt like it imparted a sense of urgency in what I was about to tell them. That I would meet them in the middle of a workout meant that it was important.

"I've been thinking about this all the wrong way," I began. "I've been looking for a traditional enemy—one of the nations involved, or perhaps a radical fringe within one of those countries that wants to sow conflict. And it could still be one of those—we can't rule it out. But who gains the most from a conflict between the Zargod and the Argazzi?"

The dozen staff members in the room looked at each other, looked at their hands—they looked anywhere except at me, like if they didn't look at me, I wouldn't call on them and expose the fact that they didn't know. But it was fine. They weren't supposed to know. They were experts in their fields but hadn't been trained to think bigger than that. So I decided to give them a hint. "Follow the money. Who benefits financially?"

More thought, and more awkward silence, until Tech Sergeant Kennedy spoke up softly. "Anyone who was invested in high-tech metals? Because the price will go up as Tanara fails to deliver."

"Good!" I said.

"Also other planets that mine the same things," said McNamara.

"Planets, sure, and what else?" I prompted.

"Mining companies," said Kennedy.

"Exactly," I said. "What if it's not anyone here on Tanara? After all, destroying the spaceport works against everybody here. Both Zarga and Argaz are losing money, and both have nationalized mining assets. But their competitors aren't."

"Ma'am, are you suggesting that a corporation is making war on the planet?" asked McNamara.

"Not exactly making war. Maybe encouraging it, though?" Some disbelieving faces stared back at me as I looked around the table. "I started thinking about what all the setbacks we've faced have in common. Our convoy was attacked by an illegal drone that should only be used on uninhabited planets. When we analyzed the wreckage, did we log who made the drones?"

McNamara scanned her pad and found the answer. "Falon Military Systems."

I glanced at Berghof, whose eyes had gone wide. "Sergeant First Class Berghof, can you tell the group who makes the helmets that you discovered were left vulnerable to hacking?"

THE WEIGHT OF COMMAND

"Falon Military Systems."

The room went silent until Hearns spoke. "Well, fuck."

The lead imagery analyst put up her hand.

"Yes, Bonner? Go ahead," I said.

"But ma'am, correct me if I'm wrong...Falon isn't a mining company."

"Good point. They aren't." I knew they weren't, because I'd checked the links via my implant while I was running. "And they're a subsidiary of Tangent Holding Company, which is also not a mining company. But they do have another subsidiary that is. Lapthal Mining. They specialize in robotic mining of asteroids and inhospitable planets. We don't have access to outside information right now, but I'd bet if we could see it, we'd find that their stock price was increasing significantly, assuming people have made the discovery about the problems here. At some point, shipments aren't going to show up and people are going to know that there are big issues. But that shouldn't stop a rival from stepping in in the meantime and snatching up some valuable contracts."

"Playing devil's advocate, ma'am..." said McNamara.

"Do it. That's why we're here. Shoot holes in the theory."

"This is a pretty complicated scenario. Simple terror attacks seem more likely."

"But nobody has taken credit for the attacks," said Corporal Collins. "They would have if it was terrorists."

"Do we have analysis from the market bombing yet?" I asked.

"Not yet, ma'am. We just got the fragments this morning," said Sergeant First Class Quinn, the lead for Explosives Analysis.

"Get that done," I said. "That will be another data point."

"Yes, ma'am," said Quinn.

"While he works that, I need some courses of action. If I *am* right, what can we do about it? Stuck here on a remote planet, with all our communications out, what can we do to stop a corporation that spans the galaxy?"

I wanted to talk to the Argazzi to see if I could learn anything from them that might corroborate my new theory, so I headed to find Captain Ana Song to get her opinion on the best method. If it truly was Tangent Holding Company that was our enemy, it made the Argazzi our allies. In theory. I almost ran into her as I opened the door just as she was coming out.

"Oh! Ma'am. How did you know I needed to see you?"

"What?"

"We just found something that I think you need to see. I was coming to find you."

"Can it wait? I need to contact your country's leadership, and I'm looking for the best option to get what I want."

"Ma'am...I don't think this can wait."

A chill came over me at her tone, and I nodded. "Okay. Show me what you've got."

She cast from her device to a wall screen that someone had installed for her. "As part of trying to re-establish communications off-planet, I had my team do a search of any planetside facility that could broadcast or a system that could launch a quantum communication platform into space for us. We didn't find any lift assets—rockets, which makes sense, since there was a working space elevator, making them unnecessary. And we didn't find anything that could broadcast. But we did find a facility that has the ability to receive data from QC satellites."

"We have receivers of our own. We tried them and weren't getting anything."

"Yes, ma'am. And we hadn't tried them again because how would there be satellites up there now that weren't there before?" She paused, letting it sink in. "But in our search, we stumbled over something. How do I put this? I'm just going to say it. I had our team hack into a civilian facility to see if they had had any luck broadcasting off-planet—"

"You did what?" I asked, cutting her off. "Whose facility?"

"It was ours, ma'am. Argaz. I'll take full responsibility."

I wasn't sure that would matter, but the damage was done, and I was too interested in what she'd found to dwell on it right then. "What did you find? Have they been sending messages?"

"They haven't. But what we *did* find is that they were *receiving* messages."

I thought about it, confused. "Receiving directly from distant stations?" It wasn't impossible, but it wasn't something normal.

"No, ma'am. Receiving from QC satellites in orbit. Or, rather, receiving from one."

"Holy shit."

"Exactly. Someone has a quantum communication satellite up there, and we missed it."

"And we can receive from this satellite as well?"

"I've got people working on it right now. But that's not the part that is going to blow your mind."

"There's more?"

"Yes, ma'am. It's what the satellite is broadcasting." She paused for effect. "They're spoofing normal messages from the planet, including messages from this headquarters."

"They're—"

"—making it seem like everything is normal here except for a critical issue with the space elevator, which they're using as an excuse to divert all space traffic."

I paused, speechless for a few seconds. "A problem with the space elevator should draw immediate assistance."

"It would if this headquarters wasn't reporting that it is under control."

Well, fuck.

"Can we tap into that satellite and change the messages? Use it to get our stuff out?" I asked.

"We're going to try. It's our first best option right now. If we can do that, then we don't have to try more drastic measures."

"Okay, stay on it."

Well that settled it. If I had doubts about my theory that an outside entity was engineering this entire crisis, this news erased them. On the other hand, it wasn't all bad news. It was *mostly* bad news, but at least now we knew more about where we stood. And if there was a functional QC satellite in orbit, there was at least a chance that we could hack into it and turn it to our own purpose. How someone had spoofed a quantum communicator that required matched particles on both ends to function, I had no idea. But given everything else I'd seen from the enemy, I had to believe that if they were broadcasting, they'd worked out how to have a hub receive and propagate it. They had it, and I wanted it. If we couldn't turn it to our purposes, maybe we could at least use it to lead us to our true enemy.

"And do me a favor," I added. "Look into the civilian company that was receiving information. I want to know who they're attached to."

"Roger. You mentioned help contacting someone, ma'am?"

"I do. I want to talk to someone regarding a theory I have about our true enemy. I think there may be a corporation that is sabotaging things here to increase its share of the lithium market."

"If that's true, that's pretty messed up."

"I agree," I said. "And if it's true, I'd like to share intelligence with your country so we can head it off together."

"I'll make some calls, ma'am. I think you'll have better luck with the military than civilians."

"That does seem likely, given what I know about the bureaucracy."

"Speaking of sharing intelligence…" She paused as if trying to come up with the best way to say something. "Am I free to share the information about the satellites?"

"Let's hold that tight for now until we know more. Once we figure it out, I might let you pass it on. But I don't want to do that until we've got a better idea of what we're dealing with." The last thing I needed was for the Argazzi to interpret us hacking into one of their civilian companies the wrong way and make the situation more volatile. "There's a chance that your leadership already figured it out, though. If there's a civilian company that knows about it, there's a chance that they've reported it."

"Yes, ma'am." If my answer disappointed her, she didn't let it show. As I turned to go I got a buzz in my implant from Watch, and I triggered a response to have them send their message.

It was McNamara herself. "Ma'am, you need to get up here to the floor. Something's happening."

"Roger. Give me the basics."

"The Argazzi are leaving their garrison locations, and it looks like they've got a significant force heading to forward deployed positions."

Shit shit shit. Not now.

"Okay. I'll be right there."

"Everything okay, ma'am?" Song asked.

"I don't know. But belay that call about the corporation interfering."

"Ma'am?"

"Instead, see if you can find out why your country seems to be back to deploying forces into the field."

"They're doing *what?*"

I read her reaction as genuine, which wasn't surprising. It would have been stupid for them to let her know ahead of time, what with her being here with us. "That's all I know, Captain. I'll take any information you can get, if anyone will talk to you."

With that, I headed for the pit to try to figure out what had changed to make the Argazzi go against what we'd agreed to regarding military deployments. I had a feeling that I'd find Tangent Holding Company somehow involved, and a stronger feeling that my earlier thought about the Argazzi being my allies had been wishful thinking.

17

There was more activity in the pit than usual, the calm professionalism replaced with people scurrying between terminals, hunching together in conversation.

"Battle stations!" called McNamara over the speaker as soon as she saw me. I settled into the command seat and put on my headphones, and a second later she addressed me. "Ma'am, whenever you're ready."

"Go."

"Current Ops," she said.

"Ma'am, Corporal Tanner speaking. At twelve-zero-seven today, a routine drone flight spotted unusual activity around the Argazzi base located here." A red dot appeared on my map. "Following up on that, we tasked collections to monitor and to dispatch assets to check on other bases. We found increased activity consistent with forward deployment at six major Argazzi bases. Tracking of elements leaving the initial base showed them heading south, toward the border with Zarga, though lead elements have currently stopped here." Ops highlighted a few square kilometers of sparse forest about fifty kilometers from the border.

"Roger," I said. "And the other bases?"

"It's still not completely clear, but we have enough evidence to suggest that all of the forces are coming toward the same general location. They're all coming south."

"But they've stopped?"

THE WEIGHT OF COMMAND

"The initial unit has stopped, ma'am, but we aren't sure if that's a permanent halt and this is their final location or if they are waiting for the rest of their forces."

For fuck's sake, it hadn't even been a week since the Argazzi told me they wouldn't do this. I wanted to get along with them. I really did. But they were making it hard. "Have they tried to interfere with our drones in any way?"

"They have taken no active measures, ma'am. They are using some passive measures, but those may be standard operating procedure."

That made sense. Many vehicles had passive measures built into them, but the Argazzi hadn't taken any offensive action against our surveillance —they hadn't tried to shoot anything down. That meant one of a few things. It could be they didn't know we were watching. Much more likely, they might not have wanted to take something that would be considered the first shot—an act of war. This could apply whether they were actually intending military action or not. Last, and most likely in my mind, was that they *wanted* me to see what they were doing. They had planned an exercise right after the nuclear attack, but I'd thought I'd talked them out of that during my visit. Perhaps something had caused them to change their mind. But I could worry about their motives later. Right now, I had to deal with their action.

"How much of their combat power are they deploying?" I asked.

"Intel," said McNamara.

"Ma'am, Sergeant First Class Delany. It is our assessment that they're moving everything. Two divisions."

Shit. Two divisions meant six combat brigades, based on how they organized. That was five more brigades than I had at my disposal. Granted, we had a significant technological advantage due to the military embargo on non-Federation worlds. But on the other hand, they had a full complement of leadership. "What do we think it means?"

Intel went through the options, laying out what I already knew. It was either an exercise or preparation for an attack, and we wouldn't know which until they did or didn't attack. And of course, we couldn't wait, because that would be too late.

"Defense, can we protect the entire city from a missile attack with our counter-indirect-fire systems?" I wasn't as worried about military assets. We had hardened vehicles, shelters, and countermeasures. Zarga's civilian population didn't.

"Not without space-based assets, ma'am," responded a man from

Defense without identifying himself. "We can protect our own base and perhaps twenty to thirty percent of the city."

"Start working a plan for what city assets we're going to prioritize in our protection plan. I need to see it ASAP."

"Yes, ma'am. We've already got options worked up and can show them to you at your convenience."

Good. I hadn't directed them to do that, but when they lost the space-based assets they'd taken it upon themselves. That still didn't help the fact that the Argazzi could rain rockets and artillery shells down on the city, killing thousands, and we couldn't do anything about it defensively. I didn't *think* they would do that, but I'd have felt a lot better if I could have ruled it out. If they wanted to start an all-out war, they'd never have a better chance. They outgunned the Zargod and would defeat them easily without the peacekeeping force now under my command. That's why the Zargod had allowed us on their land for so many years.

I realized I had been silent for at least thirty seconds when McNamara prompted me. "Ma'am…your guidance?"

"Yes. Give me a bit longer."

There were three possibilities: Attack, exercise, or assess, which fell somewhere between the first two. Maybe they just wanted to see how I'd react and they'd decide which way to proceed based on that. That meant I needed to look strong. If you walk into a bar looking like somebody that people don't want to fuck with, nobody fucks with you. I ran a couple simple simulations through my implant to give me a first draft of our needs so that I could set priorities. The staff could confirm my initial data later.

"Spin all the printers to a wartime footing. I want them printing ammunition and replacement drones and everything else we need for a high-intensity fight. Fifty percent priority is to defensive missile and gun batteries, thirty-five percent to indirect attack munitions, fifteen percent to direct fire and sundries." I paused to let people take notes and to process my next thought. "Defense, put all batteries on alert. I'll take a brief from you soon, and I want systems that need to move into the city ready to go immediately following that briefing. Watch, have the staff run simulations, and get back to me if there are any recommended changes to my priorities."

"Roger."

I took a breath and considered the implication of my next order. There was one last possibility that I had kept buried at the back of my

THE WEIGHT OF COMMAND

mind until that moment. The Argazzi could be planning a true exercise, and I could end up provoking them.

"I want the rest of the brigade on standby, prepared to move to forward locations in the grasslands north of the city."

"Timeline on that, ma'am?" asked McNamara.

"No combat force deploys without my say-so, but I want Second Battalion ready to move within thirty minutes of my order. First and Third Battalions I want ready to move within four hours."

"Roger."

As I left the pit, I debated which side I wanted to call first. I was torn because I felt like any action they took in response to the Argazzi might inflame matters, or maybe the Argazzi would use it as an excuse to attack. Ultimately, I decided that I'd have a better chance of controlling the result if I reported the information to the Zargod first, and do it myself. But before I called the senior father, I wanted Mrs. Zukov's opinion. Romero and I had built a bit of a relationship, but I figured it couldn't hurt to have an expert on the culture weigh in, just in case there was some subtlety that I didn't understand. The last thing I wanted was a misunderstanding to cause things to spin out of control.

I sent a messenger to get her and then met her outside the door of the headquarters. I walked with her, off of the path, so we wouldn't be disturbed by random soldiers rushing by responding to the alert. After walking thirty meters down the side of the building, we were effectively in public and completely in private at the same time. No soldier would approach unless they had a specific order to that effect.

"Something big is happening," said Mrs. Zukov.

"It's that noticeable, huh?"

She shrugged. "I notice."

"The Argazzi are moving troops toward the border. I've put the base on alert as a precautionary measure." Telling her that likely ensured that it would get to the Zargod leadership. I had no illusions about that. But if I told them first, it wouldn't matter.

She assessed me, but no fear crossed her face. It seemed that the possibility of an attack didn't faze her. "You don't want my opinion on that."

"I don't. That's purely a military action. What I need your advice on is that I need to notify the Zargod authorities. How should I broach it with the senior father?"

She waved her hand, dismissing him. "He will be no help in this."

"Why not?"

"He will be worse than no help. He will make it about himself, but he doesn't have any soldiers. Only the army commander will help." It was interesting that she said army commander and not prime minister, or even king. But then power in Zarga rarely followed straight lines.

"How do I approach the army commander?"

She considered it. "You probably don't. You offended him by using your own soldiers to guard the space elevator. You made him look weak."

I made him look weak? "He didn't offer to help."

"You didn't ask."

I started to snap back out of frustration but caught myself. It was my own fault, not hers. I hadn't even thought about how securing the space elevator would appear to the Zargod. "I screwed that up. I didn't know I needed to ask."

She nodded. "With the men here, you always need to ask, even when you have your own solution. When you ask, it shows respect, even if it's just pretend."

"Okay. So how do I fix it now?"

"You have to do it the hard way. Ask senior father for help, but not help with problem. If you ask his help with problem, he will tell you that he will help, but he won't do anything."

"But he'd still offer, in order to save face."

"Yes. This. But instead ask him to help set up a meeting with army commander. That he can do for you." She left unsaid that there would be a price for that help.

"Thank you, Mrs. Zukov."

She shrugged. "No problem."

She wasn't wrong. I contacted Father Romero from my office, so I'd have some privacy and he made it clear that he was very glad to hear from me, and did I get the fragments of the suicide drone that he sent, and had I given more thought to widening the road outside the base? When I finally was able to get a word in and mentioned that I had a military situation and needed to speak to the army commander, he was all for that as well, and offered to invite him to his house for a big dinner next week, and that he would be honored to have such a great man as his guest.

It took me fifteen minutes and two reiterated promises to study the road widening project to get him to understand that this was an emergency and I needed to talk to General Laughlin, and get him to agree to set up a video call as soon as possible. Romero wasn't sure when that would be, but he would try his best to make it soon, and he would use all his influence to make it happen. When we finally hung up, I wasn't sure if I had made things better or worse, and I had absolutely no idea if I'd get to talk to the general or not.

In the meantime, I went to see Captain Song, to find out if she had learned about the Argazzi troop deployment. On my way, I considered how much to share with her. There was a good chance that she and I were now at cross purposes, because while I didn't know the Argazzi's true intent, it was clear they were up to *something*.

Song stood when I entered and didn't wait for me to ask a question. "Ma'am, there is definitely a major action."

"That much we can see."

She hesitated, as if unsure how to say the next part. "They told me—and this is a quote—'tell her that it's a routine exercise and nothing to worry about.'"

"Just like that? They didn't tell you that it *was* an exercise. They told you to *tell me* it was."

"Yes, ma'am."

"Forgive me if I sound suspicious, but why are you telling me this?"

She paused for several seconds before responding, perhaps unsure of what to say, perhaps just trying to appear unsure. "Gut feeling. I'm quite sure I wasn't supposed to elaborate."

"Yet you did. And I appreciate it. But you have to understand why I'm suspicious."

"I absolutely do. And that's why I told you. Forgive me for putting it so bluntly, but what I see when I look at you is someone in a very tough spot. And it seems wrong for us to be putting added pressure on you. We should all be coming together, not pushing further division for some sort of political gain."

I studied her closely, and even with the aid of my implant, I couldn't detect any deceit. For whatever reason, it seemed as if she was actually on my side in this. I wanted to hug her. "Of course. Thank you for telling me. You can count on my discretion—I'm not going to tell anyone what you've told me. As far as the troop deployment goes, I'm going to tell you, it doesn't *look* like an exercise."

"How so, ma'am?"

"Who commits their entire army to an exercise? One division? I can see that. But when you have two divisions in your entire arsenal and you put both in the field at once?"

"Yes, ma'am. I can see how that looks suspicious. Do you think they're really planning to attack?"

"I don't know. Do you?"

"I'd like to say no. But in Argaz, the military leaders are as involved in politics as they are in warfare. More, even. And I can't begin to tell you what they might be doing, or what they're seeking. There's as much chance that they're seeking power internally rather than to gain anything over the Zargod."

"So they'd go to war to improve their own standing?"

She hesitated, as if not wanting to admit it, but said, "I'm afraid it's not out of the question."

I sighed. It was good information, but unfortunately, it didn't change the situation for me. "I think the one thing I'm pretty sure about is that it's not about training. Perhaps it *is* an exercise—an exercise in trying to gain some sort of leverage. Or an exercise to see how I'll react. Perhaps they don't intend to take any offensive action. There are a lot of possibilities."

"Is there anything I can do?"

She was there and not openly working against me. I wanted to tell her that was enough, but although it sounds cold, she was an asset, and I didn't have the luxury of wasting assets. "If you can think of someone who I can call, that would help. If not, I think I'll call Deputy Minister Trieste. She was the one who brokered the agreement to call off the last exercise, so at a minimum, she has some explaining to do." I didn't mention that she wasn't the actual decision-maker. Song didn't need my thoughts on that.

"I don't have anyone for you to call, ma'am, but I'll make some calls myself as well and see what I can learn from lower-level officers." She meant what she could learn from her *friends,* and that was good. They would at least tell her the truth as they knew it. That was more than I expected from Trieste, but I had to at least try, so I headed to my office to make the call.

They put me through to her immediately, which made me think that she'd been waiting for my call. That alone said something. I hadn't prepared myself for her perfect cheekbones, piercing blue eyes, and flawless, if cold, makeup in larger-than-life size on the wall of my office, but there she was. "Major Markov. To what do I owe the pleasure?"

I fake-smiled back at her. She knew damned well what my call was

THE WEIGHT OF COMMAND

about, and as much as I'd liked her when this whole thing started, her disingenuousness now was a pretty serious turnoff. "When we met in person, you made a commitment to me."

She paused, as if thinking about it...*commitment? Me? Did I?* It was so fake that I almost got the impression that she wanted me to see it. Or—and maybe this was wishful thinking—she wanted someone else to see it. Surely she was being monitored by people on her own side. Whether she wanted to tell me the truth or not, she was stuck in Argaz, and she didn't have her own authority. Argaz was not kind to those who didn't fall in line with the party's wishes. I had to try to keep that in mind, but it was hard. Hers was the face on the screen, and as lovely as it was, she was the one telling the lies. "Oh. Right. You mean the training exercise."

"Right. The...*exercise*."

"I'm sorry about that. I didn't think to notify you. The military leaders tell me that the situation has changed, and the exercise is now important to our security. Please accept my apologies."

"What has changed in the situation that necessitates the aggressive mobilization of all your forces?" I chose my words deliberately to force her to respond not to the question, but rather the implication. Or, possibly, to force those pulling her strings. I didn't *want* to openly antagonize Trieste, but just like she had a job to do, so did I. Mine was to stop the Argazzi troop movement.

"I beg your pardon?"

"What?" I fake-smiled again, deliberately missing her point. I was beginning to understand how to deal with her in this moment. She was playing dumb, so I would too. "It's a reasonable question."

"It's how you asked it."

"What about how I asked it? You said that the situation has changed, I asked how."

She hesitated, and I took that to mean she was receiving new instructions, perhaps through an invisible earpiece. "I assure you, this isn't an aggressive action."

"Would you know if it was, or should I be talking to a military leader?" Okay, that one was petty. But if I sowed doubt in her with whoever was really in charge, maybe I could move past the fake stuff and get to what was really happening.

Her face hardened as she realized what I was doing. "Major Markov, you called me. What do you want?"

It hurt, seeing her angry at me. It shouldn't have, but it did, and I softened a bit, and for just a second, I thought that if she and I could talk without a dozen other officials listening in, maybe we could solve this. "I just want answers."

"To what question? I've answered you."

"What has changed in the situation?"

She hesitated. "I do not know the details."

I nodded. I believed her, for whatever reason. Which meant that nobody *gave* her the details. They were using her just like they were using me. That pissed me off, not at her, but at some nameless, faceless official. Whoever that was, they weren't on the screen. But they were listening. I decided right then that I wasn't talking to Trieste. I was talking to the invisible puppeteer behind her. That made it easier to be the asshole I needed to be. "When you told me the last time that you were calling off the exercise, did you believe that to be the truth, or were you simply telling me what I wanted to hear at that moment?"

"I assure you, at the time I said it, I believed it to be the truth."

At the time she said it. "Meaning that sometime between then and now, you found out that it was *not* true."

She drew her lips into a flat line as if the conversation was making her uncomfortable. "That is correct."

"You understand that any act of aggression toward my forces or toward Zarga gives me a wide range of response options according to the treaty, right?"

"We have taken no act of aggression!"

"There's a lot of leeway for me as the commander in terms of determining where that line is. Which you know, since you've read the accords."

"It is very clear that what we're doing is not—"

I cut her off. "And me, being the inexperienced commander that I am…" I let that hang for a moment, before continuing, "I could easily make a mistake as I try to get through all that complicated language. After all, I don't have an attorney at my disposal, since both the attorney and his deputy died in the nuclear attack."

She started to speak again, but I cut the connection before she could get anything out. I let out a deep breath. Hopefully, on the personal side of things, Trieste would see through my act the same way I saw through hers. And hopefully, whoever was in charge for real would hear what I said and wonder. Worry, even. That was a lot more hoping than I'd have preferred. But I had to have hope. It beat the alternative.

Staff Sergeant Chao knocked at my door just a few seconds after I closed the call. "Ma'am, I have the Zargod general, General Laughlin's people on the line. He would like to talk to you."

I took a deep, cleansing breath. "Okay. Give me thirty seconds and then put it through." I needed the time to reset my thinking. I had to take a totally different approach with Laughlin than I did with the Argazzi. I'd tried to make them believe I might be a little unhinged. I needed to make him believe that he wanted to listen to me, a woman probably less than half his age.

An officer in the uniform of the Zargod army was on the screen when it came up, but he quickly shuffled away, and after about twenty seconds of empty screen, the general came on in full dress uniform, including his round hat with a short bill and what looked like about a hundred medals. He had a weathered face and silver sideburns, and I estimated his age at somewhere near seventy. Okay. A third his age.

"Good afternoon, General," I said.

He grunted. That wasn't a great start. "You're the new commander." Why did all Zargod do that thing where they made something halfway between a question and a statement?

"Yes, sir. Major Markov."

"We haven't met."

I wanted to get right to the point, but by Zargod custom, I was supposed to take time with social niceties before getting to business. But we didn't have wine, since it was a video call, and I didn't know what to do. I guess I could tell him how much I respected him, how great he was. If it meant stopping a war, I could subvert my own ego for a bit and do that. "I've been meaning to call on you, sir, but with the transition of leadership here there hasn't been time. I'm sure there is a lot that you could teach me about leading a large unit."

It felt ham-fisted even as I said it, but it worked. His face lit up like a kid who just won first prize in a spelling bee. "I would be happy to meet with you when it is convenient for both of us. I'm told you had urgent business for me."

"I will ask the senior father to arrange something," I said.

He waved his hand in the Zargod way of dismissing something. "He's not useful. I will have someone local contact you."

I processed that for future reference. I didn't understand the factions inside of the Zargod power structure, but Laughlin and Romero were clearly not allies. "I'm sure that you know best, sir."

He grunted. I guess that had multiple meanings.

"The reason I called, sir, is that I have some intelligence to share, and I felt I could only share it at the highest level. Do you trust the security of this line?"

"Hold on." He turned away and spoke to people off-camera behind him. "Get out. Close the door." He waited several seconds, apparently for them to follow his orders, and then turned back to me. "Now we are secure."

I nodded, pretending to be serious while internally shaking my head at his notion of security. "The Argazzi have made some concerning military movements."

His mouth dropped open for a second, but he recovered quickly. "Yes. We have heard this."

He clearly *hadn't* heard it, but I continued so that I wouldn't embarrass him by making him admit it. I had to believe that *somebody* in Zarga knew. That he had been left out of the loop was something I could process later. "It isn't a problem. We are watching them closely and have it under control."

He gave a dismissive hand wave. "They cannot do this! This is a violation, and it will not stand!"

I nodded as if taking his bluster seriously. "It cannot stand."

He paused, his face scrunched up, as if he didn't believe that I'd agreed with him. "We will marshal our forces and destroy them!"

"You would," I agreed, but thought, *They absolutely would not.* Why was this man in charge of the military? The Zargod didn't put a lot of emphasis on military service, but this seemed ridiculous. A leader should have at least understood his relative disadvantage to the Argazzi. Oh well. I had to deal with it like it was. "But perhaps we should hold your forces in reserve, sir."

He considered it. "What do you propose?"

"Let me stop them, and if I don't, then you can swoop down on them like—" For the life of me I couldn't come up with a good metaphorical swoop. "Uh…for the victory."

"Yes!" He paused. "But we should have some role. They threaten our people."

I couldn't tell if he was being coy, trying to get something out of me, or if he really wanted a viable role. I searched my brain to come up with something he could do that wouldn't get in the way or make things worse. If the Argazzi saw Zargod forces marshaling, they could use it as an excuse. I flashed back to what Mrs. Zukov had said about the space elevator and said the first thing I could think of. "We could use some of your forces to help guard the space elevator. My engineers are trying to repair it and coordinating with civilian companies. It would be great if you could take on that protection so that I can remove some of my troops in case I need them for my mission."

His face lit up, and I realized immediately that I'd made a mistake, though I wasn't yet sure what it was. I just had that feeling. "Yes! We can do that. The space elevator is very important, and we must secure the civilian companies."

And there it was. He was going to shake down the contractors for protection money. It wasn't an ideal outcome, but it was something I could deal with later. For now, the priority was to keep him from saber-rattling against the Argazzi, and I'd pay whatever price I had to in order to achieve that. It's not like it would be new for a company working in Zarga to have to pay bribes, anyway.

"Thank you, General. I need to go and prepare my unit for their mission. Thank you very much for your advice and critical assistance."

"Yes. We must meet soon!"

"I'm looking forward to it," I lied, and cut the connection.

As soon as I turned around, Captain Song approached the door.

"Did you hear all of that?" My face heated at the thought.

"No, ma'am. Staff Sergeant Chao wouldn't let me near your door until you were done."

I sent another silent thanks for Chao. "What's up?"

"I talked to a few junior officers. On the surface, they're being told that it's an exercise. But lurking behind that is a rumor that there was a cyber-attack on some critical infrastructure—the communications network and the electrical grid. They're blaming it on the Zargod."

"On the Zargod?" I asked, dumbfounded.

"Yes, ma'am."

"A cyberattack. By the Zargod." She had to know how absurd that sounded. They didn't have the technology for that. Of course, I'd believed it myself when we were attacked, so I guess I couldn't hold it against her. That thought made me stop. "Is there any chance this is from when you had our assets hack their civilian company, looking for information on the quantum communicator?"

"No, ma'am. This is definitely a separate thing."

She was telling the truth, at least to the best of her knowledge. But if it wasn't us, and it definitely wasn't the Zargod, who was it? And just like that, I was back to my suspicion of Tangent, but I decided against sharing that with Song. She'd shown some loyalty, but I still expected she'd report back to her superiors, and I wasn't sure I wanted them to know or not. Not with them deploying forces. "I don't think it was the Zargod, either."

"I'm not sure what our leaders believe, but that's the rumor at my level, and the people I talked to definitely believe it."

"Thanks, Song." I hesitated. "Perhaps you can do one more thing for me." It was a bad thought. I knew that. I'd been mad at the Argazzi for using Trieste, and here I was about to do the same thing. I wish I could say that that thought made me stop. With her own leadership setting her up essentially as a hostage, I didn't want to make her life any harder than it had to be.

But I still did it.

"What's that, ma'am?"

"I want you to deliver a message."

She looked at me like she was sizing me up. "That might put me in a tough position."

"I don't think it will, but you decide. I want you to tell them that you've heard me tell my forces to be prepared to strike first."

She thought about that for a bit. "I can do that, ma'am. I assume it's true—that you're prepared to do that."

"I'm not ruling it out. As you said before, I'm in a tough spot. I need to keep the peace, and the only way to do that might be to attack. Both sides can run our simulations and see." It was a calculated risk on a couple of fronts. First, Song might or might not believe me. She might assess that I didn't mean it, that I *wouldn't* strike first. If I'm being honest, I didn't know myself at that point. Second, if the Argazzi thought I might strike, I couldn't say for sure how they'd react. They could push up their timeline and attack first, hoping to gain an advantage. I didn't think they would, but we were preparing the best we could just in case. So my only added risk was if they weren't planning to attack but then did because of my verbal aggression. Or, without a threat, they might keep moving closer and closer to the line, trying to see what they could get away with or how much they could provoke me and my untested leadership, which could draw out the situation longer.

There were so many permutations that it became confusing. But in all of them, I felt like showing strength beat showing weakness. In my limited experience, people were less likely to push your limits when they thought you might punch them in the face.

"Do you have a preference for how I deliver the message?"

"I'll leave that to you, Captain. You can feed it back through your friends, or you can make a direct report to your supervisor. However you think best protects you."

18

I stood in the staging area, watching as bot-tanks, mobile rocket launchers, infantry transports, and various support vehicles from Second Battalion passed by on their way out the back gate. I wasn't the only one watching. The Argazzi had us under observation by aerial drone —I'd checked on that. We had the ability to eliminate them, and I'd do that at some point; unlike my drones, which the treaty protected, theirs were flying in airspace they didn't have a right to. But for now, I wanted them to see what I had coming for them.

I couldn't match their numbers; they had a six-to-one force ratio. But we had them outpaced with military technology by a wide margin, and we had better trained soldiers. It was up to me as the commander to figure out how to use those advantages. The hard part was doing it without space assets, which would have normally been a big force multiplier, but there was no sense worrying over something that I couldn't change.

I reached out with my implant to connect to the tactical network, to feel the electronic touch of the combat power at my disposal. That was why they spent all the money on the hardware wired into my brain—that link, this kind of moment. Everything else I could do with the implant was secondary. That was why I had to lead, and Hearns couldn't. Like the vehicles streaming past me, I was a weapon system. I could control the combat assets under my command with a series of directed thoughts.

THE WEIGHT OF COMMAND

The first touch of the wider network almost brought me to my knees. It was like being in a gymnasium full of people with everyone talking at once and all of them wanting your attention. Inside my brain, it came across as a cacophony of static, confusion, and more than a little pain. After a few seconds, I shut it back down. I'd controlled a platoon regularly, and I'd trained with as much as a company. This battalion was five or six times more entities than I'd ever practiced with, and it was only a third of my force.

I turned the sensitivity down, muting my connection somewhat, and I reentered the stream. The mass of systems still roared at me, but this time I withstood it. I let it wash over me like a powerful wave, immersed myself in it, tried to pick a point of focus to center myself. I located the lead bot-tank company, and then I found its command vehicle. I amplified my connection to it and dampened the connection to the vehicles around it, and the roar lessened slightly. I repeated the action with the second company and then the third, and suddenly the stream was manageable. Instead of hundreds of people screaming at me in the gym, it was just a few loud voices and the rest whispers.

The notion of command vehicles within the formation was a misnomer—I could command every vehicle myself if it came to it. But it was a useful construct for me to use intermediaries. I didn't need the fidelity of individual vehicles for what we were doing and cutting down the number that I had to order directly helped me gain control. In a better situation, I'd have had the benefit of other officers with implants in each of those formations. But I could manage it this way. I'd give an order to one vehicle and it would relay to the others in its formation. Granted, for now we were only moving to a forward position, which was the most basic of tasks. In combat it would get more complex in a hurry. But baby steps.

I muted all the combat vehicles and reached out to the sensor network to check the constellation of drones overhead. This I'd done before on scouting missions, so it came easier as I accessed their positional data and their AI's interpretation of what they were seeing. As I'd expected, I also found three of the enemy's drones via our sensor network. They were observing our deployment and undoubtedly reporting back to their masters. I flipped to the attack screen that would let me fire a range of weapons at them, from directed EMPs to lasers to missiles that turned into waves of flying pellets. I sent a message to the noncom in charge of sensor management, with instructions to keep an eye on them, let me know if any more showed up, and to develop the optimal solution for taking them all out quickly if we decided to do that.

If we decided to pull the trigger, I wanted to leave no doubt. We'd kill every drone we could in as short a time as possible. We'd send a definitive message and give the Argazzi as little chance as possible to retaliate. It was like any fight. The first thing you did was try to avoid it, but when it became inevitable, whoever hit first and hit hardest had the best chance of winning. Or maybe just causing the other side to back down.

If I could strike their drones and it caused them to quit…well that was the best possible outcome. No lives lost and a bigger conflict averted? I'd take that. The problem was, I didn't know if it would make them back off or spur them into further action.

I think I had too much data. I could see all the possibilities, but I didn't have the human element. What I needed was someone to discuss things with. Unfortunately, I could only go so far with Captain Song. I trusted that she and I had goals that were somewhat aligned, but only to a point. Discussing the intricacies of what her side might be thinking so I could use that to gain a tactical advantage was beyond our relationship. Perston would have been ideal, but our personal situation made that untenable. That left only one man, and as it happens, he'd picked that moment to approach. Hearns's body language said that he had something to say, but I launched into my own thoughts before he had a chance.

"I have to attack first if I want to win, but what if that's what they want? What if they want me to attack first in order to either justify an escalation on their part or to win some sort of political battle that I'm missing?"

To his credit, Hearns didn't give me a quick answer. A lesser man might have seen it as not his problem, made some sort of flippant quip like, "Well, ma'am, that's why they pay you the big bucks." But not Hearns. He stood there, bobbing his head slightly as he thought, probably without realizing it.

"I don't know, ma'am." I started to interject but he continued, cutting me off. "How could I know? How can you know?" He paused as if waiting for me to answer, and when I didn't, he continued. "You can't. All you can do is weigh everything you've got and make a call. I'm betting that you've already done that."

I smiled. He knew me. "I have."

"Then go with it. We'll all back it, regardless of if you're right or wrong."

THE WEIGHT OF COMMAND

It wasn't helpful in the way that I'd hoped. But it helped to have him remind me that I had unconditional support. Or at least mostly unconditional.

So all I said was, "Thanks." Then I remembered that he'd approached me and I changed the subject. "Did you need something?"

"Yes, ma'am. We've got a problem."

Shit. Even if I hadn't heard it in his tone, I'd have known it was bad. For him to approach me with an issue when I had a battle looming was significant. "What's up?"

"It's Captain Perston, ma'am. He's working to turn the unit against you."

I wish I was surprised. I shook my head and rolled my eyes, which was immature, but I couldn't help it, and if there was anyone I got to show frustration to, it was Hearns. "What's he doing?"

"You know the shortages we've been having in the mess? He's telling people that you're doing that intentionally to try to gain an advantage over the locals."

"That's ridiculous. I'd never do that."

"He has documents that you signed rejecting shipments, ma'am."

For fuck's sake. I knew immediately what he'd done. I'd signed documents without reading them, and Perston had done that intentionally. Led me right into a trap. It also explained why he was so put out by my assistant, Chao, wanting to read his next set of docs before they went to me. He'd taken those with him rather than leaving them there for her. "I hope you know that I didn't do that intentionally. He had documents, and I signed them without reading, which was stupid." I braced myself for Hearns to agree. I deserved it.

Instead he softened his voice. "I'm glad to hear you say that. I didn't think you would. Unfortunately, though, it's reached the rumor mill—"

"Shit. What should I do? Because I know my immediate personal solution to this, and that would be to punch that asshole in the throat. But I'm pretty sure I shouldn't do that." With that said, I wasn't *totally* sure.

"I can deal with the rumors, ma'am. I'll gather the senior noncoms who aren't moving out right now and make it clear that you're not doing what they're hearing. They'll believe me. But it depends on how far it's spread, and while we can limit the damage, it might take a while to completely reverse it. Some soldiers are always going to believe the worst."

I sighed. "Do it. And keep me updated. What do you need me to do?"

He wouldn't have come to me if it was something he could handle completely on his own.

"Ma'am..." Hearns hesitated, not wanting to tell me whatever was coming next. "We need to deal with Captain Perston. Like I said, I can handle the fallout from this. But he's actively working against you, and he's not going to stop on his own. Next time it might be worse."

I considered it for a second and then nodded. "I'll deal with it."

"Are you sure? I was going to recommend having some soldiers round him up and put in a cell to wait for you. You could deal with him after all this is done." He gestured at the last of Second Battalion heading out the gate.

As much sense as that made, it wasn't the right answer. I'd lock him up if I had to, but it wasn't good for the unit, seeing two officers in conflict. Better to take it head on and solve it than let it drag out "No, I'll deal with him."

"Okay, ma'am. But do it soon."

"I'll do it right now."

"Roger that. He's in his office."

The timing couldn't have been worse. I needed to be practicing my control of a large formation, not dealing with a petulant assclown of an officer. I stopped by my office on my way and got a cup of coffee, which I put in the microwave and heated until it boiled.

"Ma'am, what are you doing to that coffee? It's going to be too hot to drink," said Chao.

"I'm not going to drink it right away," I said. In truth, I wasn't going to drink it at all. I was planning ahead, and if the conversation with Perston went completely pear-shaped and he looked like he might try to get physical, I was going to throw the coffee in his face and then stomp the shit out of him. I hoped it wouldn't go that way, but I didn't know what he was thinking, and it always helped to be prepared.

I walked past half a dozen soldiers and noncoms as I wound my way back through the warren of offices to where Perston had ensconced himself in the Chief Logistic Officer's office. His home turf. That was fine for my purposes. I had thought it through, and I planned to make a scene. I wanted witnesses. There were rumors, and I wanted to put them to rest. The best way to do that was for word of our confrontation to get out, and having it get out through his people would give it more credibility. It also meant I wouldn't get the benefit of the doubt, so I needed the outcome to be indisputable. But I did have a surprise.

THE WEIGHT OF COMMAND

I flung his office door open without knocking, and it slammed into the wall, shaking the cheaply made prefab material. It didn't make as much noise as I'd hoped, but you can't have everything. I still had my coffee with me as I walked up to his desk, and with my free hand, I swept most of the stuff off of his desk and onto the floor, including an empty coffee mug which shattered satisfyingly on the bare tile. It was a dick move on my part, but it had the desired effect.

Perston leapt to his feet behind the desk. "What the fuck are you doing?"

"I know what you did." I didn't shout, but I spoke loud enough to be heard outside the office, even if the soldiers there weren't trying to eavesdrop, which they absolutely were.

"I don't know—"

"You know exactly what I'm talking about, you slimy little fuck weasel." It was a strange combination of an insult, but it worked, as Perston's face turned bright red.

"You're a fucking psycho."

"Ma'am," I said.

"What?"

"You're a fucking psycho, *ma'am*."

He glared at me but didn't speak.

"Go ahead. Say it."

"Say what?" he asked.

"Say 'you're a fucking psycho, *ma'am*.'"

"I'm not going to do that."

"Very well. We'll come back to your insubordination later. Let me ask you another question. Why did you start a rumor about me purposely shorting the rations?"

"What? I didn't. What would make you think that?" He was so full of shit.

"It's been going around."

"Well I didn't start it."

"Cool. So where do you think it came from?" I still kept my volume up, even though we were talking calmer. I didn't want our audience to miss anything.

"I haven't heard anything of the sort."

"What about the documents you had me sign?"

"What about them?"

"Let me see them."

"What?"

"Give them to me," I said. "I want to read them."

"You didn't read them when you authorized them?"

"You were there. You know I didn't. I trusted you not to let me sign something stupid. Turns out I shouldn't have because you're a traitorous little shit nugget. Isn't that right?"

"I didn't—"

"You prepared the documents, didn't you? Or did you bring something for me to authorize that *you* hadn't read?"

"You authorized them."

"That I did. Let me ask you something. How do you think this ends?"

"What do you mean?"

"When the facts come out—and they will come out when our relief arrives—how do you think this ends?"

"I think there are going to be some serious questions about how you came to be in command, *ma'am*." He spit the last word like it was an epithet. Like he was an eighteen-year-old private with a grudge. I suppose I couldn't complain, given what I'd called him in the past minute or two.

"I don't mean how it ends for me. I've made my decisions and I can accept whatever judgment comes. I'm talking about how it ends for you."

"I don't understand."

"Of course, you don't. You're not smart enough."

"That's uncalled—"

"Shut up and listen for once in your life." His face reddened again, but he stopped talking. "Good. Right now, we are rolling out in the face of what appears to be an enemy that is massing combat power with ill intent. And instead of facing that threat, I'm dealing with you and your little stunt. So, regardless of what comes of me and how I came to be in command, how do you think someone—I don't know, a court martial panel, maybe—will judge your actions and how they helped or hurt the command?"

He didn't speak right away, and it was like I could see his brain working, trying to piece it together, trying to come up with any way to frame it where his actions were acceptable. But he couldn't because they weren't.

"I doubt they'll call it treason," I continued, digging it in deeper. "But insubordination in the face of an enemy? I don't think that's a hard sell."

"You can't charge me with insubordination. You're not really a major." He said it softly, though, the fight gone from him.

"You think that whatever happens to me will absolve you? It won't.

They'll be completely separate cases. You can be totally right about me and what happens to me, and you can *still* go to jail. And I'm not talking D Cell here on the planet. I'm talking real prison, for a long time. Dishonorable discharge. Sure, maybe we'll be there together. But the difference is, I'll go knowing I did everything I could to make the mission a success, and I think that my superiors will respect that, even if they disagree with my methods. Can you say that?"

"You wouldn't."

"Wouldn't what? Tell the truth? Of course I will. But it won't even matter. When this is over, there are going to be more investigations than you or I can count. They're going to talk to *everybody* and find *everything*. They're going to study this shit in *history class*."

"I hadn't thought about that." Of course he hadn't. He couldn't think beyond himself, which was why I had to make it about him. Again.

"In the end, it's going to come down to one basic point: Did you do everything you could to ensure the success of the mission?"

His shoulders slumped as the weight of the truth fell upon him.

"Well?" I asked. "Did you?"

"No."

"What's that? I couldn't hear you."

"No." He said it louder.

"No, what?"

"No, ma'am."

"So what are you going to do to help make things right?"

He thought about it. "I don't know, ma'am."

"That's fine. Because I'll tell you what you're going to do. You're going to undo the shit you did with the rations and you're going to get the food supply situation under control. And you're going to do it before the combat units return from the field. When they get back, after we've won whatever action it is that we have to win, I expect that first meal to be a fucking feast."

"Ma'am, with the troops rolling out I don't have the assets to—"

"Perston, I have to figure out how to command and control an entire brigade at once. Have you ever done that?"

"No, ma'am."

I lowered my voice so the onlookers couldn't hear me anymore. "Me either. There's a real chance that I fail spectacularly and you get exactly what you want. That might be a mixed blessing, though, since it will probably mean that most of us are dead."

This time his face went white. He hadn't considered the real-world stakes of his little game. "I'll figure out the food situation."

"Good. Thank you. I'm going to go figure out how to win a shooting war." I took a sip of my coffee, which had cooled to the perfect drinking temperature. I hoped the Argazzi were as predictable and easy to deal with as Perston.

Somehow, I doubted it.

19

By the time I got back to the staging area, the final battalion was rolling out of the gate. I wasn't ready for my part in the operation, but at least my subordinate units had their shit together. Xiang waved at me from across the yard where my crew was waiting with the vehicle. I headed over at a walk, letting myself be seen by the drivers and vehicle commanders as they passed. Most of the vehicles—the bot-tanks and rocket launchers—held a single occupant. The personnel carriers held nine. All and all there were about eighteen-hundred soldiers moving on my order, ready to fight and die based on the decisions I made.

No pressure.

When I reached the vehicle, I plugged into the comms there to give me a boost and contacted Captain Song back in her office. "Any response to the message we sent?"

"No, ma'am. My boss was appreciative of the intel, and based on his tone, I feel confident that he passed it higher. But he didn't share anything with me about what they'd do with the information."

"Is that unexpected?"

She took a second to respond, maybe thinking about it. "I don't think so. I wouldn't expect him to share, because I don't have a need to know, and even if I did, I don't think it would be him who told me, because he's not the decision maker. If anything, he'd need to get an answer himself, and then follow up with me."

She was right. It made sense. But it didn't fit my needs, so I needed a new plan. They had my message, and all I could do in that regard was to evaluate their actions and see what I could glean from that. At least I had assets that could help. I closed down the comm link to Song and plugged into my sensor net, opening the drone feeds. We had nearly forty platforms in the sky, and each of them fed video and an AI analysis of what they were seeing. Thankfully I'd used drone feeds quite a bit, and I knew how to get what I wanted from them—not forty at a time, but that was just a matter of scale. I muted all of them but one—a forward scout with eyes on one of the major Argazzi formations.

The drone's AI gave me a scrolling synopsis of its last fifteen minutes while I simultaneously watched the live video in my mind. I got what I needed from that in a few seconds and then muted it, pulling up the feed from the next forward platform. This one had another of the major formations under surveillance. Within a minute, I'd cycled through the six most important feeds and the combined picture told me what I needed to know—the Argazzi were still proceeding with a full deployment, but they were stopping well short of aggression. Their movements were in sync with what they said they were doing: conducting a major exercise.

I reached out to the command vehicles in all of my formations and gave them an update on the situation, trusting them to pass it down. We'd move to our staging areas well short of the border, set up local security, and be prepared for follow-on operations. In three hours, once we were fully set, we'd run through a computer-simulated defense against a major Argazzi attack. We'd assess that result, and then we'd either re-play a similar scenario, if needed, or move on to the next one—an attack of our own. I could run the sims on my own, of course, but they wouldn't be as accurate as running them with the full force. Most of our fight could be automated, but there was still a human element. Besides, the training would keep the soldiers sharp.

It would also keep them busy, which I couldn't underestimate. Some of my veterans had seen combat on other planets, but for more than ninety percent, this was probably the most significant action they'd been in. You never wanted to give a soldier too much time to dwell on what bad thing might happen next.

My system beeped with an incoming message from Staff Sergeant Chao, so I shut down the feeds in my head and answered.

"Ma'am, there's a call here for you from a Ms. Trieste."

"Put her through to my vehicle."

No sooner had I said it than Liana Trieste's face showed up on my system monitor, hair and makeup perfect as always, sharp features, and strong jaw set. "Major Markov, you look ready for war." She referred, I assume, to my helmet and field gear, but she said it with a hint of a smile, taking some of the bite out of it.

I smiled back. "I'm a soldier. I'm always ready for war." Our sides were at odds, but we could still be friendly. Though I was starting to have a hard time seeing how she and I could maintain that, given everything going on around us.

"Just so. That's why I'm calling. We're a little concerned about the aggressive action your forces are taking."

"I'm not sure what you're talking about." I didn't even try to hide the lie. The Argazzi calling *my* actions aggressive was blatant nonsense, given that they'd started it. If she wanted to play dumb—or more likely, someone had directed her to—so could I.

"Your forces are currently moving toward our border."

"I'm not the one who promised not to conduct a major exercise. I believe that was you."

"The situation changed."

"It changed for us too."

"We have a right to conduct military exercises. It's not a reason for you to move your troops to our border," she said.

"We're not moving to the border. We're moving to field locations to conduct an exercise." It was technically true. I *did* have an exercise planned.

She drew her lips into a thin line. "Let's cut the nonsense, shall we? You're clearly responding to our training exercise."

"You said it. You're well within your rights under the treaty to conduct an exercise. I think you'll find that we are too."

"Your aggressive action has led some in my country's leadership to wonder what other aggressive actions you might have taken."

"I'm not sure what you're talking about." This time I wasn't lying. I really didn't know what she meant, though I didn't expect her to believe that.

"We recently came under a cyberattack that caused significant damage to our nation's infrastructure. But then, you know that."

"And that's why you're conducting an *exercise*. Because you think the Zargod initiated that attack."

"The Zargod are not our primary suspects."

That was interesting. Had the Argazzi come to the same conclusion I had about the most likely culprit? "Who do you suspect?"

"Given your aggressive action and your known capabilities, the most likely attacker was you."

I sat there for several seconds, stunned. I hadn't considered that possibility. I probably should have, but there were so many different things happening I hadn't thought it all the way through. Another mistake on my part. We hadn't done it, but I should have expected them to suspect us. I had relied too much on Captain Song's intel and hadn't thought all the permutations through well enough. "We didn't do it."

"I personally believe you. But I'm not in charge."

This time I believed her. It was clear she wasn't in charge, and the other—well, maybe I just *wanted* to believe her. Maybe she wanted to believe me. But our personal feelings weren't driving the day. Perhaps if she *were* in charge, she and I could sit down and actually iron this whole thing out. But I might as well wish for fairies to fly down and sprinkle us all with magic happy dust. "So let me guess. It would help your leaders to believe me if I stood down my forces and returned to base."

She smiled. "Obviously, yes."

That smile was screwing with my head. I liked it. I wanted to say anything I could to make it appear again. But I couldn't. "You first."

"Your exercise is clearly a farce designed to intimidate us."

"Is it working?" This time, I smiled. I tried to, at least. It certainly wasn't as polished and beautiful as hers.

"We will not be bullied by a force that is only here because we asked for it."

"And I've got a job to do. I'm going to pursue my mission—the mission agreed to by both you and the Zargod—until I receive orders that tell me to desist. And since we have no communication off-planet, I don't expect to receive those orders. But if you've got some secret communication method, I'd be very open to hearing about it."

"So you won't stand down."

"What's in it for me?"

"What are you talking about? Surely you don't mean a bribe."

"I mean what is your nation willing to do in order to secure my cooperation?"

THE WEIGHT OF COMMAND

Trieste hesitated, obviously taking instructions from someone else. I didn't know who was in charge of the call, but I assumed it was at a level where they'd be able to make a deal. Finally, she spoke. "As the military commander, you have no authority under the treaty to enter into agreements of this nature. Our treaty is with the Federation government, not its military."

"That is true. But I'm all you've got. These are exigent circumstances, and as such, I am assuming a greater role until the normal communications channels reopen. We can consider any agreement null and void once we can reach the Federation government for their orders."

She hesitated again. I'd taken them off of their planned course of discussion, whatever that was, and they were ad-libbing. I was pretty sure that was a good thing, as it meant they were actually listening to what I had to say. For a brief moment, I had hope. "We insist on keeping to the letter of the treaty," she said. "We will only negotiate with the Federation government."

I sagged for a moment, punched in the gut, before I schooled myself back to a neutral posture. So much for hope. So much for reason. What they wanted wasn't possible, and by refusing to negotiate with me, they left me no choice but to take unilateral action. I hardened my tone and made sure not to smile. We were done being nice and had moved on to the next phase, which meant I needed to intimidate them to get them to back down. My intimidating face has always been better than my smile, anyway. "Does the *letter of the treaty* allow you to fly drones in Zargod airspace?"

She turned her head this time, receiving more instructions that I couldn't hear. While she was doing it, I entered our defense network, found four Argazzi drones in Zargod air space, and locked in the optimal defense program the staff had prepared. I considered the implications of what I was about to do for a few seconds. I was firmly within our authorizations, as there were no human lives at stake, and they were in clear violation of the treaty.

"Ms. Trieste?" I prompted.

She turned back to me, but her eyes cut back to whoever was instructing her, and she didn't speak. They were trying to come up with a response where there wasn't one. They were in violation, and they knew it. If they offered to withdraw their drones, they'd be admitting it.

I used the time to gather more information on the assets in question, which my team had helpfully appended to the readouts on each drone.

Three were cheap, but one was their highest-end model, and they'd feel its loss. A message wasn't effective in this case unless it stung a bit. My own calculations also showed my odds of winning an eventual battle went up by three-tenths of a percent by taking the initiative here.

I triggered the program and our weapons went into action, hacking one drone, using a directed EMP on another, and lasers against the final two. The four red icons disappeared.

Trieste turned back to me, but then stopped and turned away again. This time I could hear a raised voice in the background. I assumed that he'd gotten the news about their drones going dark.

"Did something happen?" I asked to the side of Trieste's face.

She turned back to the camera, her perfect face fallen, and for a second her disappointment stung. She spoke softly as if resigned. "You have taken a deliberately aggressive action."

"You were in violation of the letter of the treaty. I had been ignoring your drones in order to keep the peace. But since you insisted, I've now enforced the treaty." Hopefully, they'd see that as I intended it—as a threat—and back down.

Setting the politics of my decision aside for a moment, militarily, it created a problem for the Argazzi. Now they couldn't see my forces with any kind of fidelity. They could fly drones high on their own side of the border and try to pick us up that way, but that took specialized assets that they probably didn't have. Even if they did, it would degrade their capability significantly. It gave me an advantage in case the conflict turned even more hostile.

"You have unmanned assets in our airspace as well," she said, parroting a threat that she got from someone off-screen.

"Which is allowed to the peacekeeping force under the terms of the treaty."

She paused, receiving more instructions, but she kept eye contact this time. "Major Markov, please consider our position. Are you suggesting we ignore an attack on our critical infrastructure?"

"What I'm suggesting is that you consider that you might have been hacked by someone that isn't the Zargod and isn't the peacekeeping force."

"Then who?" she answered without delay, indicating that we were back on one of her intended topics.

Now it was my turn to hesitate. My theory about Tangent Holding Company wasn't something I could prove, and not something I wanted as

THE WEIGHT OF COMMAND

public knowledge until I knew how to act on it. If it *was* Tangent, I didn't want to announce that I knew and give them warning. "I don't know. But it wasn't us."

"We are searching all possible leads to determine the source," she said.

"You could do that with your forces in garrison."

"I'm sorry. That doesn't seem logical. I think we're at an impasse." She did look sad about that, which I could appreciate. I felt it too.

"It would appear that we are. I hope your forces have a good training exercise."

"Yours as well, Major." She cut the connection.

I exhaled audibly, which drew a response from my crew, who had heard everything.

"Holy shit, ma'am. Did you blow up their drones?" asked Xiang.

I hesitated, but it wasn't a secret so there was no reason not to tell. "I took them down. We didn't exactly shoot them all down. One we hacked, one we fried with directed EMP. But…yeah.."

"Badass," said Zilla.

"Was that how you wanted it to go, ma'am?" asked Murphy.

"I'm not sure, Murph. It certainly could have gone better, but it could have been worse, too."

"They're probably pissed right now," he said.

"Probably," I agreed. "But I want them a little pissed. Pissed and scared, though. I want them to believe that if they fight us, they're going to lose."

"Are they going to lose?" asked Zilla.

"I don't know," I admitted. "That's what we're going to find out with these simulated exercises."

The next eight hours passed in a blur of data and feeds running through my brain, leaving me with a pounding headache that started at the back of my skull and radiated up through my temples. We'd finished both the defensive and offensive simulations, and now I sat outside of my vehicle on the ground, leaning back against the front bumper with my legs straight out in front of me. I wanted to close my eyes but was afraid I'd fall asleep. Zilla brought me a metal cup full of tea that she'd made over a chemical heater and Xiang was heating field rations for me.

"Thanks," I said, taking the tea and putting it to my lips.

The exercises had gone okay. I'd learned a lot about what I could and couldn't control, and that was as important as anything. I also learned that our chances of winning a defensive battle where the Argazzi struck first were only around sixty to sixty-five percent, depending on how they attacked, and even in the cases where we won we would take significant casualties. And that didn't even begin to factor in the civilian death toll, which ranged from the mid-four to the mid-five figures, depending on the scenario. That was unacceptable.

Embracing an offensive strategy produced better results, victory ranging from eighty-seven to ninety-nine percent likely, almost directly correlated with how aggressive I got. A first strike immediately while they were still in their forward staging areas gave us almost no chance of losing and potentially kept civilian casualties to a double-digit number. But that wasn't a politically tenable solution. There would be no way to frame that other than as an unprovoked attack on our part. The fact that I felt that they were being provocative with their so-called "exercise" wouldn't hold up in any sort of investigation. Technically, other than the drones, they hadn't done anything illegal, and I'd solved that violation. And more than that, the idea that both sides needed to strike first to have their best chance of winning seemed to play into the hands of someone who might want to instigate a war. I really wished there was a way to change that, but I couldn't see it.

I found myself thinking in two very different ways. Most important, I had to save the most possible lives, even if that meant I couldn't save them all. But I'd be lying if I said I wasn't also thinking about the consequences for myself after the fact. Even if we didn't fight at all, there would be independent investigators scrutinizing everything that happened under my command for years. I'd told Perston that I was willing to end up in jail as long as I did what I thought was right. And I hoped that was true. I hoped that when it came down to it, I'd be able to put the consequences for myself aside and take the best possible action for everyone. The problem was, that action wasn't clear.

And there was the absolute possibility that I could do everything right, make perfect decisions based on the circumstances, and still face repercussions. My action in taking command was unprecedented, and there wasn't much that the military bureaucracy despised more than a lack of precedent. I couldn't control that, and I needed to set it aside, so I forced it out and tried to focus on the things I *could* control.

But could I control anything? I sat there and sipped my tea, and I was stuck. If I waited for them to attack, we faced an unacceptable result. If we struck now, I faced an undesirable result. There was no way to win. And, fuck, did I ever need to close my eyes and go to sleep. But I couldn't. I was taking a short break, but if I took my eyes too far off of the Argazzi,

THE WEIGHT OF COMMAND

I might wake up to find that we were already hours into the worst possible scenario, potentially without a way back.

I needed two things. First, I needed to know who was making decisions for the Argazzi and why. I had been negotiating through Trieste with someone who didn't have the authority to stand down their forces, and that went against the first rule of negotiations. I'd taken no from someone without the authority to say yes.

Second, I needed someone to talk to. I needed to discuss the data bouncing around in my head with someone who could make sense of it and give me honest feedback on my thoughts. That should have been Perston, but obviously that wasn't happening. Hearns wasn't an option either, unfortunately. He'd tell me that if it came down to risking our soldiers or killing theirs, that there was no question we should kill theirs. I didn't hold it against him. Almost any noncom would give me that same answer. They tended to see things in black and white, which was usually a good thing but didn't help me here. This was more nuanced.

Xiang brought me a plate of food; he'd emptied the ration bags onto an actual aluminum field plate, which was unnecessary. I almost made a joke about it, but he'd clearly put in effort, so all I said was, "Thanks. You can just give me the food pouches next time. I don't need this."

"I know you don't, ma'am. But you look like you've got a lot on your mind, and I figured whatever I could do that might help, I should."

I fought to hold back tears, which was ridiculous. It was just a soldier doing something nice for a leader. But with everything else I had weighing on me, for whatever reason, that was the thing that finally got to me.

"Ma'am? Are you okay?"

I knew the correct answer to that question. As an officer, when a soldier asks you if you're all right, you say yes unless you need physical assistance. If you're bleeding, or if you need help walking because you've got a broken ankle—those are the acceptable times to say that you're not okay. Because soldiers need you to be okay.

But the fact of the matter was that I was *not* okay.

I was scared and alone and out of my depth. There was an entire nation of strategists, leaders, politicians, and military minds, all lined up against me, plotting our downfall. And on my side? Just me and my government-issued brain, sitting in the grass and crying because a soldier brought me processed rations on a plate.

I don't know how long I thought about it, but Xiang was still standing there. "No," I said, finally. "I'm not okay."

"You want to talk about it, ma'am?" asked Xiang.

"Yeah, ma'am," said Murphy. "You can dump on us. We won't tell anybody. What happens inside the crew stays inside the crew. Isn't that right, Zilla?"

"Those *are* the rules," she said.

I thought about it. By the standards of any leadership manual, it was absolutely not the right thing to do. But then, nothing I was doing was anywhere in any leadership book. "Okay. Let me tell you what's going on."

So I did. I told them pretty much everything, from the results of the simulations to the potential outcomes to my suspicions about Tangent Holding Company. I drifted and digressed and spoke in stream of consciousness. It took a while. Over half an hour. But at the end of it, I had nothing left to say and it felt good to have it out as if somehow speaking the words got some of the festering rot out of me. When I finished, the crew stood there around me, silent, looming over me like a protective wall as I continued to sit on the ground.

It was Murphy who broke the silence. "Wow, ma'am. You're pretty well fucked." The others stared at him. I stared at him. It was hard to make out his features in the dark that had swallowed us. And then I couldn't hold it in, and I just started laughing. Once I did, Zilla laughed too, and then we were all laughing and we couldn't stop for what had to have been at least a minute. We weren't directly adjacent to any unit, but we were within sixty or seventy meters of a rocket battery, and I'm sure the soldiers there heard us and wondered what was going on, but I couldn't help it.

"Thanks, Murph. That's some keen insight," I said, which started them laughing again.

"Seriously, though," said Zilla, once the laughter died. "It's got to be Tangent behind this action by the Argazzi, right?"

"Has to be," agreed Gonzalez. "No other way."

I didn't disagree, but I wanted to hear their logic without biasing them. "Why do you say that?"

"It's like when you watch a murder mystery," said Gonzalez. "There are too many coincidences associated with one character, so while they haven't told you yet, you know they're the bad guy."

I considered the *that's how it happens in murder mysteries* defense, but somehow I didn't think it would hold up in court. "That what you think too, Zilla?"

"Not exactly, ma'am. The way I see it, Tangent are the only ones with something to gain from this. The Argazzi have simulations too, and while theirs might not give them the same data yours did, they won't be *that* far off. They know their odds, and they probably know they aren't good."

"Sure." Something about what she said tickled at the back of my mind. I couldn't put my finger on it.

"And the Zargod," she continued. "They might gain something if we kick the crap out of the Argazzi, but not much. It's not like they've got the ability to capitalize on it militarily. Maybe they'd gain something politically?"

"Maybe," I allowed, but I couldn't think of what.

"And the Zargod are definitely going to take some hits," said Zilla. "Who does that leave? Tangent. They were probably behind the previous attacks, so it makes sense that they're behind the hack that has the Argazzi riled up too."

I nodded, though they probably couldn't see it in the dark. But while I agreed, I wasn't one hundred percent sure that Tangent was behind the earlier attacks. Zilla didn't have the burden of having to keep an open mind and had focused on the most obvious solution. "The problem is, I don't have any way to prove it, and I don't know who else might be working with them. I've got no way to attack it."

"We've got to find a way to go after Tangent directly," said Xiang.

He was right, but how? They weren't a physical entity. Or, if they were, they were hidden here on-planet. And I couldn't reach them off-planet. If I could find proof, at least I could present it when I finally did establish comms. "Unfortunately, Xiang, we don't have a way to do that. And even if we did, we've got a more immediate threat that we have to deal with."

And that was the problem. I should have been working on how to get at Tangent, but instead I was out here having a staring contest with the Argazzi.

The four of them grunted their assent, and as if sensing that we were through, they all drifted off, leaving me with my thoughts. I came back to what Zilla had said, about the Argazzi running their own simulations. Of course they had, which meant one of two things. Either they knew that they were likely to lose so they'd hold off on their attack, or they knew that striking first gave them their best shot at victory, so they wouldn't wait.

With that thought, I tapped back into the tactical network and looked at the sensor readouts that the staff had prioritized for me. They had shifted to the IR spectrum in the dark, casting the views into blacks and reds. There was movement on the Argazzi side of the border, but not enough to signal an attack. There were small patrols of three to four vehicles out around each of the six major encampments, but that was to be expected. Standard local security. Nothing to get concerned about. I checked the staff assessment, and it confirmed mine. Although we had to consider that the Argazzi knew they were being watched, so they'd make every effort to look normal right up until the moment they chose to act.

I thought through what that action would look like so I could put the AIs and the staff on alert for it. They'd drop our surveillance—or at least try to. Unlike my attack against their observation platforms, them attacking ours would be an act of war, and they wouldn't do that unless they intended to take it further. Our drones had some countermeasures, and they would fare better than the Argazzi's had against us, but they would likely get most of the ones deep on their own side of the border, or at least force them to flee. But our drones put them in a tough spot, no matter what they did. If they attacked our surveillance assets, it would give warning of the greater attack. But they couldn't attack me from their current location, and if they failed to drop our drones, we'd have a perfect view as they rolled out of their positions.

I considered what I would do if I was them. They had to make it look like they weren't attacking so that we'd see their movements and discount them. A key element of that included getting their rockets and artillery in range where they could strike a variety of targets. I pulled up the simulation data that the staff had plotted on a digital map. The Argazzi needed to get about twenty klicks closer for an optimal strike, and they could launch a somewhat effective strike if they got fifteen klicks closer. I sent a message to Watch to immediately notify me if specific indirect fire systems got closer to us by half that distance, in order to give myself time to react. McNamara could have her people automate it through the drones' AI if she wanted, but I left the method up to her.

And with that, I stood and climbed onto the hood of the vehicle and lay down on my back. Staring up at the stars, the evening was cool but not cold, and there was residual heat coming off of the engine which Murph had to run every so often to keep the electronics charged. The enemy might try something, but I didn't think it would be tonight. If it was, I trusted that my team would wake me up. I set an alarm for four hours in my implant and closed my eyes.

20

The sun was just rising as I woke, casting everything in a reddish hue. My back protested for a moment as I sat; I hadn't slept anywhere but in a bunk in a while, and the vehicle hood left a lot to be desired as a mattress. Zilla was in the vehicle, monitoring comms and Xiang was up with his rifle at the low ready, guarding us as we slept. Gonzalez and Murph were still down, but they'd certainly taken shifts during the night, so I left it to them to manage their own schedules. I checked our sensors while I went to the back of the vehicle and fished in my pack for a chemical heater to make coffee. I grabbed the crew pot and filled it with enough water for all of us, then took it a safe distance from the vehicle and set it to boil.

I checked in with Ops, and between that and the sensors, they confirmed what I suspected: The Argazzi hadn't tried anything during the night. They didn't have to. As long as they didn't do anything aggressive, they had an unlimited timeline; they knew that I couldn't take any action. Meanwhile, I had my troops out in the field and couldn't focus on the missions I wanted to—getting off-planet comms and digging further into Tangent. But if we were going to be in the field, we could use the time wisely, so I messaged unit leaders to send me their training plans for the day.

I had just finished sending that when I got a message from Ops that Trieste was on the line for me. I probably should have refused the call and forced her to put someone else on the line—someone in charge. But despite it all, in some sort of twisted way I still wanted to see her. It was as if some part of my brain still held out hope that things could be normal again. So I had Ops put it through to my vehicle's vid screen.

"Deputy Minister Trieste. How are you this fine morning?" I put on my best happy face. She didn't need to know that I'd slept on the hood of a vehicle the previous night. I'm sure she'd slept in her own comfortable bed and taken an hour to fix her perfect hair and makeup, though she'd have had to get up rather early to do that, given the time. I, on the other hand, had washed up in a bucket of tepid water. Funny, but when I first met her and thought about how she might keep me awake at night, I hadn't considered full-scale armed conflict.

"I am formally notifying you that our troops will be moving from their assembly areas to defensive positions as part of our exercise," she said. "This is part of a simulated scenario and is in no way indicating any sort of military action beyond that."

I nodded, understanding exactly what she was doing. "I acknowledge what you're saying. I do expect that you'll maintain a distance from the border that doesn't escalate tensions."

She glanced to the side. "What do you mean by that specifically?"

I didn't want to tell her. If I gave them the exact triggers we were using in regard to their movements, it would give them information that they could then exploit. But by not telling her, I ran the risk of them bumbling into something that looked hostile but might not actually be so. "I'm concerned that you might try to launch an attack from distance. Your military leaders will know what that looks like and should avoid any posture that creates that appearance."

Frustration crossed her face as she took that in, though whether that frustration was with me or the person in her ear giving her guidance, I couldn't be sure. "That's not very clear."

"It's clear enough, and anyone telling you that it's not is purposely obfuscating."

She hesitated, listening to more instructions. "We don't accept that as a defined term."

"Your people will figure it out. This is recorded, and I'm confident that any professional soldier will understand what I'm saying." I fake-smiled for whoever else was watching. It was the clearest thing I could say without specifically telling them that if they got too close, we were going to smash them.

"We find that you're purposely antagonizing us," she said. "Your actions are inappropriate."

"Antagonizing you how?"

"You're putting restrictions on us that aren't part of the treaty."

"The treaty says I'm to keep the peace between you and the Zargod. That's what I'm doing. I'd prefer to do it in a different way—I'd really like it if we could work together. If you want to be helpful, help me figure out who really attacked your infrastructure. Let my people help you find them. When we do that, we'll both know, and it will solve a lot of problems."

She stayed silent for at least a full minute, and in my head, I pictured an argument among her handlers. Perhaps one of them was advocating to take me up on my offer. A woman can dream, anyway. When she finally spoke, though, that dream ended. "We are not going to give you that sort of access to our network until we can determine for sure that you're not going to use that against us."

"What would it take for you to believe that?"

"I don't know," she said immediately. Then she cringed, and the feed cut off.

I considered what I'd just seen, and I thought that maybe someone had chastised her through whatever mechanism they had for that last answer she gave. The speed of her answer meant it was her own, and not her superiors', and the answer itself told me that she was frustrated with the situation. And this time I really did believe that the frustration might be with her own side. I considered calling back, taking fake blame for cutting the connection accidentally, but I decided against it. I couldn't know if calling back would hurt or help Trieste's position, and I figured she had a better chance of dealing with it if I didn't interfere. Besides, if they were having internal doubts and disagreements, it wouldn't hurt to give them time to fester. Maybe they'd come around to working together against the real threat.

I thought some more about Tangent. If they were trying to cause the war, what would they do now that they had gotten the forces arrayed in the field? I didn't like the answer I came to. Because they wouldn't restrict themselves to outside action. They could easily have people inside the government, or at a minimum have ways to put pressure on them. Especially in a country like Argaz where corruption was treated with a wink and a nod, even on a good day. What I needed was a team to analyze the political influences at play in both countries. Might as well wish for a magic spaceship.

But that, along with what Xiang had said the night before, got me thinking. If Tangent really was the enemy, how did I attack them? If the Argazzi wouldn't help, maybe I could go after them on the Zargod side. I didn't know what that looked like either, but it seemed like a better option than sitting on my ass in a stalemate for the next month.

I contacted Ops and reviewed the parameters we had and the criteria for which they should immediately contact me, no matter what I was doing, just in case the Argazzi tried something. With that done, I unplugged from the combat networks. I sat there for a minute or two, waiting. I don't know why, or what I expected to happen. Of course, nothing did. Nothing had changed. I'd delegated authority, and it was going to be fine. There was no need for me to be physically there on the battlefield. I could control the entire war from my office if I had to. The only thing that kept me rooted to my current location was tradition. Leaders went with the led, shared their burdens and their risks. They just did.

But this was anything but a traditional situation, and I wasn't being as effective as I could. At the same time, I wasn't sure how much damage Perston had done to my reputation with the soldiers, and if I left the field, that would be one more thing they could point to if they were so inclined. That's the thing with soldiers. If they trust you, they'll cut you all the slack in the world. If they don't, they won't spare you a centimeter.

I got on the comm and contacted the person who would know best.

"Yes, ma'am," Hearns answered immediately. He was at his desk, alert, and ready for my call. I hadn't needed him in the field, and I wanted him back there, keeping an eye on things on base while I was otherwise occupied.

"I need your advice on something." I laid it out to him, what I wanted to do, and he listened patiently, asking only a couple of clarifying questions. What he wanted to know was what I had planned. How I was going to get after the enemy.

When I'd finished, he sat there for a bit, contemplating. "Give me an hour, ma'am. Let me get my crew together and I'll come out there and take your spot. Once I do, you go do your thing."

"You think that will help?"

"I'll make it help," he said. "I can take care of it."

I wanted to ask him how he was going to manage the situation, but the way he said that he had it meant that if I asked, it would come across as questioning him, and not in a good way. I couldn't do that, so I let it go. "Sounds good. Bring me an escort platoon when you come."

"Roger that, ma'am."

"We ride in about an hour," I told my crew.

The idea for finding a link came from the thought that there was someone influencing the Argazzi government to cause them to give us trouble. Which got me thinking about other things that gave us trouble. And that's how I ended up, unannounced, at the compound of Father Romero. They held us up at the gate for a couple of minutes, probably scrambling to get ready for us, but they couldn't hold me outside indefinitely. I wanted to surprise him. I had questions, and I didn't want to give him any time to prepare.

Arthur and his brother met us in the courtyard, and the two of them along with Xiang and Gonzalez walked me into the office wing.

"It's not polite to visit without calling first," said Romero, his hands wide away from his body in greeting.

"I apologize. This aggressive action by the Argazzi has kept me very busy, and I didn't have time. I needed help, so I thought I would turn to my friends." Not a word of that was true, but it had the intended effect, as he smiled and visibly relaxed.

"Of course. We are your friends. The Argazzi...*pfft*." He stopped short of making a rude gesture, but he meant it. And that was good; I could use that.

I wanted to get him talking about Tangent and their influence so that I could read him and assess his own relationship with them. But I couldn't come right out and accuse him. I had no evidence beyond the fact that he'd engineered the protest at my base, although he'd also ended it. Still, I needed to get the truth from him, and the best way to do that was to exploit his adversarial relationship with the Argazzi. "My intelligence shows that there are outside forces manipulating the Argazzi."

His face remained unreadable, even with help from my implant. "Come, we will sit." He turned to his nephews. "Bring wine." I followed him into the inner office and took a seat that he offered on the sofa while he went around behind his large desk.

I didn't care for the delay, because I suspected he was using the time to figure out his response, but what was I going to do? We waited for wine, and I did my best to be patient. After I'd finished about half of the small cup, the senior father asked me to tell him my thoughts.

"As I said, our intelligence shows that outside forces are influencing the Argazzi to take the military action that they have." I didn't have any intel on that—it was just a hunch—but he'd have no choice but to take me at my word.

"Who would do such a thing? Not our country."

"No, of course not. That wouldn't make any sense. You are as much the victim here as I am."

He smiled and nodded. "Then who?"

"I believe that a corporation is bribing officials to cause problems for us."

"Really?" he asked, but he wasn't as unaware of that as he pretended to be. His heart rate had increased. He was hiding something.

I decided to push him a little and see what came of it. There was a risk, in that we'd come to a reasonable working relationship, and if I pissed him off, I put that in jeopardy. But the reward was worth it if I found out more about Tangent. "Yes. We're sure of it. And what's more, the same sources have bribed Zargod officials to cause problems as well."

Romero licked his lips, and his heartbeat was up over one-thirty now, and he wasn't a young man. He definitely knew something. "What types of trouble? Certainly you don't think we bombed our own marketplace."

"I don't know…maybe. Perhaps also the bombing of the space elevator?" I didn't believe the Zargod to be responsible for either of those things, but by accusing his people—or, at least, not exonerating them—I hoped to get him to cop to a lesser offense.

"That's not possible!" He almost came out of his chair.

"Why not? How could you know that?"

He hesitated for a split second. "I'm just sure of it."

"I don't see how you could be," I said. "Either way, I'm going to find the influence, and I'm going to hold the people responsible accountable for those crimes."

His eyes darted around like he wanted to escape. I didn't even need my implant to read his emotions at that point.

I let him stew for another fifteen or twenty seconds before I threw him a lifeline. "Of course, I'd be happy to forgive anybody involved if they worked with me—if they proved their friendship."

He started to speak—I had him—but then he stopped and thought. He sat fully back into his chair and began to calm himself. "I see what you're doing," he said, finally.

I turned my palms up and gave him my best sheepish grin. "It's a serious situation. I had to do what I had to do."

He considered that, taking his wine cup deliberately and draining what was left in it to buy himself some time. "That's not how a friend would act."

He was right, but he wasn't innocent. It was time to play my hand and see what happened. "You've not always acted as a friend, either."

He didn't get indignant with me, which was a good sign. Perhaps we were done playing games. "What are you accusing me of?"

"Someone influenced you to have the people protest outside of my gate."

"You shot and injured a child."

"We did. And someone influenced you to have people protest outside my gate." I paused, but he didn't respond. "Didn't they?"

He paused for a while longer, to the point where I thought that he wasn't going to tell me, but then he sighed and his shoulders slumped. "I was not paid."

When he didn't continue, I prompted him, "But…"

"But yes, I was asked to have the people protest."

"Why would you do that? If you weren't paid, were you threatened?"

"Not precisely. He was a powerful man. Better to have him owe me a favor instead of making him my enemy."

"But you were okay with making an enemy out of me."

"You're an outsider. It's not the same. And next year, you'll be gone and someone else will be here and it won't matter."

I wanted to be mad, but he was right. As much as we kept continuity files on things, they rarely got read, and each new commander would form opinions based on their own personality and biases, even if their predecessor specifically warned them against it. It was part of what made us great—individual initiative. It also made us inefficient. "I need to know who it was."

He considered it for a while before finally speaking. "The Prime Minister."

I sighed. Shit. The most important politician in the entire country save for the king himself was involved. I had no chance at all of putting pressure on him. I'd be lucky to even talk to him. And I couldn't ask Father Romero to set something up because that would be like putting a glowing target on him for having told me in the first place. So I'd come to a dead end.

Think, Markov. For the PM to involve himself in something local like our shooting of the child was a clear sign of outside influence. *How* he himself was involved was less clear. He may have given the order without even realizing why. From his perspective, it was pretty innocuous. Taking a bribe to create trouble for me wouldn't even count as corruption in Zargod. That was just business. And that bribe could have come from anywhere. I still needed to act, and there might be a way I could use the information I'd received. But it was clear that I wasn't going to use it there at Father Romero's office.

"Thank you for your time and for the information, Senior Father."

"What are you going to do with what you know?" He might as well have asked, *how much trouble are you going to bring down on my head?*

"I don't know. Probably nothing. What can I do?"

"Indeed."

I decided to reassure him. After all, he could have held back the information and he didn't. That was showing trust in our relationship. The least I could do was show the same. "I will do my best to make sure that nothing leads back to you."

He nodded once, but otherwise didn't respond, which was fine. We understood each other.

21

Back at headquarters, I gathered Captain Song and the heads of all the relevant departments together in the big conference room for a brainstorming session. I hated to take Song off of finding a way to communicate off-planet, but I had to prioritize, and the Argazzi threat was too great to ignore. Song *was* Argazzi, and having her there helped emphasize the message I wanted to get across to my unit.

"The Argazzi aren't the enemy," I began, and anybody who wasn't paying full attention before woke up with that bomb. "It is my belief that there's an outside actor that, for whatever reason, is trying to cause a war on this planet. I believe that outside actor to be affiliated with Tangent Holding Company, but I'm not willing to go on the record with that without proof. Hard proof. Right now, what we have is circumstantial."

"Ma'am?" One of the techs put his hand up tentatively.

"What's up, Carpana?" Corporal Carpana was one of the new additions to Berghof's team.

"We have two separate attacks using equipment from the same company, and we have the hack of the helmet via a backdoor. To me, that's pretty close to a smoking gun just on those three things."

"I need something that will hold up to Argazzi questioning. They're going to be difficult to convince. If I bring them that, they will—correctly —say that anybody could have employed the drones and military equipment, regardless of who built them originally. The helmet hack is a little harder to explain away, but it's not enough on its own." The tech had shrunken into his chair, so I tried to soften the blow. "But that's a fair point, and I'm glad you brought it up. What I want to do now is break things into two categories: What do we have for evidence, and what do we need for absolute proof? Corporal Carpana listed a lot of what we have. What else have we got?"

"Ma'am, we have a couple of partial fingerprints from the debris from the attack against our team that was headed to the space elevator," said Sergeant First Class Delany, from Intel Analysis.

"Excellent!" I said. "Do we have a database of prints to compare it against?"

"Well...uh...not legally."

"Tell me," I said.

"Cyber says that we can hack into the criminal database of the Zargod police and that their security is laughable. That would at least allow us to run what we have against known Zargod criminals."

I considered it. The risk if we got caught was significant. I wanted to talk to the Prime Minister, but not about that. With the Argazzi already agitated from a cyberattack, the last thing I needed was the Zargod pissed as well. And as a bonus, it would make the Argazzi believe even more that we were behind their problems.

"Cyber, what's the risk of getting caught if we do this?"

"Minimal, ma'am," said Sergeant Alexie without hesitating, and then he thought about it for a couple seconds. "Less than one percent that we're detected. Another order of magnitude beyond that of them tying it to us."

"Do it," I said. The upside was limited because the criminal database wouldn't include off-world actors unless they had an on-planet record. But I wanted to send a message to everyone sitting at the table. We were going to get aggressive and take this fight to the real enemy. I wanted that attitude to permeate the command, and it had to start with me. "As soon as we have names, let me know. We'll decide if we can go roll them up or not after we find them. What else do we have?"

"We've also got a signature on the explosives from the bombing of the space elevator, ma'am," said Delany.

"That's good. What can we do with that?"

"In theory, we can compare it to the inventory of potential suppliers and commercial sources on-planet to see if it came from here or someone shipped it in especially for the job."

"You say *in theory* because we don't have access to that data, either, right?"

"That's correct," said Delany. "But it's something that authorities in any country would have pretty easy access to, I'd imagine. It's commonly tracked for exactly this purpose."

"We could hack into that too," offered Alexie.

"Let's do this one by the book," I said. "The attack on the space elevator affects everybody, so there should be motivation for both sides to help us. Can anyone think why they wouldn't?"

"Yes, ma'am," said Captain Song. "If the source came from inside one country or the other, that country might not want that known for fear of blame falling on them, even if they as a government weren't involved." She'd done a nice job of keeping that neutral. It *did* apply to both countries.

"Good point," I said. "Let's still do it through formal request. Draft something for me to send to the Zargod. Make sure that it impresses on them the need for haste, and that we want to work together on this without blame. We just want to find whoever is responsible. Captain Song, I'd like you to make the request to the Argazzi. You can say it's from me, but I feel like with you asking we've got a better chance than with me doing it. They don't like me much right now."

"That's true, ma'am. I'll get right on it."

"What else do we have?" I waited long enough for even the most timid of the staff to speak up, but nobody did. "Okay. So what do we need? Or even better...what do we want?"

Alexie spoke up first. "We want to know who made the cyberattack on the Argazzi infrastructure."

"Can we find out? What would it take?" I asked.

"We can try, ma'am. We'd have to go into their network and see if we could find something residual."

"Won't they have already done that?" I asked.

"Yes, ma'am. For sure."

"How much better are we going to be at it than them?"

"For this particular thing? Quite a bit. It was almost certainly something sophisticated."

"Risk?" I asked.

"High, ma'am. They're going to be on the lookout for incursions into this network."

"Okay. That's a no," I said. I glanced at Song, who remained expressionless. I'd just contemplated an attack against her country, and she hadn't blinked. It wasn't a real attack, but they'd take it as one, and it would immediately escalate the war. "I've offered our help on this to them and they rejected it. I'll continue to offer it. So be prepared. But we don't go into the Argazzi network without their approval. Not for any reason. Everyone clear?"

A chorus of "Yes, ma'am's" responded.

"Any chance we can get prints off of the drone from the market?" I asked.

"No, ma'am," said Delany. "The folks that found the fragments put their hands all over it. It's got plenty of prints, but there's no way to link it to the source."

"Okay. Anything else?" I wanted to yell, tell them it wasn't enough. That none of this was going to get me what I needed. Instead I stood and departed.

I couldn't yell at them or even complain to them. It wasn't their fault, and it wasn't their place to listen to me whine. We couldn't manufacture evidence, and we weren't a law enforcement agency that could go out and detain people for questioning. We were stuck with looking into military things within our authority while the other side, whoever they were, wasn't bound by any such limitations. It was classic in that regard. Non-traditional enemies had been giving conventional forces fits for as long as military history could remember.

If nothing else, it gave me some empathy for some of those past commanders that I'd studied at the academy. I'd always wondered how forces got themselves bogged down and beaten by technologically inferior enemies. But I couldn't think like that. We weren't beaten—not yet. Someone was pushing us toward war, but they hadn't accomplished it. And I couldn't give up. I probably wasn't going to get enough evidence to convince the Argazzi, which meant I didn't hold a winning hand. And when you couldn't go to showdown on the strength of your hand, you had two options. You could fold or bluff. And I wasn't going to fold.

Once I decided that, the weight came off me. Because I *was* decided. I wasn't going to sit there and just let this happen without trying to stop it. So the question came down to who to bluff, and how. I hadn't discussed it with the staff; they didn't need to know. If I kept them in the dark, then nobody could prosecute them for anything later. They'd have total deniability. And I certainly couldn't share it with Captain Song. I trusted her to an extent, but not with something like this. I'd let them work on the legit missions that I gave them, and I'd take on the dangerous part myself.

But I had to tell somebody, and for this, my crew wasn't going to suffice. There was only one person it could be. I had to tell Hearns. And I had to tell him in such a way that he bought into it. If I couldn't sell him on my plan, I'd need to reconsider. It wasn't that I had to have his approval, it was that I needed an outside opinion. I was playing a hunch, but even in my own head, it seemed a little reckless.

I wanted to talk to him face to face, so I loaded up and we headed back out to the field site and found him eating cold rations on the hood of his vehicle, right about where we'd slept the previous night.

"How can you eat those cold?" I asked, walking up and leaning on the opposite side of the hood.

"I don't know, ma'am. Habit, I guess. You want a meal?"

"I'm good. We grabbed food at base before we rolled back out. How did it go out here today?"

"Good, good. We got some good training in, especially with the tanks. Simulations are great, but there's no substitute for racing around the countryside in formation."

"That's good. I think we'll be out here for a while." I wanted to ask him how his talk with the other noncoms had gone, but I didn't want to seem too eager for the information.

Probably sensing that, Hearns bailed me out. "I told people why you were going back to the rear so they wouldn't think you were shamming."

"Yeah? They buy it?"

"Mostly, I think so. There are always a few assholes, but you're never going to make them happy anyway."

"What did you tell them I was doing?"

"That was easy. I told them you were trying to win. That it was officer shit that was above their paygrade, but that we absolutely needed you to do it."

"They bought that?"

"Oh, yes, ma'am. That's an easy sell to line troopers because most of what you do is magic to them in the first place. They want to believe that their leaders are doing the things they need to do to win, and it's easy to convince somebody that the thing they want to believe is true."

"Thanks for that."

"Don't sweat it, ma'am. You've earned it."

It felt good to hear him say that, and it almost made me feel bad that I was going to try to capitalize on that sentiment immediately. "Walk with me a minute."

Hearns understood that I wanted to talk to him away from curious ears without me saying it. He gathered the remnants of his cold meal and tossed it into a recycling bag, then followed me away from our vehicles. "It's about what you said about trying to win."

He stopped near me, and we both kept our backs to our vehicles, angled toward each other. "What about it, ma'am?"

"This" —I gestured at our units arrayed around us—"isn't winning."

"I don't know, ma'am. If they come for us, I like our odds."

"That's my point, though. *If* they come for us. That gives them all the initiative. All we can do is sit here and wait to respond to them."

"Sometimes that happens," Hearns said. "Sometimes you have to let the other guy throw the first punch before you deck him."

"What if we didn't?"

"I don't think we should strike first, if that's what you're saying. Don't get me wrong; it would give us a better shot at winning. But it's also probably *really* illegal. I'm all for bending the rules, but that?"

"You're right that it would help us win; I've run all the numbers. But that's not what I'm talking about. I'm talking about going after our real enemy, which isn't the Argazzi and isn't the Zargod."

"I got you. You want to go after the corporation that makes the drones. I'd be all for that if they'd show themselves. But I'm not sure how we'd do it here on-planet."

"I've got a plan, Sergeant. It's aggressive, but I think it gives us a chance."

"Okay." His tone made it clear that it was "okay, I'm listening," not "okay, go for it."

"When I pushed on the senior father about why he had the crowds picketing our base, he admitted that he'd been directed to do it from on high. From the prime minister, to be exact."

"You believe him?"

"*He* believed it. I can tell you that much for sure. I don't know if he talked to the prime minister directly or through an intermediary. Probably the second one."

"So what does that do for us?" he asked. "We obviously can't go after the prime minister."

"What if we could?"

Hearns started to interrupt, but I held my hand up to forestall him.

THE WEIGHT OF COMMAND

"Not directly. I'm not going to try to arrest him or anything. But I do want to poke him and see what happens. He's got no reason to be worried about what happens at our base, yet he was. In my mind, that means someone pressured him."

"That's thin, ma'am. But say I buy it. How are you going to get after him?"

"There's only one person in Zarga who outranks the prime minister."

"The king? You want to get at the PM by going to the king?"

"Exactly. Normally, the military commanders of the mission don't engage with the national leadership of Zarga. I don't know that the colonel even *met* the king."

"He attended one function, early on, where the king was in attendance. They didn't speak."

"Thanks for the perspective. But this isn't a normal situation. This is a national crisis. If the Argazzi attack, it affects all of Zarga, not just the local area. And the ramifications from that attack, win or lose, *definitely* will have repercussions for years, or even decades."

"I don't know, ma'am. It's a lot."

"Hold on. Hear me out. I started thinking about this as a no-win situation, and I asked myself what the colonel would have done, if he was still alive. What we'd have done if we had our entire complement of officers. Let me ask you…do you think he'd have sat here staring across the border, waiting?"

Hearns considered it for a time. "No, ma'am. He definitely would not have. I think he'd have gone to the Argazzi and bullied them into standing down. He'd have threatened them and been willing to back it up."

"I agree. And I think he'd have been successful. Now…do you think that same strategy would work for *me*?" I knew the answer, because I'd tried it and it hadn't worked, but I wanted him to come to that on his own.

Again, he considered it. He was taking me seriously on this, and I appreciated it; it would have been easy for him to dismiss the idea outright. "You'd certainly have a lot tougher time, being younger and not having other officers to back you up."

"Right," I agreed. "Given my interactions with the Argazzi to date, I'd say almost zero chance. Because I tried. I dropped all their recon assets in our airspace, and they didn't back off a bit."

"I heard about that, ma'am. That helped your reputation with the soldiers, by the way."

I laughed. "I bet if I punched some politician in the neck, they'd build me a statue."

"Might be true." Hearns smiled. "So what's your point? About the colonel."

"If we agree that it's ineffective for me to threaten the Argazzi, and we agree that the colonel wouldn't sit here and just wait for something to happen, then the logical solution is that he'd have done something else. That's what I want to do. I want to go to the king, tell him that I have evidence against his prime minister, and use *him* to help convince the Argazzi to back off."

He pursed his lips, not buying something in what I said. "I see a couple issues with that, ma'am."

"Tell me. Be honest. That's why I'm here talking to you about it."

"First, how do you get to talk to the king?"

"I have a plan for—"

"And second," he said, cutting me off, "and more important…do you think that the king would have any influence over the Argazzi at all?"

"Is that all?" I asked, not wanting to interrupt again.

"For now, ma'am."

"To answer your first question, I lie to him. I tell him that I need to talk to him about the potential Argazzi attack, and I add on details to that as necessary. Once he agrees to the meeting, I blindside him with the accusation about the PM."

"Okay. That could work. And if it doesn't, you haven't lost anything."

"Exactly. All he can do is say no. Or, worse, try to foist me off on that useless general. But I'll deal with that if it happens." I took a couple steps and turned to face Hearns directly. "To your second point, no, the king can't directly influence the Argazzi. But if I can get him to admit to them that his own people have been compromised by outside influences, it might put enough doubt in the minds of the Argazzi about their own situation—or, if not that, maybe get them pointing fingers at each other internally—then maybe they'll reconsider their current position."

Hearns interlaced his fingers and bent them back, cracking a knuckle. He considered what I said for long enough that I wondered if he was going to speak at all. "I don't think it's going to work. I don't think the king would share that with the other side, even if it's true."

My heart sank. Without his support, I didn't think I'd be able to pull it off.

"But," he added, "I also don't see a downside. I mean, what happens if you take a swing at this and miss? The king tells you to fuck off? He can't arrest you, so what else can he do? I guess he can make it harder for us to operate here in Zarga or consider withdrawing from the treaty down the road. But those risks are small and in the future. This cold war with the Argazzi is here and now."

"So you think I should do it?" His words about the future made me wonder if he suspected what consequences I'd face after all this was done. I considered what he said about the treaty. Could the king really end it? Well...maybe. But the treaty kept the Argazzi from attacking the Zargod more than the other way around. He needed us. He could hem and haw and make official statements. Maybe he'd demand my relief. But that was happening anyway as soon as reinforcements arrived.

"I think we stand to gain more than we'd lose, ma'am. Yeah. I think you should go for it. What do we have to lose?"

I smiled. Famous last words.

22

It was the next morning before I heard back from the king's people. Getting a meeting turned out to be easier than I had anticipated. I guess an impending war would do that. They set it up for 1600 hours the same day, which I figured meant it was important enough that he had rearranged his schedule to accommodate me. That was either really good or really bad, and I probably wouldn't know until I was standing in front of him.

We couldn't make the seven-hundred-kilometer drive to the capital, so I put my people on the task of clearing our transport aircraft for a landing at the king's private air pad. It would leave us there completely without support, which wasn't ideal, but if the king wished harm upon us, there probably wasn't anything we could do about it anyway. That did seem unlikely. I also had them arrange for an aerial relay, so we could maintain communications while we were there in case something went down and I needed to command my forces. That seemed more likely.

I met with the leaders of each battalion so they could see my face and I could give guidance. On the drive back to base, I got another call from Deputy Minister Trieste, which I took in my vehicle. As always, she looked like a perfectly tailored model.

"Hello, Kiera. I trust that there were no issues with our exercise movements yesterday." I noticed that she used my first name, maybe in an attempt to restore some of the lost trust between us. It didn't work.

"No issues," I agreed. They had moved out from their positions into a defensive set, but they hadn't come anywhere near my red line in terms of positioning. It also gave me a look at what they might do if I decided to launch a cross-border ground attack, and while I didn't have any immediate plans for that, I'd never turn down intel.

"Very good," she said. "This afternoon we are beginning the offensive phase of our exercise. You'll see more movement."

We were pulling into the gate of the base and I really wanted to get a shower before I got on the transport, so I tried to hurry her along. "That's fine. My warning from yesterday still stands. Do you need anything else from me?"

She hesitated. "No, we just wanted you to be aware so you're not surprised."

"Got it. Thanks." I cut the call and hopped out of the vehicle.

Freshly showered and in a new uniform, I boarded the transport for the hour-long flight to the capital with my crew. I didn't need all four of them, but they wanted to come—traveling to a different part of the country rated as exciting in the world of a soldier—and I had twelve seats, not including the pilot and co-pilot, so space wasn't an issue. I charged Gonzalez with carrying the portable comms rig, which would link with the aerial relay and allow for high-bandwidth operations. With it, I'd be able to command and control all of our combat assets, no matter where we were.

I exited first when we landed on the roof of a wing of the capitol building in the city of Stratford. The whine of the engines died as the pilot shut them down, and I squinted against the bright sunlight. A welcoming party stood at a safe distance and began to approach once they saw me. There were seven of them, including what looked like four armed guards, which seemed like overkill given that we were inside the capital compound and hundreds of klicks from the nearest enemy. I guess they were there for us, either because they saw us as a threat or thought that they'd intimidate me.

They had it wrong. Guards didn't intimidate me. I could handle them. Standing in front of an actual fucking monarch and trying to get international policy right? *That* intimidated me.

I waited at the base of the ramp, allowing them to come to me. I didn't know the protocol for this sort of thing, so I figured I'd let them lead. Two men left the rest of their party behind and approached within a couple of meters.

"Major Markov," said the shorter of the two men. He had dark hair, a little longer than most Zargod, and a sharp, oversized nose. "Welcome to the capital. His Majesty, Robert Yannich the Fourth, sends his regards."

"Thank you for setting this up on such short notice. I'm sorry we're early. I wasn't sure how long the transit would take from the landing pad to the king's office...throne room?"

"Office," said the man. That was a little disappointing.

"Right. I didn't want to keep him waiting." Sweat was starting to drip down my face in the heat, though the cool air from the ship blowing on my back helped.

"It's no problem at all," he said. "We have about an hour to spare, but we have refreshments in the lounge inside. You can wait there."

"Thank you."

"You speak our language very well. I guess I didn't need the interpreter." He gestured to the taller man beside him.

"Thanks. I've been practicing." He didn't need to know that my implant did the work.

"If you wouldn't mind..." He looked at me as if he had something unpleasant to say, but hesitated to broach it.

"What can I do for you?"

He gestured to my sidearm. "Your weapon. Please leave that on the transport. It's not allowed in the presence of the king."

I considered it for just a second. Peacekeeping soldiers didn't give up their weapons under the treaty, but if there was going to be an exception to that, this seemed like the right time. I unstrapped my leg rig, and Zilla came down the ramp to take it from me. "Thanks," I told her. "Murphy, Gonzalez, you're with me. Leave your weapons. The rest of you don't get into any trouble." I didn't want Gonzalez more than thirty seconds away from me. If I needed the comm, I'd need it in a hurry. Murphy was the best unarmed fighter on the crew, and if we couldn't have weapons, he was my best asset. Not that I expected things would come to a hand-to-hand fight inside the capitol building, but you could never be too prepared. It took the two soldiers a minute to join me, and I stood awkwardly with the waiting envoy.

The time in the lounge passed quickly, with Murphy trying fifteen or so different kinds of finger foods that they'd set out for us. I didn't mind.

It made up for me not eating any of them. I stuck to water, my stomach a little unsettled from nerves.

The king's office was bigger than it looked on video when I'd seen him giving addresses—an octagon that was almost twenty meters across. He sat behind a huge polished-wood desk, standing when I entered and walking around it to greet me. An aide or other functionary stood behind and to the left of the desk, and the man who had met me when I landed had followed me into the room along with a photographer.

"Welcome, Major Markov." The king didn't offer his hand, so I didn't offer mine. I did smile, though, assuming that the pictures would make it to a news outlet in the near future. It made me glad I'd changed into a clean uniform before I came. He was my height, and I met his eyes. He was bald on top with hair on the sides and back in a classic horseshoe pattern, but he was one of those guys where it looked good on him. He had the weathered skin of a man who spends time outside, and it made it impossible to tell his age. He looked about sixty, but I knew from my data that he was a decade and a half older than that.

"Thank you for seeing me, your majesty."

"Please. Take a seat." He gestured to two wooden chairs upholstered in green leather in front of his desk but didn't wait to see if I took one before moving back around to his big chair behind the desk. After he settled himself in, he adjusted the hang of his suit jacket in front and centered himself deliberately with the desk. The envoy took the chair next to me without being directed, and the aide behind the desk took out a tablet as if to take notes. I guess I wasn't getting a private meeting. Without anybody saying anything, a well-dressed man appeared with three small cups of wine on what looked like a real silver tray. The aide apparently didn't rate wine. It was his loss, because as good as I thought Father Romero's wine was, this was better. But unlike Romero, the king barely took time to taste it before he jumped into business.

"You asked to meet," said the king. "I assume that it's about the enemy forces massing on our border."

I smiled and tried to look grateful for the meeting, though I could almost feel the derision coming off of him. I decided not to take that personally. Maybe kings looked down on everybody. "Yes. Forgive me for coming to you with this, but your military leader—"

"Is a moron," said the king, saving me from having to be tactful about it.

I hesitated, unsure how to continue without agreeing. "Pardon me for asking, but if you think that, why do you keep him in charge?"

He lowered his voice a little as if we were co-conspirators. "Having a strong leader who commands the loyalty of the military is a good way to end a monarchy. And we're not planning to fight a war. That's why we have your forces."

I nodded, unsure what else to do. The explanation didn't surprise me, but the fact that he came out and said it so bluntly did. I decided I should get back to a topic where I was comfortable. "Speaking of war, the Argazzi claim that they are conducting an exercise, and as of yet, there's no evidence to suggest that they're not. I'm watching them closely."

"Exercise." He waved his hand as if to shoo it away. "They are lying."

"I tend to agree with you."

He started to say something else, but stopped, looking at me confused, as if he couldn't believe that I'd agreed. It really seemed to throw him off of his engagement plan, and we sat in silence for several seconds. "Is that why you came? To tell me that you agreed?"

"No. But I did expect I'd need to address that situation before getting to my real purpose. I do want to be clear, that what I believe about the Argazzi and what I can prove are two different things, and without proof, I'm only able to take limited action."

"What proof would you require?"

"I'm not going to answer that, but"—I held my hand up, to forestall the interruption that was poised on his lips—"I have deployed my forces into a defensive posture, and I took aggressive action to eliminate Argazzi assets working illegally in your airspace."

After a few seconds, he nodded, apparently satisfied with that. "Tell me this, Major Markov. It is the most important question. Can you protect the Zargod people if the Argazzi attack?" It was the question I wanted him to ask because it was going to give me the transition I needed.

"I am not going to answer that," I said, and this time he didn't try to interrupt, instead waiting for me to explain. "I'm hesitant to give specific information about my plan or our capabilities, because—and I hate to say this, your majesty, because it is a harsh thing—there are too many leaks in your government. I trust *you* of course. You're a man who serves the people. But not all of your officials are on your level." I gave him my most sincere look as I laid on the bullshit. Mrs. Zukov would have been proud of me.

THE WEIGHT OF COMMAND

He didn't respond right away, and I prepared for him to erupt at me, but instead, he started nodding his head slowly. "This is unfortunate. A sad thing for our country." He paused. "But it is true."

"No, your majesty!" said the man next to me.

"It is true!" he shouted. He looked at the man, not me, which was about the best I could hope for, though I didn't know that he was specifically the problem. "Everybody, out. All of you. Major Markov and I will speak alone."

"But your majesty," said the aide standing behind him, "what will people say? The impropriety—"

"Out!" Despite his firm demand, his two subordinates took their time collecting themselves before departing, as if they had seen this sort of outburst before and expected their boss to change his mind at any moment. He didn't. He waited for the room to clear, and then got up and checked the door himself to make sure that they'd closed it behind them.

"Now. It's just you and me." He said it as a prompt for me to tell him about the defense of his nation, and I was going to do that. Just maybe not in the way that he expected.

"Thank you for doing that. The thing that I need to tell you is quite sensitive," I began. He was almost leaning forward in his seat, so eager was he to hear my secret information. Maybe I was finally figuring out how to get these guys on my side. "We have an unseen enemy."

He drew his lips into a tight line, and then into a frown. Apparently, that's not what he expected me to say. "I don't understand."

"The reason that the Argazzi are posturing their forces is because they were attacked. Somebody targeted their electrical infrastructure with a computer attack. They think it was us."

"So they are angry with you, and not us." Like many of his countrymen, he had the question that doesn't sound like a question thing down.

"Perhaps. Perhaps they're using it as a pretense to attack you. We can't really say for sure what they're doing."

"But it's your fault." I couldn't tell if he was missing the point deliberately or accidentally. It didn't matter. I wouldn't be baited into going down that path.

"The thing that is important here, your majesty, is that we didn't do it. And we know that *you* didn't do it. But still there was an attack. If it wasn't either of us, the only logical conclusion is that there is somebody else involved."

He considered it. I don't think he believed me completely, but he seemed ready to at least hear me out. "Then who was it?"

"I believe that there is a corporation that is trying to create conflict between you and the Argazzi in order to stop mineral production here on the planet so that they can drive up prices and make a bigger profit."

This he seemed to understand, as he nodded. But he remained silent.

"This is where I need your help," I continued. "In order to end this without bloodshed, I need to find the real criminals and stop them. But I'm afraid that the corporation has influence within your government at high levels."

"You have proof of this?" That he didn't get defensive was a good sign. He understood that I didn't mean him, and it appeared that he believed what I was saying was possible.

"Not physical proof. But I suspect someone strongly. I don't know if he is part of the conspiracy, or if he was just bribed to take on a particular task."

"Tell me. Who is it, and how do you know?"

"The prime minister. He influenced the people around my base to protest, disrupting my operations right after the nuclear event."

He sat there silent for some time, and I let him process the information. "I believe this. I will have him detained and questioned. We will find out how he is involved."

Now it was my turn to sit there stunned. Of all the things I expected when I got this meeting, immediate acceptance and assistance weren't even on my list of best possible outcomes. I glanced at the king, who sat with a suspiciously smug look on his face. He didn't look like a man who had just learned that his most important official had been accused of a crime. And then it dawned on me. The king wasn't thinking about the country, and he definitely wasn't thinking about me. I'd just handed him a way to discredit a political rival. And for a moment, I'd thought that I was being so clever. I considered trying to walk it back, but it was likely too late for that. Besides, I *did* suspect the PM, and it seemed as if the king was going to help me gather more information about him.

I could deal with the havoc I'd likely caused in the Zargod political landscape *after* I got answers and stopped a war.

"Thank you for your help, your majesty. The faster you can get answers for me, the better chance I have to end this confrontation at the border."

"No problem. I will wait a few hours after you leave to initiate the plan. That way people will not immediately assume that it is you telling me to do it."

That made sense. Finally, we might get somewhere with Tangent. I started to respond to the king, but a warning went off in my implant, so I took a second to access it. There were alerts from both staff and sensor AIs. I almost reset them to focus on the man in front of me, but something told me to check the details.

Shit.

The Argazzi had crossed my warning lines with their offensive systems. I checked the details that the staff had provided, which linked me to the right live video feeds, and found that they'd come across in three places and weren't stopping. They weren't in attack range yet, but it would happen in a matter of minutes if they kept up their current movement. I shunted it all to the back of my mind and turned to the king, who had to wonder what was going on. "Your majesty, I need a place to set up a comms system. Immediately." Simultaneously, I summoned Gonzalez via my comms.

"Why? What's happening?"

Before I could answer, Gonzalez burst through the door, one of the king's guards shouting at him that he couldn't go in there.

"The Argazzi are moving. I don't have time to discuss it. I need to talk to them now."

Something in my tone must have gotten through to him because he sprung into action. He pushed the button on the comm unit on his desk. "Get Major Markov a desk immediately. Make sure she has all types of communications access." I didn't need that last part, but I didn't want to slow things down so I let it go.

"Yes sir," responded a male voice. "She can access from my desk if that's sufficient."

He looked at me.

"Anything, as long as it's fast," I said.

"Through that door." He pointed to the door where his aide had disappeared, not the one through which I'd entered.

I stood and ran for it. Gonzales followed without being told. I didn't have much time, and I didn't know how long it would take me to get through to someone in authority. I hoped that was Trieste, but I doubted it. I'd have rather gone to my transport and handled it in private, but it was at least a seven- or eight-minute trip, and that was if I got out cleanly without anyone trying to stop me or talk to me, even if they were just being polite and trying to say goodbye. The battle could be lost by then. The King of Zarga's outer office wasn't a great option, but at least I'd get there quickly.

I paused at the door and fired a message off to Staff Sergeant Chao, telling her to get Trieste on the comm and get prepared to port it to my system once Gonzalez set it up. I sent a second message to Zilla, telling her to warn the aircraft to be ready to move if I had to head that way.

A man was sliding out of his seat at one of five desks in a large, well-appointed office done in the same style as the king's, but a little cheaper. People scrambled out of my way as I bowled my way to the desk and slid into the seat. Gonzalez shoved a bunch of stuff out of the way and hit the initialize button on the system. Then time stopped. The twelve seconds it took to put itself into operation seemed like minutes as we waited. I took a second to adjust the chair to my height while I waited.

As soon as the green light came on showing it as active, I messaged my unit leaders, giving them a warning to bring all systems to full combat readiness. The screen remained blank, waiting for Chao to get someone on the line, so I took the chance to assess my surroundings. More people had entered, likely drawn by the possibility of excitement. Murphy was one of them, and I signaled him over nearer to me to watch my back while I focused on my task. The king had come in as well, though he stood back by the door to his inner office.

The screen came on. I accepted the call, and Trieste's face showed up. Was it my imagination, or was it a little less perfect than usual? I needed to focus on more important things.

"What the fuck are your people doing, Liana?" I shouted. "You're moving troops aggressively to the border. You need to cease and desist. Now."

She was ready for my bluntness and didn't flinch. "We are conducting an exercise, as I apprised you this morning. Nothing has changed." She measured each word as if she'd practiced them.

"Tell your military leaders that your troops have crossed the line that I've deemed safe. They need to stop immediately and return to their previous locations." I put all the weight into my words that I could muster. I needed her to hear me. More important, I needed the people hiding behind her to hear me. *Please. Hear me.*

Her tone didn't change. "We are within our rights to conduct an exercise within the boundaries of our own nation."

They were and they weren't. That was the problem. They weren't in range of Zargod civilian infrastructure yet, but they were very nearly in range of my key assets. Those I could defend, though. Mostly. We had both run the simulations, and we both knew that the only way they could win was with a first strike, and they were moving into position to do precisely that. I couldn't say that to her outright, but I didn't need to. We all knew. Saying it here would only serve to announce it to all of Zarga as well, and I didn't want to do that. Three military officers entered the office just then, and two of them made their way to the king. Great. I had a strong feeling that my announcing it was now moot. They'd have sensors of their own.

I brought my attention back to Trieste. I was stuck. I didn't have any bluffs. A threat at this point would only be effective if I was one hundred percent going to follow up on it, but as soon as I put out that ultimatum, I ceded the initiative to them. If I said, "Stop, or I'll attack you," then it became their decision. But at the same time, I couldn't launch an attack without a warning. For all the work that the staff had done preparing for this moment, running simulations, and preparing both offensive and defensive responses, now that it had arrived, the decision fell to me alone. "You're putting me in a difficult position."

"We are well within our rights." Her voice shook a little that time. She could repeat it as many times as she liked, but it didn't change the situation.

I needed to get her off-script. "Remember when we first met? How we just started talking?"

She frowned, perhaps not seeing where I was going, perhaps not happy to have something personal aired in front of so many witnesses. "Yes. At the coffee shop."

"Right. I need you to talk to me like that. Just you and me."

Her lip quivered. "I can't."

"Liana, I'm in over my head. Way over my head, and your leaders are putting me in a spot where I have to make a decision. Are they willing to bet on how an inexperienced commander is going to choose?"

"That's not—"

"Please, Liana. Tell them to stand down."

She hesitated and then mouthed some words that the mic didn't pick up. I could read her lips, though. "I'm sorry."

I wanted to scream. I decided to try one last thing to shock her, shock *them*, to try to get them to see that I was serious. "If you'll excuse me, the king of Zarga is here and he looks like he really wants to talk to me." I cut the connection, not giving her a chance to respond. I hoped that rude gesture would get their attention and get them to back down without actually giving them an ultimatum.

I hadn't lied. The king had come over to me and was hovering, waiting for me to give him my attention. I checked the staff's running updates first, to get the most current information before I dealt with him. When I looked up, he spoke.

"Major Markov, you have to do something about this."

"I am doing something, your majesty."

"You have to stop them. Now."

I wanted to snap at him, but he wasn't wrong. The consensus estimate of the staff was that the Argazzi indirect fire systems would reach their ideal launch locations in just under four minutes. I didn't have to do something right *now*, but I sure as shit had to do something *soon*. "I'm working on it."

"Yes. I heard. They're not going to listen to you."

"Would you like me to deal with the problem, or would you like to stand here and talk about it?" I asked.

He looked like he was about to say something else, but he thought better of it and backed away from me. At the same time, a message pinged in my implant from Chao saying that Trieste wanted to reconnect. I directed her to put it through to the terminal.

"You disconnected," she said, as soon as she appeared.

"You weren't listening anyway."

"You have no right to make demands of us."

I was out of time. Trieste was staring at me, the king was staring at me. Everybody was staring at me except Murphy and Gonzalez, who were staring at everybody else, the way that bodyguards should. Depending on what I decided, I might need them to help me fight my way out of the building. But either way, I had to make a decision. "You have exactly two minutes from right now to turn your vehicles around and return to your defensive positions. This is your last warning."

"You can't do that."

I hardened my face and made it as cold as I could. "One minute, forty-five seconds."

"They're not going to listen!" This time she disconnected. Or someone disconnected her. Shit. I'd done exactly what I didn't want to do. I'd ceded the decision to the Argazzi. All I could do now was watch my video feeds

THE WEIGHT OF COMMAND

and staff reports and hope that the Argazzi came to their senses in the next hundred seconds.

Warnings pinged as we lost contact with an observation drone, and then another. It didn't take a strategic genius to figure out what was happening to them. The Argazzi were knocking them out—either hacking them or incapacitating them with EMP bursts or lasers. At least *that* we had anticipated. We had redundant systems, including three stealth drones that would be difficult, if not impossible for the Argazzi to pick up with their technology. Just to be on the safe side, I directed my people to deploy two additional drones from our base to replace the two—now three—that we'd lost. The Argazzi plan wouldn't work. They had no chance of eliminating all of our assets prior to the deadline I'd set for them. Part of me hoped they hadn't put all of their eggs in that one futile basket. Let me get lucky one time. Let them just turn the fuck around.

I shifted some of my AIs from observation to targeting, including all of the stealth vehicles. The enemy—because that's what they were now—had taken down one more drone, but none of those. I considered jumping the countdown. Militarily, that was the right answer. If they did manage to take out our targeting drones, it would severely diminish the initial precision strike. And the fact that they were attacking our drones—which, by their own admission, had every right to be there—was a pretty good indicator that they had no intention of turning back. But then, this wasn't strictly a military matter. I'd give them their full time, because when asked about it later—and I *would* be asked about it later, probably many times—I wanted to be as clean as possible.

Clean. That's a strange word to use when you're about to end the lives of dozens of people who didn't deserve it. The soldiers on the ground, regardless of their personal opinions about war, the Zargod, or even me, didn't have a choice in the matter. They didn't deploy themselves. They didn't give the order to move toward the Zargod border. I took a deep breath and tried to clear my head, tried to keep from crying. That would just be the cherry on top of a fuck-you sundae. The valiant commander, sitting in front of the leadership of another country, waiting for a call and bawling her eyes out. I would not. But I had a headache building from holding it back.

At the one-minute mark, with no updates from the staff that changed the situation, I called McNamara. The decision was mine, and I could execute it, but I wanted another opinion. She picked up instantly.

"Yes, ma'am."

"They're not stopping. I've got an attack sequence loaded and ready to execute. Do you see another way?"

"The staff isn't sure, ma'am. Recommendations are mixed, and they don't have the experience."

"I only have a few seconds. What do *you* think? Personally."

"I don't see another way."

I cut the connection. It didn't take any of the responsibility off of me, but it sure felt like it did.

Forward they came. How close were they going to push it? I didn't have a margin for extra time. If they didn't stop and I didn't fire, they would. After the fact, they'd claim that they were not going to go through with it, of course. They'd blame it on me. That was fine. They were full of shit. There were only two reasons for them to push forward: to attack us or to bait me into attacking them. And I didn't see what they expected to gain from the latter unless they weren't making their own decisions. If Tangent had gotten to the PM in Zarga, how high had they gotten with the Argazzi? If I could go back in time, that would be the question to answer. I should have started working that angle three days ago. But a wish was just that.

A fucking wish.

Reality said we were almost out of time.

I cut the staff updates and shifted to live video feeds, watching three at once from each of the targeting drones. They'd locked in on targets—forty-three of them in total. All the identified long-range rocket and artillery systems, the stuff the Argazzi would use to kick off their attack. Our attack plan ignored the tanks and the infantry carriers and the other direct-fire systems. It ignored their short-range artillery. It even ignored their air and missile defense assets, which would normally have been on our early target list. Not this time. We'd only hit the things that would cause us immediate problems. We'd have time to deal with the rest of it in the fifteen minutes following.

I wished that I was anywhere but the king's office. Another useless wish.

Ten seconds. They weren't turning around. They kept racing toward their own destruction, dust trails kicked up behind hundreds of vehicles drifting in perfect precision in the nine kilometers-per-hour west wind.

The timer hit zero. I gave the fire command to the prepared units.

Twelve rockets. That's all we fired. The Argazzi missile defense systems lit up, warnings flashing in my implant, but I muted those notifi-

THE WEIGHT OF COMMAND

cations. They didn't matter. The Argazzi anti-missile batteries wouldn't touch them.

Each of those twelve rockets held eight sub-munitions. When the rockets burst three kilometers up and a couple kilometers in front of the enemy's lead vehicles, each of those sub-munitions would fire a one-point five-kilogram laser-targeted tungsten penetrator at 2,400 meters per second. Ninety-six total. Enough for two per target with a few left over.

Overkill.

Because when you're going to throw the first punch, you want to make sure the other person doesn't get back up.

The world exploded on my feeds as our penetrators hit simultaneously, punching through the light top armor of the Argazzi rocket launchers and artillery systems like a bullet through a paper target. Flashes erupted all along the Argazzi line, the quick spark of metal on metal, gone in an instant, and then the blooming flower of secondary explosions as the heat and kinetic energy ignited rocket propellant and fuel and ordnance. A lone rocket spiraled aimlessly forward from the destroyed forces, leaving a trail of smoke, probably cooked off with the destruction of its launcher.

I sat there in the room, which was unnaturally silent, watching my real-time video feeds and scrolling through the staff updates in my brain as they worked to do a battle damage assessment. It would take them a minute to parse through all of their new data, but I had a good enough approximation from the naked video of the scene. Our attack had been devastating, as planned.

Vehicles swerved to avoid burning wrecks. Some stopped, perhaps unaware of what to do or unwilling to advance into what might be the face of death. An infantry carrier sideswiped a bot-tank, and then ground to a stop as the bot-tank drove on. Even a few of the Argazzi bot-tanks had stopped, which meant that their operators had overridden their commands. I checked the running staff estimate of when they'd reach the actual border. Fourteen minutes. That was the next decision point, give or take, unless something else happened to change it. I composed a quick message to my unit commanders, giving them orders to stand to full alert in defensive positions. I also ordered that by no means should anyone engage unless they were fired upon or unless I gave the order. We'd killed a bunch of Argazzi soldiers already based on my decision, and I hoped we could avoid killing any more.

After I received acknowledgements of my orders, two things

happened simultaneously. The terminal in front of me buzzed, and a Zargod officer power-walked into the room and headed toward the king. Both sides had seen what happened, and now it was time to deal with it. My heart was pounding in my chest, but I had to get control of myself. I couldn't change what had already happened. I needed to focus on the things we could still affect. There would be plenty of time for doubt and self-recriminations later. What mattered now was controlling things going forward. I took a deep breath and hit the screen to accept the call.

Trieste looked different. Her hair was mussed, and I might have been imagining it, but her makeup appeared smudged under her eyes as if maybe she'd been crying. When she spoke, there was no life in her voice. "You fired on our forces unprovoked."

"You know I didn't. You were warned."

"You killed innocent—"

"Stop," I said, cutting her off. "I'm not debating this with you. Put someone else on. Please." I couldn't face her.

She sat there for a moment until someone tapped her on the shoulder, and then she got up from her seat and disappeared. Joran Yakina took her place. My suspicions were correct. He *was* the guy in charge.

"We cannot let this unprovoked attack stand," he said.

I ignored him. "Here are your instructions: You will cease all movement toward the border. You may conduct recovery and medical operations around the area of your destroyed systems, but all units not directly involved in that effort will withdraw to their previous staging locations and prepare for further retrograde back to their bases. Do you understand?"

"You had no—"

I cut him off. "Do. You. Understand?"

He paused this time, maybe unsure of how to respond. "I acknowledge your message," he said.

I cut the connection.

The king approached, having waited at a distance for me to finish my call. "You did it! You stopped them!" The glee in his tone made me want to punch him in the throat.

"We'll see," I said.

"This is a great day. We have the advantage now. You have to follow up the attack and destroy them."

We? He'd done nothing. And how dare he presume to tell me what I *had to do*. But I held back my sarcastic response. I couldn't take out my emotions on the king. "Excuse me, your majesty. I need to check on the battle." I dove back into my head without waiting for a response. I wasn't sure if he knew the mechanism that I used for command and control, but he certainly knew about my implant, and he could draw his own conclusions. He mumbled something, but I didn't hear it.

Our new drone feeds were online now, adding to my ability to surveil the carnage, and the staff had their assessments compiled and continued to refine them for me. We'd destroyed forty of the forty-three primary targets as well as fourteen other combat systems as collateral damage. More important, though, most of the enemy vehicles had stopped moving. The staff reported that only a handful continued forward, but as I watched my live feed, even those slowed and stopped.

Good. That was the first step. Yes, they could start forward again at any moment, but their current actions meant that my decision to attack had paid off. Somebody in the Argazzi command structure was listening. At least momentarily. As bad as it sucked to have caused all that death, it would have sucked infinitely worse if I'd done it and didn't have the intended effect. I could tell myself that I'd sacrificed the lives of a few to prevent the loss of many more.

I could tell myself that, but I couldn't at that moment make myself believe it.

I messaged the staff to warn me if any more than two vehicles moved even fifty meters in the direction of the border and surfaced back into the room, where the king was still standing there in front of me. I stood.

"The Argazzi have halted their move toward the border," I told him.

"You've hurt them! What are you going to do to follow up?"

I stared at him for several seconds before deciding again to ignore him. "Murphy. Gonzalez. Let's move. To the transport."

"Yes, ma'am."

"You can't leave," said the king.

I side-stepped him and headed for the door.

"Major Markov!" He grabbed my upper arm, but when Murphy took an aggressive step toward him, he pulled his hand back like touching me had burned him. Nobody else tried to get in my way, though the liaison who had greeted me initially did scramble after us, running to catch up. I didn't need him, but I didn't stop him. Everybody had a job to do.

I checked my feeds again once I was seated in the transport. Some of the Argazzi vehicles had turned and were heading back the way they'd come. Not all, but that was reasonable enough, as they'd stagger their units. Perhaps realizing that I was zoned out, Zilla buckled me in, and then took her own seat.

We didn't speak on the trip back. At least I didn't. The team talked to each other but in tones low enough that I couldn't hear them. I wanted to tell them about what I'd done. Murphy and Gonzales were there with the king, so they already had the basics, and they'd have shared them with the others. I just wanted to let it out. But I couldn't do that to them. Not with this. This was my decision, my weight to bear, and they didn't deserve that burden.

There was a crowd waiting at base when I disembarked, maybe thirty or forty soldiers, who whooped and cheered when they saw me but abruptly cut off a few seconds later. I didn't have to look back to know that one of my team had given them a sign to stop. It made me appreciate them more. I didn't know what I needed at that moment, but the last thing I needed was hero worship. We'd done our job and we'd won. We were still alive. But a lot of people were dead, and that shouldn't be something to cheer.

I looked for familiar faces in the crowd, though I didn't expect to see the person I wanted. I needed to see Captain Song and assess her reaction to the day's events. More accurately, I needed to have someone else check on her. After all, those were her countrymen we'd killed, and that likely changed our relationship. I probably should have called back and had someone make sure she wasn't busy sabotaging everything she could get her hands on, but I hadn't thought about it. I'd been too tied up with my own problems to deal with hers.

A vehicle pulled up and Hearns got out, still in his field gear. Soldiers parted for him like a zipper opening, and he headed straight for me. I met him halfway and led him back away from the soldiers.

"You doing okay, ma'am?"

"Did my team call you?" I wouldn't have blamed them if they did. A day ago, it would have pissed me off, but now? They probably had an obligation to do what was right for the unit, and a commander who wasn't in her proper mind wasn't at all good for the unit.

"No, ma'am. I swear. I figured it out on my own. I know you, and I know that this had to be tough on you."

I kept walking for a few seconds before responding. "Yeah. I'm not proud of it."

"You did what you had to do."

"In the moment, yes. But I can't help but think that if I'd done some things different leading up to it that we never would have gotten to that point."

"There's nothing to be done about that. We can go back and *what if?* things to death, but all we can do is make the best decisions that we can at that time."

I sighed. "You're right. I know you're right." And I really did know that. I just couldn't make it register right then.

He understood where I was with it and tried another direction. "Think of it this way, ma'am. What do we do now?"

I considered it. "I've got to talk to Captain Song."

"Are you sure that's a good idea?"

"No. But I still have to do it."

"Okay, ma'am. I thought about her immediately once you made the attack and called back to make sure she wasn't causing problems. She had removed herself from the headquarters and self-confined to her room."

Of course he'd checked on that. And her response seemed to be good. Ideally, she saw the situation for what it was and removed herself from any potential conflict or suspicion, or just to get away from displays like the one that had greeted me when I got off the transport. Perhaps she was grieving. But at that moment, I'd settle for any outcome that didn't involve her actively trying to fight us.

"Good thinking on that," I said. "I'll visit her there."

"And after that?"

"Let's meet with Watch, assess the situation on the ground, and see when we think it's safe to start bringing our troops out of the field. And then...then I want to figure out how we start going after the real problem."

"Sounds like a plan, ma'am." He smiled, and I understood that. He'd wanted to take me out of my hole of self-pity, and he'd succeeded. It would come back. I had no doubt about that; this was something that was going to stay with me for a long time. But at least I was functional in the short term.

I signaled for Zilla to accompany me and headed off to find Song.

23

I asked Zilla to hang back as we approached Song's room, and she looked at me funny. "You sure that's a good idea, ma'am?"

"It'll be fine." I wasn't worried about a physical confrontation. If Song wanted to take a shot at me, it'd be verbal. That didn't mean it wouldn't hurt, but Zilla couldn't help. She nodded and took up a post a couple doors down the long hall, putting her back to one wall so she could observe both directions.

I took a deep, cleansing breath and knocked on the door. It opened, and Song and I were face to face. We both stood there for a moment, neither having thought through the next step. "Can I come in?" I asked, finally.

She stepped back to allow me to pass and closed the door behind me. "I wondered if you'd come, ma'am. I figured you would."

"Yeah?"

She shrugged. "Just the read I had on you. You didn't strike me as the kind of person who shirked the tough jobs."

"I'll take that as a compliment." I leaned back against the wall on the far side of the room, giving us as much space as possible.

"You should. It was meant as one. Which is why you don't need to say anything."

"I do," I said. "I owe it to you to tell you why it happened."

She shook her head. "It doesn't matter. I trust that you didn't make the decision lightly. But at the same time, there's nothing you say that is going to make me feel better about it. So your need to explain isn't really about me. It's about you."

I stood there, unsure what to say, and when I didn't speak, Song jumped back in.

"Not that that's a bad thing. That you feel the need to say something in itself is a good thing. It means that it mattered to you."

"It did. I really tried to come up with any other possible solution."

"Okay." She paused. "I'm not sure what else to say here. I'm not here to exonerate you. You had a decision to make, and you made it."

I started to say something else but stopped myself. She was right. I had to come see her, but there was nothing I could say. Finally, I settled on the only thing I could. "I just wanted to say it."

"Roger that, ma'am. So what's next?"

"What do you mean? I figured we were through."

"I thought about it, if I'm being honest. Quitting. But I came here to prevent a war, and while I failed, we're a long way from done. I feel like what's best for my country is to get communications off-planet and get the space elevator working again. You're my best chance to do those things."

I considered her words. I hoped that if I was ever in her situation, I could be that mature. "Thanks for that. What have you got?"

"We completely failed in our attempts to hack the quantum communicator that's up there sending false messages. It's locked down. I've been coordinating with the engineers at the space elevator, working on launching satellites on our own, and also looking for land-based options. We've got some ideas, but they're risky."

"It may be time to take some risks," I said. "Can you be ready to brief as soon as I get out of my staff sync?"

"Roger that, ma'am."

My meeting with the staff didn't give me too much that I didn't know. I'd been obsessively checking my own views of the feeds as well as following their running estimates, so the briefing was more a confirmation than anything else. But it helped to know that the analysts had the same read as I did: The Argazzi had pulled back to defensive positions but didn't look like they were going any further than that, despite my order to take their troops back into garrison. It didn't surprise me. I had no authority to give that order and had simply been relying on emotion and fear to make them comply. They probably assessed that I wouldn't attack them again, and they were right.

And we were fairly safe from them, too, in the short term. If they wanted to attack again, they'd have to rebuild capability, which was the direction that I took the discussion.

"How fast can they rebuild and refit?" I asked.

The Intel chief was ready for the question. "There are a lot of variables, ma'am. They have the manufacturing capability and the printers. If they choose to dedicate them to the task, they could have new rocket launchers in a few days. The systems are reasonably autonomous, so replacing the crews should take minimal time."

"How likely is that course of action?"

"Low probability. While they have the capacity, it's not *excess* capacity. Printers would have to be repurposed off of civilian tasks. And all it would get them would be back to the situation they were in before: Needing a first strike against a commander who has shown that she's not going to allow them that opportunity. We estimate that the probability of that type of attack is less than ten percent. If they attack again, it is not likely to be conventional."

"What should we expect?"

"The most likely attacks, starting with the highest probability, are infiltration and/or terror, cyber, and nuclear."

"Nuclear?" I sat up straight in my chair. "They have that capability?"

"They're not supposed to, ma'am. But we can't rule it out. While we don't think they were responsible for the previous attack, *someone* was, which means that those weapons may exist on the planet."

And if I was right about Tangent being behind the various attacks, it was likely they had the nukes. And I couldn't rule out Tangent giving them to the Argazzi. Shit.

"How likely is that analysis?"

"Unknown, ma'am. There are too many things we can't assess." That was a good answer, though the real answer was that it didn't matter. Any chance was too much, given the potentially catastrophic outcome. And unless I missed my own guess, the likelihood increased as we got closer to getting the capacity to get a message off the planet. That would definitely change how I looked at Song's plans. It also meant that I needed to try to engage with the Argazzi, as uncomfortable as that thought was. I had to try to rebuild the peace.

I decided to deal with that before moving on to the plans meeting, but before I contacted them, I checked the news feeds to gauge the reactions to the events of the day. Some part of me had hoped for a level-headed, neutral report on the conflict. If that existed, I didn't find it. The Zargod feeds were carrying videos of celebration throughout the country. People were literally dancing in the streets. I didn't know much, but I knew that would piss off the Argazzi, which didn't help me.

The Argazzi feeds were predictably more somber, but no more helpful to my cause. The first article, which was the *most* balanced, had a headline that read, "Peacekeeping Federation Force Attack Kills 61." Which was mostly the truth, though it didn't mention their actions that led to the attack and focused a lot on the fact that the attack occurred on their sovereign soil. It couldn't have been more effective if the Argazzi information ministry wrote it themselves. They probably did.

Firmly losing the information war, I had Chao try to contact Trieste. She couldn't reach her, but someone at the same address answered and asked to speak to me. I didn't see a better option, so I pulled it up on the screen in my office. He was a balding man with wisps of black hair coiling from the top of his head and gray at his temples. A sheen of sweat glistened on his chubby face. I didn't recognize him, but a quick search of my database marked him as Charles Stratton, Deputy Minister of Defense. That I had been switched from Foreign Affairs to Defense probably said something, but I couldn't say for sure what. It could have been worse. It could have been Yakina.

"Good evening, sir. I was trying to reach Deputy Minister Trieste."

"She has been relieved of her responsibilities." He didn't say if she'd been relieved of all her responsibilities or just those pertaining to me. Either way, it hit me like a punch in the gut. Not only had I killed five dozen people, I'd also possibly ended the career of someone I genuinely liked. I tried not to let my dismay show on my face.

"So then you're to be my point of contact from here on out?"

"As much as we see fit to deal with you, yes."

Great. I could feel the asshole coming off of him right through the screen, but that was to be expected, I guess. "Very well. I wanted to talk about where we go now. I notice that you haven't withdrawn to your garrison locations."

"Neither have you," he said. "And I think we're well within our rights to defend ourselves given that we have a known war criminal sitting right across the border."

I almost rolled my eyes at him. He was being deliberately provocative with his language, but so over the top that I didn't take the bait. I had to move forward, and if that meant letting him call me names, I'd live with it. "I think it's in both of our best interests to come to an agreement on military disposition."

"You've shown that you clearly don't have our interests at heart."

"I warned you. You persisted."

"We were within our legal rights—"

"Can we just cut the bullshit?" I'd had enough. I'd done what I'd done, and they could be mad about it, they could hate me. But I wasn't going to sit there and let him berate me. He stared at me, stunned into silence. I guess he didn't expect a woman half his age to go at him like that. Since he left me an opening, I continued, "Or if you're not capable of that, can you find someone in your government who is?"

"Your attack is not *bullshit*—"

"But your false innocence is. You deliberately ran forces into an offensive position to see what I'd do, either to precipitate an attack or to gain information for a potential future attack. I know it and you know it, and no amount of spin to the press is going to change that."

He paused and regrouped. "I guess we'll see how history judges the situation."

"Sure. But right now, I don't care about history. I care about the future. Specifically, I care about avoiding further violence."

"Then show a little more self-restraint."

I wanted to tell him to fuck off. I really did. But I took a cleansing breath and went down a different path. "There are elements working within your government to try to fan the flames of this conflict. They're working in Zargod too."

"What elements?"

"The same elements that attacked your infrastructure. Follow that lead. Find out who did that, and you'll have your real enemy. I assure you, it's not me."

He started to speak, but stopped himself, which was good. He had probably been about to say that I was the enemy they knew, because without a doubt, I'd attacked them. And if he had, I'd have cut the connection, consequences be damned. Instead, he thought for several seconds, and then said, "We will look into it."

"Thank you. That's all I ask. Now, what do you propose as appropriate actions for our two militaries?" It was a risk, letting him dictate to me, but I planned to accept almost whatever he said, as long as it deescalated things. The way I saw it, this was an opportunity for him personally. Trieste had been removed—rightly or wrongly—and this was his chance to be the hero. All he had to do was tell me something that wasn't ridiculous. I was almost holding my breath in anticipation. *Come on, dude. Act in your own self-interest.*

"You want me to decide the next actions?" He spoke tentatively, clearly sensing a trap of some sort.

"I feel like that's the best way to get to a more stable relationship. And since you're willing to look into what I've asked you to, I feel I should give something back in good faith."

He glanced to the side. He wasn't in charge any more than Trieste had been. I really wished they'd just put on the person who was pulling the strings. "Do I have to decide now?"

"Give me an initial proposal now, and we can talk again tomorrow and follow up with more actions."

He glanced to the side again, this time with his end of the conversation muted. "Give me five minutes. I'll call you back with a proposal."

"Okay. But in the interest of clarity—and I think a clear understanding is in all of our interests—I'm going to be watching your production facilities. If you immediately begin churning out offensive assets, we're going to have a problem." It was a calculated risk, letting them know what I was looking for, as it gave them a chance to try to circumvent my observation. But it was worth it, for the chance that maybe it would make them choose a different path. Or at least slow them down on the wrong one.

"I acknowledge that information," he said.

I let him cut the connection and then got up to get myself some water. I didn't like giving up control to the Argazzi, but anything I proposed they were going to reject. At least this way I had a chance. I hoped they'd give me an agreement I could accept.

I sat down and consciously relaxed the muscles in my neck and shoulders while I waited. I'd have paid good money for a backrub.

A few minutes later, Stratton came back on, and he was sweating as if he'd run laps during the break, but he was all business and looked like he was ready to pop with what he had to say. I tried to keep an open mind. "Do you have a proposal?"

"I do. We propose that within the next twenty-four hours, each side withdraws at least half of their forces back to a garrison footing."

I made a show of taking down what he said on my tablet. It was acceptable, but I wanted to hear the rest of it before I commented. "Got it. Go ahead."

"We propose that you withdraw your aerial surveillance assets back to within twenty kilometers of the border, to prevent you from using them in further unprovoked attacks."

I added it to the list on my tablet. I didn't care for the language in that one, but I could live with the restriction for a time. If they stayed back far enough, I wouldn't need to target them. The only thing I'd lose was the ability to monitor their production facilities, but I wouldn't see much there with aerial observation anyway. We had different methods for that task.

"Continue."

"We propose that within seven days, all forces on both sides resume pre-hostility dispositions. And finally, we propose that you pay reparations for the material you destroyed and the lives that you took, as detailed in the tripartite agreement."

And there it was. The ridiculous part. I kept my face neutral. "Is that all?"

"That's all for now. We reserve the right to revisit this with you in the coming days but feel that it's in our best interest to get started."

In that much, at least, we agreed. I was okay with all of it except for the reparations, which were preposterous. Contrary to his statement, reparations for military equipment were *not* in the tripartite agreement. At the same time, I really wanted to say yes to their demands so that I could move on to focusing on the real problem. But I was stuck, because there was no way I could acquiesce to paying for military equipment. Even if it was the right thing to do, that decision had to come from above me, and I didn't have a way to *get* above me. I sat silent for several seconds, which had to seem awkward on the other end, and finally settled on a half-measure. "I accept all of the terms regarding military actions. My only issue is with the requested reparations. I don't have the authority to authorize reparations, nor do I have access to the funds required."

"You have an established claims process for injuries, deaths, or property damages caused by you."

If he thought he was going to trip me up with legalese from the treaty, he didn't do his homework. I have an implant which gives me instant access to it. "That applies to non-government assets." He started to interject but I held up my hand to forestall him. "But as I said, it's irrelevant, because I don't have those funds. What I will do is this: I'll begin processing payments for the families of soldiers who died in the recent action, pending you presenting me with that information." That wasn't required, but it was a small enough amount in relation to military budgets that I could justify it to keep the peace.

"What about our equipment?"

"As I said, I'm not able to do that immediately. What I *will* do is pass the action on to my superiors for action—with my endorsement—as soon as I'm able to establish contact."

He listened for instructions for several seconds. I was passing the buck to my superiors, but I could live with that. As to my endorsement—I wasn't exactly lying. But I'd base that on how the Argazzi kept up their end of the deal going forward. Either way, my offer was enough for whoever was making the decision on their side to save face.

"We are not happy with that," said Stratton. He made a face that looked like he was in pain, which emphasized his unhappiness. "But we will accept it. For now."

"Good. I'll recall at least half of my troops at first light tomorrow."

"As will we. Goodbye, Major."

Hearns and McNamara were waiting for me when I came off of the call, and my heart jumped as I expected them to give me some piece of bad news, but they were just there because they'd been informed about my call and expected me to have orders. They were really good at their jobs and could anticipate what I needed.

"Bring Second Battalion in at first light. First Battalion after that. Give Third Battalion a screening mission, sensors and active patrols. This isn't for training. I don't want anything coming across that border without us knowing about it. Playback my call for the details on where we can and can't use sensors." That would be enough to discourage a conventional attack, which I had to prepare for, even though it wasn't likely; if an attack came, it would be something else. "That's it for now. I'm going to meet with plans and develop future actions. Questions?"

"No, ma'am," said McNamara.

Captain Song had a team assembled in a small conference room when I got there, and she launched directly into her briefing. "Ma'am, we have come up with three potential solutions for our communications issue."

"Roger. Go."

"The first option involves a ground-based transmission station relying on standard light-speed transmissions. This is the last resort. But if we can't get anything else out, it is the safest way to send a message. We'd need to build a directed transmitter with enough power and accuracy to specifically target a receiver on Tau Gamma Three. It's the only receiver in our part of the galaxy that's large enough to receive a signal of the magnitude of power we can generate, and it's one-point-one light years away. The window would be open only at short intervals when the broadcast site would align with the receiving site, so we'd be limited to a repeating message."

I nodded. That wouldn't work for what we needed, but the thought that they'd put into it was good, and I didn't want to discourage that. I also noticed that none of the noncoms around the table commented, but they all looked engaged and positive. That was a testimony to Song, and it backed up my trust in her. Noncoms could smell bullshit almost as well as I could detect it with my implant.

"We can consider that as a backup option. What else have you got?"

"We could launch our own satellite from a ground location using either commercial rockets or cannibalizing parts from military designs."

"We have the technology to put something into orbit?"

"Well...yes and no, ma'am. We don't have the technical skill to put an object into a sustained and stable orbit. That skill does exist on the planet, but those engineers are Argazzi, and we currently assess that they would not be a viable option."

"I concur."

"But we don't have to get something into orbit. We just have to get it into space long enough to get a message out. If we do it right, we need less than a minute of time in space. We think we can do that with quite a bit of margin to spare. We looked at two options—crewed and uncrewed. The crewed version gives the best chance of success, but we deemed the risk of death associated with putting a human on an untested launch vehicle as too high."

"Okay. What's the uncrewed option look like?"

"We focused on an automated communications system," said Song. "We can get that system down to about one hundred forty-five kilograms for the device itself, and another two hundred or so kilograms for the launch vehicle."

"So about three hundred fifty kilos total payload."

"Yes ma'am. That's the assumption that the space team used to calculate their data, which I'm presenting. We'd need to accelerate that mass to escape velocity of approximately eleven-point-four kilometers per second, which equates to about ten gees for nineteen minutes. The limitation of the automated version is ensuring that the quantum communication system is primed and started is a complex procedure—and one that we can't test thoroughly here on the planet. Which is why we usually do these things in space."

"What are our chances?"

"We assess it at fifty-fifty to get the system functioning remotely. But I have to caution that that's a very broad guess. Those odds would improve if we had the right civilian technicians."

"Let me guess. Also Argazzi?"

"Yes, ma'am."

"But we can do this? We can launch three hundred fifty kilograms into space?"

"We need to generate thirty-five thousand newtons of force for nineteen minutes. We have missiles right now that can do about a quarter of that for about a quarter of that time. So we'd be looking at creating something using multiple missiles in four stages."

"That's a lot of things that would have to go right."

"Yes, ma'am. We assess the chances of success at less than twenty percent."

"So twenty percent to get there and fifty percent that it works if we do. Ten percent overall."

"Correct, ma'am. But we could continue to try as long as we still have materials for the printers, and while I don't know the specifics, your logisticians say we don't have a shortage there."

I didn't want to say it, but there was one other problem with the plan. It was extremely visible. We couldn't launch rockets into space without everyone seeing us prepare for it, and that included Tangent. If they suspected what we were doing and had attacks planned, that would trigger them.

"How soon could we attempt our first launch?"

"Three days, ma'am."

"That fast?"

"Working round-the-clock shifts. I assumed you'd want us to do that."

"Good assumption. Okay. What's the last option?"

"The final option gives us the most chance of success but also involves some risk to personnel. Captain Dramovich—the engineer who came with me—has done enough work at the space elevator that she can rig a temporary lift that can get a communications device and eight personnel up to the lowest way-station."

I wanted to ask Song if Dramovich was still on board after we attacked the Argazzi, but I didn't want to do it in front of the others. I'd need to go assess that for myself. Despite that reservation, for the first time during the briefing I started to get excited. We didn't know what was up there. And there was a slim chance that we'd find people still alive.

"Tell me the risks."

"Ma'am, the first risk is that we don't have a space-worthy vehicle, and we aren't going to solve that within reasonable time constraints. Our eight-person team is going to have to make the transit to space using personal protection only. Space suits and oxygen supplies."

"Wow," I said, and thought about it for quite some time. "But it's possible?"

"Yes, ma'am. The probability of reaching the station is over ninety-nine percent. The survival of properly trained personnel in transit is also near that level."

"The risk is less than one percent?" That was almost a sure thing, but there were lives on the line, so it deserved scrutiny.

"To get there. There's uncertain risk once they're there, as we don't know what they'll find, what systems will be online, or what they'll be able to get working."

"But in theory, all they have to do is set up the quantum communicator, launch it, and we're set."

"Yes, ma'am. But to reduce risk, we'll be working with a deadline. We've got about four hours to accomplish the mission before the team would have to break station and head back down, unless there's functioning oxygen on the station."

"Is four hours enough?"

"Dram—Captain Dramovich—says that it's extremely technical. To ensure success, she proposes to lead the mission herself."

Interesting. That meant she was either fully on board, or absolutely going to sabotage the mission. But I leaned toward the former. There were easier ways to sabotage things than launching yourself into space.

"She's the only one who can do it? In her assessment?"

"She's not. But her assessment is that going along provides redundant capability that gives us a significantly better chance of mission success."

Shit. That put me in a tough spot. My best chance to reestablish comms was to send an Argazzi officer on a reckless mission into an unknown situation. Even if Dramovich herself was on board, if something went wrong, I'd set their whole nation against me, and I had to consider those implications. I glanced to Hearns, who had joined us, to see if he had a thought on it. He gave me a slight shrug and a look that might as well have said, "I sure am glad I'm not in charge." I almost laughed, despite the seriousness of the situation. He always provided good advice, but this was outside his lane. I debated internally for a few more seconds, and then made a decision.

"Okay. Do it. But I want the team going up armed as if they're hitting a hostile site. We don't know what's up there, and I want them prepared for everything. No unnecessary risks. Show me your proposed composition of the offsite party and I want to see all of their equipment personally. The oxygen tanks, the armored suits, all of it."

"Roger, ma'am."

"And Master Sergeant Hearns, give new orders to Second Battalion. I still want them to re-deploy, but I want them to move an extra security company up to the space elevator as soon as possible."

Despite what I said to Song, I wasn't a hundred percent sure I was going to send the mission—especially not until I talked to Dramovich face to face—but I could always abort later. But by setting them in motion now, if I did decide to go, it got us there faster. I messaged Chao and told her to notify everyone who needed to know that I wanted to fly to the space elevator at first light.

24

We landed at just after 0800 hours immediately outside the fenced-in compound of what used to be the ground station of the space elevator. I was beginning to sweat even before we got inside the newly-reconstructed gate. There were pre-fab towers at each corner of the compound now, all manned, and at least two vehicles that I could see patrolling outside. They were all ours. The Zargod's promised troops hadn't arrived yet, though each day we were told tomorrow. We didn't really need them now. In fact, I'd rather that they didn't show up while we were trying to do this thing. The fewer people who knew about it, the better, which was the first thing I had to get straight. I had an Argazzi officer leading the mission, and if she'd reported our plans to her superiors, which I expected she had, then we had to factor in the elements within their government who might be working against us. I had to know who she told before I could assess the risk.

Captain Dramovich met me before I reached the temporary headquarters building—also pre-fab, with air-conditioners and generators creating a comforting blanket of white noise that almost drowned out the clanking of a hammer somewhere against metal. Dramovich was a tall woman—my height—and she had a firm grip. She held my eye, and her handshake, just long enough to be a bit of a challenge. This woman shared a country with Song, but she was a completely different creature.

"Ma'am. We have the equipment and soldiers ready for your inspection."

"We'll get to that. Let's you and me talk first." I gestured for Xiang and Gonzalez to give us some space. "I need to know why you're doing this."

She stared me down, assessing. "You mean why am I helping someone who recently fired on the forces of my country?"

"Exactly." I appreciated that she didn't play dumb about it. I could work with that.

"This isn't about you, ma'am, and it's not about Argaz."

"What do you mean?"

"You asked me why I'm doing this. The answer is simple. Because I can."

My read told me she meant what she was saying, but I still wasn't sure what that was. "I still don't understand."

"I'm going to be straight with you, because I think you're a person who will respond well to that, even if you don't like everything I've got to say."

"Good assessment."

"Right. When you first assigned me out here, I was kind of pissed. You were burying me away from your headquarters so you wouldn't have to deal with me."

"That's true."

She hesitated, then nodded, apparently okay with my confirmation. "But after a day or so I got over it. I'd have done the same thing in your place. And I started to look at it as an opportunity. I was up here, and while I wasn't totally in charge—your people weren't going to blindly follow me—I had a chance to do something that nobody else on the planet could do."

"What's that?"

"I get to be the woman who fixed the fucking space elevator."

"And that's enough to put aside the issues between me and your country?"

She looked at me like I had a dick growing out of my forehead. "Ma'am—have you been to Argaz? I'm a low-level officer, and that's all I'm ever going to be. I don't have the family connections to get promoted."

That didn't fit with what I knew, but she was absolutely telling the truth as she believed it. Argaz prided itself on being a society where everybody rose on their own merits. They didn't even allow for inheritance of family wealth.

Perhaps sensing my confusion, Dramovich added, "Just trust me on this part, ma'am. I'm capped out as a captain. Unless—"

"Unless you can do something significant. Like be the woman who fixed the space elevator."

"Exactly. This thing"—she gestured behind her to the massive structure—"is important to the world economy. More significant for me, it's important to the Argazzi economy."

"Okay. Next question. Since we're being honest, how much about this have you reported to your supervisors?"

She scrunched her face in confusion. "You really *don't* get it, do you?"

"Apparently not," I admitted.

"I haven't told them shit. I mean, sure, I sent reports. Some truth, mostly lies, all meaningless. I told them it was repairable. Told them what assets you'd allocated out here, give or take. But nothing about what we're going to attempt. No way."

"Why not?"

"Ma'am, if I reported that I could get the elevator fixed in the short term, someone else would find a way to take the credit. One of my supervisors would come up with some *urgent* reason why I had to be recalled and one of their favorites had to take my place. That's how Argaz works. You think I'm the only one who wants to get ahead?"

I had a lot to learn. But on the bright side, my not knowing actually helped. There wasn't much that I trusted as much as someone's own self-interest. It seemed that the Argazzi system had a fundamental flaw. If you don't treat your people well, they'll go off script and take care of themselves.

"Okay. We're on the same page. You really think this will work?"

"All due respect, ma'am, if I didn't think it would work, I wouldn't set my ass on a makeshift elevator car on a ride into space."

"Yeah, I guess not. That's a long trip. How long will it take?"

"We're going to the low-orbital way-station, which is around five hundred kilometers up. It's a lot smaller than the anchor station, which is at thirty-nine thousand kilometers, and the way-station doesn't have as much capability. But for what we need? It will do just fine. We can launch the quantum communicator from there into a degrading orbit. It will take us under two hours to get there. We'll be moving pretty fast up the cable."

"Degrading orbit? Is that going to be a problem?"

"No, ma'am. While we can't generate the velocity to put it into a permanent orbit, we can kick it out the door and it's going to float up there for two or three years before it burns into the atmosphere."

"Yeah, that will do."

"We plan to be at the station for fewer than four hours. Long enough to try to get life support up and the control systems running again. If we can do that, we might be able to get the main lift to descend from the anchor station."

"Is that a priority?" I asked. I was much more worried about security than attempting to fix the system. Once we got a message out, we could repair the tower at our leisure.

"Not a priority, but worth doing as long as it doesn't jeopardize the primary mission or crew safety. It would let us conduct a follow-on mission to get up to the top and reopen everything, which would help restart economies on both sides." She had a good point; I hadn't thought of it that way. Getting the economies working again might go a long way toward soothing relations.

"That's a really good thought. What's your proposed composition of your team?"

"Myself, two electricians, two mechanics, a computer specialist, and two communications techs. I can go over the purpose of each if you'd like."

"That won't be necessary. Do you really think you can get the station up and running again when the people who were on it couldn't? I mean—I assume they couldn't, since we couldn't contact them. Any survivors would have tried, since their lives depended on it."

"I'm not sure what happened up there, ma'am. I'm going off of the theory that it was an EMP that took the station out. We've got a pile of semiconductor replacement parts that they didn't have. Maybe that will make the difference."

"Eight passengers is the max?"

"Yes, ma'am. I decided to trade weight for speed, and the quantum communicator is heavy. I hardened it way beyond standard against EMP. Just in case someone has the same idea as last time."

"That's good thinking. Speaking of that, I'm concerned that you don't have security."

She looked at me like she wanted to ask a question but was holding back, almost confused.

"Go ahead. Say what's on your mind," I prompted.

"Ma'am...the place is deserted. There were seventeen people who worked on that way-station when it lost power. I'd take a morgue specialist before I worried about taking dedicated security. But if it makes you feel better, ma'am, we're all soldiers. We're not taking any civilians along, and we'll all be armed."

It did make me feel *a little* better, but whatever assurance I took from that was more than negated by the fact that an electrician with a gun was not the same as an infantry soldier. "How much impact would it have on your mission if I told you I wanted to put three security personnel on it?"

Dramovich thought about it without dismissing it outright, which I appreciated. When she spoke, it was more thinking out loud, almost talking to herself rather than me. "I can't add anybody else to the roster without completely reworking the specs of the car, which is untenable without a major revision to the timeline. So it becomes a question of who I can eliminate. I've got redundancies in three areas—I could theoretically cut a commo tech, a mechanic and an electrician. And since I can put the quantum communications device into operation if I need to, the critical mission has backup."

"What's the risk in cutting them?"

She bounced her head a bit as she thought about it. "It will slow things down. And if anything happens to the personnel we do have up there—if they can't work in the zero G, or if they lose their minds when they see dead bodies—we could be in trouble. We could still do the primary mission, but it will make it a lot less likely that we get the station running, which will make follow-on missions harder."

"But it won't affect getting the communicator deployed?"

"That part of the job we can do, ma'am. The system has battery power that will keep it active for a day or so. If I have to, I'll manually force an airlock open and kick that bad boy into space. That's not the issue. You asked about risk, ma'am? The biggest risk is the crew's reaction when they come face to face with people who sat on a station asphyxiating. The backups double the chances that we have someone functional."

I hadn't thought about that in a while, about how those people must have died. It was horrifying. That Dramovich *had* thought about it gave me more confidence in her plan, more confidence in her. They could be going into a graveyard.

"We should probably run psych profiles on everyone going to see how they're going to handle this."

"Already done," Dramovich replied. "Nothing is ever completely sure, but I've picked the most suitable people I have.

"Good work," I said.

"If you want to put security with us, ma'am, we'll need to do the psych profiles for those personnel as well. If they're going to be along, I'm going to put them to work. We might need to move bodies."

"What's your plan for that?"

"The bodies? They should be pretty well preserved, assuming there's no oxygen or heat. We'll only move them if we have to in order to accomplish the mission. If we do get life support running, we'll want to get them somewhere cold so they stay preserved until we can get them properly evacuated."

I considered everything we'd talked about. She had some very known risks, but I couldn't get past the *unknown* risks. Someone had taken out that space station, and I had to plan like they were going to do it again.

"I appreciate how much thought you've put into this, Captain, but I do want to attach the security personnel."

If this disappointed Dramovich, she didn't show it. "Roger that, ma'am. I'd like to link up with the team members by this evening for briefings. We plan to launch at zero-four hundred. It gives us the best opportunities to maximize natural light on board the station."

"I'll get the security personnel to you as soon as possible."

From there we moved through the gear and Dramovich introduced me to the personnel. I didn't question them—I trusted that she had done that—but I showed an interest in each of them, made sure they knew how much we appreciated them taking on such a tough mission. The thing that impressed me most was the looks on their faces. Not one of them looked scared. They looked excited. I guess it made sense. They were doing something that very few people had ever done. They weren't at all thinking about how dangerous it was. They were thinking about how cool it was going to be.

That was okay. I was thinking about the danger enough for all of us.

It took two hours for the plan to fall apart. When it did, the news came in the form of a call from Charles Stratton while I flew back toward base on the transport. I took the call on my helmet visor, which I didn't love, but it didn't seem like a call I should refuse.

He didn't waste time getting to his point. "Given the new situation between the peacekeeping force and Argaz, we would like our two officers returned to us immediately."

I don't know what he expected, but the request caught me totally off guard. It was reasonable, but I couldn't help being suspicious of the timing. I'd just authorized a mission to solve our communications problem, and right afterward I got a request to give up the person leading the mission. I believed Dramovich when she said she didn't report the mission, which meant that if they'd learned about it, they'd learned some other way. Or maybe it really was just coincidence.

It sucked. On top of the work Dramovich was doing, I'd come to rely on Captain Song and her sound advice. But, of course, I couldn't say that. I couldn't say much at all. I hadn't told the Argazzi about the mission, exactly because I feared that someone with influence in their government might try to stop it. But I had to say something, try to forestall the action, and that meant telling him at least some part of it.

"Captain Dramovich has proven to be a big help in the push to get the space elevator working again. Losing her now would be a significant setback in those efforts, and I think we can agree that a functional space elevator is in both of our best interests."

"Even so, I'm afraid I must insist."

"I can have the officers back to you in forty-eight hours." Even as I said it, I could hear the pleading in my voice. Stratton would hear it too, and if he wasn't suspicious before, he would be now.

He didn't even pause before responding, which meant that he didn't need to seek guidance. He already had a prepared position. "I'm afraid I don't have any leeway on this. We need them immediately. You understand."

It didn't much matter if I understood. It was their call. I could defy the order, but it would lead to questions of why. And if something happened to Dramovich on her mission, the damage would be almost irreparable. "Understood," I said, and then I cut the connection. "Pilot, turn us around. We're going back to the elevator."

The response to my second landing of the morning was not quite as organized as it had been previously. It took several minutes to track down Dramovich, who was giving two members of her team instruction on some technical aspect. She had her uniform top off, wearing just a tight dry weave t-shirt that showed off surprisingly ripped musculature for an engineer.

"Pack your things, Captain. I'm taking you home."

"What? Ma'am, what's going on?"

"You've been recalled." I watched her closely, reading her body language and reaching out with my implant to monitor her heart rate.

"That's bullshit, ma'am. Did you tell them that I could get the space elevator operating?" She wasn't faking it.

"I told them you were important to that effort, though I stopped short of telling them about the mission specifically. It wouldn't have mattered. I was talking to the deputy minister of defense, and he wasn't budging."

"Fuck!" She kicked a rock, and then brought herself back under control. "Okay, ma'am. I understand. It's going to take me a minute to pack up. I wasn't planning to leave on short notice."

"Understandable." I paused. "Let me ask you something. How long would it take you to pass off the specifics of your part of the job?"

"It's not possible, ma'am. Nobody could learn that much in a week, let alone a couple of hours."

I met her eyes. "I can."

Thirty minutes later we were back on the transport. It had taken Dramovich ten minutes to pack up, and we stole another twenty as she gave me instructions and schematics of the various systems we would encounter on the low-orbital way-station for me to download to my implant—including everything the other soldiers would be working on as well so I could back them up or check them as needed. There was no way that my crammed learning could replace her years of training and experience, but it would at least get me close. Close enough, I hoped. I'd learn everything I could, but I'd focus on the most important objective: re-establish communications.

To that end, I asked questions about two aspects of the job—how to operate the make-shift elevator car and how to employ the quantum communicator. With the plans, I could study them at rapid speed, learning as much as a thousand times faster than a regular person. It might not be enough, but I'd decided the minute I cut off the call with Stratford that I was going to do it. Someone wanted me not to, and to me, that was reason enough.

When she'd finished giving me everything she had, I considered it all until just before we landed, and then confided in her. "I think it's too much. I'm going to call it off."

"I understand, ma'am. It's dangerous."

"It is, and without you, we have a lower chance of success, so the risk just isn't worth it."

I made a call to Ops on an open channel, telling them to have everybody involved with the elevator mission stand down.

I was lying. I fully intended to go ahead with the mission. I just wanted everyone to believe I aborted it, and the person I wanted to believe it most was Dramovich. Without a doubt she'd be debriefed the moment she landed in Argaz, and while she'd kept the mission quiet before, I wasn't sure it was in her best interest to maintain that going forward—or if she'd be able to. Somebody in Argaz was probably working against me. Let them think I'd given up.

When we landed back at base, I left Dramovich on board the transport and Song joined her, having received word when we called ahead. I shook both of their hands, thanked them for their service, and told them I hoped that I'd see them again someday under better circumstances. I found that I meant it. They were professionals, and I truly appreciated them. I hoped that their time with me wouldn't hurt their careers too much back in their home country, but there wasn't much I could do about that.

Once the transport took off, I gathered my crew. I didn't know how much they knew about what was going on—I hadn't stopped to brief them—but at least one of them had been near me at all times, so my guess was that they knew almost everything. Soldiers are funny like that. Just to be sure, I read them all in on what I'd be doing the next morning.

When I finished, Murphy was the first to speak. "Wait, ma'am. I thought you just canceled it."

Zilla looked at him and rolled her eyes.

"Master Sergeant Hearns is going to absolutely shit himself when he hears you're going up to space," said Xiang.

"That's why we're not going to tell him," I said.

The crew went dead silent. It was like I'd said something bad about someone's mother.

"I'm joking! But you should have seen your faces. I'm going to tell him right after we finish here. But before that, I want to tell you. There are three slots for security on the trip and I've got three soldiers with zero-G training slotted—"

All four of them put their hands up. "You were last," Murphy said, pointing at Gonzalez.

"Fuck you, it's not first come, first served," said Gonzalez.

"Are you sure you want in on this?" I asked. "None of you is officially rated in zero-G."

Again, they looked at me like I'd kicked their dog, and then they glanced at each other for several seconds until Zilla finally spoke. "Ma'am, we all train for it. We're going. We're a team. It's our job, and nobody else is taking it."

I considered it for a couple seconds and then nodded. "But there are only three slots, so somebody has to sit this one out."

"You choose, ma'am," said Zilla.

"Okay. I'll go over your psych evals and see how each of you are likely to handle some of the things we might see."

"Murph has an evaluation of his brain on file," said Gonzalez. "It's a very small file."

"It probably just says 'none'," added Xiang.

"What kind of stuff are we expecting, ma'am?" asked Zilla.

"At a minimum, I think a lot of people probably died up there. I don't know what that's going to look like. But that's not what I'm worried about. What's got me worried is that everywhere we've gone, people have tried to stop us. I want to be ready for that."

Zilla nodded. "Roger that, ma'am. Sign me up."

"All four of you prepare. Go and get fitted for space gear. Tell the printers top priority on my order."

"One of us has to stay with you, ma'am," Murphy said.

I sighed. "Fine. Rotate out and do what you have to do. I'm going to find Master Sergeant Hearns."

Contrary to Xiang's prediction, Hearns didn't shit himself. He didn't do anything. He just got quiet and sunk into himself, maybe considering the options before he spoke.

"Is it going to make a difference if I tell you it's a bad idea, ma'am?"

"Tell me why."

"Because you're the commander and we need you here. We've talked about this. You have to lead like a commander now, not like a lieutenant, where you run off and do things on your own."

I was ready for his question because I'd thought it through in some detail. "You're right. I have to do the things that only I can do and delegate the rest. But that's the thing. Only I can do this. There's no way to get anybody without an implant up to speed fast enough to take this on."

Hearns considered it. "What about Captain Perston?"

"Seriously? You want to put all of our fates in his hands?"

"No, I really don't. You're right." He paused. "So, supposing you go. At minimum, you're going to be out of pocket for half a day. At worst?"

"There's a risk in that. But what choice do we have? There's not another viable option."

"What about command down here? Are you going to leave Perston in charge?"

"I don't know. What do you think? I could name you as commander."

He shook his head instinctively. "Not when there's an officer here. Nobody would accept that. Not Perston, but also not the other noncoms. It's just not how it's done. We need as much normalcy as we can get."

"Okay. Your call."

"You could keep the command even while you're out. Only shift it to him if something happens to you or you go out of comms."

I didn't love the idea. Every unit should have a commander present if possible. But I didn't want to go against Hearns's advice any more than I had to. "We can do that if you think that's best. I added three security personnel to my team. I'm going to go through psych reports of my four and see which are the best fit."

"Take Murphy, Zillakovavich, and Gonzalez," he said. "I went through their files extensively before I picked them for you. Z is a complete pro in every situation, Murphy is immune to pressure, and Gonzalez is strong in all areas, though not the best in any one. Xiang is a good soldier, but not as good as the other three in this situation."

"Okay. I trust your call. I'm going to talk to Perston and tell him what I'm doing."

"You sure, ma'am??"

"He's going to find out anyway. Better that he hear it from me and I get a chance to warn him not to act out."

"I'll trust you on that one,."

"After that, I'm going to study some more of the technical stuff and try to get some sleep. We'll be taking off early."

I found Perston in the dining hall drinking coffee with a few noncoms. I got myself a water with electrolytes and walked over. Either on their own or at his signal, the others got up as a group and departed, politely greeting me on their way out.

"Thanks for making that easy," I said.

"Of course." Perston gestured for me to take the seat across from him. Technically, he should have stood, but I wasn't going to bother making an issue out of something as minor as that. "What's up?"

"We've got a plan to get comms reestablished, but it involves me taking a team up the space elevator in an improvised car with no life support." I don't know if I said it that way to sound cool, or to shock him. I hadn't thought it through, and that's just how it came out.

"Shit," he said. "That's the only way?"

"Originally, I was sending the engineer that we got from Argaz, but they recalled her. I downloaded a bunch of info onto my implant to take her part in the mission. So yeah. I think it's the only way."

"You want me to go instead?" he offered. I'm not sure what surprised me more—that he made the offer or that he sounded sincere.

"I need to do this myself," I said.

"That's good. For a second there I was really sure you were going to say yes." He laughed, and for the first time that I could remember it almost seemed comfortable between us. "I really hate heights. What can I do to help?"

"Support Hearns. I should be up and back in a matter of hours, but if anything happens, he'll support you."

"Hearns doesn't like me much."

"He really doesn't. Can you blame him?" I smiled, to soften the shot.

"Not really." He smiled. "I'll try. That's all I can promise."

"I appreciate it. Thanks." I stood to go.

"Hey. Kira."

"Yeah?"

"You're doing a good job."

"Yeah?"

"I just wanted to tell you that. You know. In case—" He let it trail off.

"Yeah. I got you. Thanks, Dirk."

25

The next morning, I stood with Murphy, Zilla, Gonzalez, and four technicians: Chenoweth, Davis, Winston, and Enzor. They were going through last minute checklists prior to boarding the tram. It was just after 0400 hours and still dark, though the slightest hint of a glow limned the eastern horizon. I stood still as Zilla checked my kit. When you were going into vacuum, everybody got double-checked—even the commander. Zilla got the job because she was head of the security detail. Somebody had to be in charge, and I hadn't made that call. She, Murphy, and Gonzalez decided it on their own.

Checks completed, I entered the tram last. A dozen or so soldiers had gathered around us either as part of their job or just to see us off, and I waved to them as I crossed through the door, trying to look confident, even though I didn't know what that looked like. I didn't *feel* confident. Despite cramming my high-capacity brain with as much information as possible, I couldn't help but think how many things could go wrong. When we stepped off the tram five hundred kilometers above the surface of the planet, we could be facing almost anything. No amount of preparation could compensate for that—for the not knowing.

I found my seat in the crowded space, one of four along each side separated by the door on one side and a single window on the other. The entire compartment was shaped like a disc with our seats on the bottom —what was currently the floor. They'd remain in that position until we reached the point where we started to slow, and then they'd slide along rails to the ceiling, which would then become the floor due to the deceleration force. There was no driver. They controlled the tram itself from the base station. Our equipment—the quantum communicator, tools, and a portable power generator—were strapped in the middle of the floor. We were counting on zero-G to help us get those unloaded, as they were heavy and hard to move.

Once buckled in, we accelerated gradually—at about one-quarter of a G—which pushed us down into our seats for less than a minute before the acceleration cut off and all we had left was the gravity of the planet. Several of the soldiers with me had their eyes closed behind their clear faceplates, a testament to the fact that soldiers can and will sleep absolutely anywhere. I didn't blame them. The views out the door and the window were impressive, but not much different than looking out of an airplane initially. I didn't even try to sleep. I was too keyed up, playing every possible scenario I could imagine on a loop in my overactive brain until I was treated to a sped-up version of a sunrise as the planet rotated and we simultaneously gained altitude. Only Murphy seemed to be gazing around.

He keyed his mic and said, "Ma'am, I probably should have told you this before now, but I'm afraid of heights."

I couldn't speak for a moment. We hadn't even started, and I'd potentially lost a soldier. "What the—"

"Ma'am," said Murphy, interrupting me. "I'm fucking with you."

I sat there for a second, processing. And then I laughed. "You got me. I was ready to kick your ass."

"Let's not rule out any options," offered Gonzalez.

Not long after that, our chairs automatically began to slide up the side of the tram and onto what had previously been the ceiling, and we started to slow. We decelerated at a slower rate—about a tenth of a G—probably to spare the brakes. That meant we had about seventeen minutes until we arrived. I opened a general comms feed to everybody on the mission. "Heads up. We're about fifteen minutes out. Let's go over our assignments one more time. Zilla, you first."

"Roger, ma'am. Murph, Gonzo and I are first through the door and will move to secure the landing area. We'll report on life support and power conditions as available. Once secure, we'll report, triggering your move."

"Roger," I said. "Sergeant Chenoweth?"

Chenoweth was senior among the techs, and she'd taken charge of them naturally. "When we get the word, Davis and I will debark and move aboard the station, initially staying inside the perimeter created by the security team. We will corroborate life support and power conditions, and then, based on what we find, assess our ability to improve those conditions and how much time that might take. Enzor and Winston will stay with the tram until we make a call on whether we can reestablish life support or power, and they'll either join us to take on that task or we'll scrap that option and they'll begin the procedures for a manual satellite launch."

"Roger," I said. "The satellite launch is the priority. I want everyone clear on that. We have to establish communications. Nothing else we do matters if we don't make that happen."

A chorus of rogers answered.

"And if we see dead bodies?" I expected that we would, so I wanted to address it again in clinical terms to lessen the impact when it happened.

"We avoid them as much as possible, moving them only as needed to accomplish the mission," said Chenoweth. "My team will move the bodies to places that don't affect our work while the security team maintains one hundred percent readiness. Just in case. We'll come back to the bodies and stack them in a single location if we have time after we complete the primary mission."

"Roger that." I flipped to another channel and checked my comms back to the base station. "Away team approaching landing in approximately ten minutes. How are we looking?"

"No changes, Away. Everything looks good. You're cleared for docking."

"Roger." Cleared for docking—I wasn't sure what that meant. It wasn't like we had any control over it. It did sound comforting to hear, though.

The station swallowed us whole and the views outside went black, leaving us in the dim glow of the tram's internal lighting as our chairs shifted us again to align with the station. I tried to get a sense of up or down but couldn't, and time seemed to stand still. It was probably thirty seconds, but it felt like minutes. We were in zero-G, or close to it. The door slid open automatically and the security team exited their restraints and began to float in the cabin, bumping into each other and those of us still attached to our seats for a few seconds before getting the hang of freefall and anchoring themselves. Zilla activated her mag boots and attached to the floor while Murph and Gonzalez grabbed handholds and propelled themselves above her.

Then they were gone, and my only input was via comm from Zilla.

"Landing area clear," she said. "No power, no atmosphere."

"Roger, clear." I didn't bother to relay the report to the base station since they couldn't do anything for us from down there. I hit the button to release my restraints, as did the tech team. "We'll move on your call of in-position."

"Roger." The comm went dead for several seconds before Zilla came back on. "In position."

"Moving." I used a handhold to propel me to the door, leading out the rest of the team. Beams from our helmets cut through the darkness, bouncing off walls and other reflective surfaces and creating a shifting ambient light that brought the large landing area into view in fits and starts.

Davis, the electrician, moved to a wall panel, removed it with a handheld tool, and patched into it while the rest of us waited somewhat patiently. "No readings," he announced. "I'm going to have to get to the main board."

"Roger," I returned. His finding wasn't unexpected. "Zilla, make your next move."

"Roger," she said, before dropping off the group net to talk to her two team members. Murphy worked the manual lever for the door leading to the main station and muscled it open, and Zilla and Gonzalez darted through in a maneuver that almost made it look like they trained in zero-G every day. Murphy followed not far behind. The comm stayed quiet for several seconds, and then several more, until finally I couldn't take it.

"What have you got?" I asked.

Zilla's voice was hesitant when she responded. "Nothing, ma'am. We've got nothing."

"No bodies?"

"No, ma'am. No bodies, no atmosphere, no power."

The power didn't surprise me. The atmosphere—I didn't expect *good* air, but I expected something. For it to be a total vacuum—well, that would have taken power. If people had been alive when they lost life support, they could have survived for a time on what atmosphere they had until they asphyxiated. For there to be nothing made it look more like an active venting. Could a catastrophic loss of power have done that? If it had, it would have ended the lives of the crew mercifully quicker. I ran through my options quickly and decided to stick to the original plan.

"Let's move to the central board and get an assessment of what it would take to get the power back on." Power was more important than atmosphere, because without power, we couldn't pump air even if we had it, and it supported our primary mission of getting the quantum communicator deployed. We could do that without power, but it would take a lot more work.

Where the fuck were the bodies, though?

I passed through another door and down a narrow corridor, moving slowly with the security team bounding ahead. Meanwhile, the tech team had gone back to retrieve the portable generator so they could patch it into the main power board. It wouldn't be enough to run the station, but it could bring critical systems online if they were operational, or at least provide enough power to diagnose them. From there, we'd move to the large airlock and work to get that back online so we could deploy the quantum communicator.

The heavy fall of my magnetic boots rippled through me as we moved through the empty passageways, creating an eerie atmosphere that almost gave the illusion of sound. The further we went, the more it bothered me. There's a cliché about things being *too* quiet. But that wasn't quite it. We still hadn't seen any bodies. The station looked pristine, as if someone had cleaned up and set everything in order before departing for a planned vacation. Just the opposite of what I'd imagine from a panicked crew clinging to survival. Possible explanations ran through my head as I followed Murphy around a corner. Perhaps the crew had holed up in one location and kept the air flowing there as long as they could, and we just hadn't stumbled across that spot yet.

We reached the access door for central engineering and Zilla set her people in a perimeter while Chenoweth and Davis maneuvered the generator into the narrow space. It weighed nothing in zero-G, but they still managed to bang it into the side of the door as they entered. They finally got it situated and anchored it to the floor with two magnetic clamps. Davis worked on an electrical box while Chenoweth prepared the generator, pulling out a thick plug from a recessed port and handing it over. Davis accepted the cord and seated it firmly in the receptacle, checking it twice to make sure it was secure.

"Fire it up." He stepped back toward me, leaving Chenoweth alone with the generator. It took about a minute for the mini-reactor inside of it to power up, which I knew from downloading the specs was normal. Meanwhile, the two techs traded places, and as lights started to flicker across the equipment, Davis began to press buttons and flip levers on the board, cutting power to non-essential systems and hopefully routing it to the things we needed.

"You want me to try to get life support running, Ma'am?" Davis asked.

"Not yet. Let's get the mission done, and if everything is going well, we can come back and try to bring the entire station online. Right now, I don't want to waste any time." That had been the plan from the start, but I felt even more strongly about it now. Something wasn't right.

"Roger. Powering physical infrastructure now. The airlocks should be operational in under a minute." As if to punctuate his report, emergency lights came on up and down the outer hallway where I stood, followed several seconds later by the brighter main lights bathing the hall.

"Does anybody else feel that?" asked Murphy.

I tried to figure out what he meant, but all I could make out was the vibration of systems coming online. "It's just the station starting up."

"I feel movement. Something thudding against the floor."

"People?" I asked. I couldn't get my brain around it. Nobody could have survived. There was no air, and regardless of how they had rationed emergency supplies, it had been too long.

"I don't think so," said Murphy.

"I feel it too," said Zilla. "Almost like…"

And then it hit me, too. A vibration in the floor, and not the smooth hum of equipment. "Feels like—"

Flashes erupted at one end of the cross-corridor and Gonzalez disappeared in an avalanche of sparks, flying backwards and disappearing. I froze as it took me half a second to process what I'd seen. Bullets glancing off of Gonzalez's armored space suit. Either through luck or instinct, he'd disengaged his mag boots, which might have saved his life as some of the momentum of the rounds would have dissipated as he flew backward.

"Gonzalez!" I called. No response.

By the time I reacted, Zilla had launched herself past me and took up a firing position at the end of the hall where Gonzalez had disappeared, using the corner for cover as she began to fire. "Combat bots! At least two of them."

I tried to make sense of it. They hadn't been active when we docked. And then it hit me. They'd come online when we powered up the station systems. I had to make a quick decision. If we cut power, would they shut down? My gut said no. They'd have internal batteries. Add to that the fact that maintaining power would help us to deploy the communicator.

It felt like it took me a minute to make a decision but, in reality, it had probably only been a second or two. "Try to hold them off. Tech Team Two, get the communicator to the launch airlock. Tech Team One, you're with security now. Stall whatever's out there until we get the launch complete, and then we'll exfil together."

Several rogers responded, and if the two techs who had a moment ago been powering the station had an opinion about being turned into line soldiers, they kept it to themselves.

"Still no response from Gonzalez, ma'am," reported Zilla.

A barrage of bullets flashed off the floor and the wall near Zilla just as she pulled back around the corner. "These things have a ton of firepower."

They were firing bullets, which seemed wrong for a space station. Who would send projectile weapons to a pressurized system? But then, we weren't pressurized. We were in vacuum, so it didn't matter much beyond the damage the projectiles might do to onboard systems.

And why were there combat bots here at all? They were designed for planets without sentient life. It didn't matter. They were here, and we had to deal with them. We could figure out the why's later.

Streaks flashed at the opposite end of the hall, where Murphy was in a similar defensive position to Zilla at her end. "I've got one down here too!"

Shit. They had us trapped in the cross corridor, cutting off my means to get to tech team two. Which immediately made me wonder if there were more bots throughout the base.

"Tech Team Two, any sign of bots?"

The line stayed dead for two or three seconds before a shaky male voice came on. "Ma'am, this is Winston. We don't see anything."

"Roger. Keep at your task. I'll try to reach you to help. Right now, I think we're between you and the bad guys. The team here will try to hold them off so you can work."

I took a second to fully assess our situation. Three of us were stuck in the cross corridor, hemmed in by Murphy and Zilla, who had each corner. We couldn't help them. But on the bright side, Murphy and Zilla controlled the two main passageways with their sporadic fire, and at least for the moment, the bots seemed to be content to hold us in place.

I needed more information. "Zilla, you have video? Send it."

"Roger."

THE WEIGHT OF COMMAND

A file beeped into my implant and I gave it permission to run. Zilla faced off against two Mark 47 combat bots. They were ugly things, with rectangular bodies and two pillars for legs that rotated like wheels when they needed to move fast. I pulled their specs from my database and analyzed them quickly.

Shit.

Our weapons wouldn't do much to them. When their AIs figured that out, they could blow right past us to Tech Team Two. Or right through us. Why they'd stopped and engaged from distance, I couldn't say. One thing I couldn't know was their mission orders. Maybe they were supposed to kill all humans and didn't feel the need to move on to the next batch until they dispatched these five here, conveniently pinned down.

"Is your fire having any effect?" I asked, to confirm my read.

"Nothing physical from the pulse weapon," said Zilla, "though the fire does seem to be confusing them."

"Good. Keep it up. Anything that holds them in place works." I almost added that as long as we got the communicator going, nothing else mattered. Because while it was true from a mission standpoint, emotionally, we were talking about our own lives. And they mattered.

"Murphy and I've got explosive rounds," said Zilla. "So do you. I've been holding off because of the potential damage to the station, but they might be the only thing that works against these beasts."

"Save them for now, as long as they're holding position and we can keep them away from the commo team. But if they start to advance, give them everything you've got. Murph, how many on your end?"

"Just the one. But I've used almost a third of my pulse pack already. Shit!" Murphy jerked back, and I didn't have to ask to know he'd been hit.

"You okay?"

"Yes, ma'am." The strain in his voice as he said it begged to differ with his words, but he poked back around the corner and fired off another burst, so he was at least functional.

"Fall back for a minute and let Chenoweth take your spot. Jump back in when you're ready."

"I'm good," Murphy said, so I let it drop.

"Okay. I need to get back to help out with the communicator. Your side has fewer enemy, so I'm going to try to get out that way. I need you to cover me—use the explosive stuff for about ten seconds."

"Roger that."

I moved to Murphy's end of the corridor. "On three." I counted it off, and Murphy popped out and began firing. There was no sound because of the vacuum, so I just had to take it on faith that he was doing his job. After four seconds I darted out and launched myself down the hallway the opposite direction from the bot, deactivating my mag boots and flying through the corridor in zero-G.

Something slammed into my back and all of a sudden I was tumbling out of control. I focused on the distant wall trying to get my bearings and used my implant to calculate my trajectory, which I fed directly to my suit, triggering my maneuvering jets to stabilize me.

Then the pain hit. I didn't have a suit breach—I'd have known that pretty quickly—but even through my armor I felt like someone had hit me between my shoulder blades with a hammer. Reaching the end of the hall I arrested my movement with a handhold and pulled myself around the corner and out of the line of fire.

"Fuck!" Murphy again. "I'm hit. Chenoweth, cover me." I let the chatter from the security team slide past me and focused on moving as fast as I could. They had their job to do, and I had mine. I couldn't help them now.

When I reached the airlock, the team was already in place. Winston faced down the corridor with his weapon pointed, and for a second, I thought he might shoot me. That would have been a shitty way to die. The commo tech, Enzor, was hunched over the quantum communicator, which was about the same size she was, her fingers flying as fast as they could given the restraints of the space suit.

"Fuck fuck *fuck*!" she said and pulled her hands back.

"What's wrong?" I asked.

"I missed a step in the initialization. I'm resetting and starting over."

"Take a breath," I said. "Take your time. Slow is smooth and smooth is fast."

Enzor backed away from the machine for a second and settled herself. "Right, ma'am. I've got this."

"You've got this." I turned away from her. She didn't need the pressure of me looking at her, and despite my crash course on the machine, I liked her odds of getting it right better than mine.

"Shit! Chenoweth is down," shouted Murphy. "I'm going to try and hold—" His broadcast cut out.

I didn't know for sure what that meant, but it absolutely wasn't good. "Heads up, Winston. We might have company. How's it coming Enzor?"

"Almost there."

THE WEIGHT OF COMMAND

The floor shook, and it could only be from the magnetic legs of the combat bot propelling itself at high speed in our direction.

"Done!" shouted Enzor.

"Get it into the airlock and get it deployed. Winston and I will hold this thing—"

Winston's head exploded. A spatter of blood and meat pelted my face plate. Without thinking, I disengaged my mag boots and flung myself at the ceiling, maneuvering to put my back against it. I needed to draw fire and keep it away from Enzor and the communicator. I selected explosive ammo and took a split second to let my implant analyze and aim. Slow is smooth, and smooth is fast.

I held the trigger down for three seconds and the bot disappeared in a fury of small explosions. I risked a look behind me in time to catch Enzor disappearing into the airlock with the now floating device. The door closed behind her, but that's all I saw before a bullet from the bot slammed into my shoulder, painfully reorienting my attention.

I fired another three second burst. Enzor shouldn't have closed the airlock. She needed to exit first.

"I'm not risking coming back out and trying to activate the airlock from out there," she said, as if reading my mind. "And without air in the airlock, there won't be any force to move the communicator away from the station. I'm going to use the jets in my suit."

"No! Get back in here and we'll work from—" I cut off my communication as the ceiling erupted around me.

Enzor went on, oblivious to it. "There's a manual release in here. Deploying quantum communicator now."

"Fuuuckkk!" I shouted as I fired at the bot until my weapon ran out of explosive ammo several long seconds later. I hit it, it hit me, sending me bouncing along the ceiling and spinning me away from the bot. I fought to gain control, but one of my arms went numb, making it hard. I finally got my good arm and one of my feet to latch on to the ceiling with their magnets, but I didn't have my weapon. I spun back toward the bot and found it on its side and smoking. My weapon was floating down by the floor, so I pushed off of the ceiling toward it. Miraculously, I didn't have a suit breach, but I still couldn't use my right arm. The shoulder hurt, dull and aching more than sharp, and I thought maybe something had just hit a nerve. It would wait. I attached my weapon to my side so I could have my good arm free.

"Enzor!" I moved to the airlock door to see if I could still spot her, but the window only allowed a view of the inside of the airlock.

"I'm here."

"Where?" I asked. "I can't see you."

"I overshot a bit on my thrust, I think. I'm moving away from the station pretty quickly. I don't know that I'm going to be able to get back. But the communicator is functioning."

My mind raced for a way to get her back. That was top priority now. The job was done. The communicator was floating in orbit—along with Enzor—which meant that our dispatch had already been sent. I'd kept the repeating message short—eleven seconds—and they'd receive it at the other end almost instantly. Whatever happened now, nobody could stop that. "Try to slow yourself and stay as close as possible. We'll get to you."

"Ma'am," Zilla cut in. "You need to get out of there. I can't hold them much longer. Davis is dead. It's just me here and I'm running out of ammo."

Fuck! Enzor would have to wait. "On my way."

"No!" Zilla hadn't ever raised her voice before. "Ma'am, you need to get to the elevator and get out of here. I'll hold them off as long as I can."

"I'm not leaving you and Enzor behind." I left the others off of the statement. I didn't want to leave them, either, but I assumed they were dead.

"Ma'am, they need you down below. Someone needs to make it back, and it needs to be you. We're not going to win this fight here."

I screamed into my helmet with my mic off, raging at my no-win situation. Fuck that. I wasn't leaving her. I took a few steps back toward the fight, but then stopped. She was right. It absolutely sucked, but she was right. We'd gotten our message out, but we still had weeks before we could expect a relief force, and we had an unstable situation on the planet. I needed to be there for it. I wanted to save my team. That's what a lieutenant does. A commander had to think bigger than that. "I hear you," I said, finally. "If you can get away from the bots, try to find a way to get Enzor back."

"Roger," said Zilla, but her voice told me there was no chance.

"Enzor?"

"Ma'am...I can't find the station. I tumbled some, and it's really hard to tell direction up here."

"Hold on. Someone is going to get to you." I wasn't sure that was true, but I didn't know what else to say in that situation.

"Roger, ma'am I'm not going anywhere. I'm going to float here for a while. The view is amazing. But I've only got about four hours of air left."

"Hang on."

"I will, ma'am. As long as I can. If nobody gets to me—well, when I get low on air, I'm not going to go out that way. I'll pop the seal on my helmet."

I stood there, unable to speak, tears welling in my eyes, which would cause serious problems in a spacesuit. I fought it, tried to come up with some words. But I couldn't. Because what the fuck are you supposed to say to two people who are willingly sacrificing their lives for the mission? It seemed best to simply honor the sacrifice and do what they said. When I spoke, I tried to keep my voice as even as possible for them.

"Moving to the elevator now."

Back inside the tram, I got strapped in as quick as I could and then called the control station to start me moving. The ride down was a little slower than the ride up, both literally and figuratively. I'm not sure why the tram didn't reach quite the same speed on its descent, but I understood why it felt even longer than it was. What a disaster. Everyone dead or soon to be—all seven of them, and me alive only because I was the commander. Anybody else on the team would have gone back into the fight, tried to save their teammates. I ran away. Academically, I knew it was the right thing to do. Emotionally, I felt like a cold piece of shit. And then, as if that wasn't enough, I berated myself for feeling bad, because who the fuck was I to feel sorry for myself when everybody else was dead?

I tried to put it out of my mind by talking to the base station. "Have an assault team ready to board as soon as I arrive. Eight personnel, armed to take out two combat bots."

"Roger, ma'am."

"Have you received anything back across the quantum communicator?"

"No, ma'am. The feed isn't live down here. If it's receiving, that part of the link isn't working."

"What do the comms experts say?" I asked.

"They say it's not unexpected. The QC previously relayed messaging through the station in orbit and then down to us. That link is still broken."

"But the message still got out…right?"

"We believe so, ma'am."

"But you can't confirm it."

"No, ma'am. We can't confirm it."

I wanted to yell. I'd known that that was the part least likely to function, but with everything else that had happened…it was too much.

"Ma'am?" It was Enzor. Her transmission was faint, but still readable from wherever she was in her orbit.

"What's up, Enzor?"

"Ma'am…there's something out here. It's getting bigger."

"Are you heading back to the station?"

"I don't think so. I think whatever it is, is coming at *me*." The line went quiet for a moment. "It's a ship!"

"A ship?" Holy shit. We couldn't have gotten that lucky. The odds that a ship would arrive and happen across a drifting person in time to save her were beyond astronomical.

"It's firing someth—" Enzor's transmission cut off.

And then it hit me. The odds hadn't come in. A ship didn't arrive to save her. They found her by tracking the communicator, and now they'd silenced it. And her. I immediately started scanning above me, which was difficult with only two view ports. If they'd come for her, I'd probably be next. And I wouldn't be hard to find.

But fuck them. They were too late. The message got out. I had to believe that. They could come for me, but at least I'd die with that little bit of satisfaction.

But maybe I wouldn't.

I checked the altitude from my implant. I'd just crossed below a hundred-thousand meters, putting me well inside the atmosphere. That might save me. A ship built for space likely wouldn't have in-atmosphere capability; there was rarely a need for both. Perhaps they'd go to the waystation instead. That didn't stop me from continuing to scan out the window, silently willing my tram to go faster. I was descending at about two-hundred meters per second, but that rate was declining the closer I got to the surface.

And then I saw it. A red streak coming toward me from above.

Shit.

The ship didn't have to enter the atmosphere. Its missile could.

A lot of things ran through my mind—one of those situations where time seems to almost freeze, and your brain races through a hundred thoughts, even though in reality it was probably just a couple of seconds.

Could a person survive a skydive from—I checked the altitude again—seventy-seven thousand meters? I didn't know. But the odds had to be better than taking a direct hit from a missile while in an unarmored tram.

In the end it was no decision at all. I released from my seat, hit the emergency override on the door, and launched myself into space.

I never saw the missile hit. I was spinning, and my first thought was that I was moving too fast. The tram had been moving downward at about 175 meters per second when I left it, and that momentum transferred to me. And that wasn't the biggest problem. There wasn't much air at this altitude, but there was enough resistance to start me spinning, and I couldn't gain control of it.

My suit squeezed my legs, trying to keep the blood pumping to my brain so the G-force wouldn't knock me out. That would get worse as I hit denser air and started to decelerate at a more significant rate.

"I'm…in…freefall." I managed to squeeze out the three words over what seemed like several seconds to alert the team on the ground, if my comms was strong enough to reach them without the station to boost it. Air rushing by my suit drowned out any possibility of hearing a response. Sweat dripped down my face, my neck, my back—it got in my eyes, but it didn't matter, because I couldn't see anyway. Something must have gorked in my cooling system when the bot shot me.

I couldn't find the horizon. Still spinning. My vision started to go black on the outside, narrowing my field of view. Oddly, I thought of Enzor. How she'd lost track of the station.

But I had something she didn't. I had an implant.

I triggered my suit to shoot me full of stimulants to try to keep from passing out. I had to slow my descent. I used my implant to control the thrusters in my suit, and it fired them planetward in controlled bursts when they aligned, using microbursts at exact moments that no human brain could manage alone. I couldn't focus enough to see the results in my velocity. I had to trust the machinery. I focused on each burst of thrusters and tried to ignore the growing heat that was winning the fight against my suit's cooling systems. The last temperature I remember was 41C before I passed out.

26

When I came to, I was still falling, feet first and no longer spinning, my chute open. I could make out individual objects on the ground—some buildings in the distance, the dust trail of a vehicle moving across the prairie—and I put my altitude around four hundred meters. A quick check of my implant confirmed that.

"Base, this is Markov." The words croaked out of me, and a wave of thirst hit me. I activated my suit's drinking tube and gulped tepid water, only forcing myself to slow down after a few seconds so I didn't throw it up.

The comm stayed dead. I really hoped they knew I was skydiving, that they'd received that message. I hoped that the vehicle moving across the desert was one of ours. I'd lost my weapon, and it would really suck to survive a ridiculous freefall from space only to be killed or captured when I landed.

I looked up and checked my canopy, which was bright red and white. That made sense. It wasn't a tactical chute. You don't plan to use the parachute in a space suit unless it's a horrible emergency.

And there I was, bright as a beacon, for anybody to see.

I think the thing that screwed with me most at that moment was the fact that barely four hours had passed since I departed that morning, and the sun still sat low in the cloudless morning sky.

I had about another minute until I reached ground, so I started to gather information. The dust trail had resolved itself into multiple vehicles traveling in a line, and they would reach me about three minutes after I landed if I continued on my current path. My chute didn't have an actual steering system, but I could still guide it by pulling the risers on one side or the other to angle the canopy. The problem was, there weren't many options in open grassland. I decided to head for a rock outcropping that broke the grass about a kilometer away, as it was the only visible feature in range, spikes of gray and black in a field of greenish brown. I pulled hard on the risers on that side of the chute to get me moving in that direction. I was running partially with the wind, so I ate up the distance quickly, and eventually released them so that I'd land in the grass nearby and not on the rocks themselves.

I held no illusions. The rock outcropping wouldn't hide me for long. But if someone was coming for me, I wasn't going to make it easy on them. They could come dig me out.

At about a hundred meters from the ground, I tried my comm again. Still nothing. I tried sending a message directly from my implant, bypassing the spacesuit. Nothing there, either.

Twenty seconds later I landed, feet first, and then collapsed to my side to absorb some of the impact. At full gravity, the suit was awkward at best, and trying to trek any distance in it would be nearly impossible. I scrambled to detach my chute and fought my way out of my suit. All I had underneath it was a moisture wicking undergarment. Not ideal for long term survival, but at least it was lightweight and covered all of my skin. That would give me some protection from the sun, though I figured dehydration was probably a bigger worry than sunburn. And that made me realize that my suit was my only water source. It was too heavy to carry, and I made a split-second decision to leave it. I could come back for the water if those vehicles passed me by and this turned from an evasion into a survival situation.

I reached the rocks and got behind the first one just as the vehicles crested the dune behind me. My vision was blurry, which might have been the morning heat coming off the low rolling terrain playing tricks on me or may have been a sign of something more serious going on with my body. I stumbled and went to my knees.

I may have blacked out again for a moment—I'm not sure—but the next thing I remember was someone yelling my name. I used a large rock jutting up from the grass to pull myself to my feet. A convoy of four vehicles had stopped by my suit, and soldiers were out, looking around.

My soldiers.

"Over here," I called, and then sat down to wait once they spotted me.

They bundled me onto a stretcher and someone jammed IVs in both my arms. By the time they carried me to a vehicle five minutes later, I was coherent again.

"I can sit up," I said.

"It's easier for us to keep the IVs running if you're lying down, ma'am. You've lost a lot of fluids." I marked the young soldier for a medic.

An older woman with a strong chin—I couldn't see her rank, and I didn't have the awareness to get her name from my implant—addressed me next. That would probably make her the platoon leader. "We'll be back at the elevator base station in twenty to twenty-five minutes, ma'am."

"Did the tram make it down from space?"

She hesitated, and I knew the answer before she told me. "No, ma'am."

"Then take me back to the main base. There's nothing I can do at the elevator."

"Roger, ma'am."

"I'll stay laying down like the medic said, but get me access to a comm. Something is gorked with my implant and I can't reach anybody."

"Roger, ma'am. Ezekiel!" A soldier came hustling over, and the sergeant gave him orders to get me a communicator. He disappeared as fast as he'd arrived, and in just a couple of minutes he was back and fitting a headset on me.

Funny thing, though. As soon as I had the ability to talk to anybody, I suddenly couldn't think of anything to say. What could words do? We'd accomplished the mission by launching the QC, but we didn't know if our message got through. There was nothing we could do about that.

And everybody was dead.

Everybody but me.

As I tried to get my mind to focus on what orders I should be giving, I kept coming back to that, and every time I did, it derailed me. Eventually I just contacted Watch and said, "This is Major Markov. SITREP."

It took a few seconds for a response, and when they keyed the mic, I thought I heard cheering on the other end before McNamara started speaking. Fucking cheering. As if me being alive was something to celebrate. People were watching me, so I fought hard to hold back tears, so hard that I gave myself a pounding headache.

"Ma'am, we haven't had any communications from off-planet. Nothing from the quantum communicator, nothing from the orbital waystation."

No surprises there. "Roger."

"Things are calm with the Argazzi. They've still got a small force deployed, but it's a screen line—purely defensive, and really only precautional."

That was no change from when I left. But then, how much could have changed when I'd only been gone a few hours? I tried to focus on the rest of what she was saying, but my mind slipped away from it. I'd be back in a short time anyway. They could handle it until then.

The next few weeks passed in mostly the same way. I went through the motions on things—sat through staff meetings, got the comms in my implant working, took updates, ate food when someone put it in front of me. But I couldn't *feel* anything. Nothing mattered. There wasn't anything medically wrong with me; they checked me often enough where that was more than assured. But I wasn't there.

I took a few video meetings with the Argazzi to discuss their grievances, but the fight had gone out of them almost as much as it had gone out of me. I didn't contact Trieste, and there were moments where I wondered what happened—whether she'd just been taken off the job of talking to me or removed from her job completely. Or something worse. The Argazzi didn't tolerate failure very well. Maybe it would have helped me to talk to her, but even with Trieste, I couldn't make myself care for long. If something had happened to her...well...I didn't want to know. I wasn't sure I could survive learning that I was responsible for yet another life lost. Especially that one.

The Zargod were harder to put off. They kept insisting on showing up at base and pushing hard for the infrastructure project. But even they wore down eventually when I blandly agreed to their demands every time we talked but didn't actually take any action to make them happen. There would be repercussions for that, but I figured that we could deal with all that when it came.

Xiang took it at least as hard as me. Maybe harder. He didn't say so—he didn't say anything—but he'd lost his entire team without even being in the fight. That had to suck. Granted, it wasn't at all his fault like it was mine. But something told me that wouldn't have comforted him, that he wouldn't see my culpability as a bigger failure than his own. He rarely left me, even when Hearns assigned new soldiers to my security team. They tried to relieve Xiang. I saw them. But he just waved them off most of the time. I think some nights he might have slept leaning against the wall outside the door of my quarters.

I should have talked to him about it. I know that. But I couldn't. I'd gotten his friends killed. How do you talk about that? I'm sure a real major would have known. I didn't.

Hearns didn't yell at me. I kept expecting him to, kept expecting him to explode and tell me that I was letting the team down and to get over my shit and get to work. He'd done it before. But he didn't. He didn't make excuses for me, but he did treat me with a soft touch, and he made routine decisions that I should have handled. And everybody accepted that. He didn't give orders in my name. Not directly. He just gave orders on his own and everybody assumed that I was good with them. Which...I was. I like to believe that if something critical came up—something that truly required my attention—he'd have brought it to me. But honestly, I don't know. I don't know if he'd have involved me, and I don't know if I could have handled it if he did.

We were both okay with the show.

Even Perston helped out. There it was, his chance to manipulate things behind the scenes with me too messed up to pay attention, but he didn't. I wouldn't have known it at the time, but I went back and checked later. He took on more work, and from what I could tell, he did it well.

I couldn't avoid everything, of course. The king of Zarga called. Or, rather, his people did, and then I waited on the line for ten minutes until he appeared to tell me that they had detained the prime minister, as we'd discussed, and he admitted to having been bribed. That wasn't a particularly significant crime in Zarga, so apparently the confession came easy. But it led to a dead end, as the man who had done the bribing had disappeared, and while they could link him to off-world activity, he had been too smart to leave clues to his affiliation.

The Argazzi were more dramatic in their approach, which I only learned of when Joran Yakina called for clearance to fly into Zarga airspace so he could meet with me. We met in the fancy meeting room, just him and I and Xiang. Yakina asked for Xiang to step out, but Xiang didn't move, and I didn't care enough to make him.

Resigned, Yakina launched into his pitch. "We found that some of our government leaders had been corrupted by outside influences."

If he expected to surprise me, he'd be disappointed. I barely reacted. Perhaps the only surprise was that he was here, admitting it.

"What officials?"

"We prefer to keep that under wraps, but we want you to know that the problem...problems...have been eliminated." His tone left no doubt to what *eliminated* meant.

"Liana Trieste?" She was the only Argazzi official I cared about.

"Ms. Trieste was a unique situation."

"How so?" I asked.

Yakina thought about it for a few seconds, perhaps deciding on how much to share with me. "She was not under outside influence. But she did use her connection to you to greatly inflate her position within the government after the nuclear event."

When it seemed like he didn't intend to continue, I prompted him. "And that led to..."

"Ms. Trieste has been relieved of the position to which she was recently promoted." When I didn't respond, instead staring him down, he added, "She's alive."

I nodded. "That's good."

The first thing that really cut through my malaise was when the relief force appeared in orbit. They had commo equipment on the transport ship that let them hail us from space. They'd brought along an escort of three combat ships, too, which gave some early indication of how they saw the situation. They were ready in case somebody wanted to try them in space.

I did my homework on the commanding officer, Lieutenant Colonel Tariq, while he was on his way down from orbit in a shuttle. Colonel Tariq was a veteran of multiple combat tours and had a reputation as a soldier's soldier, a man who didn't play politics and got the job done. He was a rare officer who appeared, at least from what I could find on the net, as a man loved by both his seniors and subordinates alike. None of our external material had been updated recently since we'd lost comms, so of course I couldn't find out why they selected him for the mission.

About an hour after that initial contact from orbit, the first shuttle touched down. I should say shuttles. Four of them, loaded with two dozen soldiers each—mostly staff officers and sergeants, but with a fair number of combat troopers mixed in. I tried not to think about why they'd thought they might need those on their first wave. Were they treating me as a potential hostile entity? There was at least some chance that I was about to be arrested. I wouldn't fight it. Whatever happened, whatever my fate, I'd take it. There was plenty of time to do an investigation and sort things out later, and honestly, spending some time in a cell with nobody talking to me didn't sound horrible.

I approached Lieutenant Colonel Tariq as he debarked, stopping about thirty meters short of his shuttle, as befit a greeting party. Hearns was with me, of course, and Xiang, who posted himself a dozen or so meters behind us.

"You must be Major Markov," said Tariq, returning my salute. He used the rank without any inflection, as if it belonged on me. "I'm Lieutenant Colonel Tariq, commander of the rapid reaction battalion. We departed four hours after we got your message."

"Thank you, sir. We appreciate your haste."

"You're a little young-looking for a major." He said it with a smile that infected his whole face, and he clearly meant it without harm.

I responded flatly. "Yes, sir. I am." I think he got the hint that I didn't find it funny, because he schooled his face back to professional. Thinking back on it, I like to think that as a combat veteran, maybe he recognized something in me in that moment that let him understand. Or maybe I'm just an asshole. It's hard to say.

"Do you want to go inside and spin me up on what's going on? We can figure things out and schedule a formal handover of command at your convenience."

Handover of command? I hadn't even considered that. I assumed that he would show up and just take charge. Instead he was treating me like a peer. It seemed my thoughts about being arrested were without basis. At least for now. They could still charge me later, *after* the investigation. But the fact that he hadn't shown up and immediately taken the reins was a good sign. "Yes, sir. But before we do, I need you to do something for me. I ran a mission up to the lowest way-station on the space elevator—that's how we got the quantum communicator functioning. I had to leave soldiers behind. There was at least one alive when I left. There's not much chance that any of them survived, but we have to check. Just in case."

He nodded solemnly. "Yeah. We can do that."

"You'll need combat troops. Last I knew there were two enemy combat bots active on the station."

"Combat bots? So it's true."

"What's true, sir?"

"I got a download of information as soon as we arrived and got our communications running back to base. I haven't had time to go through all of it, but the long and short was that an entity worked specifically to cut you off from the rest of the galaxy. A corporation."

"Tangent Holding Company?"

"Yeah." He stared at me for a moment. "What the fuck went on here?"

Tangent. I'd been right. "Happy to fill you in, sir, but I'd really feel better if we did that after we put things into action regarding the orbital way-station."

"Right. Of course. I've got orders to retake and revitalize the elevator anyway. I'll get an assault force in there immediately."

"Thanks, sir."

He nodded, and then paused, probably sending instructions via his implant. With a full staff of officers, they'd be able to disseminate orders almost instantaneously. I wandered off while he was zoned out. They were professionals and they had things under control. They didn't need my help.

Zilla lived.

It was impossible, but there she was, standing on the landing pad. She walked with a limp but otherwise seemed unharmed. At least physically. Chenoweth made it, too, though she was in worse shape, riding on a stretcher with a bunch of high-tech medical monitoring equipment hanging off of it. Four body bags told me that they were the only two, and that likely nobody had recovered Enzor's body yet.

I approached Zilla and she saluted. I returned it with a messy salute of my own, and then I hugged her. She didn't seem to know what to do, which was completely reasonable on her part since soldiers don't hug each other and she probably thought I'd lost my mind. But I didn't let go, and eventually, she sagged into me and hugged me back. After a few seconds, she apparently realized we were drawing attention, and she gently pushed me back.

"How?" It was the only word I could get out through the tears.

After I'd made it off station, Zilla said she figured she had nothing to lose, so she used everything she had against the bots, including grenades. If she damaged the station, so what? She was dead anyway. She didn't go into a lot of detail, but she'd won the fight, destroying one bot and crippling the other to the point where it couldn't move, and she could avoid it. She hadn't thought it mattered at the time, as she waited for the ship that destroyed the communicator to come for her. But it didn't. She had cannibalized the oxygen from the dead soldiers to buy herself time, and she'd found Chenoweth alive, but in bad shape. But she could talk, and she walked Zilla through how to power up a small section of the base using the portable generator. They minimized their power usage, only bringing the small medical room online. It had its own air system, separate from the rest of the station—probably for quarantine purposes in an emergency—and it sealed. It also had enough medical equipment to keep Chenoweth alive.

Zilla was able to recharge her portable units and made daily forays out into the station proper for supplies. They hadn't eaten well, but they'd found enough to survive, and the medical facility had its own water recycler, so once she got that running, they had everything they needed.

It was a hell of a story, and it was all I could do not to hug her again. That was weird for me. I've never been a hugger.

It wasn't long after that that Lieutenant Colonel Tariq found me again. "Come on. Let's go sit down over a cup of coffee. I'm sure you've got some stories to tell."

"Yes, sir. I do."

We went to my office—the commander's office—which I realized was a bad choice as soon as I hit the door. I should have picked more neutral ground. Did I go sit behind the desk, or take one of the visitor chairs and leave that to him? Thankfully, he made it easy and plopped down in the first chair he came to. I decided to follow suit and took the other visitor's chair, putting us on equal footing.

I reached up to my collar and unpinned my rank. "First things first, sir." I tossed it to him.

He tossed it back. "Nope. That's yours."

"Sir—"

"Not my call, Markov. Not yours either. That decision was made well

THE WEIGHT OF COMMAND

above either of our pay grades. Speaking of pay, you'll get back pay for the difference in rank, retroactively."

I held the rank in my hand, all three point one grams of it. It still felt heavier than that.

I had things to tell him. If my promotion held, I wanted to lobby for Berghof's to hold too. I wanted Zilla promoted, and Hearns because both of them had worked way over their assigned stations. I had so much to tell him.

But right then, I couldn't speak.

ACKNOWLEDGMENTS

A lot of people do a lot of work to get a book out into the world, and I'd like to thank some of the people responsible for this one. This book wouldn't be here without my agent, Lisa Rodgers, who went out and found it a home. She continues to be the best advocate a writer could ask for both creatively and on the business side of things.

Thanks to Steve Feldman and the crew at Audible Originals for taking the initial chance on me and Kiera's story. Thanks to John Hartness and the folks at Falstaff who gave me a home for the print and e-book versions and for all the work they do to get books in the hands of readers. They're one of the best small publishers in the business.

Thanks to Dan Rowinski and Ernie Chiara for their early reads and insightful feedback, and special thanks to Keena Roberts who really challenged how I was thinking about the book and pushed me to make it a lot better. Thanks to Dan Koboldt and Jason Nelson, who have read everything I've written before it has gone out into the world. Not only do they make my books better with their feedback, their advice on all things related to the business of writing is invaluable.

More than anybody else, I'd like to thank my wife, Melody. She is unconditionally supportive, which is a blessing both in life and especially in the capricious business of publishing. I love you, and I couldn't do this without you.

Lastly, I'd like to thank every reader of any of my work who took a moment of their time to find me at a con, or via email or Facebook or Twitter, to tell me that they enjoyed my work. Those moments make the hours working alone worth it, and they matter more than you know.

ABOUT THE AUTHOR

Michael Mammay is a science fiction writer and former US Army officer. He is a graduate of the United States Military Academy and a veteran of more wars than he wants to count. He lives with his wife in Georgia.

ALSO BY MICHAEL MAMMAY

Planetside

Spaceside

Colonyside

The Misfit Soldier

Generation Ship (August 2023)

FRIENDS OF FALSTAFF

Thank You to All our Falstaff Books Patrons, who get extra digital content each month! To be featured here and see what other great rewards we offer, go to www.patreon.com/falstaffbooks.

PATRONS

Dino Hicks
John Hooks
John Kilgallon
Larissa Lichty
Travis & Casey Schilling
Staci-Leigh Santore
Sheryl R. Hayes
Scott Norris
Samuel Montgomery-Blinn
Junkle

Made in the USA
Monee, IL
06 January 2023